A Stranger in Need

"Sick." Gabriel lowered his gaze again so I couldn't read it. "Back to . . . bed . . ."

I removed my waterpack, then bent down to ease his own off. Then, carefully—careful for so many reasons—I maneuvered his arm over my shoulders and led him to his blankets.

In doing so, I couldn't help breathing him in, my lungs tight with the struggle of trying to keep my senses fortified at the same time. But I lost the battle, becoming saturated with the scent of him—a vague tinge of earth where there should've been musk and the tang of skin.

Without hurting him, I made quick work in setting him down, then backed away, my limbs weak and quivery.

It was only when he reached for his flask that I succeeded. I concentrated on how he gulped down its contents, how he closed his eyes and reveled in the shuddering pleasure of the liquid—a mixture that left his lips flushed red.

Then, obviously satisfied, he capped the flask and slumped to the blankets, keeping the container close to his chest.

Damn. *Damn.* What had I let in?

BLOODLANDS

Christine Cody

ACE BOOKS, NEW YORK

THE BERKLEY PUBLISHING GROUP
Published by the Penguin Group
Penguin Group (USA) Inc.
375 Hudson Street, New York, New York 10014, USA
Penguin Group (Canada), 90 Eglinton Avenue East, Suite 700, Toronto, Ontario M4P 2Y3, Canada
(a division of Pearson Penguin Canada Inc.)
Penguin Books Ltd., 80 Strand, London WC2R 0RL, England
Penguin Group Ireland, 25 St. Stephen's Green, Dublin 2, Ireland (a division of Penguin Books Ltd.)
Penguin Group (Australia), 250 Camberwell Road, Camberwell, Victoria 3124, Australia
(a division of Pearson Australia Group Pty. Ltd.)
Penguin Books India Pvt. Ltd., 11 Community Centre, Panchsheel Park, New Delhi—110 017, India
Penguin Group (NZ), 67 Apollo Drive, Rosedale, Auckland 0632, New Zealand
(a division of Pearson New Zealand Ltd.)
Penguin Books (South Africa) (Pty.) Ltd., 24 Sturdee Avenue, Rosebank, Johannesburg 2196,
South Africa

Penguin Books Ltd., Registered Offices: 80 Strand, London WC2R 0RL, England

This is a work of fiction. Names, characters, places, and incidents either are the product of the author's imagination or are used fictitiously, and any resemblance to actual persons, living or dead, business establishments, events, or locales is entirely coincidental. The publisher does not have any control over and does not assume any responsibility for author or third-party websites or their content.

BLOODLANDS

An Ace Book / published by arrangement with the author

PRINTING HISTORY
Ace mass-market edition / August 2011

ISBN: 978-0-441-02062-1

ACE
Ace Books are published by The Berkley Publishing Group,
a division of Penguin Group (USA) Inc.,
375 Hudson Street, New York, New York 10014.
ACE and the "A" design are trademarks of Penguin Group (USA) Inc.

PRINTED IN THE UNITED STATES OF AMERICA

10 9 8 7 6 5 4 3 2 1

To Sajen, my creative and brilliant buddy in the fantastic.
Love you a million times over!

ACKNOWLEDGMENTS

Thank you so much to everyone at Ace—Ginjer, Kat, the art and marketing and sales and editing staff, and every single person who made these books happen. Hats off also to my team at the Knight Agency—Pamela, Deidre, Elaine, Jia, and the gang. And to Judy Duarte and Sheri Whitefeather—you guys are the best partners a crazed writer could ever hope for!

Thank goodness for the *New Yorker* magazine, one of the best idea-generators a writer can treasure.

Lastly, a big shout-out goes to all those Westerns that provided us with High Plains Drifters, Shanes, and Pale Riders, plus all the greedy ranchers and gunslinging villains, feisty homesteaders and rugged pioneers. I wanted to twist and reshape those wonderful tropes into something new while recalling the old. Most important, though, I wanted to pay homage to the mysterious cowboys who have wandered across dusty landscapes to face down the bad guys.

I've taken licenses with this work of fiction, so please forgive any flights of fancy or mistakes. Any errors are my own.

1

They called this ravaged, sun-sucked place the New Badlands and, under the gray-hazed shine of the swollen moon, it certainly lived up to the name.

Bad because of its dull, apocalyptic scape. *Bad* because of its throttling day heat.

Bad because it allowed a night monster such easy, easy hunting.

Hidden behind a boulder perched on a withered hill, one such monster waited patiently, its hunger knocking against its skin, its saliva stinging its jaws.

Tonight, nature forced it to hunt, and someone was coming. Someone with blood, hot and nourishing. Someone who could quench a bitter, desperate thirst.

Its mind went as fuzzy as ether-soaked cotton, pulled apart by fingers of appetite. As it gripped the boulder and felt the stone crumble under its fingertips, its vision, which turned the murky night into a blue-tinged, throbbing haze, caught small animals that looked like electric blurs while scurrying for cover.

Heat. Food. Blood . . . The cadence echoed, called, invited the monster to feast.

Its breath came faster, faster as the prey shuffled closer . . .

Unable to help itself, the monster eased to the side, peering round the boulder, craving a look. It saw the buzzing outline of a human mazing through the Badlands scrub. The male was slim, almost painfully so, stick-legged and awkward-gaited. His face was near featureless in the creature's neon sights except for lips gaped in a wobbly attempt at song.

The creature's hearing picked up the low, whistled tune. Melancholy. Something that might speak to another wholly human heart, if one was beating within range.

The monster's nostrils flared from the strength of the man's flesh, sweaty and musky beneath his tattered clothing: a wide-brimmed hat, a poncho, boots. There was also a trace of turtlegrape alcohol, cheaply made and readily available on the black markets found in any city that was still standing.

Mouth even wetter, the creature ran a tongue over the pierce of its teeth. It recognized this smell. It had tracked the scent tonight.

Heat, food, blood . . .

Anticipation ran cold and urgent in its veins. Its body stiffened as the prey tripped on a rock, cursed at himself, then started to whistle again—sad notes reminding the monster of something lost. . . .

He was coming closer, closer.

The wobbly song warped into a death dirge that competed with the quickening call in the monster's mind as the scent and pulse of blood became unbearable.

Heatfoodblood . . .

It winced, yearning, as the man pulled within mere feet—

A rock skittered from the creature's hiding place as it shifted.

The human startled to a halt, peered round. The creature heard the prey's heartbeat thudding, smelled his blood heating.

Food—

Like dark mercury, the monster unfurled from behind the boulder, fully showing itself. It flashed its teeth.

Heatfoodblood . . .

With a thin cry, the man tripped into a run, his hat toppling off his head. But the creature was faster—so much faster.

It sprang, arcing through the air, grasping its prey's booted ankle and hauling him in.

"No—" the human begged, panting, clawing at the dirt for purchase and sending up abraded wisps of dust instead.

Beyond pity, the creature pulled at the man's hair to expose his throat and, for one beautiful moment, the thing thrilled to the engorged strand of a jugular vein as it pounded.

Food—

Just before the monster sank its teeth into the man's neck, it helplessly groaned, so hungry, so needy.

The human swiped at his attacker, drawing red stings, scratching, scratching—

But he couldn't stop the feeding, the flood of hot liquid coating the monster's throat in frenzied comfort.

The man's last stand didn't endure. Neither did his last screams. They gurgled to nothing as the monster ripped into his throat, sucking and tearing and reveling in wet, thick heatfoodblood—

When it was over, with the taste of fulfillment still vivid on its tongue, the monster sank to the dirt. A twinge of consciousness bit into it as the carcass of its victim sifted back into focus.

The human, the prey, was staring at the sky, the shadow of what would soon be many carrion feeders blocking the moon and spreading darkness over a horrified death gaze.

The monster closed its eyes, but then the scent of blood consumed it again and the moment disappeared, replaced by the hunger and thirst.

Diving back to the man's neck, the creature continued gnawing, feasting. Glutting.

That was all it knew, all it felt—at least right now.

Only when its body was heavy with satiation did it look back up, touching and testing the wounds its prey had inflicted—injuries that were already healing. Then it scanned a wary gaze over the New Badlands for other creatures that used this night to hunt.

All that stared back was the blue-bathed desolation of a world gone terrible.

2

Mariah

Eighteen Hours Later

When I saw the stranger weaving through the newly settled dusk on my visz monitor, he looked like a lie—a mirage, half wavering fantasy, half dust in my eyes. Chaplin didn't even believe me when I told him about it, but then again, he knew that I'd stayed partway sane only because of one altered version of the truth or another. It always took him some good thought before he ever put stock in what I did or said, and I wouldn't blame him, or anyone else, for that. Lies and omissions were how we lived out here in the nowheres. It was how we made sure strangers like this one on the visz never paid mind to us.

We lied about reality to survive.

Hell, I would lie to anyone, even you.

When I grabbed my old revolver from the wall arsenal, that must've lent some credence to the situation for Chaplin. He looked at the visz, seeing that I was telling him true about a stranger coming toward us.

"Think he's another one of them?" I asked, while keeping an eye on the screen. "Think this guy's one of Stamp's?"

My dog chuffed, then padded over close to me, leaning against my leg. His long tail curled over my boot, like a child wrapping an arm round a protector.

Not that I'm all that good at protecting. Sometimes I even think that Chaplin does a better job of guarding me than the other way round. There's a lot of ways a person needs to be protected.

Strung tight with tension, I adjusted a knob on the visz's side to get a better look at the approaching stranger. The long view was gloomy with the surreal blur of the camera's night vision, streaking his movements as he lurched even nearer to my underground home. Could he somehow see this earthen dwelling, even though I'd taken great care to disguise the entrance amongst the scrub and mounded landscape?

Chaplin made a garbled sound, and I rested a hand on his furry head.

"Don't worry," I said. "I'll bet he saunters right past us."

I didn't even believe myself this time.

My dog softly yowled, as if chewing on words. To anyone not trained in Canine, his sentiments would be inarticulate. But years ago, when I was no more than a pup myself, I'd begged my dad for one of the Intel Dogs he bred and trained at his lab. Dad had obliged only much later, just before we'd been forced to flee our Dallas home; then Chaplin had become necessary for survival—a watchdog genetically tooled to be more intelligent than most humans. Stronger, too. He was also a balm for us after my mom and brother had been murdered right in the home we'd abandoned.

I guess I needed Chaplin more than ever now, long after the murders and one year after my dad had taken his own life. My dog wasn't just my best friend—he was my only friend. In particular, he was nice to have round at night. Nice to have round whenever I thought about what waited outside the dirt-packed walls.

Just thinking about outside made the phantom scars on my body itch, but I forced myself not to touch them. They'd only bring back what had supposedly healed.

Now Chaplin growled low in his throat, his brown-haired ears lying flat against his skull as he backed toward a door barring a tunnel that connected our domain to one of the underground caverns.

I offered him a nod, a show of unity that didn't need to be voiced between the two of us. Then I turned back to the visz, which showed the stranger in post-stumble pause.

When I found him staring right back at me, my heart jerked, sending my adrenaline bursting to a hum that I fought to contain. His eyes were rendered luminescent by the camera's night vision and . . .

It was like he could somehow see the camouflaged lens. Like he knew we were in here.

Pacing my breathing, calming myself lest I lose control—God-all help me if I did—I hefted down a mini-crossbow from the wall, then stuffed my revolver into a holster built into my wide belt. I loaded the bow with a bolt because it'd be quieter than the bullets if I should have to defend my home. Bullets might attract attention.

"If he's one of Stamp's men," I said, "I'll show him a lesson about coming here when he's drunk and looking for trouble. Stamp's got to be sending his crew to poke round, just like that other man who was already here."

My dog didn't make a sound, and I was glad about that. Neither of us wanted to talk about Stamp's workers. Meanwhile, the stranger loomed closer on the visz, his features coming into shocking focus.

Something in my stomach fisted at the sight of his facial wounds, but I battled back the clench, the emotion. Battled hard, until all that was left was a tremor that only reminded me I wasn't safe.

Then my dog crept to my side and stared at the visz, too, almost like he'd been drawn closer. He let out a long, sympathetic whimper.

Hurt, was what Chaplin's sound meant. *The man is hurt.*

I tried to glance away but couldn't. The blood enthralled me, even more than it had when I was young, back before my family had been attacked and before we thought the world was going to end. Back when the media had first started entertaining the masses with violent news images, films of close-up war casualties in North Korea and public executions that people had clamored to witness in real life. Carnerotica, it had come to be called, until that form of amusement had become old hat under the new thrill of the subliminal fantasies I heard they were airing on TV now.

This man was a lot like one of those old executions.

The visz's pale night vision showed his face to be a wounded map to nowhere, etched with open gashes on his forehead and cheeks. Blood and dirt seemed to crust his short-sheared hair. His battered mouth opened round a word.

"Help."

Chaplin whimpered again. *Hurt.*

"Maybe that's what he hopes we believe." I gripped my crossbow all the harder, sweat breaking out over my skin, even though summer was a season away—a dry, brutal time that made staying inside my shelter all the wiser.

When Chaplin cocked his head, I realized that, for the first time, I couldn't exactly translate what his gesture meant. He was acting addled, off-kilter. Off-guard.

Inexplicably, a sense of isolation expanded in my chest, filling me up so there was no room for much else. I didn't like this sudden lack of simpatico that separated me from my only real ally left from better days.

"You're posing like you're going soft, boy. Where's the wariness in you?"

Chaplin turned his big brown eyes in my direction, emitting a series of whines. I still didn't understand, even though I could translate. It was his gaze that befuddled me, because it brimmed with foreign haziness, an utter lack of focus.

The dog wanted to help the stranger?

"You think we should open the door and let him in for nursing and shelter?"

Chaplin wagged his tail.

"Jay-sus."

He still wagged.

"Hell, it doesn't matter that Dad and I spent sweat upon

sweat trying to disguise the dwelling so it'd be quiet and unnoticeable. It doesn't matter that, if Stamp's sending his men round to search out more water for his property, he might resort to trickery to get one of his guys inside here and drag us off the property. Most of all, you know what we have to lose by letting anyone near. No, you're just sitting there cocking your head and flashing your browns and begging like none of that is of consequence."

The dog just kept cocking and flashing while the stranger's visage hovered in the visz, as if gauging the hidden device.

Chaplin gnawed out a few more muddled sounds. *He asked for help.*

I turned away, forcing my concentration on the visz again. It was as if I were stuck in one of my nightmares, where Chaplin had finally given up on me and had decided to go his own way, leaving me behind.

On the screen, the stranger crumpled to his knees and hunched over in what looked to be agony. Chaplin winced, then stamped round, fidgety.

But letting the man in would be too much of a risk . . . in so many ways. Yes, he was wounded, and I felt for him. I'd been wounded, too, way back when. But that was exactly why I couldn't drag him inside. I knew better than to welcome anything in.

And I knew the rest of the community would probably feel the same way. From the sights I often saw on the viszes, which were trained on the underground common area where other New Badlanders had begun gathering again recently, I could tell that the world hadn't changed fast enough for anyone to be trusting strangers. The bad guys were still out there, and Johnson Stamp might prove to be one of them. According to gossip, he'd permanently moved here about a month ago, establishing a setup for uncovering water in the area, seeing as the earth didn't produce a whole lot of it for regular folk these days. Of course, corporations had the means to desalinate ocean water and seed clouds, but their services came at a steep price few could afford without indebting themselves body and soul. Water was life, especially in an out-of-the-way place like the New Badlands.

The stranger made one last pain-ragged appeal over the visz.

"No . . . harm," he croaked out, lifting his head back up in supplication.

Then I saw something I couldn't be sure of. His eyes, already whitened by the camera's night vision, flared, reminding me of a gunslinger opening his jacket to show that he wasn't armed.

I sucked in a breath when he hit the ground again, dust wisping up round his flattened body like smoke seething out of the earth.

Chaplin whined deep in his throat, an accusation.

Well, screw him and his dog brain. Maybe his Intel was rubbing off him, what with living out here in the wilds. Maybe we'd all have every last bit of sense bleached from us soon. Wouldn't surprise me, seeing as I was halfway there already.

I ignored the visz and clung to my crossbow, still remembering that odd flash in the stranger's eyes, riddled by it.

Chaplin put his paw on my boot and I said, "I'm not falling for his tricks."

Hurt, he repeated.

"And his hurt trumps what might happen to us should we let him in, whether or not he's Stamp's man?"

No answer from Chaplin on that, because he probably had enough brain cells working to realize that this stranger could be a million things spelling a last mistake. Besides exposing our home, there was a chance that he was one of the bad guys himself—and bad guys would pull anything to make their way in life. See, after old prophecies had come to a head—things like pestilence and earthly change—the bads had taken advantage of all the chaos. The mosquito epidemic had wiped out and separated much of the population in the old States, and terrorism had coerced the normal, law-abiding citizens to take homebound jobs, where they only face-to-faced with their core families. But that was only the start.

U.S.-based terrorists had rigged massive charges along the quake faults of the West Coast to blow off some of the "devil-ridden" area, and the government had extended full security for the good of the country. But a lot of people thought the government could be just as bad as any enemy, and they'd left the urban hubs, seeking safety on compounds or isolated places like the New Badlands. From that point on, bad guys had risen from the ashes all over the place. There'd been a spike in identity theft, so we'd dug the ID chips out from under our skin. We stopped using the Internet and mass tools of communication. We basically wiped ourselves off the face of society since the government—which had even stopped pretending that it wasn't composed of many a bad guy itself—had been too slow to regulate privacy information legislation.

That was when bad guys seized even more identities and properties with impunity. Basically, to live nowadays, even if the government was said to have been weakened by out-of-country monetary sanctions, you had to decide whether to eat or be eaten. And, right now, I wasn't about to put myself on a banquet table.

When I checked the visz one last time, I saw that the screen was empty. A trickle of sweat slid down my temple. *Eat or be eaten,* I thought again.

But Chaplin didn't seem to get it. *If someone had helped you when you needed it . . .*

"Stop," I said before he could really cut into me. "Don't be talking about that. You know better."

The dog merely waited me out, big-browning me with those eyes. It was almost like I could see exactly what he was thinking, too: images of my mom and preteen brother reaching out, screaming while covered with blood as the bad guys got to them. To us.

If someone had helped us when we needed it . . .

Damn it all. Maybe the only thing separating us from the

world we were hiding from was moments like this, when you could make the choice to do more than just stand by while someone else fell.

Could I just help the guy a little, then send him on his way? Was it possible? I did have an arsenal of weapons on my side, after all.

I had a lot of things he'd be afraid of, except I wasn't so willing to use everything at my disposal. He could thank me for that later.

Damn it. *Damn* it.

I raised a finger to Chaplin, but it trembled. "You'd better be right. If this man's fooling us with those injuries, I'll gun him off good and make sure Stamp knows we're not buying whatever he might be bringing. Then you and me are going to have a talk about common sense."

My dog shifted from one paw to the other, happy as could be. His gaze seemed . . . what? Inappropriately misty? Bright?

Adrenaline thudding, I set down my crossbow and rechecked my revolver. It'd been made in the early 2000s but would work fine, bolstered by the modifications and the old ammunition, plus the homemade, I'd loaded into it.

I couldn't believe I was doing this. Stupid. But Chaplin would never let me forget that I was no better than a bad guy if I didn't at least see if the stranger was truly wounded. The dog had put up with a lot from me, and someday, I'd push him over the line. I didn't want that day to be now.

With a hard glance at him, I tucked the revolver back into its holster, grabbed the crossbow, then moved toward the wooden ladder. I slowly climbed toward the exit panel, wanting to take the high ground in case I needed it.

God-all, when was the last time I'd willingly been outside? To hell with Chaplin for reminding me that this was the right and decent thing to do. To hell with him for playing that horrific card.

I heaved in oxygen, held my breath, slamming open the panel and emerging into the darkening dusk. Through my night sights, I scanned the area for traps.

Nothing amiss.

Or maybe not.

I scanned a second time while the night air baked over me: dragon's breath, they called the extreme conditions forced by all the changes.

Heartbeat tangling, I smoothed myself out as I breathed. Breathed.

At the same time, I kept thinking: *Outside. I'm outside. I should get back in. . . .*

Trying to shove my doubts away, I maneuvered over the dry, rock-bitten hill until I slid to the ground. A few sharp blades of cockroach grass, named because it'd sprung up in defiance of the harsh weather, pricked through my pants.

Inside. Get back inside . . .

Now I went a step farther, shutting myself from feeling altogether: smelling, intaking, *experiencing.* Then I approached the stranger, aiming my crossbow at his chest. It'd be quite a sight when he opened his eyes. Hopefully, he'd report back to Stamp that there was nothing near here worth even a third look.

Unless he was really hurt.

Peering closer, I discerned that the stranger's wounds seemed genuine enough, not to mention his obvious pain. Then, as I knew it would, the blood on his skin zoomed in at me, and I clamped off the sight before I could have a reaction. A contained tremor blasted through me and, when I was strong enough to open my eyes, I saw that his knees were drawn to his chest as he clutched his long coat round him. His jaw was clenched, as if holding back another fruitless request to allow him inside my home.

With a brief glance at the visz lens hidden amongst the scrub, I wondered how everyone seemed to be finding the equipment when I'd done such an expert job at camouflage.

Inside! Get yourself inside!

I cleared my throat so my voice would come out strong. "You one of Stamp's drunkards?" I was still targeting him, my lungs so tight I could barely talk.

The harmless moon caught a gleam in his eyes as he

opened his gaze. He grimaced, dragging himself over to me. I stepped back.

"Shelter," he uttered.

Definitely not faking. I'd heard so many screams in my head over the years that I knew what agony sounded like.

Even so, I scanned him over for weapons with my bow monitor. Unarmed. But a quiver reminded me to keep clamping myself off from his wounds, his hurt.

The stranger stirred on the ground.

Inside! Go!

But I couldn't move. The sight of his blood was transfixing me again, owning me. Frantically, I grasped my mini-bow one-handed and jerked a dust kerchief out of a pocket, holding it over my nose.

"Do anything dumb," I said, "and you die."

"Understood." His whisper was barely discernible.

I wondered if I should get my dad's old med equipment and take care of him out here, but that would mean lingering in the elements. That might be more dangerous than bringing him in.

A sound behind me persuaded me to swing round my crossbow, but I yanked it up once I saw what was happening.

Three feet away, a scrub-shrouded trapdoor that served as another entrance to the domain had spewed open. And damn it all if Chaplin wasn't waiting right there like the most hyper welcoming committee ever.

He barked, intoning an invitation for the stranger to come in.

"Chaplin!" What was the mutt thinking?

Before I could react, the stranger rolled to the opening, his body disappearing as the entrance swallowed him up.

The thud of his weight hitting the dirt of my home pounded in my ears. I ran to the opening, peering down to find him sprawled near Chaplin, who was already licking the man's wounds.

"Are you crazy, dog?" I jumped to the floor, too, crouching to ease the fall. Right away, I reached over to secure the trapdoor again. Then I pressed the kerchief to my face. "You don't know what's in his blood!"

But that wasn't true. Intel Dogs had an even keener sense of smell than their ancestors, than any type of canine, in fact. Chaplin could warn me about the proximity of any intruders after taking an outside hunting trip; he could tell me if the man was carrying disease or not, too. My dog must've known the stranger was otherwise healthy.

Chaplin avoided me while tending to his patient. Keeping the crossbow in hand, I put some distance between me and the stranger as I headed for my living space.

Breathe, I thought, thankful, so thankful to be back inside. Lucky to have come back without bringing trouble with me.

You can breathe now.

In the food prep area, I leaned against a cupboard, where I could still my racing blood and my tremors. Then, after getting hold of myself, I pulled out some linen that could stanch the stranger's bleeding. I also ditched my bow and brought out antiseptic and a general first-aid kit, from which I opened a bottle of antiseptic gel and smeared the contents under my nostrils.

Back in the day, I would've been able to access the Nets to see if I was nursing a person correctly, but since the bad guys had taken over, that wasn't possible. I'd trashed anything—the computer, the phone, the personal devices—that could possibly allow criminals access to my life. There wouldn't have been good reception out here in the nowheres, anyway.

When I came back and sat down next to the stranger, I realized that Chaplin had licked off the blood, giving the man's features clean definition. Unhindered by crimson, there was something stoic and haunted, his nose slightly crooked, his barely opened eyes gray, his skin pale, just like everyone else's since day-walking without a heat suit was dumb business.

Looking at him did something, curling me from the

inside out until I felt twisted up. Heat surged through me, but I couldn't stop, even though I knew I should.

It was just that . . . Well, in what looked to be all the clothing he owned—a long, battered coat that matched the misery of his trousers, a frayed bag slung over his chest, plus three shirts layered and weather-beaten—he seemed like one of those storied cowboys who used to wander the landscape of mid-twentieth-century cinema. I'd seen a few of those old movies Before, previous to the world's degradation. Hell, most all New Badlanders dressed in this kind of gear, but . . . it wasn't the same. Maybe it was the silver-star color of the man's eyes or his civil way of asking for help that'd done it. Maybe I was a right fool, too. But there was something about him that brought back a link to the comfortable, the soothing fiction of myth.

The stranger watched me just as well. Something seemed to tweak the front of my mind again, calming me down, making me think it was okay for him to be here.

When Chaplin tilted his head at me, I blinked, pushing the stranger's influence out of me. I was real good at pushing.

Feeling oddly unburdened now, I straightened up, then busied myself by pressing the antiseptic-dipped linen to the stranger's head wounds.

Weird, though. He didn't seem to be breathing. But he was alive all the same.

I glanced at Chaplin. "Does he ring familiar to you? I've never seen him wandering round on any of the visz screens before."

Chaplin shook his head, and I continued to apply pressure. The quicker I nursed him, the quicker he'd be out of my hair.

"Just because he doesn't register," I added, "it doesn't mean he isn't a part of Stamp's crew."

Now, it seemed as if the stranger had fallen into a light stupor after expending enough energy to get himself past the trapdoor. He closed his eyes, his muscles relaxing. His lips opened slightly, and I found my gaze on the cuts and bruises that were making his mouth swell.

That weird heat started making me uncomfortable again, so I pushed it back. "How do you think he got himself hurt, boy?" I asked Chaplin.

My dog growled out an answer. *Beat up by one of Stamp's guys.*

"Makes sense, I suppose." I grabbed another cloth, dipped it in the gel, then kept right on nursing. "One of them could've gotten blazed on turtlegrape and found a distraction in this unfortunate."

Although Stamp and his men had been more aggressively exploring the area very recently, none of my neighbors were willing to fully reveal themselves so Stamp could be shooed off. They were still hoping to stay unidentified.

But it looked like we'd been discovered anyhow.

I used a corner of linen to wipe down the stranger's face, then paused. Hadn't there been a scratch round his cheekbone?

Chaplin wagged his tail faster, enthused about my willingness to nurse. Darn the dog.

"Bag," the stranger whispered, his voice raw. "In my bag . . ."

I touched the leathered carryall strapped over his chest, and he grunted in the positive.

"Unguent," he added before going silent again.

I searched the contents of his bag, taking care not to discomfort him. A comb, a scrap of fragrant pink cotton, a flask that seemed cool to the touch, a jar . . .

I grabbed it, screwed off the porcelain lid to find a solidified pool of goo, then scooped out a gob. It tingled on my skin.

As I slathered it over his wounds, I minded my breathing again. It'd quickened in these last seconds, fighting with my pulse and making me much too aware of the scratch of slight beard on his face, the coolness of his skin.

I caught a small smile right before the creases round his mouth went slack and he succumbed to rest.

And that was how the next few hours passed, with the man resting. Oddly, his head wounds hadn't been as bad as

I'd first thought; they certainly seemed to have been humdingers at first, but I was no medic. Still, expert or not, I took care to mind every bit about him, even his lack of breathing. But he was alive enough, so I didn't search for lung activity too diligently.

In the meantime, I brewed some loto cactus–flavored water for when he awoke. He'd be sorely thirsty, no doubt, and the concoction would make him heal all the quicker.

As the water boiled in a stainless steel container I'd once salvaged from an abandoned highway weigh station a few miles distant, I sat on my ground couch. Chaplin cuddled up next to me and, out of enjoyable habit, I petted him between the ears. But I kept tabs on the slumbering stranger. In fact, I was so vigilant about watching him that something outside caught me by surprise. It took Chaplin's growl to shake me to the present—to the other visitor showcased on a visz monitor.

Chaplin kept growling. Even I felt myself tensing until I forced myself to better serenity.

"Lo?" the second visitor called out in greeting.

Like the other intruders from Stamp's camp these past few nights, *this* guy was speaking Text, the shorthand English that had become so prevalent because of chat rooming, texting, and the like. Since the Badlanders had long ago cut themselves off from all that crap, they'd clung to Old American, just like the shut-ins who tucked themselves away in their urban hub homes and the businesspeople who communicated also in Hindi and Chinese with the global community.

I hunched toward the visz, my heartbeat tapping against my breastbone. Chaplin growled louder at the silhouette on the screen. The guy wore his long hair back, most of it secured into a bun by what looked to be chopsticks.

"C'mon ot," the silhouette said, strolling round the area as the camera tracked him. A jangle accompanied every footstep. *Clink, clink.*

He was still too far away to recognize in the night vision, and thank-all he wasn't looking straight into the visz's lens like visitor number one of the night had done.

Yet that didn't mean my defenses went down. I felt the threat of this one in my very cells, which collided and heated up.

As I got off the couch, Chaplin followed, going to the sleeping stranger's side as if to guard him. I didn't have time to ask him why he thought that important. I also had no time to indulge in the disappointment of seeing my dog's loyalty spread to another.

For the second time that night, I took out my revolver from its waiting position in my holster, then headed toward the ladder. While passing the visz on the way, I gripped my firearm, palms sweating and—

Crash!

I whipped round, my revolver aimed.

But all I found was Chaplin barking up at the trapdoor as it closed, darkening the empty spot below where the stranger had just been resting.

3

Mariah

'd thought the stranger was down for the duration.

Wrong.

Darting to the visz bank, I discovered just where he'd gone—to the surface, standing behind the new arrival, shadowing him while he belatedly turned toward the sound of the already-closed trapdoor.

Obviously the stranger hadn't been hurt all that much, because there he was on the visz, with his ragged clothing and taut body providing an ominous threat to the unknowing visitor. Even more unsettling was the fact that, although the stranger wasn't in close range of the camera, his eyes seemed to be shining in the night.

Belowground, I readied my revolver, my blood racing.

"Wh'r u?" the intruder asked. Then he stopped, spun round, as if he felt his spine tingling.

When he found nothing—at least, that was what *he* probably thought—he walked toward the now-hidden trapdoor. "Whooz thr . . . ?"

The stranger kept mirroring the guy like a true shadow,

and I inched closer to the visz, my heartbeat hammering my lungs flat. But I didn't let myself panic.

When the intruder reached for some jagged scrub five feet from the trapdoor, the stranger spoke in Text, stopping the other man.

"I wodn't."

He sounded strong, but I sensed the effort beneath the words.

A stretched hesitation marked the reaction of the man with the chopstick hair; I wasn't even sure whether that pause lasted for a second or a full minute. At any rate, it was enough time for me to realize what was coming next.

The man with the chopsticks moved his arm, clearly going for a weapon.

I hitched in a sliver of oxygen, then sprang toward the ladder, not really knowing what I'd do once I got up it.

The stranger's voice filtered through the speakers. "I sed *stop.*"

His tone halted *me* cold, turning my veins to lines of ice. The after-slice of his words cut and echoed through me, a shattered whisper.

On the nearby visz, I saw the new intruder startle to a freeze, too. Nearby, Chaplin's growls doubled in volume. Dog was pissed.

As if hearing Chaplin, the stranger's shadow tilted toward the camera. But he couldn't have heard. The viszes were one-way hookups.

In the next moment, he was back to facing the intruder, sauntering closer, leaning toward the man's ear, whispering.

I couldn't hear what he said, but the new guy took off running, jangling madly as his form faded into the darkness.

Chaplin and I didn't say anything for a long moment. Then, finally, my dog made a *hmmm* sound. We watched the stranger touch his head, probably to adjust the bandages there, then inspect his hand. Afterward, he stumbled forward, carefully making his way back to the trapdoor.

Chaplin ran to it, releasing the button to let our guest back in.

Without ceremony, the stranger made his stiff journey down the ladder, the door closing behind him. Then he fell the rest of the way to his blankets, offering no explanations. Nope, he merely removed his long, beaten coat, then his bag, while his bandages slumped over his forehead. He reached into the carryall.

Again, I just stood there, brain-fried.

But that didn't seem to attract the notice of our guest. He casually went on to extract the flask from the bowels of his bag and gesture to us with the container.

"Excuse my indulgence."

I had to absorb the Old American. Absorb the fact that he could be so nonchalant.

"That's it?" I asked. "No expounding on what just happened?"

He paused, a melancholy look passing over him.

As sure as the moon had started its waning phase tonight, I wasn't about to let him off the hook. I narrowed my eyes at him, and he must've known I meant real business. I hadn't saved his hide earlier for him to come in here and toy with me.

The stranger sent me a lowered glance. "The way you talk . . . I haven't heard Old American for a while. Haven't ever seen a real live Intel Dog, either."

I was about to ask him why he seemed more comfortable speaking Old American when he continued, just not in the way I would've liked.

"Seeing as our visitor won't be back tonight," he said, "I'd like to settle. Talking can follow, if you don't mind."

Oh, so he thought it'd be that easy.

"Exactly what did you say to make him run off?" I also wanted to ask about his wounds. How was the stranger all of a sudden functioning well enough to *be* scaring off others?

He smiled, and it was a sad sort of gesture. But then he winced, holding a hand to a cut near his mouth. I noticed *that* gash wasn't nearly as bad as I'd first made it out to be, either.

Just seeing his injury brought the smell—the nightmare, the adrenalized sight—of blood back to me, and I blocked it off again.

"What I conveyed to him," the stranger said, undoing the top of his flask, as if resigned to being interrogated for a bit, "is between Chompers and me." He toasted the pronouncement and took a gulp. When he finished, he closed his eyes, shivering.

"Chompers," I said. "Who's Chompers?"

"Our flown visitor. That clinking he was making? From some silver-capped teeth strung around his booted ankles. Human teeth, I gather, since animals don't generally subscribe to that sort of dental work."

A chill tumbled down my spine. Even Chaplin began to pant, stressed out by the thought of what kind of creep Stamp employed, if indeed that was who Chompers had been—one of Stamp's henchmen.

I reached over to console my dog, but my other hand still held the revolver. In the light of the dwelling's solar-batteried lamps, I could see that *all* the stranger's wounds seemed to be healing quickly.

What was in that scentless unguent of his?

"How'd you stalk up behind that man so easily, especially since you could hardly even stand a short time ago?" I asked.

The stranger shrugged. "I just did it quietly." He faltered slightly, seeming to lose energy. "Now, if I could . . . ?"

He gestured to his flask, then swigged another gulp. Again, he quaked in the aftermath, hanging his head to hide his expression.

Like a genial host, Chaplin trotted over to the stranger and gave him a thankful nudge with his nose. It caused our so-called friend to crash back into his blankets with a grunt.

"See, here's someone who understands the beauty of rest," the stranger said wearily. He closed his eyes.

"I'm still talking with you."

"I'm listening through my eyelids."

Chaplin brightly glanced at me, obviously expecting me to enjoy the humor, too. But all I could focus on was my dog's bright eyes. Had the stranger brought some kind of crazy bug with him and had Chaplin caught it? Outside held all sorts of dangers and disease that might weaken even an Intel Dog.

But Chaplin had seemed off *before* the stranger had actually come into our home, so our guest couldn't have brought on any kind of bug.

"I'd like just a few more moments of chatter, if *you* don't mind," I said.

When the stranger answered, the voice that'd been so persuasive outside had turned to an exhausted whisper. "I understand. You want to know who you've taken in."

Yeah, and who I'd be throwing out just as soon as I could.

Chaplin sat on his haunches by the stranger's side, his long fur like dark root tea in the lamplight. His quick affection might be a show of gratitude for what this man had done with Stamp's guy, and I should be expressing the same, really. But I could ill afford parlor manners beyond what I'd already extended.

The stranger's eyes were still closed, his hands clasped on his chest in ease. "For the record, I'm appreciative of your kindness. Truly. But I'd just like to allow my medicines to get on with healing."

A beat passed, heavy with my unanswered questions. Heavy with the look I found myself running over him, too— a look that made me weaken, my bones starting to turn to something like liquid.

I went back to pacing my breathing. Hell, it wasn't as if I'd never been near a man before. It'd just been a while. The attack in Dallas had scarred me in a lot of ways, and I wasn't used to people anymore.

As if sensing my interest, he opened his eyes, and I saw the gray of them.

"I suppose, manners-wise, I should at least offer that my name's Gabriel."

I nodded, hoping he'd go on.

"Not much else to tell," he said.

When he smiled—just a slight, pained gesture with those

injury-swollen lips—I swallowed. My mouth had become dry, but not the same dry as outside. Not at all.

The realization brushed over me with shame, with awareness, with . . . I didn't want to give name to it. But something lingered in the way he was watching me.

And what did he see exactly? A tallish twenty-three-year-old woman with red hair sawed off to the jaw by frequent knife cutting for the ease of care, her eyes narrowed in eternal distrust and self-loathing. A flinty hostess sheathed in dusty garb and an impregnable attitude.

His smile . . . For some reason, I thought it meant that he appreciated the way I looked. It made me want to peer into my rarely used mirror to see what he saw, to discern if I'd changed somehow since the last time I'd checked. It'd been a long time since anyone had told me I was pretty.

I glanced away from the stranger . . . Gabriel. With harsh reluctance, I tucked my revolver into its holster. Then I fixed my gaze right back on him, letting him know that even though there was one less gun in his face, I'd still have it handy.

Chaplin woofed softly. He was chiding me for being prickly.

Hell, since when had *he* gone lax? Oh, yeah—right when the stranger had shown up.

"I look forward to the rest of your story, Mr. Gabriel," I said, prickly indeed.

"Just . . ." The stranger's smile disappeared. ". . . Gabriel."

"At the risk of keeping you awake, can you at least tell me why you're in the New Badlands, in the middle of the nowheres? It's not on many itineraries."

He sighed, as if willing to give up this one last inch. "I've been passing through what's left of the States for . . . well, it'd be about twenty-five months now. After everything that's gone down the last twenty-odd years . . ." He paused. "I lost my family in the epidemic way back when, and though I haven't been wandering all that long, I never did find any place to root since they died. Not with substitute families, not with anything much."

The mosquito epidemic. I softened at this; a lot of people had lost their loved ones then. "I'm sorry to hear that."

"Afterward, everything fell apart. But you already know."

A burn stung my throat. I knew.

His words were weighed with something I couldn't even begin to comprehend. I didn't want to, anyway, since Gabriel wouldn't be round long enough for it to matter.

"I guess I've been . . . searching . . . for a while, even when I stayed in one place. Now I think I've found somewhere quiet—what people call the New Badlands since the original ones were wiped away by that freak earthquake that came before the West Coast attack. I suppose the name of this place had a noble ring to it for me." Slowly, he slipped his flask into the bag, then kept one hand on it. "But more importantly, I heard there might be a chance for survival and keeping to myself out here."

This wasn't good. The community had taken in stragglers before, but it'd been closed off to any more newcomers for about a year now. Circumstances—our very existences—had . . . well, required it. It didn't matter if Gabriel turned out to be the greatest man in history or not, he wouldn't be invited to stay.

Then the bigger implications of what he was saying barreled into my brain: Just how much had he heard about the New Badlands? How many others out there knew that there were dwellers here, and when would they be coming, too?

My skin bristled with its hair standing on end. Gabriel. Dangerous.

I tried to let him know that this was no paradise. "Since word is that the government went bankrupt during all that economic sanction trouble with India, we heard that there haven't been U.S. satellite sweeps here." That was the most recent update from the last visitor we had, anyway, but I didn't want to talk about her. "We heard rumors of mercenary investors from different parts of the globe bailing out our treasury, and we've been fearing that the sweeps will start up again."

"Those rumors about the investors are true enough,

though I don't know if the government's secured any satellite coverage."

"What I'm saying is that this place probably won't be any more private than others, come the future."

"*You've* remained unscathed," Gabriel said.

I wouldn't get into personal stuff with him. "Supposedly," I said, still trying to scare him off, "Stamp heard about the so-called serenity, just like you. And the water, too."

"Stamp?"

I nodded. "Johnson Stamp probably sent that goon you just chased away."

It looked like Gabriel was turning the name over in his mind. Then he seemed to store it away and move on. "At any rate, I came out here to see if this was what I've been needing in life. I might be mistaken, though, based on the trouble that's already greeted me."

"You mean those injuries?" I motioned toward his healing face, injecting the right amount of suspicion into my voice.

Gabriel nodded, and when Chaplin tilted his head in sympathy, the man laughed, reaching out to pet the dog. Chaplin, of course, reveled in it.

Affection whore, I thought, trying not to feel envious, because Chaplin had always been *my* friend.

"How I got bloodied up is an involved tale." Gabriel cleared his throat, as if losing the words. "I was only resting out of the sunlight when they found me, just before dark was about to slant down."

Folks hardly went outside here without heat suits—which he didn't seem to own—during the day anymore. The weather could be that hellish, but probably that was why he'd been resting out of the light and traveling by night.

"The next thing I knew," he said, "I was yanked out of my cave and roughed up for straying onto someone's claimed property."

"You couldn't see who it was?"

"Not with the scarlet in my eyes."

The reference to red made me dig my nails into my palms. Blood, attacks. Bad guys everywhere, even in the places you least expected them to be.

"This stinks of Stamp's guys," I said. "Word has it they'll mess with anyone they find on the surface round here. Their boss doesn't seem to exercise much control over them."

"So you don't go out there often." Gabriel was rubbing Chaplin's neck, bringing the dog to the throes of ecstasy.

"Only a few of my neighbors do—unless we're gathered somewhere else."

I jerked my chin toward the east wall, where more visz screens showcased the sparse common area in a cavern not far from my home. Everyone had a tunnel leading there, although few had been using them to meet in the open.

Not until lately.

Propping himself up to see better, Gabriel stopped petting Chaplin for a moment. The dog scratched out a paw in entreaty, and our guest grinned, then resumed his work, much to the whore's satisfaction.

Unable to watch much more, I went over to a screen that showed a middle-aged woman and a stocky, dark-haired man near the same age sitting at a rickety crate table. Zel Hopkins and Sammy Ramos, two fellow Badlanders who'd recently started to venture into the common area since Stamp's arrival. Unlike with the outside visz lenses, Stamp hadn't found this secluded gathering spot yet, so Sammy and Zel obviously felt secure in meeting there tonight.

I turned up the volume; doing so would automatically lower the feeds from the other viszes.

The sound of chatter emerged from the speaker. Earlier, when I'd been listening in, they'd talked about how one of Stamp's guys—a spindly-legged youth whom Zel had nicknamed "Twiggy"—had been slaughtered last night. I'd turned down the sound, not wanting to hear more because it revved up something vengeful and bloodthirsty in me.

Bad guys getting their due. A reckoning. Justice.

I lowered the volume again. "This is the common area.

Back when we all found each other and decided to settle in a tight community, Dad connected viszes to this spot where a few Badlanders used to gather. They stopped meeting for a while"—here, I took care to keep myself controlled and subtle, even if Chaplin lowered his head and averted his gaze from me—"but now people are meandering out again. They're worried about Stamp moving into the area and letting his wild men run free." I crossed my arms over my chest. "This is how I hear the news that goes round."

Gabriel had stopped petting Chaplin, and the dog didn't ask for more this time. "You really don't go out of your home much?"

"Not if I don't have to. They know I listen in on them, though." Sometimes my neighbors even addressed me, asking me to join them, but that had to be just a civil habit left over from the days my dad used to socialize with the locals. "We respect each other's privacy enough to keep a distance when it's required."

Saying it out loud, I realized how cold I seemed, but that was the state of things everywhere, not just here. Neighbors who lived close but never much communicated.

"How do you sustain yourself if you don't go out?" Gabriel asked.

I stuck to safe answers. "I'm able to do my own water mining. I also use a hydroponics system to farm enough grub for me and Chaplin, and we supplement that by trading for more supplies with the others on a leave-it-by-my-door basis. There's not much out there for vegetation anymore." Quite a few old herbivores had died off because of that. "We make it just fine, though. And if there's a threat?" I gestured toward my wall, where the archaic collection of guns, knives, projectiles, and chains hung in a dare for him to ask more intrusive questions.

Hardly getting the hint, he said, "Where'd you gather all that?"

"Salvaged from abandoned materials round these parts. As I said, we make it just fine."

He grinned, like he respected my defensiveness. "So this Stamp . . . ?"

"Why, Mr. Gabriel," I said, "what happened to your need for sleep?" He'd just been trying to avoid conversation, hadn't he? Something had sure changed that.

"My unguent works its wonders." He ruffled Chaplin's fur, smiled at me again, then squeezed his eyes in pain, lifting a hand to the cuts near his mouth.

But his gesture struck me all wrong. *Now* it seemed like Gabriel was acting, like he was belatedly faking his hurt.

Yet . . . that smile of his. It heated my belly again, and that heat slipped right down to my center, tightening into an ache I felt most mornings when I woke up to realize there'd be no way to fully satisfy the brutal longings of the night.

A mixture of anger, confusion, fear stretched me, but I lowered my arms, pressed them against my stomach.

Better. Still, this stranger was making me awful uncomfortable.

"I don't get it," I finally said. "A bit ago, you were bleeding like there was no tomorrow. And now . . ."

He'd gone stiff, his eyes shuttered to emptiness.

"Now I'm wildly improved."

"The gel healed you that fast? What's in it?"

"Trade secret. But I might be persuaded to share because of your kindness. In fact, I feel compelled to offer more."

At the innuendo, my body flared up and the ache between my legs intensified, sharpened.

Panic really flooded me this time, overtaking my self-control. And, damn it, did I ever need some, because control balanced the world, inside and out.

Gabriel must've realized that he'd crossed a line with me, because he raised his hands in a mild type of surrender. "Listen, I wasn't getting fresh. I'm only thinking that maybe you'd like an extra hand around to chase off this Stamp and his guys for the time being. You do me a kindness, and I return it. That's how things should work."

I looked at my wall of weapons and then back at him. "I've already got good company."

"I see that. And I had years of wildlife hunting with my dad before the Second Amendment was struck down. Hunting made me good at using most of what you've got."

"All the same, Mr. Gabriel, no thank you."

"Hey, I couldn't sleep well if I left you in such straits. . . ."

"Your sleep isn't my concern. Chaplin, c'mere." I patted my thigh, hoping my dog wasn't so taken by the stranger that he'd refuse me.

But when Chaplin trotted over—just after one last glance at Gabriel—I hugged him. Hugged him hard.

My voice was muffled by fur. "You can convalesce here as you require. But after sufficient time, you and your miracle gel will have to walk."

"Then I'll just get my rest, miss."

Jay-sus. It'd do no good for him to be "miss"-ing me all the time. "The name's Mariah. You might as well call me that. But don't think it's an invitation to stay."

"I understand, Mariah." He sank down to his blankets and closed his eyes, his lips spread in a bruised grin.

Not trusting him an inch, I sat on the couch and faced our guest, my hand near my holster. Then, since I had nothing to occupy myself for the coming hours, I ended up just watching him: taking in his wounded features, his . . . lure. Yeah, that was what it was. I couldn't *not* watch the stranger.

Little by little, I even allowed myself to open fully to him, to be saturated with him. All the while, my blood heated, simmering until every pop was agony.

It wasn't until Chaplin nuzzled my hand that I got hold of myself. Then, in control once again, I continued my vigil, counting the moments until Gabriel would thankfully leave.

4

Mariah

Just after dawn broke on the visz bank, I gave up on guarding against Gabriel, who was still resting, and got to work farther belowground. I left Chaplin lying next to him, but I wondered if my dog was too taken by our guest to sentinel properly.

Hoping he'd be as ferocious as Intel Dogs could be, I retreated to my living area, where I dressed in work garb and strapped on my helmet, which featured a lightweight solar-battery lamp that Dad had once contrived. I left Chaplin to do his thing while I went to work. I had no other choice, because there were too many things to see to, like mining water down below the dwelling, culling enough food for today's meals, and molding more ammunition for my revolvers just in case Stamp saw fit to bother us even after Gabriel had chased away his man last night.

After one last look at Chaplin nestled all content and happy at Gabriel's relaxed side, I headed for the north tunnel's door, went through it, and switched on my headlamp as I turned round to ease the door shut.

The light showcased the wooden barrier I'd handmade out of a salvaged billboard from an old highway. On it, the faded sign of a crucifix stood at an angle, rays of light emanating from its glory. GO WITH THE ANGELS, it said, right above a church address that had long since been torn asunder, just like most religions before organizations of personality had replaced them: Web leaders, saviors of society, pop culture idols that substituted for spirituality.

All that remained of this church's address was CALIF.

And then a tear, right down the side, cutting off the name of a state that pretty much no longer existed.

I turned my back on the sign, but that didn't quite do the trick. Most days I could look at that crucifix and derive a sad bit of optimism from it, reminded that there were people who'd once believed in something they thought was pure. It made me think there had to be more waiting for me in the future than things that'd been ripped and nearly shredded. But today, after Gabriel's bloodied arrival, that crucifix only reminded me of screams, red, agonizing gashes, my mom and brother red-soaked and reaching blindly for life as Dad opened fire on the burglars, spraying bullets over his loved ones in the process, too.

Unsteadily, I picked up one of the waterpacks that sat near a table made out of an old fruit crate. While sliding the straps over my shoulders, I caught sight of myself in a mirror that canted over the table, something I avoided doing as much as possible because it was too hard to see how much I'd changed.

But now . . . now I did look, averting my helmet so as not to shine the light directly into the mirror. My red hair was slicked back from my underground-pale face, making me too stark, too hard. On my skin, I searched for any sign of scars, although I knew none would be there.

I shrugged one shoulder, as if using it to hide the cleared skin on my neck. I could still feel the scars, old and new, itching just beneath the surface.

The light flashed in the mirror at me, a reminder that I was lollygagging, and I turned from the image, the woman

I didn't know anymore—the true stranger—and descended
the stairs, the ominous drip of water tapping and echoing
against the rock below. My helmet's lamp provided a fuzzy
glow, creating dancing fingers of shadow. The lower I went,
the cooler the air became. That was why I liked it down
here; outside during the day, I would've needed cool-
modifiers to stay healthy. Here, hidden away, I had everything a person might need.

Actually, we did get occasional rainfall in the New Badlands, and that resulted in the area holding just enough water
for survival, although who knew how long things would last
for the Badlanders and the wildlife, most of which consisted
of mutant animals that had come out after the changes
because they were better able to survive than the old species
in these conditions. But, for the time being, me and the
others depended on pumping liquid from aquifers, where
water collected in porous layers of underground rock. My
dad, even after losing his faith in the science that had
employed and sustained him, had devised a hand-pump
system, as well as the camouflaged solar panels that provided what little electricity we required.

When I reached the bottom, I headed toward a small
opening that led to a massive cavern. A network of hand
pumps decorated the rock walls opposite a UV-lighted,
climate-controlled hydro-garden. Upright tubes stood filled
with homemade nutrient fluid, most of the ingredients gathered as a result of trading with the locals. I normally left
water from my abundant claim near the common-area tunnel leading to my home, and my neighbors left what I needed
in return without face-to-facing—things like seeds, meat,
materials they'd salvaged from outside. As a result, my garden gave me items as varied as tomatoes, lettuce, peppers,
and even strawberries and melons.

I prepared myself for some hard labor, not only out of
necessity but because . . . hell, I was the first to admit that
it often cleansed away my reality. So I spent hours working
the pumps, farming as much water as I could directly into

my container packs, which I'd use to transfer my booty back home. After that, I'd repeat the process with more packs kept here below.

When I'd run five packs to the stairs, I returned to get more water, to complete my afternoon until night came round.

Night, always night. It never failed to arrive, with Stamp and his men, with the bad things lurking out there . . .

Throwing myself back into the flow of labor, I retreated to a corner of the cavern—a workshop Dad had created. I cleared the area of the chains I'd recently brought out from storage, tucking them in a chest, my throat tight. Then I resumed work.

Cleansing, wonderful work.

I shaped revolver ammunition out of the cache of lead my father had come upon once during a salvage trip. He'd found a store of it under the frame of a broken house and, since we'd never had much cause to use weapons before Stamp arrived, the ammunition had lasted. But now I didn't want to be caught lacking.

After melting and then molding bullets, I tended my garden, plucking out enough to normally appease me and Chaplin . . . and now our guest, too, I supposed. Then I transferred all but one of my waterpacks upstairs.

Exhausted, but in a bone-weary way that meant I'd worked a good day and might just sleep like a rock, I strapped on that one last pack and returned to my living space, where Chaplin rested at the foot of Gabriel's blankets. When the dog saw me, he perked up, lifting his furry brown head and wagging his tail.

"Hey, boy," I whispered, bending down and opening my arms right up.

Chaplin crashed into me, and I grunted at the impact on my overworked body. Still, I held on to my friend. Then my gaze strayed to the sleeping Gabriel. He seemed peaceful, if not still banged up and bandaged.

When I found myself peering a little too hard at him—I

still couldn't see or hear him breathing, couldn't hear any other signs of life—I ruffled Chaplin's fur and scratched his ears, refocusing on my friend.

"Any trouble up here while I was gone?" I asked.

Chaplin chuffed and lowered his gaze, scolding me for being so insecure about his abilities to sentinel a man.

I paused, and he tilted his head, probably wondering if I was going to lay into him with some chiding. But then I attacked him with playful petting instead. Chaplin was right—he'd never let me down, even now.

The dog pounced on me, dominating until I wrestled him to the floor, where he barked, calling uncle. I backed off, suddenly realizing that I shouldn't be roughhousing in front of even a snoozing guest.

I'd been raised better. I could just hear Mom now. *How about some etiquette, lady-girl?* she would've said, smiling and going back to restoring the old dresses that I, so many years ago, had unearthed from abandoned dwellings and brought home, just to see Mom light up. Dad would've listened to the exchange and laughed, going back to smoking his pipe and thinking about some brilliant solution for getting the world back to normal.

I softly clapped my hands for Chaplin to get to his feet, then headed for the water storage unit and completed my daily work by transferring the contents of my packs into the massive contraption. Then I got started on a meal. Earlier, I'd fed my dog and myself a big one consisting of a fat sand-rabbit Chaplin had caught this morning while I'd still been dozing. Gabriel had been out like a burned bulb, so he hadn't eaten anything yet.

By the time I whipped up salads and fruit blooms and cooked the rest of the mouthwatering sand-rabbit, dusk had arrived on the outside-view viszes. I carried a metal plate to Gabriel.

But when I got to his blankets, Chaplin was snoozing away and the stranger was gone, the only thing left of him being his discarded coat.

Pulse jerking, I barely got his full plate to the ground instead of dropping it—food was far too valuable to drop— and reached for the revolver I'd put in my holster earlier. At the same time, I shook Chaplin awake.

"Where'd he go?" I asked. "You've got to keep an eye on him!"

The dog blinked, his eyes fuzzy. It didn't take but a second for him to sniff, then train his gaze on the empty make-shift bed.

"What happened, boy? Come on, don't tell me you sacked out while on guard."

Chaplin made a low whimper—an apology. His expres-sive face arranged itself in confusion as he got up, then sniffed round for his new buddy.

"Damn it." I stood, training my revolver round the room. *Had* Gabriel been one of Stamp's guys? Had he been instructed to infiltrate my home by any means necessary, even with a ruse that played on my better instincts?

Or had he just up and left, as I'd wanted him to do all along?

I pushed back a rush of odd disappointment at that.

I heard Chaplin bark for attention, and I whipped round, aimed and ready, only to find my dog near the north under-ground entrance.

The billboard door had been left open, its crucifix-postered back to the inside wall.

"What's this?" Once there, I realized that an empty waterpack I'd set by the fruit crate table was gone.

I dashed back to get my helmet from my living area. What was Gabriel up to?

Chaplin was right behind me as I pointed my revolver down below.

"You think he's stealing water?" My voice was near trembling with anger. "You think he'll be reporting back to Stamp with what he sees down there?"

Chaplin merely panted, shaking his head a little and posing no theories of his own. With a whimper-grunt, he indicated that I should be careful, that he'd be waiting up here for me.

"If the cretin comes back upstairs with me chasing his tail," I said, "get him."

Without waiting for a response, I closed the door behind me—but not all the way. Then I descended, hoping Chaplin wouldn't go and fall asleep again. Not that I thought he would, because he no doubt also felt betrayed by the thought of Gabriel stealing something so valuable from us.

I crept down the stairs. Instead of hearing the soft call of water, a different sound pulled me forward. The sound of pumping, fast and smooth.

What the . . . ?

I reached the mining area, and what I witnessed made me slowly lower my revolver.

There Gabriel was, head bandages and all, in the near dark except for a solar-lit lantern he'd filched from the living area. His bag rested a few feet away from him, as if he couldn't bear to be away from it. His motions were tireless, almost effortless, about ten times faster than *I* could've ever managed.

And I was pretty hardy, if I said so myself.

Speechless, I watched him, so strong and capable, dressed in his rough white shirt, which had been rolled up at the sleeves. His trousers molded his long legs, and the vision sent tugs of that awful awareness through me.

But for a moment—just one taboo moment—I allowed myself to cling to it. Then I thought, *Wouldn't it be something if he really was helping? If he wasn't going behind my back to steal?*

All of that slid through me, and I must've made some barely audible, silly sound, because he abruptly paused, lifting his head. Then he turned all the way round to face me. Heat tore through my body double-force, a lonely, needful blast that made me clutch my revolver tighter.

I tried to say something, failed, then tried again. "Like I said before, you're not looking so ill."

He wasn't even sweating, but suddenly his chest was rising and falling, as if he were making himself out to be more tired than he'd first seemed. It was almost as if he were just realizing that he shouldn't have gotten so damned much done.

As he lifted an arm in modest greeting, I noticed how the muscles in his forearms strained.

"Guess I got carried away," he said. "You were busy in the food prep area, so I figured I'd do some exploring around here. Your system is easy to decipher, easy to work. I even seem to have found a pretty efficient way of speeding things up, pumpwise. Lucky I've done some water farming here and there myself, so I thought I'd get down to it and thank you for helping me out at the same time."

He'd filled about a third of the waterpacks that had been stored down here. God-all.

"How long have you been at it?" I asked.

Gabriel planted his hands on his hips and surveyed the packs. "Since dusk closed in on the outside viszes."

After doing the math, I was so stunned that my arm loosened, letting down my revolver to my side. He couldn't have been working for more than a half hour.

He seemed to understand my bewilderment. "I've done my share of manual jobs. Been real good at them, too. Strong as a bull, that's what my dad used to say back Before . . ."

Gabriel cleared his throat, as if chasing away the pain. He nodded toward the pumps. "I could do well at a job like this."

It took a moment for the words to sink in. "I hope you're not expecting me to take you on."

He grinned, wiping a hand over his mouth. "I guess I'm not."

A beat passed, laden with more than the air's dank must. Awkward, this lack of knowing what to say.

Finally, I settled on something simple. "Mr. Gabriel, I really do thank you for your endeavors." Not that I was fully convinced he wasn't stealing. "But dinner's ready for you."

"If you don't mind, I thought I'd work on through some more."

His refusal once again surprised me. "Aren't you still under the weather?"

"Feeling better," he said. "Work's good for recovery."

His comment should've made me trust him a little more. In this world, there were mostly two kinds—those who worked because it made them forget, and those who ran and played because it made them forget. The hubs were supposedly full of the latter now—overstimulated hordes that didn't have the sense of animals.

Gabriel capped off his comment with one more. "Far be it from me to lay about and be waited on, anyway."

The tough part of me wanted to say, *If you're feeling so fine, then get out of my home*, but before I could even shape the words, he'd turned away, clearly intent on continuing his labor.

And, without any more fuss, he did just that. I wasn't sure how to handle that, so I just kept standing. And standing.

While I watched, one thing I saw was that his pace had considerably slowed, as if he knew I was gauging his more efficient work system and wondering how it could possibly trump my own.

He obviously sensed me still standing there minutes later, too. But, unfazed, he grinned at me, then carried on.

Well then.

I went back upstairs and set to feeding both me and Chaplin. The dog kept casting me inquisitive glances, but I didn't even know how to begin explaining what I'd just experienced.

Finally, after cleaning up, I ventured back down, only to find Gabriel still pumping away.

Although his pace had languished, all but four of my waterpacks were full.

Maybe he *was* a true sort of guy. Or maybe he was real good at playing some kind of confidence game that would explode into my getting double-crossed. Any way I looked at it, he'd done some nice work, and I couldn't complain about that part. Instead, I came over to don a pack, then carry it to the foot of the stairs. I continued moving each one in preparation to transfer them home.

Soon, he joined me, silent in his labor.

Side by side we worked, connected by these rote motions. For the first time in . . . ever . . . I got a clue about what it meant to be at ease with a person who wasn't family, what it was like not to feel on guard or threatened in the presence of someone new, and that was certainly a switch from what I'd been feeling round him before—worked up, bothered, strained by the boundaries of control.

Maybe I was getting used to Gabriel. Too used to him.

In the end, he slid his carryall over his chest and we both secured the first of the packs on our backs. But before mounting the stairs, Gabriel sent a glance at the pumps, smiling in his quiet way. My helmet light bathed his facial injuries, which were all but gone.

A question tipped my tongue, but I hesitated, half of me not wanting to interrupt whatever was going on in his mind. I suspected it was something like pride, and I could respect that, even if I had no idea what the rest of him was all about.

But I would be questioning him later. No doubts there. You need to question everything, even if you think you know what's happening.

Finally, when silence went as far as was comfortable, I spoke. "Hungry now?"

At that, he drew in a long breath. His gaze went blurry.

I stiffened, on high alert. His look was frightening. Exciting. Both.

As he fisted his hands, his veins popped to the surface of his skin. He trained his gaze on the ground.

"The thought of food presently turns my stomach," he said. "I'd rather sleep that off, Miss Mariah."

"You need something to eat—"

His voice came out garbled. "Don't." Then he composed himself, lifting his head, his mouth tight. "Don't mention hunger again."

I itched to put my hand on the revolver I'd tucked back

in its holster, but something told me it was a bad idea to make a move. Instead, I stared right back at him, testing him until his mouth relaxed and he shook his head.

"What I'd like," he said, "is some rest. I believe I overdid it."

My instincts said to kick him outside again where he belonged. Even though we'd worked in a smooth partnership down here, it didn't mean I'd be okay with having him hang round.

I must've given away my thoughts by allowing them to settle on my face. In fact, his eyes got that intense gleam again before he clenched his jaw, then relaxed it.

But I couldn't help noticing it was a forced type of relaxed.

"Please, Mariah," he said quietly. "I'd just like to stay a fraction longer."

He sounded so in need that I couldn't turn him out. What kind of thing would I be if I did? Chaplin had been right about one matter—if I'd had someone to help me when my family had required it most, life would be so different. Besides, Gabriel hadn't caused me trouble yet. One more night wouldn't be a tragedy.

Sometimes I hated that I had a conscience. "A fraction longer," I said, beginning to walk toward the stairs. "And that's all, Mr. Gabriel."

From behind me, he said, "Thank you." It sounded as if he were smiling, as if I'd done good.

Right. Good wasn't a word best applied to me. My neighbors might even testify to that if they were less guarded.

We ascended the steps, with me in the lead, his lantern and my helmet lights bobbing over the rock walls as we got closer to the door. The stairs made way to the closed door and the crucifix billboard poster with the holy image coming into focus like a piece of impossible heaven; it always seemed so close as I came back home day after day, but when I got to it, the image always turned out to be a painted lie.

"Chaplin's going to be foaming at the mouth for company," I said, moving aside and turning to Gabriel as I reached the landing. "So expect—"

I heard, more than saw, Gabriel crashing to his knees on the stairs. Unthinkingly, I extended a hand to grab him, only to grip air.

But when my light's dim beam showed him on hands and knees, safe, I exhaled.

Yet . . . he didn't seem right. Not with him on all fours, his head bowed and his fingers clutching the step in front of him. His waterpack was like a hump as he heaved in tortured breaths.

"Open that door." His voice was as mangled as it'd been in the mining area, when he'd told me not to mention hunger again. "Please, *open it.*"

Without question, I darted to the door, pulling it toward me until the billboard faced the wall, just as it had been doing when I'd found it open earlier.

"Okay," I said. Would I have to drag him the rest of the way up if he'd thrown out a knee? Had he overdone our labor to such an extent that he couldn't function now?

Slowly, he crawled up to the rickety stair landing, keeping his head lowered. It was only when he reached level ground, past the door, that he raised his gaze. His eyes were filled with a wary terror that seized my veins and tried to shake them free of my body.

He stayed like that for a minute, regulating his breathing. Chaplin bounded over to him but hung back at the sight of his new friend's state.

"What—?" I began to ask.

"Sick." Gabriel lowered his gaze again so I couldn't read it. "Back to . . . bed . . ."

I removed my waterpack, then bent down to ease his own off. Then, carefully—careful for so many reasons—I maneuvered his arm over my shoulders and led him to his blankets.

In doing so, I couldn't help breathing him in, my lungs tight with the struggle of trying to keep my senses fortified at the same time. But I lost the battle, becoming saturated with the scent of him—a vague tinge of earth where there should've been musk and the tang of skin.

Without hurting him, I made quick work in setting him down, then backed away, my limbs weak and quivery.

It was only when he reached for his flask that I succeeded. I concentrated on how he gulped down its contents, how he closed his eyes and reveled in the shuddering pleasure of the liquid—a mixture that left his lips flushed red.

Then, obviously satisfied, he capped the flask and slumped to the blankets, keeping the container close to his chest.

Damn. *Damn.* What had I let in?

I went to pull the door shut, thinking of the billboard crucifix on the other side and how it'd affected Gabriel.

5

Gabriel

Gabriel lay on his blankets, feeling Mariah's gaze press down on him.

Unlike last night, when he'd been too beaten to think straight, he'd remembered to breathe this time, showing her that he was capable of it, though his body was undead, his soul and life as he'd known it long gone. Under better circumstances, he was good at rolling back his full powers so as to blend with regular society as best as he could. And he'd done such a decent job of survival out in the world that he'd even fooled himself into thinking he *wasn't* a preter sometimes.

But his recent errors—especially after encountering the crucifix he hadn't seen on the rear of the door until he'd come back up the stairs—could've all added up for Mariah by now.

Could she tell he was . . . different?

Shit. It was times like this when Gabriel wished he were a demon or were-creature, which were supposed to be tough to recognize when they were in human form. The latter were even rumored not to have access to their extraordinary powers or animal habits when in their "people bodies." Vampires had to be way more vigilant than either variety.

Now, here on the blankets, he held back from opening his eyes and catching Mariah's gaze to peer into her mind, as he'd attempted to do upon meeting her last night. He'd only meant to do a scan, to see what she was all about, maybe even to sway her into offering unquestioned shelter. And until she'd blocked him with a wall of mental caution, he'd been hopeful, too, mostly because it'd been easy enough to read Chaplin's thoughts—energy, lines of translated communication that a vampire could understand no matter what language the other party used. As a vampire, Gabriel had an affinity for canines, plus Chaplin was so eager to know who Gabriel was that the dog had opened most of himself right on up.

In fact, when Gabriel had taken the risk of using his gaze to sway whoever might be watching that visz monitor on the other end from where he'd been on the outside, the dog had sensed Gabriel's good intentions, welcoming him, even in the face of the recent activity with Stamp, and immediately acquiescing to become Gabriel's familiar. He had agreed to shield his new master's identity, plus silently vowed protection.

Mariah hadn't been quite as cooperative.

However, even the canine had proven to possess his own protective limits. Heck, the dog was even now beginning to shake off Gabriel's sway pretty well. Too bad Gabriel, a young vampire as far as power went, had gotten only basic information out of Chaplin so far.

But with Mariah? Gabriel had hardly gotten a flash of sharing from her before she'd blocked him without even knowing it. She was a tough one. Smart. On constant watch. Dangerous if he should push too far.

He could've tried, all right, for an experienced vampire was supposed to be able to sway a subject after mind-reading them, persuading them that nothing was amiss. Yet even after just a couple of years, Gabriel was too green to depend on that ability, and he'd preferred to just back off and leave

Mariah's mind alone this time out, especially after Chaplin had invited Gabriel inside his home, where the visz screens had revealed the other New Badlanders gathered in the common area. Others who might just turn out to be much more sympathetic to a man with questions.

Mariah was closed off, as if wanting to hide something from him, and since she'd set herself at such a distance, he couldn't pursue any sort of interview with her.

At least he had Chaplin.

After the dog had mentally shared a very casual introduction of the neighbors, Gabriel had decided that he would definitely use them, not Mariah, to do what he had come out west to do—ask all that was required to track down the one person he was out here to find.

Abby.

On the back of Gabriel's eyelids, he detected a needling wisp of memory. A woman who'd left him with a puzzle of a broken existence that he'd been trying to piece back together ever since she'd left him.

Keeping his eyes shut—more because of the pain of remembering Abby than the threat of Mariah's realizing that he'd recovered—Gabriel heard his hostess shift position from her spot across the room. He guessed that she'd rested her hand on that revolver snuggled against her hip.

The weapon wouldn't do harm to him unless it contained silver bullets that could poison his system. But her geared-up caution told him that the crucifix image had given her ideas about what he might be.

Okay then, he thought. *Time for damage control.*

But before he sought it, Mariah began walking out of the room; he could hear the fading of her vital signs. Most people only sounded like a tune to him, their blood humming and calling, but she sounded like patterns of angry, thrashing, spellbinding percussion that kept time with his bloodlust. To a certain degree, he'd heard the same music in Abby, though she'd been more like a symphony in driving minor chords than this stormy mess of primal beats in Mariah.

He was also taken with the scent of her—again, so similar to Abby's own. Yet both were different from any others. It was something he couldn't describe in olfactory terms as much as how the aroma provided another layer to the sounds.

Gabriel had to fight the push of his incisors against his gums. There was something about this woman that got to him, even if, physically, she was nothing like Abby, whose face had reminded him of a demure portrait he'd once seen of a near-ancient Victorian lady on a Nets museum site. But Mariah, with hair the color of blood, wasn't soft.

Not when she thought he was looking, anyway.

Gabriel's ears tuned in to the shuffle of Chaplin trotting out of the room to follow his mistress, and he opened his eyes, sat up, then helped himself to just one more swig of the blood in his flask. It wasn't the freshest way to nourish himself, but the liquid was kept cool thanks to the solar battery in the device, which he often buried in the sand with the uncovered battery-side up while he tucked his own self away during the day.

He shoved it into the back pocket of his trousers, spied the plate of food Mariah had meant for him to eat, then took out a swath of oiled material from his bag and wrapped up the vittles. He would find a nocturnal creature outside that would appreciate the sustenance simply enough, and then after he'd lured it, he would, in turn, take the blood it offered during what Gabriel always hoped would be an uncomplicated hunting session.

Though it didn't normally turn out that way.

He put the food into his carryall. The crucifix had stunned him for a gut-tearing few moments, but now he could move with the best of them as he stood, tracking Mariah's scent.

It led him to a room that was lined with rickety shelves, all of which bore books. Real books, too—not the e-backs that everyone in the world read on screens. These novels and encyclopedias and almanacs had actual paper and, thanks to the thousands of vampire-heightened olfactory receptors in his nose, he could inhale to smell the battered leather and pulp.

He wondered if this had been her dad's private room. Chaplin had mind-flashed on Dmitri Lyander last night, but the dog had blocked Gabriel from knowing deeper details, such as where Mariah's father was now. Dead, probably, since Chaplin hadn't been able to hide a tinge of profound sorrow that had come with the image of the pipe-smoking, mustached scientist.

Mariah, who had her back to the shelves, still maintained contact with her revolver as she faced Gabriel, a book already laid open in her other hand as she perused a page.

In spite of himself, he looked up and down the length of her: the rough boots; the low-riding cloth pants that seemed practical save for some delicate lacings up the sides; the loose white shirt she'd donned that made him imagine what might be beneath.

His incisors pushed as he listened to the cadence of her blood, and he concentrated on those bookshelves.

"Thought you were resting," she said in her usual accusatory style.

But she'd taken him in, and because of that alone, he would cope.

"Not to worry," he said, playing up his aw-shucks nature in the hopes that it would steal the attention away from everything else he preferred to keep under wraps, like the pulse of famished longing he felt whenever he was within range of her. "I'm pretty sure I was only temporarily weakened. But your meal just remedied that."

"Good to hear."

Damage control, he reminded himself. He was determined to lead her away from any suspicions without getting himself into more trouble by using the power of sway to distract her. She just wasn't easily opened to him. Besides, it was altogether simpler to slip by unnoticed when he wasn't utilizing his abilities. Simpler to fade into a groove of survival.

But, most of all, Abby had made him wonder if trading his monster in for a better self truly did improve him.

"The books," he said, nodding at the shelves. "No wonder you're so steeped in the Old American language. You study how everyone used to talk and you've kept yourself away from all the dialects out there."

"There're too many to keep track of, anyway." Mariah set the book down on a crate table and turned the page, all while keeping touch with that revolver. "You speak Old American pretty naturally yourself."

All right, so she wasn't very distracted just yet. Like most shut-in citizens in the hubs, she was relatively focused.

Mariah didn't even glance up from the book. Chaplin squatted on his haunches next to her, bright-eyed as he wagged his tail.

Gabriel winked at his familiar, who, in spite of his helpfulness, still retained such loyalty to his mistress. Then he addressed his hostess's comment, which had seemed conversational, though he was under no illusion that this was anything but a continued interrogation.

"I speak Old American," he said, "because I lived in a sanctuary in the Southblock. We cut ourselves off from society there, just as you folks did out here. There're a lot of places that outside forces haven't corrupted yet."

The mention of the Southblock finally merited a glance from Mariah, probably because it was a mass of states—the remaining part of Florida that hadn't been consumed by encroaching waters, and what used to be known as Georgia, Alabama, and Mississippi—that had been born from chaos. They'd once tried to secede from the Union, and it was the first part of the United States that the government had officially locked down with martial law.

By then, Gabriel had already become a vampire, saved by a young, anonymous, self-appointed female with frizzy dark hair and eyes like the shine of a firebird. She'd come to him a few years after the mosquito epidemic, when he'd been, like many others, still consistently drunk off his ass after the loss of his family. But that hadn't stopped her from continuing her personal crusade to lure every human she met into a shadowed place, where she would bite, then exchange blood with one of her "lambs" to keep them alive, because monsters had proven immune to existing diseases and were said to adapt to new conditions quickly.

At first, he was grateful for what she'd done, and to hear her whisper her intentions to him during the exchange. She'd offered hope and what he thought would be a path to sobriety in such a time of darkness, but that was before the blood-lust had really hit. Still, he'd tried to locate her that night after he'd recovered, wishing for some real guidance in this new form. When he'd been unsuccessful in that, he'd spent weeks on her trail, only to hear that she'd been caught by a government-sanctioned slayer—one of the "Shredders." However, for some reason, this Shredder hadn't terminated her. Gabriel would've known if the slayer had done it, too, because, during his initiation in that black alley, his creator had left him with a slim survival pamphlet he'd eventually destroyed because it could prove easy evidence of his preter status. He'd read the thing before getting rid of it, and at least it'd said that his maker's termination would result in the return of his humanity.

But that hadn't happened just yet. And even if he got his soul back, he highly doubted he'd ever get rid of his monster, something he clung to even as he wished he could cut it out of him.

Once exposed, always mentally infected, he thought.

"I've heard of the Southblock," Mariah said, still in investigatory mode. "Why'd you leave?"

Because Abby had disappeared without any warning.

But he didn't mention it, even if Chaplin sensed what was haunting Gabriel and lowered his tail, tilting his head in empathy.

"I've already told you why I came out to the Badlands," Gabriel said instead. "It's not as crowded here. The Southblock sanctuary was filling up, and I thought that'd lead to a raid all too soon. I got out before bad guys got hold of us and took what was left of what we had."

And then he'd hunted clues from east to west, tracking rumors of one person having seen Abby, then another. The path had finally guided him out here, into the New Badlands, to this community.

With every passing second, Gabriel was itching to say Abby's name—to ask Mariah if she'd ever seen a woman with kind brown eyes and a smile that had all but disappeared on the night Abby had discovered Gabriel wasn't like her. But he held back, knowing his questions would only be shot down.

Even Chaplin had blocked Gabriel's initial queries about Abby. Both mistress and companion were protective about their hidden community, about the details of their lives and those of the other Badlanders. Gabriel had the feeling they'd been burned before, yet they were only hosting him based on Chaplin's instincts that their guest truly wasn't there to do them any harm.

Mariah finally closed that book, but when she gripped the butt of her weapon, Gabriel knew he hadn't passed any kind of test.

Then she fired away—just not with her revolver.

"The crucifix," she said. "Your cold skin. Sleeping all day. Everything else about you . . ."

Too late, he spied the cover of the old book she'd been reading.

Monsters.

He would need more than damage control here. Someone like Mariah might have it in her to disable him and then turn in his body to high authority for compensation. Before monsters had been deemed "cleared away" by the government, they used to be worth decent bounty, even to a recluse.

But he'd come a long way, and it would require more than a revolver to scare him. He had taken the gamble of living among humans in the Southblock, just to follow Abby there. He had risked going outside the sanctuary when he required feeding. He had been ready to die just to be near her because being away seemed even more suicidal.

Now, in this moment of possible exposure, Gabriel forced a grin that was even more seemingly careless than before.

"Vampires?" he asked Mariah, as if her question were too amusing to pursue.

She didn't draw her weapon, but she didn't release it, either. Next to her, Chaplin's eyes weren't bright anymore as the dog watched her, as if he dreaded having to make a decision between defending his new master and helping his old one.

"Hey," Gabriel said, his voice low and calm as he held up his hands in placation. It was still a better option than swaying her; that would be the worst thing to do, testing her wariness. Last night when he was injured, he hadn't cared as much. "If I *were* a vampire, I'd daresay you've got the wrong weapon with you. Aren't they supposed to be killed by stakes and the like?"

She gestured with her free hand toward the book. "Or fire or decapitation."

"Come on, Miss Mariah. Vampires and other preternatural things are only tales. Surely you know that, even out here."

"And that's why they have Shredders running round?" she asked.

Even the word itself was enough to send a shiver of wariness up Gabriel's spine.

"They say society used to have Shredders," he said, hedging the truth. "Back in the day when paranoia was at its height. Back when there was a run on sustenance and rumors about monsters were at their peak."

Back when the Nets had whipped people into a frenzy after offering proof of preters.

There'd been hunts, and the surviving monsters had to hide their true natures. Some, like Gabriel, even masqueraded among the humans who called preters "parasites," which was just a dirty name for creatures who used humans for food and water. The fear was actually that the monsters would feed off mortals—who were composed of a lot of water—for secondhand sustenance and would end up extinguishing the already-threatened human race altogether.

Gabriel added, "I haven't heard rumors of Shredders for a good while. Stories say that they ran out of work after they supposedly extinguished what monsters there were, and after regular people killed the rest off with impunity. But that's all bullshit, if you don't mind my candid description, Miss Mariah. Monsters were always a product of the fearful collective imagination."

"Urban legends," Mariah said. "Is that your take on it?"

"I have no other."

A hard smile shaped her lips, and he wondered anew just what'd happened to make her this way.

"Where do you get your information?" she asked. "The Nets?"

The toxic Web. Years ago, it had led to the demise of newspaper journalism, giving way to bloggers who weren't subject to the fact-checking process. Rumor had become truth and truth, rumor. In fact, real truth had seemed to die a nonresurrecting permanent death.

"I suppose," he said, leaning back against a wall, showing he had nothing to fear, at least from a revolver, "that I picked up some commentary about monsters during my travels. You probably also heard stories about a cure for preters, and that's another reason for the sharp drop in their supposed population."

"If monsters exist . . ." She narrowed her eyes, as if compensating for some vulnerability in his presence. "The bad guys would use the rumor of a cure to draw out any remaining creatures. Besides, there've always been stories, including the one about a cure for lyncanthropy."

It was a condition that had introduced itself in full after the mosquitoes had been dealt with. But it wasn't the same as actually being a werewolf; it was supposed to be a product of melancholia, which ran rampant after the world had altered. Lycanthropy had accounted for a lot of the "monster rumors," and Gabriel had been reluctantly thankful for the diversion, even while wondering if the condition had made humans more aware of monsters—fake or real—than ever.

He continued using a calm tone while avoiding hypnosis. "The only monsters out there are the human ones."

Mariah's gaze wandered to a wall. But Gabriel thought that maybe she was looking beyond it, outside, where there really were monsters who only needed to be invited in.

Just as Chaplin had invited *him*.

He watched her for a moment, caught a shard of some memory cutting through her gaze that made him tilt his head.

"What happened to you?" he asked, genuinely curious. "Why did you leave the world?"

She flinched, then turned back to him and, unable to control himself for a terrible instant, Gabriel sought her gaze and peeked into her temporarily unprotected mind to hear the cries of what he thought to be loved ones.

He saw blood on a woman who might've been her mom . . . then her brother . . .

Then there was a tearing wipe into a second, even more painfully vivid memory, blood . . .

The red of it clutched at him, and he dropped the connection. A tremor lined his veins, and he hungered. Yearned.

That was why he couldn't afford to look into people— because they might jigger his worst instincts with careless thoughts. That was why he should've been able to stop himself this time, too.

Chaplin winced, as if feeling his anguish, and Gabriel silently commanded the dog to keep this secret between them.

The dog quivered, as if the effort of separating secrets were too much.

Control. Gabriel needed to find it, to access it. Control was key to a monster's survival. It was almost all they had.

He took the reins of the conversation, leading it to where he thought it'd be safer.

"Ask me anything," he said to Mariah. "And I'll tell you so I can ease your wonderings."

He'd lie. He'd dodge. He'd hide.

"Okay then," she said. "The crucifix. Your reaction to it . . ."

"Coincidence." There—simple enough. "You know I hadn't eaten properly after I was injured, and I overtaxed myself while working." Gaining strength by the moment, he stood away from the wall, his tone lightening. "Besides, I'm an atheist. Always did have an aversion to crosses and the like."

Another lie—he'd had religion in his day, and the symbols of his own church burned at him every time he witnessed one. In a cross or crucifix, all he saw was hopelessness.

"Healing," she said, taking a step toward him. "You got rid of those injuries as if all you had to do was wish them away."

"The unguent I had you put on my wounds," he said. In truth, it was meaningless, slightly-tampered-with lard that he carried and used as part of his masquerade. "An old woman—an herbalist—made some for me before I struck out of the Southblock sanctuary."

Mariah still didn't seem won over. Steel, this one was.

"Your flask. What's in it? Blood?"

He laughed, as if that were ludicrous, but he knew he'd have to bury the object outside before she could check it. Chaplin had vaguely revealed to Gabriel that Mariah didn't leave the shelter unless necessary, and even then she didn't stray far, so the odds of her discovering it out there were slim.

"A concoction," he said, adding lie upon lie, "made from a nutrient powder and what water I manage to find. The old woman gave it to me, as well."

"Sleeping all day . . ."

"It's relatively cooler out here at night. Everyone knows that. Better to sleep when the weather is unkind."

As Mariah stood there, he could see that she was stuck between wanting to believe this stranger who'd proven so helpful today and disbelieving him out of wise necessity.

She glanced around the room, her gaze resting on a crate

with some sticks poking out of a metal cup, as if she or her dad used to char the ends to write on paper.

Walking over, she grabbed two of them, and Gabriel knew exactly what she was about to do: construct a make-shift cross to flash at him.

But Chaplin also must've sensed her intentions, because he sprang up on the crate, knocking it over, spilling the sticks to the ground, barking and making those strange yet patterned canine sounds at her.

He'd said something to her while blocking Gabriel, and he wondered what it was. Before he could mind-ask his familiar, the dog opened his thoughts.

Don't worry—I won't let her kick you out, Gabriel.

Mariah had already backed off, seemingly bothered by her companion's defense of Gabriel.

Chaplin yipped and yapped, stringing together a sen-tence, and Gabriel could hear what the dog was saying to Mariah now, because Chaplin was allowing him to.

He chased off Stamp's no-gooder. He can help. Monsters are serious business. Take it back.

"Just hush," Mariah said, her voice ragged with the betrayal of her friend. "He could be dangerous to us, and you know it."

The dog added a few more yaps. *We need him, Mariah. Trust me.*

She stared at Chaplin, as if wanting further explanation, and the dog added more, though he blocked Gabriel from knowing what he said.

Mariah sent Gabriel a strange glance.

He hoped whatever Chaplin had said worked. He needed the dog on his side, needed all the Badlanders to confide in him so he could find out about Abby. And after a short time, after he got some answers about why there'd been rumors about his lover's presence in the New Badlands, he'd leave Chaplin to Mariah, just as it should be.

She'd crossed her arms over her chest, as if she were trying her best to hold in the apology that came next.

"The dog . . ."

Her voice faded, but Chaplin barked at her.

Out with it.

Her flintiness returned with the spark to match. "The dog," she said louder, "means for me to apologize. Monster talk is a serious thing, he says, and it isn't supposed to be thrown about lightly."

This was progress. "You had your reasons."

She searched his gaze, then glanced at Chaplin, raising her brows as if to ask, *Is that a good enough sorry for you?*

Meanwhile, Gabriel couldn't help but feel the beats of her blood running, hot and passionate, notes crashing into each other to make that music he couldn't resist. He imagined running his mouth over her, reveling in her heightened scent until he was drunk on the hunger that was consuming him even now. He could almost feel his fangs sinking into her flesh, popping it open to let the blood seep out so he could fill himself with the anger—or was there something else combined with it that drew him?—that made her seem so alive to him.

Near dizzy, he fisted his hands, wrestling the emergence of fangs, the reddening of his irises, which would betray him.

He turned around before that could happen, ducking out of the room just as Chaplin barked after him.

"I'm off to that common area," Gabriel said, his voice low enough to barely disguise how garbled it was.

He could hear Mariah sucking in a breath to ask a question—probably *Why?*

But he cut her off.

"Don't wait up for me," he said as Chaplin darted ahead of him, obviously intending to show his new master to the tunnel that connected Mariah's home to the place where the Badlanders gathered.

"Chaplin!" Mariah called, her voice rushed.

It'll be okay, the dog thought. Then he mumbled something else to Mariah that Gabriel didn't catch since Chaplin had blocked him out again.

She didn't say another word.

Gabriel followed Chaplin beyond a steel door that stood adjacent to the one that led to her own underground work-shop. Shutting the barrier behind him, he leaned against the wall of the tunnel, not moving another inch as he yanked his flask out of his pocket. He gulped the last of the blood, trying to imagine Mariah's own life liquid coating his throat, then bursting into every part of him.

Once, he'd wanted Abby's blood like this, as well.

He lowered his empty flask, knowing that this appetite for Mariah would only end just as badly if he gave in to it.

6

Gabriel

By the time Gabriel reached the last door separating the tunnel from the common area, he was in as much control of his faculties as he could be.

He'd always needed to battle for any kind of handle on himself since Abby had gone. But even as his hunger had threatened to unleash itself whenever he was around her, there'd always been something about the rhythms of her heartbeat, her breathing, that kept him together. Even on that first night, when he'd found her running from a gang of bad guys through the streets and he'd saved her solely because the smell of her fear—and only *her* scent—she had gotten to him.

He'd needed to feed properly around Abby. Properly and frequently so her blood wouldn't pull at him with such a lack of mercy. But the extra effort had been worth it because she'd lulled his system, and he hadn't heard such rhythms in a person since he'd followed the low, stifling wind of the New Badlands and ended up finding Mariah.

Now that he even thought about it, Gabriel realized what Mariah's and Abby's vital sounds might have in common . . .

Fear, stronger and clearer than in most people?

Was that what made them stand out to him? He suspected that he liked to feed on that quality just as well as blood itself. . . .

Flushing himself of anything but the pressing desire to find answers about Abby, Gabriel rested his hand against the heavily locked common area's wooden door, taking a listen to what was going on inside. There were three distinct, muffled voices—what sounded to be a mature woman and man, plus an even older guy whose speech wasn't much more than a creaking of hooked-together words.

Gabriel's blood seemed to spiral through his veins. *Resources. Answers.*

But then his thoughts turned ruddy, soaking his memories with the useless answers he'd already come up with.

Abby, lying in her blanket-piled bed in her room—just one of many honeycomb-like nooks in the underground South-block sanctuary. Mosquito netting was draped so that it barely allowed a peek of her undernourished body curled in slumber, her light hair loose and tumbled. Up until that point, Gabriel had refrained from ever drinking from her, drinking from *anyone* down there. It would've been a death wish, possibly setting off an alarm that there was a monster in their midst.

Yet there she was, on the edge of disappearing from life altogether—a woman he'd known for only a couple of weeks, but one who had already ensnared him. She'd lost so much weight since he'd met her, lost her appetite for the processed foods sanctuary smugglers were able to acquire since any natural resources were scarce in the area. Abby had even been shying away from Gabriel as well as all others, and they could only guess that she was exhausted from existing this way. That she was letting go so she might pass on to what they said would be a better place.

Up until then, he'd loved Abby from a near distance, assuming the part of her protector, and she had been his mainstay. Sometimes she even wondered aloud if he'd stuck by her because rescuing her had validated him in some way she would never fully understand.

Gabriel had wondered about all that, too. He even thought that she had become his own mission, much like the one his creator had been following when she had saved *him*.

Even after he'd rescued Abby, she hadn't realized he was a monster. And he'd embraced the charade, sneaking off to the outside to hunt and then bury himself under the dirt just before dawn. He was determined to never let her see how he died a little every day, and knowing that she might be able to love him back, in spite of what he was, had made him that much less of a dreaded being. He'd loved her for that gift—for resurrecting him yet another time, even in this small way.

But that night, as he'd stood by her bed, seeing her slip away from him, seeing her chest rise and fall while he longed for the need to breathe right along with her, he'd been willing to do anything to keep her.

Anything.

So he'd gone closer. Closer.

Then, before he could register what was happening, he was at her neck, his sight red, his fangs sprung.

She'd awakened on the sharp inhalation of a coming scream, her eyes closing tightly when she saw his reddened gaze. But he'd registered the fear in her scent and thrashing pulse first, pushing his hand over her mouth to stop the sound, whispering that it was only him. And when she'd calmed, then opened her eyes, even without going into her mind, he saw that she knew what he'd been doing.

Then, by some miracle, as he'd taken his hand away from her lips, she invited him into the gift of her still-guarded, superficial thoughts.

He'd seen and felt wonder from her—at least as much as he *could* feel. She'd believed that he'd been rescuing her again, but this time with the bite and exchange of their blood, and she'd been grateful for his intentions.

My one, my only, she had thought to him. *My savior.*

But though he was inside her head, she had no idea how famished he was. How he'd wanted to gnaw and feed and condole something that could never really be assuaged.

"I won't tell," she'd nevertheless whispered to him, believing that he hadn't meant to kill her or hurt her, that he never would. "I won't tell any of them, Gabriel."

Though he'd never bitten and then exchanged blood with her to turn her, he'd taken Abby at her us-against-the-world promise, because if not her, then who? And she'd repaid him by growing stronger during the following week, eating, getting out of bed, though he often caught a distance in her gaze when she thought she was alone. She'd even blocked him out whenever he tried to access what she was feeling. Actually, she blocked out *any* type of persuasion, telling Gabriel that she needed to get used to how things had changed between them. She needed to think about where they should go now, what they should do. . . .

And then, one night after he'd slipped back into the sanctuary from his sleeping and hunting, he found that she was gone.

No good-bye. No nothing. She'd been ruthless, leaving just an empty bed with her scent still permeating the blankets. Just dead ends he'd slammed into after leaving the sanctuary to find her.

After months of getting nowhere, he'd finally come upon a good enough clue from a scuffer who sold black-market goods at the no-name hole in the ground near what used to be Kansas City. Gabriel had purchased the information for the price of his last meaningful possession—one of Abby's abandoned ruby earrings that he'd wrapped in a piece of cloth from a shirt of hers.

Then, armed with the knowledge from the scuffer that she'd purchased a higher grade of heat gear for her trip west, Gabriel headed toward the New Badlands.

Now, as he tuned back in to the chatter on the other side of the tunnel door, he found Chaplin watching him cautiously, and Gabriel realized that his gaze had gone reddish and his eyes would look bloodshot and brutal.

Reaching for control again, he gritted his teeth, hating his loss of self-containment. Hating the red that was braided throughout his every vampiric instinct.

He had it in him to overcome it. Abby had shown him it was possible. He just needed the chance.

"Didn't mean to worry you, boy," he whispered, bending down to pet the dog, whose heart rate had quickened. But when Gabriel grinned at him, Chaplin's vitals sounded like those of most other domesticated dogs, even if he was an Intel.

Though Chaplin was highly evolved, he was still a pup somewhere under all that fur, and his gaze brightened, his tongue lolling out. Gabriel knew he could look into the dog's mind without harm out here in the deserted tunnel, so he connected with the canine, sharing placid thoughts.

When he was done, he said, "Sure do appreciate you keeping mum about all this. But you know I'm not like the others out there—whatever it was that hurt you and yours."

And Gabriel almost even believed it himself.

The dog smiled, not giving any more than that, and Gabriel smiled back as Chaplin shared other thoughts: the pure joy of being loved, of being petted and appreciated.

So Gabriel obliged his familiar, stroking over Chaplin's smooth brown coat. At the same time, he tried once more to see if this version of a relaxed, happy dog might have it within him to parcel out anything more about Abby or Mariah.

Gabriel tried to slide right into the canine's head again, but the dog blocked him out with the usual wall of mental blackness.

"You're really that protective of her and the rest of the people here," Gabriel said.

Chaplin nodded, whining, though Gabriel didn't understand what he was saying.

But then the dog shared his thoughts again: an image of Chaplin standing guard next to a younger version of Mariah, who was huddled under a thermal blanket in what looked to be a stripped-down house in the night.

The picture made Gabriel long for her all the more. He liked the idea of saving her from ever being that helpless again, just as he'd felt with Abby.

After one last pat to Chaplin, Gabriel stood. "I suppose I'd be a guardian, too, if I thought my best friend needed extra care."

Even so, Gabriel's limbs felt colder, and he chalked that up to disappointment in the dog's lack of full complicity. An older vampire who had more control of his abilities might've been able to overcome the canine's resistance, but Gabriel was unguided because of his creator's absence.

After one last listen to the voices behind the door, Gabriel unbolted the locks, then stepped inside.

Everything seemed to freeze as he stood there, taking the measure of the community area. The same dirt-packed walls as he'd found in Mariah's place, except for the various doors around the room that no doubt led to other tunnels connected to the Badlanders' homes. The same dust-bitten type of crate chairs and tables under a line of solar-driven lanterns dangling from the ceiling. And, also, what seemed to be roots and rock stuck out in various patterns from a single wall in particular.

Then there were the people.

At one table sat a fiftyish woman with wide gold-tinged eyes and a little beak of a nose. Gabriel could tell her hair used to be black, but now it was spun with gray, tucked behind her ears into a tiny ponytail. She'd pushed her floppy hat off her head, and it hung from entwined strings around her neck; her clothing was dirt-worked and as utilitarian as she seemed to be.

Across from her was a compact man in his late forties, with a dusky complexion, his skin pocked, his curly hair dark. It looked as if he hailed from Mexico, but since that country's economy had surpassed that of the United States, Gabriel couldn't guess why the man would want to be here instead of there. His orange-brown hemp clothing seemed hand-woven, made with care.

The third person was an old man with fuzz for whiskers, wearing ancient earth-toned jeans and a matching vest over a white shirt. He hung out near the roots on the wall, an old canteen halfway to his lips, as if Gabriel's interruption had put off a good drink. Gabriel hadn't seen any elderly people for a very long time, and he looked at the man for an extra second.

Meanwhile, their vital signs and scents had spiked at the intrusion, and Gabriel absorbed them. Like Mariah's essences, these seemed more appealing than most other people's, perhaps because they lived on clean air and unpolluted food out here, just as Abby had; she'd been raised on a farm until it'd been seized.

Chaplin barked at the crowd, and they seemed just as baffled at the dog's presence as Gabriel's.

Gabriel shut the door, affably nodding at each person as they gaped at him. Chaplin continued to make his educated sounds until everyone seemed to relax a bit.

The woman was apparently the only one who understood the dog as she translated for the rest. "Chaplin says he's brought a guest—Gabriel." She'd recovered quickly, her tone wry, as if she were used to curves in life. "He had a rather intense meeting with one of Stamp's guys outside, as I suppose we all could infer by those bandages around his head. Mariah took him in to get him back in working order." She addressed Gabriel. "Which night were you ambushed?"

"The one before last." He neglected to add that he didn't actually recall fighting Stamp's people. He'd been worked over too badly. He just knew that, afterward, there'd been pain and the news of a dead body.

Zel stared at him as all went quiet around her. Then she spoke to Chaplin.

"I have to say that it isn't enough that you show up out of the blue, boy. But then you bring in a random from the outside?"

Gabriel had known an introduction wouldn't be easy goings. "Chaplin's the one who persuaded Mariah to play hostess to me. She wasn't thrilled about the prospect . . . to say the least."

The old man squinted at Gabriel from across the room. "Mariah opened her place to you? *Mariah?*"

The Mexican had his hand out to Chaplin, as if to welcome the dog, and the canine trotted right on over, looking real happy when the man began petting him.

"Chaplin was the one who persuaded her," the man repeated. "Chap, you gave your approval of him?"

The dog yipped.

Gabriel stuck his hands in his pockets, looking as nice as possible, though he was constructed to be anything but. "Before you ask, just know that all I'm looking to do is keep quiet and at peace."

The Mexican man rose from his chair, almost reluctantly at first, then moved to Gabriel, extending his hand in stoic greeting.

"Sammy Ramos," he said, carrying no accent except for the Old American one. They shook hands. "You'll have to excuse this rude bunch. We're not used to newcomers, but Chaplin's endorsement speaks enough for you."

Then he retreated, and Gabriel wondered just how welcoming Sammy really felt.

"That dog and Mariah really saved my hide." Gabriel hoped she was monitoring the visz right now, so buttering up to her seemed the thing.

Sammy gestured toward the woman, who was still sitting down. "This is Zel Hopkins. You've probably ascertained that she's standoffish. She won't trust you as far as she can shoot you."

She kept staring at Gabriel, even as he donned his most charming smile. At least, he'd once thought it was charming back when he'd been a human craftsman with a wild streak, who'd learned the hard way to shut off his propensity for making more trouble than was needed.

Sammy started to introduce the old man, but then stopped himself. "I'm not sure what to call you." He glanced at Gabriel. "The oldster changes his mind about everything, even his name, once every few days."

The old man looked sullen. "None of us has a name anymore. Not out there."

Zel rolled her eyes. "But we're in here, kiddo. Get over it."

"He won't tell anyone his real name," Sammy added. Then, almost as if he were still cautious, he reluctantly motioned toward a crate, inviting Gabriel to take a sit. "Never has and I doubt he ever will."

"You wouldn't if you were me, either," the oldster said, drinking from his canteen and leaning against a root that had seemingly clawed its way out of the wall.

"Thinks he's a real badass, too," Zel added.

Then she turned her attention to Gabriel while reclining in her chair and checking him over even more conspicuously. He got the feeling she was good at taking the piss out of people, and he wondered what she'd been before she came out here. He didn't dare look into her mind right now, lest he raise an alarm as he'd done with Mariah.

"You know," Zel said, turning her focus toward a corner where a visz lens was barely visible, "it'd be great if Mariah would show one of these times, just like Chaplin finally decided to do. We keep telling her over the visz that the community shouldn't split. Her dad wouldn't have wanted that."

The visz lens seemed to stare right back at Zel, silent, unmoved. Gabriel guessed that Mariah was probably the same. According to what he knew about her, he surmised that she had only come outside the other night to save his skin, and she didn't often venture forth for a less pressing reason.

He decided to investigate. "She does like her solitude, doesn't she?"

Taking his hand away from Chaplin, Sammy cleared his throat, and both Zel and the oldster looked down. The dog rested on the floor, his head on his paws, his gaze shuttered, too.

They seemed to be dodging something, and Gabriel cocked his head slightly.

Sammy said, "Mariah's just her own kind of hermit, all right. But maybe she'll change her mind soon. Bit by bit, more of us come here to commune. Maybe Hana and Pucci will be by later tonight when they aren't able to withstand the thought of hanging back while trouble draws near."

Zel's tone hardened. "Stamp's presence really brings a crowd together."

The oldster stepped away from the rooted wall, and from his loose walk, Gabriel could fully see now that he was nothing more than scrawny elbows and knees contained in denim.

"Good neighbors don't force introductions," he said. "Stamp's boys don't seem to understand that. They're tone-deaf as to what was happening in the hubs, with the bad-guy raids and the attacks coming from every which way."

Zel took up where he left off. "Too true—Stamp's gotta get a grasp on his men. Those fools seem to have no restraint, and it's going to amount to a terrible something."

Gabriel could read it in them—these were people who'd retreated more than any of the sanctuary-bound ones in the hubs. A lot of good citizens had done the same. It was much easier to keep to yourself than to put yourself outside your walls.

He knew that more than anyone.

The old guy came to stand a few unsteady feet away from the table, and Gabriel wondered if there was some turtlegrape alcohol in that canteen. He couldn't smell it on him, though.

"We could take Stamp on," the oldster said. "Him and his guys."

"Smart," Zel said, engaging the old man, who seemed to have been waiting for just such an interaction. "While we're at it, let's just kill him. Let's ignore that he might even have connections in the world and his death could spark off a thousand shit scenarios that'd bury us under more than dirt."

"Aw, we've suffered worse before with terrorists and the like. Zel—*you* could bust them up all by yourself. You and Mariah, with all those weapons her dad collected before he—"

The oldster stopped when he saw Sammy glaring at him. Even Chaplin kept quiet.

This would be a good time to look into someone's eyes and scan his or her thoughts, if Gabriel had more confidence in doing it.

The oldster grinned as if nothing had just happened, and he ran his hand over his wire-gray hair, casual as could be, while he changed the subject. "Zel used to be a cop, you know."

Gabriel focused on her, realizing now that she could communicate with Chaplin because police forces used to employ Intel Dogs until the government had retired them, leaving the cops with more primitive devices that were hardly a match for lower-level bad guys.

Zel sighed and lifted an eyebrow at the oldster. "Didn't you already point out that nothing we had out there matters anymore?"

"Your aim still matters," he volleyed. "And Sammy made a lot of money fixing junk like TVs, tech screens, and computers. He's valuable enough these days, too." He paused. "We're not as helpless as we act sometimes."

Everyone went silent, and the old guy made a disappointed sound. As he wandered back to the rooted wall, his gaze remained on the woman a moment too long, and Gabriel noted this, right along with the rest of this group's dynamics.

He didn't blame the denizens for keeping shut-mouthed. Everyone had learned to ease back from standing up to any threat that might turn out to hold a danger. Once, just before things had gone to ruin, people had believed in the law of this land. But as it broke down, folks lost hope, retreating into their families. Into themselves.

Into almost nothing.

Gabriel could see the evidence of that here, among the shadows on the walls, among the silhouettes of what these people used to be.

He glanced at the visz lens. Even Mariah had been different, no doubt. They all had.

He rested his forearms on his legs, hunched over. Now was the time to step into the reason he'd sought out this area. It didn't even matter that Mariah would now hear the true motivation he'd possessed for coming to the New Badlands.

"Bet you all don't get many wanderers coming into your sphere," he said.

Sammy shook his head. "Not many at all. There are a few who've come. Less who've gone."

"I know of a certain woman who headed out this way." Gabriel glanced around the room, finding that he'd captured everyone's focus again. "Abigail Trenton. Truthfully, I was also hoping to find her even as I found myself a new home."

Again, none of them met his gaze, so Gabriel couldn't scan their thoughts even if he deemed it safe to try. And if he vocally swayed them, Mariah would see it on the visz— their change in personality would be that obvious, just as Chaplin's had been before Gabriel had toned down the hypnosis with the dog. He'd seen how Mariah had noticed the change in her companion, so Gabriel had needed to adjust.

He would go about it the old-fashioned way, questioning these people, just like any normal human would do. In fact, Gabriel liked the notion of that quite a bit.

Just like any normal human.

Abby would've approved.

"You ever hear her name?" Gabriel added. "Abby?"

Both Zel and Sammy shook their heads, but the oldster motioned toward one of the doors in the room. "We had an Annie here not too long ago, but not an Abby."

Gabriel's gaze locked onto that door as he straightened in his seat.

"She left a while ago," Zel said, but her tone held some warning for the old man.

He clearly didn't like being told what to do, and he stared at Zel while he spoke, as if savoring this act of defiance.

"About a year and a half ago, she laid claim to a piece of water-rich land round here."

Chaplin huffed a bit, as if anticipating what the oldster would say next.

"But that was before," he continued, with a challenging glance at the dog, "Stamp and his boys came along."

Gabriel's spine stiffened. Stamp? Had he gotten to Annie . . . ?

Abby?

Bloodlust ripped heat through his veins, and he fought

the fangs, the urge to let loose and just peer into anyone who'd look at him.

But he wouldn't let himself, and it felt . . . decent. Safe, even.

It felt right, way out here, in a place where no one knew just what he was. Abby would've liked that, he thought. A new start.

The old man's eyes were shiny while he watched Chaplin, as if he hated this story of what had happened to Annie. As if he were angry and sad all at the same time.

It was hard to decide what the oldster was feeling. Vampirism had taken the raw emotion out of Gabriel, leaving only memories of what he *should* feel. Sometimes he even told himself that this was why he'd been so drawn to Abby— because she made him go beyond experiencing mere hunger and need. Because she was a way to access what he'd lost along the way.

Seeing the oldster made Gabriel want to feel the rage and vengeance, too, because to Gabriel, empathy was what separated the good guys from the bad, and the absence of it had put him on the wrong side. But he still had to have some good within him, and he meant to discover it again by finding the woman who'd disappeared from his life.

He summoned the concept of anger and how it used to feel.

"Are you insinuating," he said to the old man, "that Stamp got to this Annie and that's why she's not around anymore?"

Zel interrupted. "Annie left. That's it."

"And," Sammy added, "since Annie's gone, you might think of moving on, too. If you've got no reason to be here beyond your friend, you'll want no part of our business."

Gabriel shifted in his seat. So Annie had just up and left. It sounded enough like Abby.

Being this close to finding her inflamed his vampire instincts, and in spite of everything he'd just told himself about being a better man—a real man—Gabriel found himself looking at Sammy, compelling him to connect gazes.

As if unable to resist, Sammy glanced at him, and Gabriel peered into his eyes.

Slam!

A wall of black, just like with Chaplin.

His body ringing with the force of being blocked out, Gabriel lost patience. When Zel looked at him, he peered into her, too.

Slam!

The oldster, who seemed to have finally taken Zel's silent warnings to heart, also proved to be a block when Gabriel glanced at him.

Slam!

Gabriel fought the loose clench he had on his control, felt it slipping, sliding as he yearned to throw one of them against a wall and *really* look into their eyes.

But going deeper into them would probably expose *him*. Worse yet, it would cause him to lose the possibility that there was more to him than appetite and destruction.

He fixed his gaze on the visz monitor where Mariah might be watching, and the thought of her disgust at what he really was made him build a facsimile of despair that felt real enough.

It was only when one of the tunnel doors creaked open that he lost his focus.

Gabriel turned toward Annie's door to find a man with long, trimmed sideburns and an expensive whale-hide hat stepping through, a genial smile on his face.

Zel, Sammy, and the oldster tensed, as if frightened to be discovered in the open.

This wasn't one of their crowd, Gabriel thought. And he was coming through *Annie's* door.

As a second man entered, he knew they were Stamp's crew—they stank of the hubs: dirty, used. Their vital signs varied from one another, but there was an excitement in their pulses that confused any sure rhythms because the blood had to drag through arteries clogged by too much processed food.

Spastic. Hopped up on chemical sustenance and entertainment. These men had to be what they called "distractoids" in the hubs. The appeased ones who lived among the bad.

Last night, after the heat had waned, one of these people had found Mariah's visz lens and had harassed her. And tonight, they'd found a real entrance. . . .

Gabriel tuned his hearing to a longer range, trying to detect any near-distant cries from Mariah, even back in her home, but he heard nothing.

And that was when he reached out with his mind, not thinking about it at all, merely reacting.

He mentally shut down her visz lens so she wouldn't come running down here with her guns. He would handle this, just as he'd done last night with Chompers.

Two other men came through the door.

They were all dressed in the sand-colored heat suits they'd probably been wearing in the elements while they'd been wandering through the last of the daylight, nosing around. The bulk of the material was pushed down to their waists, kept up by suspenders while revealing hemp shirts and long gloves on one arm that protected the small screens many urban hub people had implanted in their arms for easy, lazy access.

Even when Gabriel's old buddy Chompers took up the right side of the group, the teeth around his boots jangling, Gabriel didn't react.

No, he didn't do that until Chompers stepped away from the person who was taking up the rear, revealing him in full.

A tall rangy youngster in his early twenties, almost disappearing into the background except for the gun-barrel black of his eyes. A presence more than a person—a near specter who seemed to fade in a crowd though you realized he was there more than anyone else. His pulse was slow . . . cool.

Unlike the other bad ones.

Without introduction, Gabriel guessed who he was, and the threat of the infamous Johnson Stamp made his fangs pulse at his gums while his gaze heated.

7

Gabriel

Through the seething film of Gabriel's peripheral vision, he caught Zel and Sammy trading looks, as if neither one of them knew what to do. Chaplin even backed up toward Gabriel, pressing himself against his master's legs, awaiting a command or maybe even . . .

Gabriel didn't want to think it, but he did.

Maybe the canine was as reluctant to stand up to Stamp as Mariah and these others were.

But when, near the wall, the oldster took a bold step forward, Gabriel revised his thought. The old-timer was either the bravest of any of them or just plain foolish.

He pointed toward the door through which the four newcomers had entered, and Gabriel's vision went that much hotter, though he tried to dial it back, lest his irises reveal the change his body was battling.

Annie.

Abby?

Either way, *had* Stamp and his crowd been instrumental in whatever had happened to her?

Gabriel lowered his gaze to the ground while bringing his level of ferocity down to a manageable limit, then looked up again.

The man-boy in charge of the newcomers leveled his gaze at all the other doors around the room, including Mariah's.

The old man was pointing at Annie's door. "That ain't your quarters."

Three of the men glanced at their apparent boss, seemingly for direction. But the youngster remained mute, refocusing his dark gaze from those doors to every single denizen instead.

His employee—the smiley one wearing the whale-hide hat—spoke in his place. "Weer ur nu frndz."

We're your new friends? Gabriel thought. This clown wasn't gauging things so well, but that was no shock. Most times, Text speakers were better at reading screens than actual body cues.

The oldster stared at Whale Hide for a tense moment, and the room itself seemed to slant during the rough pause.

As Whale Hide opened his mouth to say something else, the old man chucked his canteen at the intruder, and it clipped him at the shoulder, splashing his shirt with water.

The man and his cronies flinched, their lips parted as if to protest, and Gabriel hunched, ready for whatever came next.

But he held back.

No vamp powers if you end up fighting, he thought. *Don't let any of them know what's in their midst. You'd be signing a death warrant for these people because Stamp would think they're sheltering you.*

Ever so slowly, the youngster with the cold eyes turned to survey his comrade's shirt.

Chaplin seemed to chew on some muttered canine sounds as the three intruders looked to their boss once more. But the young guy merely sighed, hooked his thumbs into his suspenders, and stared at his boots for a moment.

Zel and Sammy planted their hands on the crate table,

as if bracing themselves. Gabriel's body shuddered, still fighting his instincts.

When the youngster finally glanced back up, his tone was even. "I find the waste of water to be more offensive than the gesture, sir."

Old American. Gabriel hadn't expected to hear it from this kid's mouth. But if he'd come out to the New Badlands to capitalize on the water, it'd make sense for a businessman, who'd still use the formality in the world at large.

As the kid locked gazes with the oldster, Whale Hide pulled his watered shirt away from his chest, then bent to touch his tongue to the moisture. Without even glancing backward, the youngster's hand whipped out to lightly smack the man.

Gabriel's shoulders hunched even more.

The kid tore his gaze away from the oldster and addressed everyone else. "We've been looking high and low for neighbors, and just today, we happened upon an entrance in the ground. Cleverly hidden, all right, but finding it was inevitable."

"Did ya ever think," the old man asked, hardly scared off, "that we weren't making an effort to welcome you? Round these parts, housebreakers are shot."

"Around these parts," the youngster said, "I imagine it's survival of the fittest, just like everywhere else." He was still visually taking inventory of every one of them, as if committing all details to memory.

Then, just as if he'd deemed the lot of them safe, he switched gears, taking a step forward, sauntering toward Zel without a hint of menace, yet still as serious as could be, while he extended a hand toward her in greeting. Gabriel even thought that the kid was genuinely happy to find some fellow nonspastic humans of his own ilk out here.

"Johnson Stamp," he said.

But Zel didn't make a move to accept the strange gesture. Instead, she recoiled ever so slightly.

From where Gabriel was standing, there was nothing physically repulsive about Stamp, who seemed well kempt and proper. It was more of a curdle to the blood that the kid brought on, and Gabriel could understand her reluctance to engage him.

If Stamp's employees were Text-blind to body language, the boss himself sure wasn't. He read Zel's message loud and clear but didn't make issue of it, as he then offered his hand to Sammy.

But the Mexican angled his body away from Stamp.

That seemed to do it, causing the kid's gaze to darken even more as he drew back his hand, almost like it was a weapon about to be holstered.

"This is how it'll be, then," he said, his arms curved at his sides in stiff rejection.

The old man piped up from his corner of the room. "Maybe you'd have gotten a different version of hello if your men had seen fit to stay away in the first place."

Stamp faced the oldster again, as if interested in his sparkiness. Meanwhile, the three employees loitered near the door, their arms crossed over their chests. They were assessing Gabriel and his head bandages, and he returned their stares with an outward composition that didn't quite match the creeping heat of his vision.

Had one of them harassed Annie, just as Chompers had done to Mariah over the visz screen last night?

Had one of them chased Annie away?

In particular, Gabriel watched Chompers, whose trophy teeth clanked around his ankles as he shifted position. He was watching Gabriel right back with a strenuous curiosity. But Gabriel knew that the guy hadn't gotten a good gander at him in the dark last night, so he wasn't in the process of recognizing him. However, Gabriel *did* fear that the thug might be able to recall Gabriel's whispered threats, which had suggested that Chompers leave before he got torn apart.

Shit. See what happened when he tried to sway somebody?

Still, scaring off Chompers last night had actually been worth it in the end, with the thug fleeing Mariah's home.

"Sir," Stamp finally said to the old man. "I don't think

you realize that I'm not after anything you own. Not unless you count company. I've found it isolating out here, and being a hub boy, I'm not used to it, even though I'm all too happy to get away from the masses."

"Is that so?" the oldster said.

Stamp nodded. "Like you, I'm out here to just exist like nature meant us to, without all those abominations you find in the hubs." His mouth curled up at one side—an unsaid, bitter reminiscence. But then he smoothed himself out again. "I'll admit to you that my men need a firmer hand. I'm not used to employing anyone, seeing as I always made my way solo before now. I apologize for this tough start. But I'm also here to tell you that I don't take kindly to the way the people around here have been dealing with the temporary waywardness of those on my payroll. If you give us the opportunity, we can be nice enough. I brought them out here to teach them better. I'm even gearing up to teach them polite language. I tell them that speaking Old American is the first step in becoming the entrepreneurs and successes we can all be." He jerked his chin toward Whale Hide, as if the man's smiliness provided all the example anyone might require of their intended goodwill.

The oldster glanced at Zel and Sammy, who were still keeping to themselves.

Then Stamp's olive branch seemed to snap. "I should add that, unfortunately, one of my men was picked off the night before last. We found his remains under the circle of some carrion feeders, and I'm also here to see if there's anything I need to do about it."

It was as if someone had aimed a bullet at the ceiling, silent debris raining down as Zel, Sammy, and even Chaplin went taut.

But not the old man. "Death is a risk of living out here in what remains of nature. By leaving the hubs, you've just bought yourself a stake in the ultimate craps game, so you might want to inform your boys that flitting round at night isn't for the wise. *That's* what you need to do about it."

Stamp turned to all of them now, even Gabriel, who knew that just because the kid hadn't singled him out didn't mean he hadn't been fully aware that Gabriel was there, waiting, nearly quaking with the effort of watching and wondering what any of this had to do with Annie . . . or Abby.

"If another one of my men ends up with his belly torn open," the kid said, "I'll be back here for better answers. But I think we can agree to live alongside one another well enough instead. Understand?"

Zel's voice was low as she spoke. "We understand. But you won't find any answers about what happened to your man in this room, Mr. Stamp, I promise you that. There really are wild things out there at night. Nature hasn't been shy about providing them."

Sammy was quick to support her. "If you'd just keep your men inside, you won't find any of them attacked from now on."

For a second, it seemed that Stamp and his men would leave without further ado.

Until the old man said his last piece.

"Hence, screw you and the horse you rode in on—"

Seemingly resigned, Stamp gestured toward Whale Hide, who yanked a contraption out of a long pocket of his heat suit and zap-flicked it toward the oldster.

Too late, Gabriel saw that it was a taserwhip, the length of it sizzling through the air toward the old man's neck.

Gabriel felt himself going into a crouch, automatically preparing to spring and intercept the lash by wrapping it around his hand, reeling the culprit toward him for a pre-emptory reckoning. The electricity would give him a charge, yet he'd heal quicker than the oldster.

But, near his feet, Chaplin pressed hard against Gabriel's legs, the dog opening his mind, pushing in images of what would occur if Stamp's men realized that they had a monster in the room:

More whips, zap-flicking toward Gabriel, lashing around his neck and arms, capturing him. . . .

The images caused Gabriel a second of hesitation—one in which the taserwhip sang out to curl around the oldster's neck.

The smell of burning skin hit the air.

As the man gurgled out a whimper under the grip of the lash, Gabriel could just about feel it, too. And when the old guy's hands came up to pull the wire from around his neck before the thug could fully energize it, Gabriel couldn't help but start forward, consequences or not, thinking that his own capture would be nothing compared to the pain of knowing something could've been done to avoid the old man's anguish.

But Chaplin disagreed, fixing his teeth to his master's trousers, urging him back and connecting to his mind with ferocious strength.

Mariah, the dog thought. *All of us. Don't make it worse.*

That brought Gabriel to his senses.

If they saw how he withstood the electricity, they'd know, and he'd be no good to anyone right now if he exposed himself, bringing this sanctuary into the sights of the authorities for harboring a monster.

So he hung back, digging his nails into his palms as he fisted his hands by his side, as helpless as he'd felt that night when he'd seen Abby wasting away.

The other two employees already had their whips out, eyeing Zel and Sammy, and the tips of Gabriel's fangs pierced him.

But he pressed his lips together, narrowing his eyes.

"Don't even think about it," Stamp said to Gabriel. "Not unless you want the electricity turned on high and your old friend to really dance."

Chaplin tore his teeth away from Gabriel's trousers, barking at Stamp.

The kid's gaze slid down to the dog.

Gabriel bent to wrap an arm around the canine's neck, holding *him* from jumping in to defend Mariah's friends now.

Outplayed, Gabriel thought to his familiar. *Too much to lose, boy. You should know that.*

But the notion abraded him, anyway. They'd *all* been retreating for a long time, and look where it'd gotten them—underground, hiding, always on the defensive.

Yet he carried on, knowing that Chaplin had been right when he'd reminded him that now wasn't the time for his vampire to come out. Not if he wanted to finesse his way into answers about Annie or find what he was looking for and then somehow move on. Not if he wanted to keep these people from further trouble.

But he could still help.

"Why're you really here?" Gabriel asked, his lips barely moving so that he could hide his teeth.

As the oldster let out another, weaker trembling sound of discomfort in the background, Stamp glanced toward it, as if it might answer Gabriel's question.

He'd come here to show he was serious about keeping his men secure.

Gabriel's hands tightened in Chaplin's fur, and the dog stirred beneath him.

Obviously content with the upper hand, the kid took a handheld black unit out of his suit pocket. It looked like a gun with a flip-up monitor as he turned it on and aimed it at Gabriel.

At first, Gabriel thought to cloud the device, just as he had done with Mariah's visz monitor, but Stamp adjusted a knob, and the machine proved too powerful to interrupt.

So, Gabriel withstood it, realizing that the kid was only using a scanner with a built-in facial recognition database to determine who his neighbors were. Really, there'd be no big harm since Gabriel had never been identified as a monster, so it wouldn't give Stamp much to go on. Also, he was only a couple years older than his vampire appearance let on.

The bottom line was that Gabriel, like many other society dropouts, had destroyed his identity long ago, and the history stored in the database would end just before it got interesting. Thank-all for that.

Stamp touched the screen, no doubt accessing more

information. Then he flicked a glance at Gabriel, his features never changing, never revealing what might be on that monitor.

All the same, Gabriel put on a show of breathing quicker, just as he'd done with Mariah. He just hoped that the machine didn't have anything that could register his vital signs, because he'd be in trouble.

But when Stamp turned away from him, Gabriel supposed the scanner wasn't equipped with such accoutrements, and he laid his hand flat against Chaplin, patting the dog, telling him that things would be okay if they could just endure another few moments.

Stamp went on to scan Zel, who had her hands pressed flat on the crate table again, a muscle working in her wrinkled cheek, as if she were drawing on every ounce of restraint she had. All of them seemed to be doing that, especially the old man, who shook under the pull of the lash.

"All of this," the kid continued as he accessed the screen, "could've been done in a friendly enough manner. 'Hello,' you could've said. 'Pleased to meet you. I'm Zelda Hopkins, ex-lieutenant of police forces in the Northlink. I went off the Nets a while ago, but I'd be pleased to show some kindness to someone else who could enjoy a fresh start.'"

When the oldster yelped from his corner, Stamp glanced at Whale Hide, who seemed to be getting more and more impatient to mess around with his prey.

"Lay off him," the kid said.

His command was so even and forceful that Chaplin shrank back. As for Whale Hide, he held up his free hand, murmuring something like a Text apology.

Stamp turned the scanner on Sammy, looking just as blank-faced as he had with Zel and Gabriel. "All of your ID chips went dead a while ago," he said. "If I didn't intend to show you what a good neighbor I can be, I'd report that."

"But you won't," Zel said. "Not if you want to get along."

Stamp lowered the device, sending her a glance that could've been either detached or threatening.

Zel shut up, then seemed angry at herself for backing down.

The kid wandered over to scan the oldster next, and Stamp adjusted the machine as a high squealing sound made Gabriel and Chaplin cringe. Gabriel tried not to show it, but when he saw that the pitch had caused Zel, Sammy, and the oldster to react, too, he relaxed. The response wouldn't set him apart.

Stamp finally lowered the device. "You're not even in the database, sir."

"Intrusive technology came after my time," the oldster said, the lie a mocking last punch to show he still had some fight left in him.

By now, he was on his hands and knees, breathing hard and unsteadily, the whip still looped around his neck. Gabriel knew that Whale Hide hadn't even turned up the electricity to high, either. He would've smelled the crisp of it.

Nearby, Chompers humphed, acknowledging the unlikelihood of anyone not being in the database. But his friends didn't find the oldster's gumption quite as amusing.

Gabriel kept his gaze trained on Stamp, wondering what would come next . . . if the oldster's continued resistance would finally break the kid's patience.

Were it possible to scan these assholes right back, he'd probably find reports of brain readouts classifying these guys as repressed psychopaths.

His blood surged through his veins, and Chaplin sensed it, pressing against his chest again in warning.

I know, boy, Gabriel thought. Because after seeing that these men weren't just thugs—they were carrying weapons in those pockets, some of which might kill a vampire within a second flat—he felt even more powerless.

Still, as Stamp put away his scanner, Gabriel caught a jitter of movement from Whale Hide, who still seemed up for playtime.

His thumb moved to press the electric-pulse button and—

That was all Gabriel was going to take.

With all his will, he pushed back his inner monster, rising to his feet as any decent human would do, and then avoiding Chaplin's teeth again, he took a few long steps across the room. He took Whale Hide by the wrist with one hand, preventing him from pressing the button and, with the other, he denied his true strength and used street smarts instead, positioning his thumb against the jerk's eye, feeling the curved, gelled softness beneath.

"Enough," Gabriel said.

No one moved except for the oldster, who'd rolled to his back for a better view, panting, as if holding himself back from getting angrier.

Gabriel prepared himself for the feel of a shocking lash around his own neck, but it never came.

Only Stamp's voice did.

"He's right," said the kid. "Undo your lash, Teddy."

The thug did so, and Gabriel held up his hands, making a show of backing off, too.

The entertainment over, Stamp packed up his facial recognition gear and herded his men toward the door. But before he got there, he paused near Gabriel.

Their gazes snagged, and it was all Gabriel could do not to peer more deeply into Stamp's eyes, parting the dark of them to get to what was beneath.

But more than the instinct to look, he remembered the images Chaplin had given to him about what might happen if he got caught.

Someday, Gabriel thought. Someday soon when he found Stamp alone, he was going to peer inside, and then he was going to leave before the chance of getting caught turned into a reality.

With a nod that could've denoted a warped respect for Gabriel, who'd finally shown what he was worth, Stamp followed his men through Annie's door, then shut it behind them.

Gabriel kept his gaze on it. He wouldn't look into any minds right now, but he was sure going to go through that door to see what was inside *it* when the time was right.

He didn't turn around, even when he felt Chaplin's tail curl around his leg. Even when the oldster clambered to his feet.

"Ain't *you* the shit?" the man said gleefully.

As Gabriel mentally restored the visz lens to where Mariah would be able to see the common area again if she was watching, he realized that maybe he wasn't a fraction of the hero Abby used to think he was. Maybe he never would be.

But when he finally turned back to the Badlanders, they were looking at him as if he just might be wrong.

A World Gone Mad

8

Mariah

When the visz finally came back on, I stopped messing with the wall-bound control panel. The common-area connection had fritzed out, leaving me hanging, although none of my other cameras had broken down. But the viszes weren't perfect, and sometimes they failed me like this.

I pushed shut the panel's door, then stepped back to get a better scope of the screen, which showed what was going on in the commons now. Unlike before, when the group had generally been conversing at the crate table, Gabriel was now standing by a door while facing my neighbors.

Annie's door.

I backed away from the monitor, rubbing my hands over my arms, which carried a chill. Before the visz had gone out, Gabriel had been talking about a woman he'd come to the New Badlands to find. Abigail. Abby for short.

Or maybe even Annie.

At the echo of her name, a tide of violent despair edged its way over me, so I backed away from the visz to create distance. Annie and I . . . Well, we hadn't gotten along.

On the visz, Gabriel walked away from Annie's door, nodding to the other Badlanders as he made his way toward my own entrance. The sight of him made me come out of my momentary numbness as I waited for him to arrive.

I realized that the sight of him had the power to drag me a little ways out of my melancholy. Somehow, Gabriel piqued my interest. He piqued more, too, and now that I knew he wasn't just here as the harmless wanderer he'd pretended to be, I went on double guard.

We didn't need a stranger to get too close to us, especially if my suspicions proved correct and Gabriel was thinking that Abby and Annie were one and the same. We didn't need the floodgates from outside to open into our hiding place.

I heard Gabriel saying a farewell to Zel, Sammy, and the oldster, and I muted the visz's sound and headed toward the food prep area, intending to seem otherwise occupied when he returned.

It'd be bad form for him to know I'd been keeping tabs. Hell, it'd been awful enough that I'd accused him of being a vampire. Why did I even bring that up with him? Sure, I knew, contrary to what Gabriel had told me, that there *were* monsters, but to go round accusing people of it . . . ?

Dumb. Best to keep quiet. Best to keep safe by pretending I knew less than I did. Chaplin had been adamant about backing off the questioning, too, and I trusted my dog's judgment more than anything in this world; he'd told me he would handle Gabriel. He'd also told that to Zel, who would spread it round to the rest. I'd let the dog do what he needed to with our guest, even if it included bringing him to the others, who'd no doubt blame me for his introduction, anyway.

But there was something even more that kept me from challenging the dog—I also kind of felt decent about having Gabriel round, monster or not. He'd chased off Chompers and made such a productive day out of work. Not that I really needed his help, of course.

The tunnel door opened, and I grabbed a cloth, starting to wipe down a cooler while trying not to feel the thud of Gabriel's footsteps in my chest.

Chaplin trotted into the prep section, brushing against my leg, and I smiled at the dog, masking all my concerns about what I'd heard on the visz.

Shortly thereafter, I heard Gabriel stop just before he entered the room. Awareness trickled over my skin, a simultaneous warm and cold that came to settle in the center of me. The sensations were confusing, turbulent. I hadn't ever enjoyed such a reaction before he'd come along, and I felt the heat separating itself from everything else, stretching through my limbs, enlivening every cell.

While my breathing upped its pace, I kept wiping the cloth over the cooler, telling myself not to turn round, to keep working. *Stop,* I told my body. It needed to stop what it was doing. . . .

Chaplin nudged my leg, because he knew that I was off balance. But then Gabriel spoke, his low voice only adding to my ever-growing aches.

"Mariah."

Hearing him say my name . . .

I pushed back with the only thing that had ever saved me before—defiance meshed with the fear of what might come.

"Why didn't you just tell me about this Abby before?" My voice was low and grating, but it sounded better than I'd thought it would. "You lied about why you were here. You could've asked me about her and I would've told you that she hasn't been round. Then you could've gone on your way to find better solutions."

"You wouldn't have told me squat, and you know it." Gabriel shifted, as if he'd come to lean against the doorframe. "I'm glad I visited with the others. Now I know the extent of your situation with Stamp . . . and I know that he very well might've had something to do with your Annie not being here any longer."

My hand gripped the cooler.

"But you must've heard all of that on the visz," Gabriel added.

There was something in his tone that sent up another red flag in me, just like the one I'd detected when he'd seen the crucifix on the back of the door. An out-of-place, what-doesn't-belong-here? inflection in his words.

Could a vampire mess with a visz if he put enough mind to it? Was that what'd happened when the screen had gone on the blink? Had Gabriel wanted to keep me out of Stamp's way, just as he had with Chompers?

I finally turned round, and the sight of Gabriel punched at me, made me twist inside with unsettling force and motion.

He was indeed leaning against the doorframe, head bandages and all, the length of him as casual as always. But there was a stiffness to him, too, although he was doing his best to cover it with the raising of his brows.

"I'm afraid I didn't hear any such thing on the visz," I said.

"I know you were tuned in. Let's not fool each other about that."

Okay, I was willing to give him this much, especially because I did want to know what I'd missed while the reception had been down. "The visz did blank for a short time."

Now he frowned. "So you didn't see when Stamp and some of his boys found one of the tunnels to the common area? That they paid us a greeting?"

Whether he was perniciously omitting that he'd interfered with the visz or not, I stood away from the cooler, my pulse coming faster, pushing under my skin now, but it wasn't just because Gabriel was in my full sight.

Stamp. Here?

Everything else—Gabriel's "differentness," Gabriel's search for Abby—went by the wayside as fear crowded me.

"You already know that Stamp lost one of his men recently," Gabriel said, "and he wanted to inquire as to how it might've happened. If a member of your community had anything to do with it."

I warded off the accusation. "He should've read up on the area before coming out here."

"That's pretty much what everyone told him."

Gabriel was running his gaze up my body, then down, and even though I knew that he was reading my physical reactions for the truth, I couldn't help feeling the skim of his attention, how it left scratches of sensation behind, inch by inch.

"And after everyone set him straight," I said, "Stamp left you in peace?"

"After some play with us, yeah, he did. His men had taserwhips, and one of them—he wore a whale-hide hat—used the lash on the oldster because the guy couldn't keep his dander down."

A lash? On the oldster?

Anger licked at me, pushing my temper. But I'd just seen the old man on the visz, and he'd looked okay. . . .

"He's fine," Gabriel said. "Stamp meant to ring a warning bell, is all."

"He's going to stay away, then?"

"I think he realizes that he can't force friendship, so maybe he will."

"And you place stock in his word?"

Gabriel seemed surprised that I was actually asking his opinion, but it wasn't long before his expression became a cocksure grin instead. A sign that he liked how I wasn't fighting him right now.

I melted, just a little, but won myself back when I thought I heard Chaplin chuff.

Then Gabriel seemed to become reflective again. "I don't trust his boys in the least, and that's reason enough not to trust Stamp by extension."

As I tossed the cleaning cloth onto a counter, I was still all too cognizant of Gabriel thinking that I'd gone and accepted him or something.

"Then I'll take that into consideration after you're gone," I said.

He didn't move from his spot against the doorframe, and that told me everything about how long our guest intended to stay.

But having him here was impossible. He'd bring too much damage. "You seem fit enough. How long do you think you're going to be round?"

"Well, Miss Mariah," he said in that mild tone of his, "I think it'll be for a while."

Chaplin gnawed on his words. *He's fine here, Mariah.*

I almost argued with that, but then I remembered that Chaplin had a handle on Gabriel. My dog probably wanted our guest round here as backup in case Stamp acted out. Sounded reasonable enough, I supposed.

Gabriel said, "I made a vow to Chaplin about staying on and giving a hand here, and I don't break promises easily."

I shouldn't have been even slightly happy that he was persistent about this. Best that he went soon, after Stamp had calmed down and decided to back off. Best that he—

He was talking again. "If I have to, I'll find myself a place outside your home so I can keep watch. In good conscience, I won't leave just after a man like Stamp has escalated matters."

But it was more than that, wasn't it? He wouldn't leave just after he'd heard that Annie . . . or maybe Abby . . . had disappeared from the New Badlands under shady circumstances. He'd be looking into that, too.

God-all, I had to be realistic about this. Smart. Think . . . *think* . . .

All right. Gabriel was serious about staying, whether it was inside my home or outside. Was there a way to lead him to answers that would satisfy his curiosity about Annie for the time being? A way to keep life just the same as it had been until things with Stamp could be resolved and Gabriel could move on and leave us in solitude?

I went out of the room, past Gabriel, feeling the tingle of his presence over my skin, even though I didn't touch him at all.

Chaplin barked. *We'll make sure Abby* isn't *Annie—at least as far as Gabriel knows.*

I understood what he was getting at. He wanted me to

visit Annie's domain to cover anything that'd reveal the truth about her.

So, for Gabriel, I laid out my first real big deception.

"Seems that the dog's heart is gonna break if you do scoot," I said over my shoulder while I moved toward my private quarters. "So *he* can play host until he gets tired of you, I guess."

"Good enough," Gabriel muttered. Then, louder, he said, "Meanwhile, don't mind me while I take a look-see outside to make sure Stamp and his boys have really gone home. I'd like to be thorough, so it might take a while."

Maybe he was going to try to find Annie's outside door. God-all, I hoped not. It wouldn't give me time to edit her belongings.

As I entered my quarters, my body was still quivering, clenched with heat, mostly because of that near brush against him. "It's your hide, but make sure you take a weapon from the wall. You might need it."

"Got you, Miss Mariah," he said. "I've endured his crew a couple of times now, as well as what's outside, so don't worry about a thing."

For a second, I wondered just how he'd survived out *there*. He hadn't brought any weapons with him that I knew of.

I addressed Chaplin, hoping my voice wouldn't tremor. "Boy, stay inside. Gabriel seems to have this covered."

I heard our guest gathering materials in preparation to go outside, heard Chaplin jumping round and Gabriel telling the dog he'd have to stay put. All the while, I walked the length of my room, pushing down the tension that didn't seem to want to leave.

Annie had never talked much about her personal history. Who *had* she been? More important, who was *Abby*?

And what had she been to Gabriel?

A noise in the background signaled that Gabriel had climbed the ladder to the top entrance and, suddenly, my place seemed a bit emptier. I wasn't really sure why, but the thought of not having him round was just about as bad as having him here.

Chaplin woofed in the main area, and I heard him settling down, probably near Gabriel's blankets to wait for his return.

Blankets. Bed. Gabriel.

I tried not to think of all that, but I did, anyway.

Him, lying in those blankets. These past couple of days, I'd been free to look at him when he didn't know it, and my temperature had come to near withering as I imagined what a man might feel like. . . .

Throwing the feelings away—they made me too afraid of what might happen if I gave in to them—I decided to cool off my sweltering body, the simmering of blood and cells beneath the skin. I needed it badly before carrying out what I'd need to do about Annie *if* Gabriel wasn't already going over there. So I went to a corner where the dirt met a wall of metal—my sensor-driven cleaning station, which allowed water to stream from the wall more efficiently than with the old-fashioned showers.

I began to unlace my cloth pants, starting at the ankle just over my boot, one strip uncrossing another.

Then, as the taboo thoughts returned, my pace slowed.

Blankets. Bed.

Gabriel.

With one side of my pants undone, I went to the lacings on the other, reaching my knee before I felt . . . something.

The same tingling that had licked at my skin when I'd passed Gabriel in the doorway.

My fingers hovered near my knee, over the rest of the lacings. He'd gone outside, right?

Or was he still . . . here?

A thrill swiped me, winding between my legs and making me go a little damp. Something within me shifted violently, and even if Gabriel wasn't anywhere round, I imagined what it might be like if he saw me, one hip bared, one thigh . . . a calf.

Controlling my breathing, I got a little bolder, telling myself it'd be fine to entertain these new feelings for a moment. Just a moment. Bold was easy when I didn't know if Gabriel was really here or not, and I continued unlacing myself, strip by strip, up my other thigh now, to my opposite hip, picturing all the looks Gabriel had previously given me—the visual strokes that I couldn't help wishing were a show of his own thwarted need to be touched, too.

A languid throb made me ache in my sex, and as only a few lacings still held my pants in place, I hesitated, my hands shaking while I listened for any signs of movement, even of the breathing I didn't always hear from him.

But . . . nothing.

Yet, even if he wasn't here, I pictured that he was only holding his breath, and I inched my hand to my belly, under the edge of my shirt, where the cloth gaped away from my skin.

I rested my fingertips there, and the muscles jumped, unused to contact. I'd been taught to treat the body as a temple, but years had passed. Time, and circumstance, had altered everything.

And no one was round . . . at least, I was pretty sure no one was.

Maybe I could make this new pressure in my body, this new frustration, go away. So I slid my fingers lower, hesitating, a tremble lining the inside of my stomach.

Careful . . .

I slipped my hand even lower, biting my lip as I touched the slickness between my legs.

Closing my eyes, I inserted my fingers into the folds there.

Wet. And when I pressed up against the sensitive bump, I drew in a breath as hunger emerged, eating at me.

But I kept on imagining him, my repressed yearning unfolding, opening me up now that I was alone in my room, solitary enough to let go for a minute, lonely enough to need it.

Fantasy took over. What if he hadn't gone out yet and he *was* still here, watching? Maybe his fangs were going sharp, just as my fingers were pressing harder against my sex, as I stroked myself, my legs going weak, my blood heating, my bones beginning to melt.

My knees gave out, and I sought my bed for balance, grasping at the covers with my free hand while the other one got me wetter, higher, more excited than I'd been in . . .

Ever.

I sank all the way to the floor, my cheek against the bed, my eyes open enough so that I could see through my lashes the sparsely rendered room—the walls, the darkness of the doorway . . .

Then beyond, where I thought I saw something in the shadows.

A glimmer . . . Two glimmers . . . Red . . .

Watching.

The threat of complete exposure, real or fantasized, interrupted my rhythm, my fingers still insinuated in my sex, my breath suspended, my skin pounding.

I wanted this too much to stop now. I craved this. Had to have him there, even if he wasn't.

So I stroked myself again, harder, never tearing my gaze away from the red eyes . . . the watching.

Redder, I thought as I imagined how he might want me, too.

Redder . . . the hunger building . . .

Then, just as I came to the edge, so close, so near, the red . . .

I groaned and grabbed at the blankets on my bed.

The red blinked out, extinguished, and I wondered if it'd even been there at all.

Either way, the loss of the illusion tore at me, and when I tried to get back to where I'd been at the height of the fantasy, when I could've chased this tight agony all the way out of my body, I failed. Failed again. Failed until my throat burned with a sorrowful tightness, burned right along with my blood, which wouldn't stop its heating rise.

My body still pushed at itself, still stimulated to the point where I pressed against the bed, the pains growing and stretching, my gaze going dark as I kept thinking of Gabriel. . . .

. . .

9

Teddy Danning had imbibed way too much turtlegrape after tonight's work shift for him to go straight to sleep.

He was still too wound up after what had happened earlier, when he and the others had returned from the scrub-dweller gathering where Stamp had allowed them to put the fear of ages into the Badlanders. Sure, the crew had come back to Stamp's domain after that, to continue installing a water-farming system in the aquifer, but that hadn't killed Teddy's energy.

So he'd ended up here, outside under the cloud-mottled night sky, drinking himself halfway to boredom as the rest of the crew obeyed directions and stayed underground for the night.

Pushing back the whale-hide hat he'd purchased in the hubs, where Stamp had recruited him, Teddy wondered what he'd gotten himself into by signing on to this job. He missed the urban hubs. Missed the games there, especially, because if there was one thing Teddy was, it was a doer, and the Badlands wasn't offering much in the way of allowing him to exercise that quality.

But doing was what had drawn Teddy to his boss in the first place, even though Stamp was just a youngster. The boy was what this country was about—a well-spoken, educated leader who seized his opportunities. It was said that his parents had been obliterated by a human bomb in a marketplace, and that had brought out the aggression in the boy, yet this was a good thing. Teddy knew that there was a time in every life when the aggression had to emerge, or a person would perish.

A rustling sound came from the brush to his right, and from his seat on the flat rock above the New Badlands in all its stark fucked-up-ness, Teddy took up a stone and heaved it at the disturbance.

He smiled while a fox scuttled out, its eyes capturing the glow of the moon as it fixed its gaze on Teddy.

Aggression.

They'd see who was king of the rock here.

He found another stone and sent it at the creature just to watch it dance.

The little thing hissed, flashing a sharpened tongue, but Teddy wasn't afraid of the desert mutant.

He set down his canteen and stood, reaching to the belt of his trousers for his taserwhip, thinking it might be fun to see if the fox whined as much as the old man had earlier.

Unfortunately, in the time it'd taken for Teddy to change position, the creature had already disappeared.

Teddy hopped off the rock to the dirt below. That damned little thing had been fast, but there weren't a lot of places to hide out here, and he was in the mood for fun.

"Hya, Foxy," he said, creeping over the dirt, his whip unfurled. "Dn't b shy."

After their shift, Stamp had told his crew to stay inside—to mind the dangers of night—but Teddy had never been great at taking orders. Not in prison, not on the streets, not even in the organized gang he'd tried out before he'd quit it. Besides, he wouldn't venture too far.

"Foxy," he said again, wandering away from his own rock, coming upon a stand of boulders piled against each other in a semblance of a hill.

The taciturn moon peeked over the ragged top of it, lending light as Teddy caressed the "on" button of his whip.

"C'mon," he urged.

When something broke out of the brush at the base of the hill, Teddy jumped back. But lickety-split, he enabled the whip's electricity, and the device hummed as the fox scurried past him.

"Spooked?" he asked, starting to go after it.

As he raised his whip, rocks shifted in back of him, and Teddy turned around just before something else sprang, knocking him over after a whistling burst of speed.

Pulse choking him, all he saw before he hit the ground was a shadow with livid eyes and long teeth flashing in the moonlight before it disappeared.

WTF . . . ?

His vision fragmented, Teddy rolled over, seeing nothing around him except the night, the boulders.

He scrambled to his feet, wobbling, then brought the whip back, ready to strike.

Again, the whistling burst came out of nowhere and toward Teddy, but this time it swiped out, catching him upside the head.

Half of his sight went black, and it took him a few seconds to realize that there was pain where the left side of his face used to be.

Uselessly, he snapped the whip, yet it caught nothing but air just before he dropped it.

It buzzed on the ground while Teddy raised his hand to touch what was left of his cheek.

Mush.

With his working eye, he looked at the grounded whip again—buzzing, buzzing, just like the cacophony in his brain—and he saw something weird lying next to his weapon.

His other eye, bulging, streaming gore.

Teddy started to scream, but before a sound came out, a growl—or was it a demonic laugh?—ripped through the night.

It struck such fright into Teddy that he pissed himself.

Another whistling burst—clawed fingers swiping at him?—and Teddy held up his hands, as if to ward off a blow. But when something grabbed his neck and teeth sank into him, his arms dropped to his sides.

Ripping. Tearing.

As if in a convulsive dream, he heard the buzz of his whip in the background, the slurping of the creature as it feasted on him, and Teddy realized that the tables had been turned. That this animal was playing with *him* tonight.

While the creature had its fun, Teddy Danning stayed alive long enough to wish he were dead way before he actually, thankfully, was.

10

Gabriel

Twenty Hours Later

When the next dusk arrived to settle into Gabriel deeply enough to rouse him from his makeshift bed, he didn't move at first.

His head. His . . . body.

He held back a groan, knowing that, again, he'd overdone it. Once a reveler, always a reveler, and vampirism hadn't managed to change that.

Back when he'd been human, entire nights of binging had disappeared clean from his memory, too. Holes in a calendar that he'd never been able to fill up. And that was what he felt now: a little bewildered, searching for a trace of recollection in the dark of his mind.

Thing was, this was also how it'd been a couple nights ago, just before he'd woken up with those injuries outside and come crawling to Mariah's visz lens.

Knowing full well that he needed to hide this hangover if he wanted to avert even more suspicion with her, he reached out with his senses to see if she was around. But he got nothing—no scent, no presence.

He decided that she was down in her workroom, so he sat up, shrugging off blankets that he didn't really need. Next to him, Chaplin slept, keeping watch over him. The dog probably thought that Mariah might have it in her to come at Gabriel with a crucifix while he rested, and Gabriel was thankful for the canine's loyalty. He only wished Chaplin had been just as vigilant last night when Gabriel had been drawn to Mariah's private quarters. . . .

As the images came to him again, he had to fortify himself. But he kept seeing her unlacing those pants, one side, then the other. Kept seeing her pause, as if she'd heard him behind her, watching. Kept seeing Mariah touch herself, as if she'd been driven by the possibility of his voyeurism.

Even now, his vision pounded. Before seeing her like that, he'd genuinely been preparing to go outside, where he'd hoped to hunt, eat, then refill his flask while making sure Stamp and his crew had left. So Gabriel had eased into Chaplin's mind, surprisingly successful in getting the dog to sleep so he wouldn't follow his new master. But Gabriel's intentions had been thwarted by a whiff of Mariah's skin, stronger than ever, as if it had been exposed and the air was carrying it to him.

He hadn't meant to watch, yet he'd sure gone and done it.

Bad enough that he'd wanted her from the first. Even worse that he hadn't been able to stop himself from following the scent of her arousal to her room, where he'd yearned to jam his fangs into her, joining with the building rhythms of her body.

Yet, just in time, he'd saved himself, forcing himself to back calmly out of the shadows and up that ladder, his reddened sight nearly blinding him. And, once in the cleansing outside air, he'd rushed to a spot far away from Mariah so he could hunt and appease the thirst that battered him in the aftermath of such a tease.

He didn't remember much more—just waking up a little later, his stomach full, his mouth ringed by crusted blood. After cleaning up, he'd arrived back at Mariah's, hearing

noises down in the work area, where she was clearly laboring away, even in the dead of night. Thinking avoidance
would be a fine idea, he'd gone to the study, looking at all
those books, taking down the one called *Monsters* to see
what it said about things like him.

Soon after, the noises downstairs had stopped, and when
sunrise approached, he'd fallen into the blank rest that he
often considered a gift.

Tentatively, Gabriel rolled out of bed, coming to a
smooth stand and awakening Chaplin, who must've been
up and about much earlier before returning here to guard
him. The canine stretched so casually, without any indica-
tion of question or judgment, that Gabriel knew the dog had
slept right through last night's shenanigans; Chaplin had no
idea about what Gabriel had seen with Mariah . . . or the
aftermath.

Thank-all, Gabriel thought. However, it might've been
convenient if the dog could've provided enlightenment about
last night. It would've been nice to know whether Mariah
realized Gabriel had been watching her undress, or if the
situation would cause them even more tension around here.

"She's still working?" Gabriel asked the dog.

Chaplin nodded.

"She was going at it last night when I got back, too."

The canine got to his feet, in no rush, just as if he were
used to Mariah's near around-the-clock labors and didn't
feel a mite of guilt about lazing through them.

I'm off, then, Gabriel mind-shared with the dog. *My
flask's outside where I buried it after a refill.* Just for good
measure, he added a lie to cover the fact that he didn't
remember just what he'd eaten last night, only that his flask
was full. *Blood from a sand-rabbit.*

Chaplin stared for a moment, then shook his head, clearly
catching the fib. *You're not going out there for your flask,
Gabriel. Annie's place. Didn't you go last night? Are you
going back now? What's to see?*

Lying might be useless with this dog. Chaplin was smart,

and it seemed he was getting better and better at resisting Gabriel's sway.

I didn't find her old home last night, Gabriel thought, *so, yeah, I'm going now, just out of curiosity, boy. It's just something I've got to do.*

He didn't mention that there hadn't been much of a chance for him to search out Annie's last night. A tad too much going on in the frenzy department.

Gabriel waited for the canine to talk him out of going, to tell him, just as the other Badlanders had done, that Annie was nothing, that she'd just up and gone and that was the end of that. But when Chaplin merely sighed, it took Gabriel aback.

Maybe the dog knew that Gabriel was going to do what he needed to, no matter the barrier.

Whatever it was, Chaplin took his *que sera, sera* attitude across the room and to the door that led to the workroom, then camped out near it, waiting for Mariah.

After scanning one of the outside-view monitors to make sure the coast was clear, Gabriel grabbed his carryall and exited by using the ladder entrance, verifying that it was hidden all neat and tidy afterward. Then, in the stretch of darkening sky, where carrion feeders circled in the distance, he concentrated on the job at hand, making his way to where he thought the Badlanders' common area might be located below the ground. He was planning to map his way outward from there, seeking Annie's home via where he thought her tunnel led.

Before he began, Gabriel opened his senses wide, taking in everything: the dryness of the air and ground, the smoky hint of a brush fire somewhere, probably near Stamp's property. Those carrion feeders.

But it all turned his stomach, so he lowered his intake.

All the same, he identified Annie's entrance soon enough, because when Stamp and his guys had discovered it last night, they'd decimated the otherwise camouflaged doorway behind its mound of scrub.

Blood rushing—this could be it, Gabriel thought, *Abby*—
he opened the entrance, sending tiny four-eyed lizards scurrying.

He waited until they were gone, then lowered himself
through the hole, where a set of rickety steps led to the
ground. Then he opened his senses as far as he could again.

Even before he was partway down the stairs, the scents
of Annie's place attacked, rushing him with a mélange of
skin from all the people who'd been through here recently,
probably Stamp and his men, though the components were
so mashed together that Gabriel couldn't separate them.
Then came the scent of old sage that someone might've used
to smudge and cleanse after Annie had departed. Then old
wood and cotton.

Gabriel reeled under the combination. He'd been too
quick to open his perceptions this wide. He'd only done so
because he'd wanted to isolate Abby's scent right away, but
he didn't recognize her. Not in this crowded assault.

Gabriel lowered his intake once more, letting his visual
senses come to the forefront. There was no light to speak of
but he could see well enough, even without the rusted solar
lanterns that dangled cockeyed like a spindly chandelier.
There was a deadened visz screen, too, as well as walls
crumbling with dirt, like diseased faces.

All the way into the room now, he looked around some
more, soon discerning the cause of the old cotton smell;
Annie had evidently been in the middle of braiding several
rugs that hung on the walls, most only halfway finished.

Abby hadn't ever practiced a hobby like this, Gabriel
thought. But maybe she'd taken up this trade out of necessity.

He ran his fingers over one of them, trying to feel her in
the rough material.

No. Not there.

Yet, he didn't stop searching, and he found a spot in the
corner where she must've slept, because there was a pile of
those rugs there. Touching the top one, he felt for an inden-

tation where her body would've lain, then pressed his face to the material.

A faint smell. An impression ghosted from months and months of abandonment. . . .

Blood tugging through him, Gabriel took out a piece of pink material from his carryall. A swatch from a shirt Abby used to wear. When he'd seen her one of those last nights, her shirt had been so worn that the sleeve had begun to separate, and soon after he'd revealed his true nature to her, she'd ripped the material all the way off, giving it to him.

"You know what they say about wearing hearts on your sleeve," she'd said in that sweet, lightly affectionate way of hers. But there'd been a slant of sadness, too, and in hindsight, he should've known what had been coming.

Now he held the swatch to his face. These days, there wasn't so much a scent as much as something like a note he'd forgotten, and he tried to get it back, to save the last of her because he was afraid that, before long, it might all be gone.

Then he went back to the rug, absorbing the last remnants of smell.

Something jerked in his chest.

Was there a similarity?

He kept testing the difference, desperate for a match, but if there was, Abby hadn't been here for a long time.

Longer than Stamp's first appearance in the Badlands?

As Gabriel tried to construct a timeline, he stuffed the swatch back into his bag. Nothing was coming together yet.

When he searched further, the process seemed equally fruitless . . . until he came to a little cove where the shadows melded.

A cleaning station?

Then his own perception seemed to imitate the shadows, flowing together, ebbing back into his mind, where thoughts of last night weren't far from the surface.

A place where a watcher could stand undetected, just as I did with Mariah?

While he lingered, he experienced the vision of her all over again, and his gaze heated right along with the blood thrusting through him.

Then he realized the sacrilege of seeing Mariah in a domain that might've been Abby's. Raw need versus a pure love.

He backed out of the cove and found another room, and one scent untwined itself from all the others.

But . . . it couldn't be.

Mariah? Or was he confusing Abby's scent with hers?

At first, he rejected the notion, thinking that his lust for her had eclipsed everything else. Then, as he followed the smell and wandered closer to another side room, where stacks of old material for those braided rugs was stored, Mariah's essence overcame him.

Her. He could feel Mariah priming him, the scent so overwhelming that either he was losing his mind or she'd been here very recently.

He grabbed the swatch of material from his bag again, used it to cover his nose, and reality crept back on him, second by second, enough for him to focus on what else was in the small room: nine containers for water that looked as if they'd been culled from a sporting complex; a long stick leaning against the wall, near twenty-eight faint hash marks that looked as if they'd been hastily erased; fifteen sharpened poles, plus chains and cables, that could've been used as defense in case of an attack.

As he continued around the rest of the domain, he noticed that most of Annie's belongings had clearly been picked over, and he suspected it was more due to Stamp's trip through here than anything else. In the end, he still had no answers about why Annie had left or if she'd ever been Abby at all. Really, wishful thinking had been the best evidence he'd found.

If he had the ability to naturally feel anger, he knew that it would've been mastering him right now, but as it was, Gabriel walked toward the door that led to the common area and followed the tunnel there instead. Annie's visz screen had been disabled, and he wanted to see if any of the Bad-landers were out and about yet, just to pose a few follow-up questions.

He was in luck when he got there, because Zel Hopkins was exercising, using a root-constructed bar on the one wall to do pull-ups.

From what she was wearing—a khaki tank top and can-vas pants—Gabriel could see that the middle-aged woman was still in great shape, her arms and shoulders toned with muscle while she methodically pulled herself up, then low-ered herself down. She was so deep into her routine that she didn't even seem to know he'd entered until she dropped to the floor to face him.

Her unfazed expression told him that he'd been wrong about her not realizing he was there.

She wiped her hands together, nodding at Annie's door. "I knew you'd be coming through, sooner or later."

"Were you keeping guard, just to catch me if I did?"

His query was casual but entirely serious; he remembered last night, when he'd run into the blackness of her blocked mind, and was even somewhat relieved that he wouldn't even need to try anything but this humanlike questioning with her.

"I wasn't spying so much at all," Zel said, chuckling, and he wondered if she was trying to make him see that this needn't be a confrontation. "I use this wall here a few times a week. That's why the oldster arranged some of that wood to stick out among the roots, to give me something to do besides yoga and running up the walls of my own home."

"Kind of him."

She assumed a more serious grin, and he knew the small talk was over.

"If you hadn't taken up against Stamp last night, I might be a little put off with you being here. There's just something about you, isn't there, Mr. Gabriel?"

"And why's that?" he asked, interested in her candor. "Because of my interest in Annie?"

"Because we already told you there's nothing much to know, and you're still at it."

She went back to the wall, where she jumped to the bar and raised herself up, spinning herself over feet first until she balanced, her stomach to the bar and her back to him.

"Can I ask you something?" he said.

"If you think I'll give you anything worthwhile, sure." Now she perched herself over the bar, a flying position, her muscles delineated with the effort.

"Can you at least tell me what Annie looked like?" He didn't have pictures because Abby had shunned technology, like most of the other Southblock sanctifiers. He couldn't illustrate worth a lick, either, or else he'd have drawn a portrait.

Zel didn't even wobble, though her voice revealed her effort. "Brown hair, brown eyes, thin as a stick. Independent cuss, too, but you pretty much have to be out here."

Abby had blond hair, but she could've colored it if she wanted a change. But why would she have wanted to disappear to such an extent?

He crossed his arms over his chest. "How long ago did Annie . . . ?"

"Leave us?" Zel breathed out, then in one motion, brought her legs over the bar and sat on it, facing the wall. Her shoulders were stiff. "Over a year ago."

"I thought Stamp arrived only a few months past, and I was under the impression that Annie's problems started when he got here, based on what the old man said."

"Did you ever think that maybe Stamp and some company came out here to scout around before that?"

Her response offered a welcome condolence—an explanation. With Stamp out here that long ago, the timeline would make sense. If he and his guys had been scouting land and they'd found Annie's visz lens, just as they'd eventually found Mariah's, maybe they'd threatened her. As a single woman, she might've been scared off.

But would Abby, who'd had the stones to run away on her own, have been that affected by a threat?

"Listen," Zel added, looking partway over her shoulder but failing to meet his gaze, "she's gone, Mr. Gabriel. She hasn't come back in all this time, and I highly doubt she ever will. Dragging Stamp into this isn't going to bring her back, okay?"

It was as if a brick had been pulled out of him, making him crumble a little. Now he hoped that Annie *wasn't* Abby. Hoped that, somewhere out here in the Badlands, the woman he loved had found a place where she was living in quiet away from Annie and this place. He would find her someday.

Then again, *hadn't* he sensed Abby in Annie's room . . . ?

He managed to speak. "I appreciate your help, Zel."

She positioned herself so that she was fully in front of the wall again, like a bird on a wire. "You can thank Chaplin for bringing you here and getting you into our graces in the first place. He's a smart one, and he wouldn't have accepted you if there wasn't a good reason." After a pause, she added, "We're all family here, including anyone who's allowed in by one of us."

Little did she know that family wasn't for monsters.

Thinking she might be warming up to him, he decided to push his luck, especially since Mariah still might be down in her workroom, where he'd seen no visz monitors, just lenses. She wouldn't know that he was about to ask Zel about her.

"I only wish I knew more about Mariah," he said. "There's a lot that goes unspoken at her place. Even when it comes to her dad—"

Without warning, Zel dropped from the bar, landing gracefully before standing. Her expression gave nothing away as she finally turned to him.

"Best to not wonder. I mean that, too. Family respects each other. Am I clear?"

She moved past him and toward her door, going through it and shutting it behind her with a soft click, then the sound of locks being engaged.

In the disquieting aftermath, Gabriel looked at Annie's own door, thinking that there had to be more to everything than seemed apparent.

A *lot* more.

11

Mariah

Over the last hours, I'd washed myself in a lot of cold water, then worked at the aquifer pumps, as if that would clean me through and through. But no matter how much I scrubbed or labored, I knew consequences were on their way.

Gabriel was upstairs.

But, worst of all, so was the rest of the world.

Sweat was clammy on my forehead, my skin, as I pushed back my lamp helmet to wipe off the moisture, panting while I rested my hands on my hips. The next time I saw Gabriel, I'd see a reflection in his silver gaze, and I wasn't sure I could handle it.

You see, the last few hours had been . . . well, bad. Not even Chaplin knew what I'd done, and I was dreading how he'd respond when he found out. Guilt was punishing me, along with the ache I still carried from the sins of my body.

Furthering that punishment, I donned a waterpack and trudged toward the steps. Long ago, Mom would've said, "Our bodies are temples, Mariah. Treat yours accordingly." Over the years, I'd tried my best to remember that, but last night I'd crossed a line, and it was because of Gabriel and the way he affected me. I'd let myself go too far.

Thing was, I'd liked it.

But there was something else putting me on edge now.

After my loss of control, I'd gone over to Annie's to re-arrange the remnants of her life in the Badlands. Hell, I'd even sucked up my courage and taken the outside entrance, where dawn had been flexing, while Gabriel was bundled in his blankets and it was still decent enough not to require a heat suit.

Annie's wasn't far off, and I'd kept telling myself that as I ran there as fast as I could.

When I arrived, I could feel her all over the place, but I forced myself to go about adjusting her possessions to my satisfaction, even if Gabriel had already been there. I couldn't tell if he had, though, because it was obvious that Stamp and his men had already been present to confuse things, the bastards.

Nonetheless, I collected the only objects that might've given personal clues as to who Annie might've been during her pre-Badlands life. I took her hairbrush, a flame lighter that she'd used to smoke the feyweed that grew round here, the few items of worn, coming-apart-at-the-seams clothing she'd left behind. Then I quickly used my hand to wipe over a makeshift calendar Annie had carved into the dirt.

I got the possessions out of sight and blessedly out of mind, stuffing the items well below the ground, shoveling dirt back over them, moving a hill of rugs over the site and hoping that would suffice to hide the burial. I returned home as fast as I could, shutting the entrance behind me and head-ing straightaway to my workroom while trying not to look over at sleeping Gabriel.

So it was done, and I should've felt all the better because of it. But guilt's a wily thing that sneaks into you and hides real well, coming out every so often like a ghost under the bed, just to remind you it hasn't left.

Now, weighed by it, I looked round my workroom, the last waterpack on my back. My body was about to collapse on me. It'd been through too much, and although there was a lot left to be completed down here, I couldn't put off going upstairs any longer. I'd have to do it sometime.

I slogged to the top of the steps, where I stood on shaky legs in front of the shred of crucifix billboard image on the door. I rested a palm against the beaten image. I should've taken it down a while ago, yet the symbol of it had given me such hope when there was so little of it nowadays.

Unable to look at it any longer, I unpinned the poster, and it unfurled, cringing to the ground. I rolled it up and propped it in the corner, near a crate.

Inhaling, my lungs almost too tight to take in much oxygen, I shed my helmet and opened the door.

Luck be with me . . .

I held my breath, my nerves jumping as I listened in. Quiet, except for a . . . chuckle?

I hesitated, and another laugh filtered over to me from my dad's old fortified quarters, which were hidden by a wall.

Grasping every ounce of control I could muster, I tried to remember that Gabriel might not have been privy to my waywardness last night at all. He might have been outside the whole time, and I'd just imagined him as an audience, with those red eyes in the dark. Still, my belly tightened as I heard him say my name to Chaplin, and the tautness in me turned fluid, warming me in the places I'd touched so recently.

"You sure this ain't hers?" Gabriel said, and just hearing him talking about me made me feel owned by him in a small, disturbing way.

I'm sure, Chaplin woofed, and I wondered if the dog had been with Gabriel all along.

Our guest continued the conversation with my dog, although I was pretty sure Gabriel didn't understand Canine. Or was he misrepresenting that about himself?

"I can't imagine Mariah would've been so keen on dolls," he said, "though a tough role model like this Princess Leia would've been her speed, if any doll was."

I quietly positioned myself at the lip of the room, behind

the fragmented wall, already knowing what they were up to. Chaplin was obviously showing Gabriel my dad's vintage geek collection, which the equally geeky dog had always gone silly over. Dad had kept the items locked safe, all the components vacuum-bagged just in case our Badlands hideout failed us and we needed to trade for essentials with some urban hubite who still cared about old movies and nostalgia. Also, my father had once told me that geeks just plain packed up their collections like this. It was a sign of caring.

I could just hear him in my head, clear as the day used to be. Dad. He felt near to me right now, because of those damned dolls. Maybe that was why I'd kept them in the safe, even after his death—because bringing them, and him, out was too painful.

Peering round the corner, I found Chaplin and Gabriel looking at the bagged dolls. There was Princess Leia, Arwen, Apollo, and Batman. As a girl, I'd never touched them, but it hadn't been because I hadn't wanted to. Dad had made it clear that these weren't for play.

Even though Chaplin, at least, had to sense that I was nearby, he and Gabriel still kept their backs to me, chatting away as if things were dandy and lovely in the world at large.

"Know what I wish, boy?" Gabriel asked.

Chaplin cocked his head.

"That you and me could have a real discussion." Gabriel put the doll back. "About things like Mariah having a predilection for dolls."

My skin went hot again. I was embarrassed and, okay, also angry that he'd been riffling through everything in *here*, not maybe just at Annie's.

Or I could've been flushing because of something else. Something like . . .

My heart started pounding because, last night, I wouldn't have minded some riffling.

Gabriel was talking again while he shut the safe's door. "You and I could also chatter about things like how I suspect your mistress isn't quite as thorny as she'd like most to believe. It's an idle theory, but I've seen her be nice enough to you, so I know she's not *all* fireworks and vinegar."

The dog laughed, and right before my temper got riled high, Gabriel slowly turned his gaze on me, his crooked grin revealing that he'd known I was there.

But was he also remembering my behavior?

Had he seen me . . . ?

"I heard the door shut a moment ago," Gabriel said. "Chaplin's ears perked up at the sound, but I told him to play along with me."

He was acting as if he hadn't seen anything untoward at all in me. As if all my fears had been for nothing.

Thank-all, a million times over, thank-all.

I breathed easier, at least for now, and deigned only to cast an exasperated look at Chaplin and Gabriel, then walk toward the food prep area so I could get a meal on its way.

"Mind that you shut that safe up tight," I said. "Dad's gone, but he wouldn't have ever taken kindly to anyone pawing through his stuff."

Thank-all, thank-all, thank-all . . .

I passed the visz wall, glancing at the common-area screen. The gathering place was empty. Then I went about brewing some loto cactus–tinged water. When I heard Chaplin bark near the workroom door, I realized that I'd neglected to shut it all the way, but that was fine. The gape of it often allowed a stream of cool to enter our domain.

Chaplin kept barking, so I went to him, seeing that he'd nudged through the door and to the other side. He was sticking out his head, jerking his chin toward the spot where the crucifix billboard used to be.

You took it down, he said.

I shrugged, but not before I detected a faint slant of thanks on Gabriel's mouth.

I didn't ask him why he might appreciate my taking down the poster shred, mostly because pursuing the subject of him being a vampire had done me no good the first time.

"I've got cactus water on," I said to him instead. "You going to want a mug of it?"

"Don't mind if I do."

I'd expected him to refuse. Vampires didn't drink regular stuff, right?

"I suppose," I said, gearing up for what would surely prove to be the night's big discussion, "you'd be pretty thirsty after a day of searching round for Annie."

I waited a beat. And when his light gray eyes went dark, I knew I'd arrived somewhere.

"I don't know you all that well," I said. "But in some ways, I can predict you to a T."

He hooked his thumbs into his belt loops. "You got me then. I did go to Annie's after this last sunset."

Tonight? He'd gotten there *after* I had . . . ?

"I didn't want to be out too long searching for her place last night, after it was plenty dark," he said, "so I waited until today's dusk. I don't have a heat suit, or else I could've gone earlier."

I *had* beat him to Annie's. Hell-a-lu-jah.

I said, "You could've used my father's old suit, but Dad didn't quite possess your . . ." I refrained from scoping out Gabriel's body. ". . . dimensions. Although having it's not a bad idea for when you do take it upon yourself to leave."

"Much appreciated, Miss Mariah."

Now I was wondering about why he might've put off his search for Annie's until after the sun had settled. I'd read that some breeds of vampire couldn't go out in the daylight without burning right up.

"You could've also gone through the common area to get to Annie's room," I said. "Unless you thought someone might try to stop you from entering her place once you were down there."

"That did occur to me." Gabriel was so still that I wondered if he'd shut down altogether. Then he took in a deep breath, as if recalling that humans needed to do this to survive. "Actually, I didn't want to fly in anyone's face, flaunting my going into Annie's. It's true that I didn't want anyone to stop me, either."

"Did you find anything?"

Gabriel stared at the ground. "Not much. Not what I'd hoped."

My knees went weak with relief. "And what were you hoping for?"

He began to respond, then halted.

But I'd already predicted his answer. "You do know that Annie isn't the same as your Abby, right?" The comment emerged quieter than I'd expected.

"How would you be sure of that?"

Because I didn't *want* Annie to be Abby. Yet I could hardly say that out loud.

Instead, I shrugged again while, in the background, the boiling water moaned, like wind through stripped, deadened branches.

He started to walk away, and I blurted a question. "Who *was* Abby?"

Who was she to you?

Gabriel spread his fingers as his thumbs kept hold of those belt loops. "Wish I could tell you that, Miss Mariah. But I suppose I'm here to find out."

He finally glanced up at me, as if wondering if I wanted to hear more. I was fairly sure my face couldn't hide that I did, so he kept on going.

"Abby was . . . special to me."

I didn't know what to say, how to feel, so the numbness overtook me.

Chaplin shifted from foot to foot, sensing my disquietude along with enduring his own. I backed into the food prep area, going to remove the water from the burner.

Special. Damn it all, Abby had been *special*.

"You don't need to continue," I said, my words sounding strangled. "I didn't mean to get personal."

"Of course not."

His tone was dry, and it could've denoted all kinds of things, none of which I quite understood.

If Abby was so special, why didn't I hear it in him?

Trying to keep my hands busy, I steeped the hot water with a loto cactus–filled wire mesh strainer. I hoped Gabriel didn't see how my hands shook.

When I was ready, I brought the steaming mugs out, handing one to Gabriel, then taking my own toward the study, where I thought it might be a good idea to hole up for a while.

But halfway there, something on the visz stopped me.

Sammy Ramos and the old man had taken up space in the common area, yet they weren't sitting round lazily gabbing with each other. They were in front of the lens, where the old man was waving his arms, as if to get attention.

Gabriel and Chaplin were drawn to the visz, too. Our guest even turned up the volume.

The oldster yelled, "Mariah!"

From the way he was shouting it, he sounded more worried than ecstatic. I froze in my very steps.

Sammy chimed in. "If you didn't hear us before, another of Stamp's men was found dead. Gutted. Half-buried in the dirt with that whale-hide hat of his sticking out. Come over here if you hear us!"

"We're gonna keep repeating ourselves, Mariah, because we can't get through the inner locks barring your doors!"

My hand darted toward the monitor to shut it off, blanking the screen.

Blanking everything. And, for a blessed second, the darkened visz truly made me feel as if nothing were there.

If it wasn't there, it couldn't affect me.

But Chaplin was whimpering, and I couldn't shut *that* out because it sounded like puncturing yells. And when Gabriel reached out to turn the visz back on, one look at his face told me that the hiding was over.

Thanks to another dead body, Stamp was going to be coming for us.

12

Gabriel

Beyond Mariah shutting off the visz screen, it was obvious to Gabriel that she didn't want to hear anything else from Sammy and the old man. Her rejection of their news was in the remoteness of her expression, the drag of her heartbeat.

And, just as if she felt Gabriel's gaze all over her, probing, wondering, she stepped over to a second monitor—one whose lens was trained on the wide, desert-empty view outside. She adjusted the definition of the picture, her pulse taking up its normal time again, then speeding up with every passing moment.

"Why'd you turn off the common-area visz?" he asked. "The news doesn't concern you?"

Her throat worked around a swallow, and Chaplin sat on his haunches, resting his paw against her leg while sending a troubled gaze up at her. Otherwise, the dog had shut his mind.

Gabriel heard Mariah's pulse stretching, a weak vibrato in its tremble, and the sight and sound of it moving in her neck vein dug into him.

"Mariah," he added, "maybe we should be planning to batten down the hatches."

She backed away from the monitors, as if this were the only way she could escape any trouble. Then she went to the weapons wall, running her hands over the deadly choices as she faced away from him. "Stamp didn't listen," she said unevenly. "And they're paying the price. But he'll be putting the cost on someone else."

He could understand her anger. It was delivered out of fear, and the two often went hand in hand. Miles yonder, where Stamp lived, he would also be angry—enough to retaliate against those he blamed—and it would've come out of his own fear for his men.

A vicious circle, Gabriel thought, just like a formation of carrion feeders in the sky.

"Tell me, Mariah, just how *would* Sammy and the oldster know about this new death? How can they be sure it's even a reality with the way everyone keeps to the sanctuary?"

Her shoulders were slumped, like she was trying to clamp down on a burgeoning pain inside her. "Unlike some of us, Sammy puts on a heat suit and ventures a decent distance away from here before most dusks hit. He hunts for meat out there, brings it back for trade, and that's how he discovered the . . . first body." She seemed to fold into herself even more. "Then a second one tonight."

Gabriel's eyes rested on the outside visz screen, which showed the moon, the grasping shadow of the nearby loto cactus under which he'd buried his blood flask.

"Stamp's gonna be back," he said. "He told us he would be if this happened again."

Now she was breathing faster, approaching panic.

Where had the woman who'd initially confronted him with that crossbow gone? Was he so much less scary than Stamp that she'd been able to stand up to *him* but couldn't bring herself to do the same with the kid?

Ironic, Gabriel thought. He, a vampire, seemed less intimidating to her than a regular bad guy, and he had to wonder why that was. Letting him into her home might've been the worst decision she'd ever made; it was even possible that *he'd* been the one who'd brought Stamp's ire upon them. Gabriel only wished he knew what had happened during every one of his blackouts, wished he knew who or what his meals had been consisting of lately.

Instinctively, as if to compensate, he moved toward Mariah, lifting his hand. What if he could manage to soothe her with just a touch?

For some reason, Chaplin growled at Gabriel. *Back off.*

He let his hand fall to his side, seeing the dog's glare.

It wasn't okay to be a vampire with Mariah, Gabriel thought to himself. That was what he believed Chaplin was getting at, anyway.

And the dog was right. It wasn't fine to act that way. He didn't even *want* to. Besides, either she would be wise to what he was doing or she would shirk him off altogether. Also, last night, all he'd had to do was take a gander at her undressing, and it'd sent him off the deep end.

Gabriel shouldn't be getting near her.

After a conflicted glance at Gabriel—a look that made him back off even more—Chaplin went to the trapdoor, making agitated woofing sounds. Mariah angled her face toward him.

"No," she said, her voice lower and far more jagged than he'd ever heard it. "I don't want you out there."

The dog opened his mind so Gabriel could understand the discussion. *No worry. I can scent Stamp's men far off if they're coming. I go out, I come back in. Give me fifteen minutes.* The dog shot a glance at Gabriel. *Meanwhile, you stay away from her.*

Gabriel didn't argue—not about staying away and not about the prospect of Chaplin going outside. The canine's abilities weren't anything to scoff at. Back in the day, Intel Dogs could fight almost as well as any monster, and that was why the government hadn't wanted them around. They'd started to rebel in some circles, and the bigwigs had feared the dogs would turn on them one day.

Addressing Mariah, Gabriel pretended that he didn't

understand what Chaplin was saying. "Is he asking to go outside?"

"He's asking," Mariah whispered, "but he's not getting."

"Then I'll go."

Chaplin jumped in with a direct mind-link to his temporary master as Mariah emphatically shook her head.

Don't, Gabriel, the dog thought. *My nose is better than yours. I can see if Stamp is on his way and how many he might be bringing with him. I won't take long at all.*

His last words were more warning to keep a distance from Mariah than Gabriel had ever heard from the dog, and without waiting for a response, Chaplin hit the trapdoor release, scrambling up some ledges that circled the wall while sand poured down. The dog jumped through the rain of it, disappearing outside, the door automatically shutting behind him.

Chaplin!" Mariah started over to where sand still dribbled, landing on Gabriel's blankets.

He darted over to grab her arm and stop her from doing something impulsive.

But, curse it all, he'd moved too vampire-fast out of concern, and she jerked back from him, her eyes widened.

Oddly, he didn't so much care what she thought about him right now.

"Stamp's coming," he repeated, as if she hadn't heard the first time. "You want to be out there, too?"

Something flickered in her gaze, and her voice turned cold, even rougher than it'd been before. "*No one* should be out there."

"Then cut it out, Mariah. Chaplin's gonna be back soon. He'll be okay."

She took in a long, tremulous breath, her gaze changing once again, allowing him to see for the first time the complete terror in her green eyes. It'd taken over any bluster or bravado, and she seemed just as bare as she'd been last night, when her skin had called to him.

Her vulnerability struck Gabriel so hard that his instincts

got the best of him. Fear. Invigorating, inviting *fear*. His fangs nudged, his gaze heated, his voice twisted as he spoke.

"Don't be afraid." He realized too late that his words were coated in hypnotic sway. It'd just . . . happened, and he couldn't take it back.

In spite of all the fight she'd put up before, she was in a perfect state of openness now, with her best friend outside and in possible danger. Her defenses were already so wilted that her gaze went soft at the sound of his words, her head tilting back slightly while she got tangled in them.

Falling, he thought. He'd been successful enough to finally make her fall under his power, and he was here to catch her. He *liked* being the one to do it.

But though she'd lowered her guard, there was still an inner wall holding her up, one last mental barrier, and it blocked him from reading her beyond the surface.

"Mariah," he said again, and that wall wavered, as if it might not actually exist.

Her heartbeat resembled low, raging chords, strings taut and played by his voice until something dark and rough-edged ran through him, too. The blend of her vital signs drew him even closer, and aside from Mariah's angrier disposition, the sounds reminded him of the night he'd gone to Abby when she'd been lying on her bed, so near to giving up on everything.

He pulled Mariah closer to him. "Just trust me. . . ."

Need kicked at him, and he imagined piercing her, brutally sucking and taking.

Mariah's eyes drifted closed, but remained halfway open, her mouth parting on a mellowed exhalation.

And with that breath, he could feel her letting go of the hurt, but not anything else. Not her guard.

Even so, her pulse became his—strong, livid—and he leaned toward her, attracted to the rage, pressing his face to her neck, his lips on her jugular. Each beat rammed into him, and he tasted her skin: salty, sweet, hot. Saliva pooled in his mouth, stinging his jaws, making the emergence of his fangs smooth.

His vision pounded hot, keeping time with her, with them. He wanted to bite but was somehow able to hold back, reveling in how this particular hunt had differed from the ones he practiced so often. It had more clarity. It existed on a different tier of violence, more personal, that made him want to rip into her before the inevitable blackout came on him. It conjured a shaking urge that made him want to feel every moment of blood washing through him until he came out feeling as he had whenever he'd been around Abby.

But Mariah wasn't the same as Abby. Would never be. Abby had never made him *this* ready to brutalize.

Resting one hand at the back of Mariah's head, Gabriel grabbed her hair, easing her back so that her neck arched. He wanted more of her. More of an expanse of flesh, more area for him to explore and sniff and agonize over before he drove into her.

Beneath his lips, he could feel the vibration of a groan in her throat, and her last sign of resistance traveled in him, too. Her sounds, his sounds. Her blood, his, just as Abby's blood should've been his . . .

When Mariah groaned again, louder, he heard her body rhythms change—from slow to fast, from smooth to restless. All her chords sawed through him.

He lifted his head, separating himself from the fantasy he'd fallen into. He looked at her face through his warped sight. Really looked.

Mariah's face.

Then the lust kicked back in. Not just any lust. *Blood*lust—hot, pulsing, needful. The type of crazy he'd been able to endure up until now because of the promise of someday finding redemption with a woman who made it seem so possible.

But he knew that this wasn't the way he'd get redemption—the validation that he could exist outside a hideout, among others, passing for anything but a bad guy.

He covered Mariah's neck with his free hand, as if to block it off from his senses, and then he let go of her hair.

"Don't remember," he whispered, swaying her with as much power as he could, hoping it'd work a second time and she'd come out of this with a blank slate.

Then he lowered her to the floor and began to count down. The closer he got to zero, the readier he got to defend himself from any explosive waking reaction.

"Three," he said, backing off and holding up his hands to show his innocuous intentions, though appetite kept snapping at him.

But he continued the countdown, knowing it wasn't just about allowing her to gain consciousness again. He was doing it so he would come back to himself, too, and with every passing moment, his body cooled.

"Two." He was five steps away from her now, and he needed all the distance he could get.

When he arrived near the common-area visz, where Zel and two other people Gabriel had never seen had joined the oldster and Sammy, he ended the countdown.

But instead of saying, "One," he said, "Stamp." He was banking on the hope that the enemy's name would divert Mariah's attention when she regained consciousness.

Gabriel still had his hands up when Mariah blinked, frowned, then straightened up from where she was lying on the floor. She glanced around her, discombobulated.

Unmoving, he waited to see if she would recall anything.

Waited.

And waited.

He let his hands fall back to his sides, and Mariah stood, as if she were taking right up where they'd left off, with Chaplin jumping out the trapdoor.

She glanced at the visz and, for a second, it seemed that she was wondering what she'd been doing sitting on the ground. Then, just as quickly, she hurried back to her weapons wall, where she took down an old-fashioned double-barreled shotgun with night-vision modifications.

Gabriel's strategy of putting Stamp uppermost in her mind seemed to have worked. He'd gotten away with losing control because of pure, dumb luck, hadn't he?

Mariah loaded the shotgun with ammunition from a sack hooked to the wall.

"What're you doing?" he asked evenly.

"Getting ready for Stamp. Chaplin should be back soon with a report."

She didn't say anything about going outside. Would she end up gathering her courage to face Stamp out there? And how far from her home would she go to defend it?

She went to stand below the trapdoor. There, she could still watch the viszes, one of which even now showed the neighbors having words with each other in the common area.

And while she watched, she absently laid her fingers against her neck, like she was feeling a latent tingle.

Shit, Gabriel thought. *Shit. Shit.*

Maybe he wasn't so great at swaying, after all.

But when she took her fingers away and adjusted the shotgun in her grip, Gabriel realized she probably hadn't recalled anything. That as far as she knew, there was only a tickle on her skin.

The close call chipped away at him. He'd vowed to protect her and Chaplin from Stamp, but funnily enough, Gabriel himself seemed to be the one she needed protecting from more than anything.

They waited for Chaplin for what seemed like hours, though Gabriel knew mere seconds had ticked by. Proof of that was in the way the Badlanders in the common area hadn't moved around much, their visz monitor still silent because Mariah had turned up the outside viewer instead.

Were the neighbors monitoring what was happening outside from a viewer in the common room? Gabriel didn't recall seeing any screens down there, so they couldn't be watching, though he did notice that Sammy Ramos was staring at something in his hand.

A portable visz?

It would make sense that he'd possess such a device out of everyone—though the New Badlanders had mostly rejected the more intrusive technology, Sammy had a background in it. He'd probably welcome simpler devices.

Gabriel turned back to the monitor that showed the outside, where there was nothing but near silence, too. Sounds of the wind raking the dirt. The hum of nothing . . .

. . . until a dog barked in the near distance.

Mariah stared harder at the visz. "Chaplin," she said. "He found something."

But when they didn't hear more, he saw her knuckles whiten as she throttled her shotgun.

The desire to go outside pulled at him, but he wasn't about to leave Mariah alone, whether he'd seen her take care of herself in the past or not.

When she fixed her tortured gaze on the ladder, as if getting ready to head toward it, he saved her by saying, "Just wait a little longer—"

That was when they heard it on the outside visz. A whimper.

Then they saw it.

Chaplin's face, shoved front and full on the screen, blocking almost everything except for the night-vision glare of metal cords that bound his muzzle. The dog's glowing eyes were at half-mast, and he was weaving back and forth on his feet, unbalanced.

Something like anger whipped through Gabriel, but he recovered to read the dog easily enough.

Stay inside. The canine's thoughts were slurred, as if he'd been shot up with a drug.

"Chaplin," Mariah whispered, dropping to her knees, one hand wrapped over her midsection as she lowered her head. Her next words were a sobbed plea. "Please, no."

On the visz, Chaplin was trying to talk through his muzzle bonds, but, simultaneously, he sent more thoughts to Gabriel.

Six, he relayed. *Chompers, plus five. They got me instead of one of you. . . .*

So this was Stamp's revenge.

Gabriel's blood popped inside him. He was tired of lying down. Tired of the good always suffering.

How long could beings like him and the people in this community take it? When should they stand up and make it stop?

Though Chaplin had warned Gabriel to stay inside, he went toward the ladder, anyway. He even grabbed a weapon from the wall—a revolver. It'd take away the need for fangs. The last thing he wanted to do was expose his vampire and get himself and the community in bigger trouble.

"Gabriel!"

At the almost unrecognizable, torn fervor of her voice, Gabriel trained his gaze on Mariah. Her fingers clutched his bed blankets, her chopped hair covering most of her face and making her look wrathful enough to take on Stamp's whole crew herself.

Their body rhythms beat in time to each other's, her anger his anger. It was even as if they were one of a kind.

"I know this is a trap," Gabriel said, "but Stamp's gone too far."

He glanced at the common-area visz to see if the others were there, and they were, still talking, still huddling together.

Maybe Sammy *didn't* have a portable visz with him. Maybe they didn't know what was happening outside. Shit, Gabriel wished he and Mariah had been audibly tuned in to the common area to know for sure what their neighbors were planning . . . if anything.

On the outside visz, someone pulled Chaplin away from the lens, leaving the screen empty again, except for a voice.

"We b at Stamp's!"

No more time to waste.

"You coming?" he asked Mariah.

He thought he saw her mouth curl downward in a grimace, but she lowered her head, pulling at the blankets harder.

"Chaplin's your best friend," he said, disbelief coloring

his question. Didn't saving Chaplin trump her fear of straying too far? Wouldn't this be worth going all the way to Stamp's place?

Slowly, she raised her head, her eyes still covered by hair. But he saw something in the silent cry of her mouth.

A reckoning. Her own desire for revenge, and it was making her limbs quake as they struggled to hold her up.

His own body responded, leading him to his inner vampire again. But he wasn't going to fight that way. Wasn't going to give in to it . . . or them. He was going to do this on his own terms, as Abby had made him want to do.

Mariah only pointed to the workroom door, and he caught her meaning. When he'd farmed water down there, he'd seen a trapdoor in the big cavern, and using it might offer an element of surprise if Stamp's men were nearby expecting an exit out of Mariah's primary doors.

"So you're not coming," he said.

A second passed, and he thought she just might pull through. But then she shook her head: harder, then faster, as if trying to jar something awful out of her.

Then, with a dry sob, she started to move toward the common-area tunnel. Was she going there for safety, to be with the others in case the voice on the visz had been lying about taking Chaplin to Stamp's and the thugs were actually going to infiltrate the homes below instead?

Now he understood why she might stay, though if it'd been him, he'd have gone after Chaplin for miles and miles.

But that was why she had Gabriel here.

"Gabriel," she said, her voice low and ragged as she neared the tunnel door. "Go."

Her eyes, which he could barely see shining through her hair with tears and grief and rage, made him realize that he'd do anything she needed him to do.

With one last look, he opened the door to the workroom, taking the stairs, blanking his mind, not dwelling on Mariah. He couldn't. She had her wall of weapons plus the other Badlanders to back her up if she needed it. Chaplin had nothing.

After he'd made his way through the workroom, then crept out the trapdoor, which was hidden among a hill of rocks, he tracked Chaplin by scent, going farther and farther away from the sanctuary.

Tracking made for slow going, yet he did it, inch by inch, foot by foot, as fast as he could.

When he heard the gunshot from back in the direction of Mariah's place, he was too mired in Chaplin's trail to go back there to see who'd fired.

Or why.

13

Cedric Orville had thought that the silver-capped teeth he wore around his boots would be too loud for a cat-and-mouse exercise like tonight's, so at dusk, he'd taken the baubles off and carefully stowed them in his pocket.

He'd gotten them from a stay in an East Coast sanctuary, sneaking around when the others had been snoozing, targeting his marks and then giving them a drop of lazy-donna, a black-market drug that would ensure unconsciousness while Cedric used his pliers to extract the teeth. Precious metals weren't as useful as they once were—water was king—but they sounded pretty when he put them on his boots and walked.

When Johnson Stamp had discovered Cedric one morning, ditched in a gutter where some vigilante sanctifiers had thrown him after catching him red-handed during a silver extraction, the boy had found Cedric's jewelry interesting. That had led to their conversing about how Cedric had been tossed out and left for garbage, and how no one in society should suffer that.

Stamp had offered him a second chance. Said that everyone deserved one, although if the recipient spit it right back at you, the slight should be accounted for. Cedric had agreed, knowing he wouldn't be doing any spitting. The boy was big on giving people new opportunities, and Cedric had heard once that it was because Stamp was looking for some himself, so he could distance himself from the things he'd done that no one dared talk about now. Stamp seemed to have some sort of moral code that Cedric found quaint—it'd kept the kid from outright killing the Badlanders until there was good proof of guilt.

As Cedric saw it, Stamp's whole second-chance attitude was probably the reason he'd been so downright disappointed when the scrubs over at the nearby community had seen fit to throw Stamp's graciousness right back in his face; who was to say that they *weren't* guilty of killing another one of the crew? Cedric was all for hanging them high and getting done with it.

Thinking about Teddy and his half-buried remains was all the reason Cedric needed for action. They'd found him under the beaks of those shades—the black-winged crow ancestors who'd grown in size and appetite since Before, just as things like scorpions and lizards and all manner of mutants had so rapidly done out here.

Thinking of Teddy made Cedric mad.

As a gunshot rang out from the west, back at the scrub compound, he stood up from the ground where he'd been resting, ready for any come-what-may.

He'd been tasked with transporting the dog to Stamp's place, but shooting the critter with the drug gun and capturing it had been the simple part. It sounded like Cedric's comrades were currently experiencing worse times back with the rest of the scrubs at the community.

Damn, he hoped his partners had gotten one of those *Homo sapiens* and not another dog to drag back as a captive. The crew hadn't gone over there tonight to wrangle *dogs*.

In a bid to see if his buddies were okay, Cedric quickly shoved up his shirtsleeve, then tugged down the long, protective glove over his left arm so he could access the small personal computer embedded in his inner forearm. It was wired to the chip in him, but then he remembered that they were too far from even the nearest server, and reception out here stunk. Communication wasn't an option. He yanked the glove back up and the shirtsleeve back down, shifting from foot to foot.

Aside from the lamp affixed to his head, he couldn't see much in the dark, and he squinted down at the dog, who was trussed up in cabled bonds and making weird noises in its throat. The thing had needed a rest, even though it could move surprisingly jiffy when properly motivated.

Cedric smiled. Stamp had told them that they could throw around some payback tonight. The scrubs were territorial, the boss had said, and putting them on warning obviously hadn't been enough. They needed a stronger lesson in being good neighbors, so the crew had gone to the compound, thinking to lure one of the scrubs out by using a visz lens that the gang had already found. But then a dog had emerged instead of any humans, and Cedric had drugged it before it could bite, then taken what they could get for a captive.

"Tym 2 go," he said to the dog.

The critter didn't move, but Cedric hadn't expected it to. Lazy-donna was potent stuff.

He fired up the power on the jet-propelled speed braces he'd fitted over his boots tonight, then fixed his taserwhip to the creature's bound muzzle. All set now, he sprang away, hitting the ground running, dragging the dog behind him.

His soles skimmed the ground, and they traveled in leaps and bounds, the sound of his running like quick flaring gasps. The FlyShoes elevated him about two feet off the ground and dug into his calves, up to his knees, but they felt like an extension of his legs, too.

In the meantime, the dog tumbled behind him, and Cedric toyed with the notion of turning on his whip to give it a good shock.

He saw a rock jutting out of the ground ahead and, electing a different mode of *giddy-up, dog*, he headed straight for it, knowing he could clear it while the canine would get a sharp thunk to the hide.

Pushing off with one foot, Cedric sailed up, yanking the dog with him. He landed, expecting to feel the airborne animal wiggling on its whip-leash, then crashing to the ground.

But he didn't feel anything, and he slowed down, then came to a skidding stop. When he jerked at the taserwhip to retrieve it, the lash snicked right back to him, as light as could be.

Empty.

He stared at it, then ran a hand along its length to the end, where it was frayed.

Damn it, he'd have to get a new one, and they didn't come cheap.

Grunting, he turned back to where the dog had probably gotten caught on the rock, then took an aggressive leap back toward it.

Something came toward him—a thick branch?—and Cedric caught it in the stomach, flipping, head over heels, then smacked the ground face-first.

As he lay there, his nose, chin, and cheeks vibrating to numbness, he thought he heard a mumble. A chewing wordy sound.

He was barely able to glance up, where the cracked lamp attached to his head showcased the dog, who stood in wobbling, drugged confusion while it moved its whimpering mouth like a drunkard.

Its unbound mouth.

Cedric absorbed that. Had the rock snagged on the muzzle and stripped it off?

But what about the dog's other bonds? What'd happened to . . . ?

He never finished the question, because a grating laugh took its place.

It'd come from behind Cedric, and shivers spiked every inch of his flesh.

While wincing and semibarking, the scared dog backed away from whatever it was.

Then the creature made a seething sound—an awful hiss—and the dog scrambled, fell down, and began crawling off, impeded by the drugs.

Cedric stared after the critter, his mind taking a million years to catch up until he heard footsteps behind him.

Slish, slish, they went over the dirt.

As Cedric foggily watched the canine stumbling even farther away, he felt the thing behind him going through his pockets. It found the silver teeth, then tore off a piece of material from Cedric's shirt, as if it were reluctant to touch the objects.

The teeth jangled, and Cedric let loose with a curse. Fuck these stupid animals out here in the Badlands. When he got up, he was gonna . . .

Then Cedric felt one of those teeth placed against the back of his neck, where it was traced down his spine, creating a batch of chills.

But he wasn't going to be a pussy.

"Cut it ot," Cedric said. His lips didn't work so well. "Im gonna work u ovr whn I . . ."

He choked on a fragment and realized it was part of his own incisor.

The thing removed the silver tooth from Cedric's spine, and silence followed.

More silence. And more.

Then, after a few heartbeats, Cedric told himself it was gone.

He was just preparing to push off the ground to get back on his feet when something punched into his back and jerked his spine out, surprising him for the last time ever.

14

Gabriel

Three Hours Later

After Gabriel returned from tracking Chaplin, he found Mariah in the common area, safe and sound, sitting on a crate in a corner, wrapped in an all-encompassing gray thermal blanket and wearing a knit hat that pulled over her ears, as though she wanted to shut everything out. Her neighbors surrounded her, and all of them—including two denizens he'd never met before—looked up at his entrance, sticking close to Mariah, still cocooning her.

Their faces were a study in unreadability, though Mariah's own features practically screeched of the terror that even now dogged her.

Gabriel froze under the larger unresponsiveness, because it looked a whole lot like a prelude to group accusation, as if they were thinking that he might've brought all this trouble from Stamp down upon them.

Or maybe he was imagining it. A guilty, blacked-out, blood-glutted conscience tended to do that when it had no other explanations for those two dead bodies that'd been found before tonight—the reason Stamp had descended on them now.

Gabriel endured the scrutiny, until, from behind, Chaplin came stumbling out of the tunnel as best as he could while still under the effect of the drugs that Stamp's crew had used on him. When everyone saw the dog, the room came alive, the neighbors separating from Mariah as she stood.

"Chaplin!" she said as the dog accelerated and then jumped at her, knocking her to the floor so that she was turned away from the rest of them, allowing for a private moment. She opened her blanket to embrace the dog, not even seeming to mind that his coat was damp from the quick shower he'd taken after Gabriel had escorted him back home.

Earlier, when Gabriel had found Chaplin, his fur had been matted with dirt, which the canine had coated himself with to distract from the scent of his blood out there in the night. Chaplin had initially warned Gabriel away, telling his temporary master that he was bleeding from being dragged along with a taserwhip, so Gabriel had kept his distance while ushering him back. Then, while Gabriel had checked Mariah's common-area visz to see that she was secure among her neighbors, Chaplin had used the sensors in the cleaning station to water the blood off him, and Gabriel had lent a hand in toweling the dog dry. All the while, Chaplin had kept fixing a cryptic half-angry, half-regretful look on Gabriel.

No telling what that had been about, but it made Gabriel think that something had really changed between him and Chaplin, who was blanking him out yet again. Something bigger than Gabriel was grasping.

Now, in the common area, the weight of all these silent stares from the Badlanders pressed him near to the ground, too.

One by one, he met their heavy gazes: Zel, Sammy, and the oldster, people he'd already met who suddenly came off like strangers. Then he acknowledged one of the new people who'd joined the crowd tonight—a short, hardy woman with doe-brown eyes and dark skin who wore a brownish-gray scarf that covered her head, plus matching robes that swathed her body. She was holding hands with a man wearing khaki trousers over his long legs and a brown henley over his barrel chest, his hair brown, his skin a natural tan that was made all the lighter by time spent under the ground.

Was this Hana and Pucci, the neighbors who didn't leave their shelter as often as the rest?

Speaking to the group, Gabriel jerked his chin at Chaplin, where the dog was licking Mariah's face and she was hugging her friend as if he'd come back from the dead.

"I found him making his way back to the sanctuary," Gabriel said, "all padded down with blood and grime. Your delightful neighbors shot him up with drugs and bound him. They were taking him back to Stamp's place, probably so they could get some captive leverage in this war they've declared."

From beneath Mariah's blanket, where she was still cradling her dog, he heard Chaplin talking.

Zel translated. "He says that Chompers was wearing FlyShoes when he captured him, so he was dragging Chaplin along the ground until the ropes rubbed off and freed him. He hid from the thug until the guy just gave up and left."

As Gabriel watched Mariah and Chaplin in their corner of the room, he felt cold to the bone. For some reason, he doubted the dog's story. Chompers had just given up and left? Right.

But even under the thrall of drugs, Chaplin's mind was strong enough to bar Gabriel. Maybe, when the dog could think straight, he'd let his temporary master in again.

The oldster stood by Zel's side, his spine curved as if in protective caution as she fired off what everyone else in the room had to be thinking.

"We thought you might not be coming back, Gabriel. You were gone a real long time."

The comment didn't exactly condemn him, but he thought it might lead to a sort of trial—one that could include questions about where he'd been on the nights when the first victim, and then Whale Hide, had perished. One that would explain how the community had found itself in Stamp's vengeful sights tonight.

Maybe his time here had come to an end, Gabriel thought, but he wasn't going to go that easily. Not without knowing more about Annie.

"After I came across Chaplin," he said, explaining just what had taken him so long out there, "we almost ran into a party of Stamp's men on their way back from messing with you all. They were about a half mile from the community, laughing and springing around on their FlyShoes, acting like little kids until they ran off and left the way clear for us to get the rest of the way here. I'm guessing they were going back without another captive because of that gunshot I heard early on."

Sammy was watching whatever he had in his palm—the item that Gabriel had seen him with earlier, over the visz. Now Gabriel realized that the man *did* have a portable screen in hand, and that he was monitoring the outside with it.

"Zel scared them off with a warning shot," he said. "It was enough to give the thugs some distance but not enough to make them run all the way home, because they taunted us from a spot where they felt safer. 'C'ot, c'ot,' they kept yelling. 'Cum git ur woofwoof.' They had on those Fly-Shoes, so they moved fast. We didn't engage them, especially since Mariah said you were out there on Chaplin's path."

So that was what the shot had been all about, Gabriel thought. And here he'd toyed with the idea that maybe *Mariah* had sucked it up and gone outside to defend her home.

He watched her, disappointed that she hadn't emerged yet—not from those blankets, and not from much else. Maybe she never would. But he wouldn't think of her as a

coward, because she'd been the one to save his hide by letting him into her shelter. All the same, the notion that she
might be yellow underneath it all had already carved its way
deep into Gabriel.

Everyone was watching Chaplin, whose muzzle was
peeking out of Mariah's blanket, just over her shoulder. He
was nudging aside her knit cap and whispering something
to her while keeping his mind closed.

Zel obviously heard what he said, and her gaze whipped
over to the others, her jaw tight as she clearly strove for
composure of some sort. She cursed, making Gabriel flinch,
and turned her back on the dog and his mistress.

Mariah's face only lowered farther into her blanket.

What had Chaplin told them?

After several beats, Mariah rested her forehead against
her dog's.

Gabriel caught her raised profile. She wasn't crying now.
Actually, he found a sort of strength in her that he thought
she'd been missing lately.

A desperate resignation, though he couldn't say why.

Gabriel was just about to ask what Chaplin had said when
Zel stepped in front of Mariah, canceling Gabriel's view. "I
think it's best that you say your good-byes now. The more
strangers that come into this territory, the more the wildlife
comes out to prey. We've handled the situation well until
Stamp came here. Before . . . you came, too."

Along with the oldster, Sammy backed Zel up, his eyes
dark.

"You have no idea," Zel added, "what kind of damage is
going on and how you only make it worse."

Gabriel got the feeling that no one was blaming him for
those deaths now that they'd already come to a vigilant
acceptance of possible danger as a course of living out here.
But like Stamp, Gabriel had interrupted that flow of survival.
He was an interloper—a symbol of the change that was
ruining their lives.

When he didn't respond, Zel sighed.

"Chaplin just now told us that there was another killing

tonight," she said. "Chompers, the thug who was taking the dog to Stamp's place. Chaplin says that, after he got free, he came across Chompers's mutilated body and then got as far away as he could."

At first, Gabriel just stood there under the onslaught of the news. Another death . . . ?

Then he realized Chaplin hadn't said anything about it to him on the way back.

Then the weight in the room seemed to lift right off Gabriel altogether.

Wait . . . He hadn't blacked out tonight.

He couldn't have killed Chompers. . . .

As Zel shifted, Gabriel was able to see Chaplin, who was assessing him, his head against Mariah's.

He wished he'd been close enough to scent tonight's carnage, wished he could've done some investigation to see what was killing Stamp's men. After all, not long ago, these people had looked *to* him, not *at* him, and the difference mattered.

He wandered over to the crate table and took a seat on it. Zel looked at him as if he were thick in the head. And maybe he was, determination-wise.

Chaplin spoke, his mind opened for Gabriel, his thoughts a bit slurred, though they were articulate. *Nobody's accusing you of doing this, Gabriel.*

Support. Thank-all, it was about time from his familiar. But when the dog talked, including the group now, Gabriel rethought everything.

Normally, Chaplin said, *I would be the first to tell Gabriel to get himself out of here.*

It was as if the dog were trying to persuade his neighbors of Gabriel's worth. But Gabriel tried to come off as if he didn't understand the dog without a translation. At the same time, he accepted the dog's statement to mean that if Gabriel hadn't taken on Chaplin as his familiar, the canine would've rejected him.

The dog, who was pressing his head against Mariah's cheek, glanced at Zel as she frowned; it was almost as though she didn't understand where he was going with this.

But, Chaplin added, his sounds lazy with the remnants of the drugs, *we know that we might need all the help we can get with Stamp now that it's too late to do anything about the trouble and it's come to a peak. There's no turning back what's already happened, so we need to strengthen up in whatever way possible.*

Reluctantly, as if she didn't agree with what Chaplin was suggesting, Zel translated for the group. Meanwhile, Gabriel dwelled on what Chaplin had only hinted at with his comments.

The dog was hoping that Gabriel would eventually reveal his vampiric side when the time was right, wasn't he? Was he also hoping Gabriel would spring the surprise on Stamp when there was no other recourse? But surely Chaplin knew that his new master wasn't about to do that. If Stamp were as tech-savvy as Gabriel suspected, he probably had high-grade viszes all over his property, and if recorded images of a vampire attacking his place were to ever surface beyond the Badlands . . .

Well, the Badlanders could kiss their secure existences good-bye. They'd be on the run forevermore for associating with him, and Gabriel wouldn't do that. He wouldn't do it to himself, either. Not after what he'd accomplished out here as another person. A vampire learning to be a man.

From her spot against Chaplin's head, Mariah subtly glanced at Gabriel, and a burst of disturbing blood-need made him look away.

A man, he reminded himself. *Not a vampire.*

When Zel had finished translating, the oldster nodded, as if agreeing with Chaplin's comment about strengthening up, even if they kept a stranger like Gabriel around to do it. "The times," he said. "They are a changin'. Chaplin's right. We need to face Stamp, and if need be, face him with whatever we have."

Sammy shook his head, his eyes flashing with the same growing terror he'd seen in Mariah's earlier.

The oldster addressed the younger man. "Stamp's gonna

pay us a nasty visit—that's the reality, Sammy. We're done with the way things were. Now we have to do whatever it takes to get ready for the inevitable."

"And risk being assaulted from this night forward, even if we were to win any kind of fight with Stamp?" Sammy asked. "He's an urban, oldster. He isn't hiding out in the New Badlands as much as retreating from something in the hubs. He'll still know people there, and if we prove to be trouble for Stamp, they'll come out here to find us . . . and our valuable resources, just like all bad guys do. It's safer to stay quiet."

Chaplin garbled out a series of sounds, causing Mariah to startle. Then she shared a glance with Zel. They both seemed resigned now.

But resignation wasn't what these people needed.

"Then what comes next?" Gabriel asked. "What do you intend to do besides sitting around here talking about it?"

When the oldster glared, Gabriel knew he'd gotten somewhere.

"You think your smart mouth gave Stamp any thoughts about backing off when he first visited?" he asked. "He was intrigued by your sass, I'll give you that, but he wouldn't hesitate to whip you silly again."

The oldster's skin flushed, and he turned his back on Zel, as if he didn't want the woman to see it.

Gabriel addressed her now. "And you. The ex-cop. The one who should be doing more than firing warning shots at these morons. Do you get all your frustration out by running around these rooms, exercising, wishing you could gut up enough to make Stamp leave you alone for good? How's that been working for you?"

She seemed to resent his words—and maybe even herself.

"If you're trying to shame us into action," Sammy said, the visz still in his palm, "you're—"

"Doing a fine job," the oldster finished. He glanced at his neighbors. "Gabriel took it upon himself to be the only one to rationally confront Stamp last time the kid was here. It seemed to work, too. I was even hoping Gabriel might do us a favor and voluntarily keep being the one who takes the chance of facing down our troubles while we just stand by. Truth to tell, I was still hoping he'd keep on doing it since it'd allow us to stay where we like to be—out of sight, out of mind."

The instinct to sit taller claimed Gabriel, but he didn't do it. He only watched Mariah, who hadn't contributed anything. But Chaplin kept looking at her with those big brown eyes.

Again, the faint discomfort of cowardice defined her in Gabriel's thoughts. Why wasn't she saying something? Where was that gumption he'd seen on the night she'd stuck a crossbow in his face?

From the back, a lazy voice cut the conversation. "This is nonsense."

Everyone focused on the tall man with the wide chest who'd draped his arm over the scarf-wearing woman.

"I've never heard this kind of discussion here before," he added, "and I can't believe I'm hearing it now."

Zel spoke. "Well then, Pucci, I suppose you have a better idea about how to handle matters? And you haven't exactly been round much to hear us talking before now."

"Dmitri gave me and Hana a visz, just like each of you, so we've been listening in." He hugged the woman to him. "I say we can mollify this guy Stamp in some way so he'll step off. If we show him that we want to work with him, he'll be more receptive."

The oldster rolled his eyes. "Genius idea. Why didn't I ever think of it? Negotiating with bad guys always leads to success."

Hana joined the conversation, her voice smooth, unruffled, even what some would call sisterly. Her tone carried an exotic accent, and if Gabriel had to guess, he would've said she was from somewhere in Africa.

"As far as Stamp thinks," she said, "*we* are the bad guys. He needs to see we are not. If we could bridge an understanding—"

"You don't know how this kid builds bridges," the oldster said, rubbing his hand against his neck, as if the taserwhip were still there. He had his collar buttoned up tonight, so any burn marks he might've had weren't visible. "Besides, who's gonna go over to his place to bow before him, apologizing for the troubles with his men? You, Pucci? You, Hana?"

She actually seemed to consider taking up the option, but the tall man pulled her closer to him, as if telling her not to commit.

At least the oldster, Zel, and Sammy were actually looking as if they were sick and tired of Stamp's shit. That was a start.

Even Mariah, who was so quiet in her corner while petting Chaplin with the dedication of someone who'd almost lost a vital part of herself, seemed as if she could be open to new ideas.

If she was capable of it. . . .

Any way you sliced it, Gabriel thought, these people would have to decide to do something he could back them up on. Something that wouldn't involve using a vampire, and he trusted that Chaplin was keeping quiet right now about who Gabriel really was because he knew the group would turn on a monster, even if it could aid them.

Maybe the dog also thought Gabriel would have to be the one to volunteer his services after a battle with Stamp was in progress, and, at that point, the community wouldn't mind the kind of defense Gabriel could bring. . . .

The Intel Dog, with his strong, secretive mind, made so much more sense to Gabriel now. And here he'd thought that he'd swayed Chaplin into welcoming an injured fellow into his home. But the canine had turned the situation to his advantage, hadn't he? That was probably why they called them *Intel Dogs*.

Typical. He'd had to go and get himself a familiar who might just be controlling him more than the other way around.

Gabriel tried to take back some of that control. "Seems

to me that you all are taking up a whole lot of time to come up with a plan of action."

Pucci grunted out a laugh, and Gabriel concentrated on him—the seed of complacency in the group.

Maybe he could slap that useless quality down a little. "Power can be lost easier than most might think. First you suspect there's something bad going on out there, but you only hear about it—you haven't so much run into it yourself. You think that your life can never be taken over, and trouble's gonna pass you right by if you're just quiet enough. Then, while you're sitting there, hoping time is going to take care of the situation, what power you took for granted is replaced by something bigger. Something worse." Gabriel looked around the room. "Together, you guys can make a stand before it's too late."

Pucci and Hana stayed mute. Mariah kept holding Chaplin to her. Zel and Sammy meandered away from the crate table. But the oldster's lips were pursed, as if he remembered times Before.

It wasn't lost on Gabriel that though he'd been preaching "take back your power," he didn't intend to do any such thing himself by using his abilities. Hypocrite.

The oldster finally tossed his hands up. "We're just gonna sit here?"

Pucci sounded off from his and Hana's corner. "I think just sitting here would've solved our troubles very nicely before we got into this pretty fix."

What did that mean?

With a loaded look toward the rest of the crowd, especially at Chaplin and Mariah, he guided Hana toward a door, which he opened.

At the same time, Hana gave a helpless shrug.

They left and, one by one, the others ultimately retreated, too—Sammy to his door, Zel to hers—leaving just the oldster, Gabriel, Chaplin, and Mariah, who pulled the blanket closer around her as the dog laid himself down, his adrenaline no doubt spent and the drugs taking over.

She'd been under the blanket for such a long time that

Gabriel started to wonder if, maybe, she'd gone through some trauma, and he'd been too quick to judge her.

Just as he was about to try communicating silently with Chaplin to find out if she was okay, the oldster hunkered down on a crate, his expression serious.

Gabriel quietly asked him, "What did Pucci mean by just sitting here—and that it might've been a good thing if you'd done just that?"

He heard Chaplin stir, but the oldster was already answering.

"Pucci's a malcontent. He's . . . not happy about letting in new people"—the old man jerked a thumb toward Gabriel—"or new situations."

The explanation didn't sit quite right with Gabriel, but the oldster was changing the subject. "So if we were to do anything about Stamp, what would be your way of going about it?"

He was asking for guidance, and Gabriel was gratified.

"Seeing as I've never played four-star general before," he said, "why don't you just lay it out?"

The oldster did so, and Gabriel listened to what amounted to a bunch of crazy revenge fantasies. But at least it was a start.

Especially since Mariah sat there listening, too, just as if she were hanging on every idea and considering it, even if it would require going outside.

15

Mariah

After I listened to Gabriel talking to the oldster, me and Chaplin followed him to my domain.

It was the time when night was at its coolest, with the sun a few hours away from starting its rise, but Gabriel clearly wasn't ready to rest. No, now that he'd given us his opinions about what we needed to do, I could see he was itching to grab a weapon and go outside, because he wanted all of us to see that he wasn't afraid, and we shouldn't be, either.

Right. Hell, I could still feel my neighbors' gazes on each other, watching. Waiting. Seeing what I would do next, too.

In the end, the oldster had been full of his own ideas. Gabriel had obviously revved him up to a level where he could spit fire, but I knew the rest of the community wouldn't act. There was too much to lose.

Still, a part of me had listened to Gabriel and wanted to follow him, ready to face down Stamp, whatever the cost. And part of me knew it was just a plain bad idea, because

once we came out of hiding, there'd be no holding back—
that'd be it. Our lives would change.

They might even end.

Gabriel perused my weapons wall, and I retreated to my
room with Chaplin, who was still sluggish. There, I shed
the knit cap and blanket I'd been huddling under, my hair
still damp from an earlier bracing shower until I took my
time now in drying it more. Then I put on my nightclothes—
a simple linen sleeveless top and pants. I intended to bury
myself under my covers, just as soon as I made sure Gabriel
wouldn't be causing any trouble.

Though my getup wasn't an outfit a woman would wear
to entice, I think I ended up doing it to Gabriel, anyway,
because when I came out of my quarters, his gaze lingered
on me, making me aware that the material showed off much
more than my usual baggy shirts.

Even half out of it, Chaplin seemed to notice Gabriel's
attentions, too. My dog positioned himself in front of me,
close to my legs, his fur seeming to bristle, his gaze lowered
at our guest.

Gabriel sure enough caught my friend's protectiveness.
But would he also recognize that Chaplin was just as put
out with me, too?

I rushed to get this over with so I could bury myself in
bed. "You going out again?" My voice was flat, and it
sounded as if something inside me had lain down and
wouldn't get back up after the drama with Chompers and
Chaplin. It sounded as if I'd already been beaten by the
trouble that was bound to rain down on us now, with this
newest death.

Gabriel checked over my shotgun, which I hadn't
unloaded after I'd used it to cover him when he'd arrived
that first night. "No use in my staying in here. You just go
on and get some sleep, and I'll hammer my time out by
patrolling for any activity until the sun arrives. Maybe
Stamp hasn't discovered Chompers's body yet. Besides, I
think the heat will bar any imminent attacks, even if Stamp's

crowd has got suits to withstand the day. If you ask me, I can't see anybody coming at us until dusk, but it's good to watch the entire landscape for signs of them now. The viszes wouldn't give me such a wide view from down here."

I couldn't believe it. "You want me to *sleep*?"

"It's either that or go outside with me."

He said it like it was a challenge, as if he suspected I was some sort of coward for using walls and blankets as cover.

I was just about to go back into my quarters without giving him the satisfaction of an answer when Chaplin woofed at me.

He was talking nonsense, and I bent down to quiet him. Gabriel stood there, uncomprehending.

He's right, Chaplin said. *Let's go outside, Mariah. It's time. It'll make you stronger. It'll whip the fear out of you, bit by bit, until you can master it.*

"I don't think so."

But before I could rise to my feet, the dog took his paws and pushed at me, making me stumble back. I fell on my ass, my breath jarred from my lungs.

Gabriel took a step forward, but Chaplin slumped away from both of us, muttering something angry that not even I understood.

Had the mutt lost his senses? His behavior was almost enough to make me think he was pissed at me for letting him get captured. Didn't he know I'd been out of my head with fear when I'd seen him bound up and drugged on the visz? I'd been so upset that I'd even lost some time or . . . I don't know what I lost, but there'd been a blank spot in my emotions and thoughts, a blip, just like I remembered a television looking when you switched from one channel to another.

But I knew Chaplin was angry about more than my staying inside.

"Going out there wouldn't result in anything constructive," I said. "It wouldn't mean I was gaining control of any kind of fear, and you know it."

Gabriel's expression told me that he was using my side of the conversation to build a whole one, as if he were thinking that Chaplin was asking me to go outside in order to make up for not coming after him earlier. No wonder Gabriel looked at me as if I were a coward.

I could feel my face flushing, my blood boiling.

Chaplin turned round to bark at me, his comments sleepy yet irate. Gabriel's expression changed, as if he suddenly understood what the dog was saying. But how?

Unless he was a vampire and Chaplin was allowing him access to his mind . . .

Get it together, the dog said to me. *I told Dmitri I would see to your survival. Told him I would help you get better. Yet, how can I if you won't allow it?*

"But what if—" I started.

Try, the dog said with a yowl.

Instinctively, I held up a hand in front of my face, rearing away from his livid sounds. But just as my own frustration and rage was welling up, Gabriel reached out, offering his own hand to help me up.

I turned my face away from him. I breathed, settling my pounding heart, the rise in my blood temperature, the quaking that threatened my body.

Chaplin smoothed out his tone. *This is the situation we find ourselves in, Mariah. I'm doing my best with it, and you need to, also. Prove to me . . . to yourself . . . that we will get over this. Do it now while we're still offering to help. While* anyone *is still offering.*

Gabriel picked up where the dog ended, keeping his palm outstretched. "Just come outside for a short time. Give Chaplin what he's asking for. It clearly means a lot to him."

He was apparently trying to keep the peace in this household, because the last thing we needed was to be divided in the face of Stamp.

He added, "Chaplin would be able to sense any of Stamp's men if they do come around, Mariah, and I'd get you inside pronto if need be." He leaned closer to me. "Just take one step forward, because you're going to need all the ground you can get underneath your feet from this point on."

It seemed as if Chaplin had given Gabriel some background on me, and I glanced at the dog. Tears were making my vision wavy, so I saw Chaplin through the heat of them.

None of this was fair. I hadn't asked to be like this. I hadn't let those men into my family's home in Dallas to do what they'd done.

I'll be out there, too, Chaplin said, *just in case. And Gabriel . . . having him with you is going to do a world of good. You'll see.*

Gabriel . . .

He still had his hand out to me, and I knew if I refused him, Chaplin would give up on me altogether. There was nowhere for me to go, really, no other choice for me to make.

I had to move forward.

Closing my eyes, I gripped Gabriel's hand, expecting the body-electric awareness I got just from touching him.

A second zinged by. I don't know what he was thinking, but his fingers seemed to tighten, as if my flesh on his shocked him just as much as me.

Then he hauled me to my feet and helped me to a stand.

Chaplin clumsily rushed over, as if hurrying before I changed my mind. He nudged me to my quarters, and it wasn't a minute later when I emerged wearing a large, pea-colored coat and my boots. Afterward, with the dog panting at the foot of the ladder, I ascended, one rung at a time. Gabriel followed, and Chaplin went to his trapdoor to get out.

When Gabriel came up top, he immediately covered the area with his weapon, just in case something was round. But we were all clear. Then Gabriel helped me outside, Chaplin's gaze trained on me, as if proud to see me taking this step. But there was concern there, as well, as he again sniffed the relatively cooler air, which was traced with dryness and the grit of wasteland.

Gabriel took up position at my shoulder. "Looks like Chaplin didn't find anyone out and about who shouldn't be."

I merely stared into the distance, toward the rock-jammed hills. Stamp's place would probably be just beyond.

Chaplin lethargically circled round to bump the back of my legs, urging me to move. My heart rate seemed to take me over, fast and frail, likely to snap at any minute into a run. I breathed, told myself I could do this, if only to show Chaplin I could.

"So where's your usual perimeter?" Gabriel asked me. "I mean, how far do you normally go at any given time you need to be out here?"

"My normal perimeter?" My mouth turned up in a mirthless grin. "I don't go past the cusp of our community, if I come out here at all."

Thud-a-thud went my pulse.

I had the coat bundled round me as if it were a life jacket in this sea of dirt and gray-cast, waning-mooned night. A slight wind cuffed at my hair, and I thought that it just might be with enough force to send me back inside.

Gabriel grabbed hold of my coat, discouraging me from going anywhere while clutching the shotgun in his other hand.

"Come on, then," he said. "Might as well make the dog happy."

He pulled me along, Chaplin following at a distance. Smart dog.

My flailing pulse beat harder when we came to the edge of the community caverns. I stopped, unwilling to go any farther, my breathing strained as I lowered myself to a knee.

I wanted to break free . . . wanted to run . . .

Couldn't . . . do . . . either.

"Far enough," I said. "Can we go back now?"

Chaplin barked. *No. You've been doing fine, so now you'll sit here and face it for once.*

"And this is your way of helping," I said, wishing I could just kill him.

Stop being afraid. Chaplin was glaring at me via his sleepy eyes. *Fear destroys this control you're showing right now. Don't. Fear. We can't afford for you to be weak—not anymore.*

Gabriel stood by, as if knowing that this was something he had no business in. Still, he said, "Mariah, you're going to be stronger now, for when trouble comes again. Just remember that."

Listen to him, thinking he had his finger on the pulse of what was happening. As I sat there, cursing Chaplin, I almost hated Gabriel, too, for seeing me like this, shame-faced and put in my place.

Surveying the area, the dog acted as a sentinel, and I kept breathing. One inhalation, one exhalation. In. Out. Before now, the rhythm had been outpacing me, but miraculously, I seemed to be catching up.

Maybe Chaplin had been right. Maybe I just needed to face what was out here, master it.

That was when I stopped hating my dog.

"You okay?" Gabriel asked.

I stopped hating Gabriel, also, and I started to shake my head but then halted, nodding only once.

That seemed to be good enough for him. He was peering at the sky now, as if concerned about the coming sunrise. I watched him carefully, wondering if he was going to bolt for shelter if we stayed out here for too long. If he would finally admit to what he was.

Funny, but there wasn't much of a monster evident in him. It could be that he really was one of the good ones and I'd only misjudged.

"You know," I said softly, "I can normally tell my bad guys from good."

"Can you?" he asked.

"Don't ask me to explain, but I've had my time with evil. Every one of us out here has, and that's why I'm glad Stamp's men are dying. Bad guys deserve their comeuppance, and they sure don't get it back in society. There, unchecked greed is rewarded. Out here, it's punished, and that's why you don't go outside if you've got something to answer for. That's the way of the world here. Everyone but Stamp seems to know it."

"Not all bad guys are like him. Some don't try to be greedy. Some are grouped in with the rest because they had no other choice."

He sounded like he had something to defend, and the hair on my skin reacted.

Vampire, my common sense whispered. I wished he would just tell me, because there was so much I wanted to know. Could all monsters be good? Could vampires read minds?

Then it hit me: Could they soothe a person and give them peace merely by looking in their eyes and willing it . . . ?

Chaplin barked. *Time to move farther on, Mariah.*

Damn the dog. He was going to hold my feet to the fire.

My heartbeat picked up again.

"Ready for a yard more?" Gabriel asked. "I think that's all Chaplin is asking right now—for you to cross over from where the community is beneath you. Then maybe you can go on home."

I was about to tell him to screw off, but then I slowly got to my feet. He was right. Chaplin wouldn't let me off the hook until I did what he wanted.

"Just a couple of steps," Gabriel said, putting his hand on the small of my back.

The bulk of my coat didn't really erase what he did to me: sending a buzz up my spine, fingers of energy thrusting out to every part of me.

He gave me a little push, and I all but tripped a few steps forward.

And there I was, across that imaginary line between here and there—the borders I'd tried so hard to keep myself to. My heartbeat was a crash of panicked keens roaring together.

In the midst of my chaos, I inadvertently looked toward Stamp's place. He was the reason I was so vulnerable, the reason I was in a crisis.

But when I heard Gabriel behind me whispering,

"Mariah?" I came to myself, stunned by my remaining emotion.

What would I have to do to overcome it? Would I ever be able to?

Without Chaplin's approval, I turned round and bolted back home, craving the serenity of my workroom.

But once I got inside my domain, I never quite made it there.

16

Gabriel

Gabriel watched as Mariah ran ahead of them, darting inside the entrance. He'd heard her flailing body rhythms this entire time, connecting to them, so he hadn't been at all comfortable with what'd just transpired. Before Chaplin could get to his trapdoor, Gabriel stepped in front of the dog.

"Good enough for you?"

Yup, Chaplin answered. He'd been mind-connected with Gabriel most of the time, except for there at the beginning, when the dog had first confronted her in the domain. What'd been said between the two, Gabriel couldn't be certain, but he'd pretty much put the puzzle of the conversation together, along with the images the dog had shown him about Mariah's attack a couple nights earlier.

"Angry, ain't she?" Gabriel said.

Chaplin finally seemed unable to avoid the drugs in his system as he answered in a dragging cadence. *She'll probably go to the workroom, as usual. It helps her calm down. Maybe she'll sleep well with you outside. At the very least, she just learned something about her limits, and she needed that. Badly.*

"You want me outside," Gabriel said. "It sounds as if you hope I'll keep my distance."

Chaplin paused, then thought, *There's a hunger, Gabriel, and it's been building.*

So there it was. "If you can sense that in me, you probably also know that I'm getting better and better at conquering it."

The dog hesitated again, as if carefully setting out his musings. It almost struck Gabriel as too deliberate until the canine thought, *Maybe you should just consider drinking some blood from that flask of yours. It might even help to dig a good spot out here under the dirt for your coming rest.*

That stung. And it also made Gabriel determined to prove the dog wrong. He could overcome the hunger just fine.

He jerked his chin at the dog as they came to the main entrance. "Understood, Chaplin. You need me around because of Stamp, but you're going to make sure you protect your mistress, too. I get it. You're a jerk when you need to be."

I'm only doing what I have to, Gabriel.

"Aren't we all?" He lifted a brow. "Including you?"

Gabriel meant to broach the subject of any plans Chaplin might have for him, but the dog was spent, stumbling to the trapdoor and going through it while Gabriel made sure the spring-loaded dirt spiller covered the entrance sufficiently. He shouldn't have bothered.

As he vowed to talk to Chaplin later, he searched out his flask in the ground, took a good drink, and assumed his guard duty, the shotgun tucked in his arms. But the longer he stayed outside, the longer he wanted to show Chaplin that there was nothing to worry about with him.

Carrying a chip on his shoulder had been a shortcoming as a human, too, Gabriel thought. Throughout his life, he'd been doubted by teachers, not responding to so-called cures for dyslexia, feeling stupid except when it came to working with his hands on the intricate patterns of handmade furniture only the elite could afford. Of course, when he became a vampire, the dyslexia had started to fade after about a year and a half, and by now, only a little remained, just as if his extraordinary body was healing it.

Now, Gabriel just wanted to show that he could be just like the rest of this community. He wouldn't go inside for long before he came back out to bury himself beneath the dirt. Just enough time to make his point to Chaplin. And himself.

After entering the domain through the ladder door, he put the shotgun back on the wall and found Mariah's coat bunched on the ground, like she'd just shed it there in a fit of disgust with her pet.

Yet the dog hardly seemed bothered, since he was already sprawled out near the common-area tunnel door, unconscious. Gabriel poked him, and Chaplin didn't even stir.

Out for the night, all right.

Then his heightened hearing picked up Mariah in the food prep area, where she'd shut a folding pocket door to block everyone out. After a moment, she opened it, looked at him, then went back inside, leaving the door open.

He took that to mean *Come in*, so he did. Unexpectedly, she shut the door behind him, as if making her own point to Chaplin, though the dog was beyond seeing it.

"Is he knackered, the little dickweed?" she asked.

"Yup, down for the count."

She was still dressed in her nightclothes, her fists at her sides as she stood before a counter littered with pieces of uncooked sand-rabbit she'd been chopping up.

He recognized her pique, because her eyes were still a flashing green, just as they'd been outside. Obviously, she needed to get her frustration off and away, and Gabriel was a fine target.

Okay then.

"That mutt thinks he knows everything," she said, cleaning the cutting blade and shoving it in a drawer, tossing the meat in a bowl, then washing her hands in the pump sink. Gabriel couldn't help but notice how her nightclothes clung to her, offering a view of her curves. Along with the heightened noise of her body he'd experienced outside, it all made him shiver with want.

As if spent, she leaned back against the tall, metallic cooler, wiping her hands down her face. "I'm just tired of all this."

"Tired of . . . what?"

When she lowered her hands, he saw the same exhaustion he'd witnessed in Abby when she'd curled into that invisible womb on the bed in the Southblock sanctuary. His instincts responded to this, following the same pattern, the same need to make things right for Mariah now.

But with Abby, he'd wanted to bite her to save her. With Mariah, he knew it'd be out of the greed he tried so hard to keep in check.

Bad-guy greed?

Maybe that quality was all too obvious in him, especially with her standing there in her nightclothes, nearly as bare as she'd been the other night.

Too late, he realized that he was seeing Mariah through a red haze, that it'd gone so far that his eyes had to be revealing his cravings—and they weren't just about blood. They were about *her* blood.

The drink from the flask hadn't done any good. He'd been wrong, shouldn't have come in here, should've listened to Chaplin.

He should get out. Now.

But then he saw the wondering expression on Mariah's face, and it enthralled him.

"Gabriel?" she asked.

He tried to tamp his need down, like dirt over something that refused to stay buried. But when she slowly pushed away from the wall, he heard the raging tempo of her vital signs, an exposed need in her, too.

He'd spent too long fighting his want of her, and he was losing.

"Don't," he said, and his tone was deep, hollow. "Don't . . . move any closer."

This was the end, he thought. He'd failed to restrain, failed in all his best intentions.

But she hadn't heeded his comment, clearly fascinated as she continued to come toward him. "Would you . . ." She seemed to lose her courage, then blurted out the rest. "Would *you* be able to make it all go away?"

He kept pushing at his urges, but he might as well have been laboring to get a boulder uphill.

She continued. "Can you go into a mind and wipe certain memories?"

He noticed she was trembling, holding something back, too. He saw the goose bumps ruffling the skin of her bare arms.

"I read in my book that you could sway others." She was only a few feet away now. "That you don't even have to bite to accomplish something like that."

Did she even remember how he'd swayed her earlier? He doubted it, but the question remained hanging there.

"Mariah, I told you I'm not a vam—"

Her anger seemed to return, blazing through her, her blood heating, her temperature flaring as she clenched her hands. "Stop it! You're lying. I . . ." She swallowed. "And I'm real familiar with lying."

The smell of her skin . . . hot . . .

Gabriel's fangs knifed out, and his body moved of its own accord, his conscience a red blank as he took one big step toward her, darted out his hands, and grasped her by the straps of her top, which he used to lift her onto the counter. The bowl of food clattered to the floor.

He was closer to her neck now, and the bloodlust was all-consuming, a summons to resume where they'd been last night, with her undressing and him following through to ram inside her, taking, taking, taking, because this woman burned hot and she could fill him up, making him even more than just an animated, walking body.

He heard her top ripping as he wrapped his fingers in the

straps, but he didn't let go, not even as she pushed her knees and hands against him.

Why couldn't he get himself in check? Why—?

"No bite," she said, her voice nearly hysterical. Unable to stop what was coming now, he flashed his fangs, looking into her eyes. His mind switched gears, from lucid to scrambled.

Time to sway her, his instincts told him. *Time to calm her and then get the bite, just as I should've done with Abby, who could've been mine.*

Could've and should've.

It was all too much to stop.

He tried to thrust his sway into Mariah's head, but he hit the black wall of her mind, and the shock of that loosened his hold on her.

He took a step away from the counter, just beginning to realize the horror of what he'd been about to do.

The assault had put Mariah in fighting mode, her eyes wide, bright, her hands in front of her, open and gnarled and ready to scratch out his eyes if he should come near again.

And her scent . . . the same as it had been last night, when she'd undressed . . .

Much to Gabriel's surprise, she grabbed his shirt, hauling him back to her, then clamping a hand on the back of his head, just below the bandages still hiding the injuries that had healed too quickly for any kind of human.

She forced him to look into her feverish eyes. "Try again. *Try*, Gabriel. No bite. Just my mind. Please. Maybe I wouldn't have to stay inside this house if you gave me that soothing. Maybe . . ."

He was beyond backing off again, and this time when he peered into her, she was open. He fell right in, surrounded by the black of her pupils, which seemed to clench around him, tight and hot.

Her blood. The lust for it controlled him.

Since he was inside her mind, she sensed his intentions.

With more brute strength than he'd guessed she had, she looked right back into him.

Peace, she thought. *Can't you give me just a little peace . . . ?*

Needing no more invitation than that, he used his sway to soothe Mariah, and her limbs went pliant as she kept engaging him, hooking him to her.

He sent her the best images he could conjure: Images from movies, when lawns were still green. The happiness of staring at a peaceful sky. What it might feel like to have a fresh, moderate summer wind comb his skin. The smell of what real grass used to be like and the feel of its soft blades against skin.

When she broke eye contact, the thoughts sliced to the present, with her still holding his shirt, his head. She was relaxed now, but he was drained, and he leaned forward, bringing his face to her shoulder. Her body moved with each breath, making him feel as if it might be perfectly natural for him to breathe right along with her.

But . . .

Blood.

He could feel it flowing and pumping in her, and he rested his fingertips against her neck, finding the pulse. There was nowhere for him to go but this way—even the tearing sound in his mind, the last clutches of what he'd grabbed on to out in the Badlands, couldn't hold him back from doing what his nature needed.

"Is that what you want in exchange?" she whispered, still floating in the peace he'd given to her. "A bite? My blood?"

In answer, he groaned low in his throat.

"It wouldn't make me one, right?" Her breath warmed his ear, where she'd rested her mouth against him. "Just a bite. It wouldn't make me a vampire? Because I can't imagine what that would do to me—"

He shook his head, unable to talk. If there was one thing he knew about being a vampire, it was that an exchange produced progeny, and he didn't spread his seed around. He wouldn't have Mariah take his blood.

Her vital signs had calmed, though they were still unstable, and they got even more so when she tentatively ran her hands down his arms.

From her touch, he could sense inexperience, and he thought he had to be wrong. The woman who'd stripped off her clothes and touched herself had all the right knowledge. She couldn't have been that innocent.

When she slid off the counter and allowed her entire length to coast down his body, her breasts over his chest, her sex skimming his belly as she came to a shaky stand, he was further confused.

She went on tiptoe, nestling her lips just under his ear, and he recognized intoxication in her tone. He'd felt it enough times before to know.

"This peace . . ." she said. "The cost of some of my blood is worth more of it."

His veins seized up as she leaned back to meet his gaze. Though she was calmed by the sway, her eyes still had a wild glint.

But then she asked something that made him go back to thinking she *was* innocent.

"What do I do?"

He snagged her gaze, and through the red, he could see the trepidation. So he eased more of his sway into her, and her breathing settled, her exhalations vibrating with what remained of her nerves.

He hated that her skin was irresistible to him, but he slowly ran his mouth down her neck, anyway, over her collarbones, then back up. He unbuttoned her top, and she gripped his arms.

"It's okay," he said. "You'll heal fast with my help, but I don't want to leave a mark where it'll glare out at anyone who looks at you before it fully mends."

As he murmured it, he realized that, somehow, giving her peace had made him feel some of it, too. He still wanted to rip into her, but then again, he was able to keep himself from doing it.

Not knowing how to interpret that, he spread the material of her top, revealing her breasts. Small, just heavy enough to curve into his hands, the pink tips stimulated.

He bent to one, taking her in—musk and the clean perfume of water. Then he tasted her with his tongue, and she stirred under him, whimpering.

The sound thrust at him, and he took all of her into his mouth, easing his hands against her back to bring her closer. He avoided nicking her with his fangs, but he was so giddy on her aroma and taste that he could hardly see through the heated mire of his vision.

Almost shyly—but with some aggression—she latched her fingers around one of his wrists, then guided him between her legs, where she pressed his fingers against her.

She was already slick, and he leaned his cheek against her breast, flattening it, her nipple near his mouth as he groaned. Her arousal . . . it took him over, and he stroked her through the linen of her nightclothes until her hips wiggled with each coaxing rub. Her excitement built in him, too, and he found himself tearing at her pants so he could get at all of her: the wetness of her sex, the tightness as he slipped a finger into her, priming her just as she was priming him.

He heard his shirt tear as she pulled at it, and he took his fingers from her and, mindless, put them to his mouth, where he sampled what she would bring him with her blood.

Her. Mariah. So different than any other taste.

An implosion sent white spots over his sight—a red background needled by pure blankness—and he went back to her sex, inserting two fingers into her now. Then he rubbed his body back up hers so he could come in for the bite. If he brought her to climax, a bite would have that much more impact in him.

He urged his thumb against her clit, and she gave a little cry. He could see in her eyes that she was fast losing what composure he'd given her with his sway, but he was beyond restoring it.

He worked her toward climax with his fingers, his gums pounding around his fangs, and she panted, back arching, as if she were fighting decimation. Her nails cut into his neck, letting blood, but he'd heal within moments.

Still, the scent of his own blood combined with her drove him onward, and, bending to the underside of one of her breasts, he gnawed gently before opening his mouth wider.

He heard her suck in a breath, her pulse suspending on a throb, her nails digging into him—

He sank his fangs into her, and her hips lifted as he pushed his fingers farther inside her body, curving them up to find a spot that would get her hotter. When he found it, she mewled, sounding so far gone that he didn't recognize the sound of her as he sucked, sucked, dizzier and dizzier.

Then she came, renting him apart inside with her heat, her taste, which seemed at one with him, something he could call and it would answer.

Blood trickled down his neck from her nails; it tickled his skin, and everything faded, melding together in his sight as the red lifted and his fangs receded.

He was close to going under, blacking out, but his body was too awake to let him go. He was lifted, not weighed down.

After removing his fingers from her, he raised them to touch his neck. She'd scratched him hard, and as he looked at her, she was still hitching in quick, shallow breaths, shaking. It even seemed as if she were about to explode again.

And there was . . .

He didn't believe it at first, but there was terror in her eyes.

"Mariah."

Without another thought, he peered into her, swayed her, and she accepted it, her body relaxing until she sank against him.

Yet even as he held her, she still looked up, watching him. Did she think he might take more blood or force an exchange?

Shamed by that, he sat her on the counter so she wouldn't fall, pressed his fingers to the breast wound to start healing it with his energy, wiped the rest of the blood off with a nearby cloth, then adjusted her clothing around her—what was left of it. He'd forgotten all the better parts of him, and now he doubted he'd ever be able to find what he was looking for out here, so far away from where he'd started.

Why hadn't he been able to keep himself together?

"You should eat something," he said, almost awkwardly. "Drink fluids. Rest. Make up for what I took."

"Okay."

"You're still afraid of me."

She shook her head. But no matter what her answer was, he could see that he was right, and he moved away from her, not knowing what to do now. She looked like Abby had at the times she'd thought she was alone, preoccupied by an ominous worry, an agitation about what might come next with him, though he'd never dared to touch her like he had just done with Mariah. A bite with Abby would've been far gentler.

But as Mariah sat there, holding her top over her breasts, everything about her struck him hard—her skin, her rhythms, the way she'd made him feel worthwhile, even if it was in an uncommon manner.

In the bubble of this reality, Abby seemed to be no more than an idea.

Mariah got down from the counter, wobbling slightly from the blood loss, and headed toward her private quarters, where he knew he wasn't allowed to follow. Not this time.

Remorse, he thought. This was what it surely felt like.

Was she going to tell the rest of the community what he was now that she definitely knew? Was she going to force him out of her home because he couldn't contain himself?

Based on past experience, he wouldn't even be able to get into the part of her mind that allowed him to sway her into forgetting. . . .

Gabriel wasn't sure where to go, though he seemed to be headed for the workroom, which was funny, because that was where *she* usually went for composure. But he thought it might be a good idea to wash Mariah off him before Chaplin woke up and sensed what had happened.

Before the rest of the community knew what they were truly dealing with in Gabriel.

17

Gabriel

By the light of a lantern, Gabriel pumped out some water and rubbed it over himself until he thought all hints of Mariah were gone from him. Then he got dressed again, taking care to adjust the bandages around his head, keeping up the masquerade. But as much as he wanted to look human in those bandages, he felt in the core of him the approach of sunrise, which couldn't have been more than two hours away by now. He thought it might be wise to be buried outside, as Chaplin had wanted, when the day arrived.

Until then, he decided to lend a hand with Mariah's hydro-crop, hoping that going through the motions would create room in his mind for something other than this new situation he'd put himself in. But her blood was inside him, and he couldn't stop moving under the palpitating burn of it.

Unlike any other blood he'd ever taken, hers was like old cocaine to him. It was a powder he'd tried during his more experimental human days. He might've even gotten addicted, too, but for the world's calamities. After that, chaos itself had been enough stimulant.

As he sheltered himself down in the workroom, he cleared his mind for a while . . . until one of the last people he ever expected to see in Mariah's domain descended the stairway behind Gabriel, the light from a solar lantern suffusing the cavern.

It was the oldster. But why was he here? Had Mariah already told the others about Gabriel taking her blood? Had the community already planned to run him out with machetes and stakes before Stamp could get wind of the monster and drag the authorities over here to ruin the residents' lives as they knew them?

Gabriel stopped packing some tomatoes into a tub and braced himself to endure the consequences of his hunger for Mariah. But when he turned around, the old man smiled, and that didn't seem to Gabriel to be an introduction to a run-him-out.

The other guy gestured toward the staircase. "So I came into Mariah's place through a trapdoor. Sue me. I couldn't contact Chaplin on the visz, but that's because I found out the pup is still sleeping off those drugs."

A worst-case scenario came to Gabriel. Maybe the whole community was actually up there with Mariah while the old man was down here making Gabriel think everything was hunky-dory until they could spring a trap on him when he returned. It sounded like the kind of half-assed plan the Badlanders might whip up.

He almost laughed at the ridiculousness of it. His harbinger of doom: a feisty slip of an oldster, armed with only his flapping gums. Then again, it wasn't wise to underestimate anyone in this day and age.

"I take it Mariah doesn't know you're in her home," Gabriel said.

"No, she hasn't a bit of an idea. Mariah's abed, and good thing, too. The girl had a . . . hard night." The oldster rubbed his knuckles over his whiskers, as if measuring out everything he was saying. "It's just that I've been thinking since our last conversation. Thinking long and hard. That's why I thought it important to seek you out."

"To announce the miracle of you thinking?"

Gabriel was just testing the other guy, and the old man chuckled. But the sound died quickly as he shuffled his boots.

"Why don't you just come right out and tell me, old-timer," Gabriel said. He hoped that he'd truly washed Mariah off him, including the blood that had gotten on his shirt from those already-healed nail marks.

Once more, the old guy cleared his throat, then started up again. "I just wanted to assure you that we're doing something besides depending on you. I've persuaded the others—minus Pucci and Hana, of course—to arm up with all we've got in the common area. They're watching their viszes diligently, too."

"You came here to report that?"

"I also wanted to talk more, one to one. Mariah and Chaplin were still with us at the end of the gathering, and I thought privacy wouldn't come amiss for what I want to say to you." The oldster waited, as if reluctant to go any further.

"So you wanted to talk to me about . . . ?" Gabriel prodded.

He glanced back toward the staircase, then at Gabriel. "Well, you're bent on finding out what you can about Annie, then getting on out of here, right?"

Some kind of dull twang hit Gabriel. "That was the plan. Then Stamp came along."

The oldster looked gratified to hear that Gabriel gave a care, and that seemed to encourage him. "I got to wondering . . . Just what did you find in Annie's place? You've been there. Zel told us."

Just from saying the woman's name, the oldster shuffled around a little more.

Gabriel pretended not to notice. A blind fool locked in a box could see how the guy had eyes for Zel.

But why was the oldster even quizzing him about this? Could it be that he and the others wanted to know if he'd figured out anything about who Annie was?

Could it be they were nervous that he *did* know?

Gabriel decided to be honest. "I didn't find a whole lot at Annie's place. I suppose you wouldn't be much more of a resource, would you?"

"Afraid not. She came out here to leave something behind, like all of us. She was friendly, but not too friendly. Made most of her conversation with Hana, but that's about it."

"Maybe I should chat with Hana then."

"Not worth your while. Even after Annie left, Hana didn't have much to say. She told us she'd promised Annie discretion, and she aimed to preserve it."

Hearing Annie's name frustrated Gabriel. He was already on pins because of Mariah, and the agitation weakened his restraint. He found himself looking at the oldster, *into* the oldster, not caring if he was caught or not.

But once again, he was blocked by that black wall that all of them seemed to have erected against him.

Ringing with the denial—and with the disappointment of even reverting to a vampire trick—Gabriel went back to the tomatoes, picked up the tub, and started to walk away, pushing back the desire to spring at the old guy and throttle him human-style until the truth did come out.

The oldster halted him with a question. "You love your Abby? That's why you came all the way out here to find her?"

Gabriel just nodded, but instead of seeing Abby in his mind's eye, he saw Mariah. Still felt her on his skin, her blood even now throbbing through him.

The old man continued. "I'd probably go to the far reaches for someone like that, too."

"Didn't you?" Gabriel asked, meaning Zel Hopkins.

The oldster seemed to understand just who Gabriel was talking about, his skin going ruddy. "I came out here on my own a long time ago, when the sky began to figuratively fall."

"Long enough not to be in the facial recognition database that Stamp was using."

He grinned. "I had a few friends who knew how to hack computers. Let's leave it at that."

Gabriel allowed the old man to go on.

"I was the first," he said, "and the rest trickled on out here. I let them in if they seemed to my . . . liking."

"And Zel was to your liking."

The other man laughed, but it was a reflective sound, not his usual amused cackle. "She'd never know it."

"Then why don't you tell her?"

"No, no." The oldster swatted at the air, and Gabriel heard the man's heartbeat string together bump after bump, disturbed by this very discussion. "It's enough that she came here and hasn't left. Not that Zel or I would ever swagger back into civilization, anyway. She's no spring chicken, but she's not quite as useless as I am in my waning years. Still, the hubs are no place for anyone over forty. If it was hard for oldsters there before, it's even worse now."

No doubt, Gabriel thought. Recently, it'd become commonplace for all oldsters to be locked away in rest homes, which were casually referred to as "pounds" now. Everyone knew that once admitted, the ancients were put down like unwanted dogs. No one talked about it. Society just pretended that it didn't happen, and it allowed the pursuit of happiness to continue for those who were young and rich enough to afford it.

"No sense of respect from the young back in the hubs," the oldster added. "A fifteen-year-old can post most kinds of work on the Nets—especially in graphic arts, which was my bag. They can get a job without a lick of experience, so there's no laboring a person's way up the ladder of success these days. And who could stay caught up with all that technology except for the young?"

"Phased out," Gabriel said. "But you made it here instead."

"That I did." The oldster shrugged. "Don't you let me catch you gossiping with the others about this."

"Don't they know?"

"Just the basics. But talk leads to conjecture, and I don't need anyone coming up with stories about me." He kicked at the dirt. "And I don't need any foolish stuff circulating about me and . . . anyone."

"I know how you feel about getting too personal."

As the oldster nodded in confederacy, Gabriel got caught on the words he'd just said. *I know how you feel . . .*

For the first time since Abby—and in spite of how he'd lost his control tonight—he thought that maybe he *was* closer than ever to feeling. Even as a human who'd chased away emotion and pain through the flow of drink, he'd been looking to feel.

The oldster was aiming himself toward the stairs. "Guess I should scoot before Mariah wakes up. She sleeps in fits and starts. That's what Chaplin told Zel, anyhow, and I predict a privacy-monger like her'd throw a fit if she caught me skulking round."

"Why do you think she sleeps that way?"

Another shrug. "Because, as much as we try, sleep doesn't get us away from the living nightmares. But we *have* to try, anyway."

Without elaborating, the oldster departed. All the same, Gabriel knew exactly what he was talking about.

Living nightmares. Everyone was just doing their best to get through them, no matter who or what they were.

As he picked up the tomato tub and went to set it by the stairs, he couldn't help remembering what he'd managed to glimpse in Mariah's head when she hadn't been guarding herself properly: a younger Mariah cowering. A wave of red.

Again, he felt her blood stirring in him, but even though that much of her was a part of him, he couldn't absorb anything else about her.

He felt dawn coming upon him and headed for the stairs. But the oldster had distracted him from keeping good track of time, and Gabriel sank to the ground at the foot of the steps, knowing he'd never make it all the way up before rest claimed him.

At least he was away from Mariah, he thought as a black yawn seemed to envelop him, sucking up all his energy until . . .

When he awakened at dusk, fully aware, his gaze fixed on the cavern wall, which was lit from a lantern burning illumination from behind him, for some reason.

Then his skin tuned in to another presence.

A hand on his waist. A warm body stretched out against his back, nearly fitting to him except for a vibrating chasm of inches.

Mariah.

18

Mariah

The only reason I knew he was awake was that his body stiffened under my hand. Otherwise, he wasn't breathing.

I had sneaked down here out of . . . I don't know. Gluttony? Neediness? A spark of addiction that made me finally appreciate all the stories I'd read about being with someone?

Or maybe it had to do with what Gabriel had given me earlier—a sense of peace. Floating on a calm lift of water, my hands spread to the sky, my body weightless and held up by something other than my own exertions. I'd been so tired of living that his peace gave me rest. I was even experiencing remnants of it now, my thoughts dizzy, my body soft and sharp at the same time, as if I were still being raised from the inside out.

It was almost like the time I'd smoked feyweed, shortly after arriving in the Badlands. What Gabriel had given me temporarily made me forget everything that hurt. But it was more, too, like a song that played in me, bonding me through notes both high and low.

At any rate, I'm not sure if I'd meant to awaken him by

coming down here. I'd just wanted to put my hand on Gabriel because it felt nice. I'd just wanted to be next to someone because it made me feel that I wasn't so alone, I suppose.

"Mariah," he whispered, and there was a choke to the way he said my name.

Now I felt as if I'd been caught doing something naughty, too intimate. So I covered my discomfort by saying, "I saw the oldster sneaking out the trapdoor earlier. Was he talking to you while I was asleep?"

"He just wanted to make more plans about Stamp."

Gabriel must've realized that I wasn't here to talk about the oldster, because he rolled to his back, onto the blankets I'd brought down here from above. They were bunched round us, where we lay at the foot of the stairs. Those bandages were still on his head, but I doubted he needed them. Probably had never needed them much at all.

I was on my side, cradling my hands against my chest now. He ran his gaze over the nightclothes I'd changed, seeing as he'd mauled the ones I'd worn last night. And I'd sure enough allowed him to do so.

As my skin went flush, my mom's voice tried to make its way out from under the remaining peace and to the top of my thoughts.

Your body is a temple, said the echo of her.

I didn't want to hear it, so my next words rushed out of me. "Would it be possible for you to . . . ?"

His body clutched as he sensed my excitement at asking for more of his vampire hypnosis.

I saw a flare of red in his eyes, as if he were remembering what'd transpired between us upstairs. "I shouldn't have done it the first time."

"I was already pretty certain you were a vampire, so you didn't give anything away on that account."

"That's not exactly it. If I oblige you, I just might take more blood this time. It's hard to stop the inner greed for it. I tried to stay away from you—that's why I came down here—because I didn't know if I could handle a second time."

Little by little, the peace was leaving me, and I almost wanted to cry. I already missed it. "I don't feel sick from the lack of blood. I'm fine. You shouldn't worry about that."

"I'm not. But when would the whole community find out? And how far of a head start would I need to get?"

"I'll make sure they don't know." I think what was left of the peace gave me more courage than I would've normally possessed. "I don't believe you're here to harm us, Gabriel. If you wanted to, you would've tried already. That's why I did what I did when I saw your eyes in the shadows near my room . . . that night."

Again, something in his eyes flashed in the dimness, a turn of thought, as if he were imagining me taking off my clothing. His eyes began to glow a hotter red.

The color made my belly tighten. I wanted to bring him to the point where he couldn't say no to me. I wanted *more*. "I haven't told anyone about you."

"Your dog already knows."

In my pool of serenity, the news didn't come as any shock. Chaplin had said he had a handle on Gabriel, and I'd put my faith in him, because he often knew more than I did.

So what was my dog up to? I'd have to have a real sit-down with him.

"Did you *tell* Chaplin to stay quiet about you?" I asked.

"I insinuated that I wasn't a threat, and I needed him to help me out by keeping mum. I didn't want to alarm you or the community."

Right. He'd wanted to search for Abby, and being identified as a monster would've gotten him run out. But I didn't want to have Abby interfere with what was between me and Gabriel now.

"If I haven't revealed anything about you to the rest of the community by now," I said, "you can rest assured that I won't be doing it anytime soon."

I hesitantly touched his arm, and his muscles clenched.

"When you came into me," I said, "you gave me something I thought I'd never find. You made me forget about . . . outside."

"And you want to keep forgetting."

My escalating desires were eating away at me, and I pressed a hand to my stomach, as if that could control them.

He seemed to know how much I craved his aid, and he rested a hand on my forehead, as if he were feeling guilty about withholding from me. As if he were reminding himself that he could ease me, even temporarily. He could make the nightmares go away. And wasn't that better than not helping me at all?

Gabriel stroked my temple with his thumb. My skin burned, and he looked into me, as if wanting so badly to cool me down.

I let him mentally enter me, let him go to the only place inside myself that I kept undefended. Right away, my breathing smoothed out. I smiled, relief bubbling through me in a small laugh as he offered magic, soothing images, like how people used to climb trees with leaves.

By his coming into me, I could intuit his musings, too. He was thinking that good thoughts came so very easy with me. The positive notes of the past, the decency of what we all used to be. I could also sense that he was clinging to this peace just as much as I was. He *couldn't* let go, because doing so would plunge him into bloodlust.

And he didn't like the bloodlust. He despised that about himself, mostly because of . . .

Abby?

The name was like smoke in the wind, and I couldn't hold to it as it floated off. But that was fine, because Gabriel was now riding the peace with me. The vibrations distracted him from jabs of appetite, sending us into a hushed place. A limbo, electric and welcome.

I took enough of him to last me, then closed my eyes, laughing until the happiness almost turned to crying again. Besides the peace, something else from him stayed with me—a yearning. A plea for humanity. His profound longing for it choked me up.

"What?" he asked, as if unable to comprehend what was happening with me.

I guess not even a vampire could go deep enough into me to see everything.

"It's only that . . ." I couldn't draw any words from my confusion. So I settled for something safer to say. "You just bring out the wicked in me. But you bring out some good, too."

I opened my eyes, and he tilted his head at the sight of them. I'm sure fever was burning in my gaze, just like earlier, during the first time we'd been together. I didn't want him to see it.

"I need the good so badly," I said.

"Don't need it too much." He was still staring at my eyes, and I breathed and breathed, calming myself until I felt better. "This can't become a pattern, Mariah. I won't facilitate it."

"An . . . addiction?"

In my floating state, the idea almost sounded ridiculous. His tone told me it wasn't.

"I should know addictions, because I used to depend on booze. Then I graduated to blood."

And then finding Abby?

I stroked his face, over all the scars that had basically healed since that first night. His eyes went redder, and I could've sworn he peered past the fever in my eyes and deeper for an instant—one in which I could see how he'd taken lovers during his human days and they'd laid hands on him just as I was doing. But there hadn't been many instances of tenderness after he'd turned vampire, because the worse the world had gotten, the more interested he'd been in fast and easy than slow and meaningful.

I scooted nearer to him, gently pushing until he lay on his back as I balanced myself on an elbow, then bent down to impetuously brush my lips over his. He shivered at the softness, the care of my actions, clearly not knowing how to react.

I kissed him again, experimenting in how far I might go without causing him to rage for another bite. I also wanted to know how things worked between a man and woman, and the peace made it seem okay to find out.

He was looking into me again, and my surface thoughts seemed to meld with his. He was picturing a man and a woman, too, but not in a regular way. Sex without a bite, he was thinking. He hadn't experienced it in a long time, not since he was human. Nowadays, he didn't get his pleasure like they did, although he was capable of bringing it to a human he was biting.

Was a bite *his* means to satiation?

"Mariah—you know what you're asking for. These aren't garden-variety . . . relations . . . you're inviting."

"I've read my dad's medical books. I know the difference."

As I hovered over him, I could feel the moistness of my breath bathing his mouth.

"I dipped into your blood last night," he said, almost as if talking to himself, "and it should've been enough to keep me."

"Maybe you want something more."

And then I saw it in his eyes: how devastating it'd been to lose any semblance he'd created of his humanity out here.

Emboldened, I kissed him again, lingering this time, spreading warmth through his coolness. I touched his cheek, his chin, his neck—a vein that was bulging because of the push of blood.

I asked a question against his lips. "How old are you?"

"Not very."

I skimmed my fingers over his collarbones, and he jerked.

"What you do to me . . ." he said, then laughed a little, just as I had after receiving the peace. "My skin isn't sensitive like a human's, but . . ."

I waited him out, not sure what else to do as my body pounded. It felt like my heartbeat had been pushed under the water, muffled, taking up every inch of space round me.

He sighed, bringing my hand to where his heart should've been beating, had he been truly alive. "Your touch brings these rays of energy. Like . . . like a living imprint."

He didn't have to say that he'd never experienced this before with a blood victim. I got a perverse thrill out of knowing he hadn't felt it with Abby.

"How old are you?" I repeated, wanting to figure out how many bites there'd been before me.

"Mariah—"

"A century?"

He gave in. "Only just over a couple years in vampire terms."

I was unbuttoning his shirt now, rather proud of myself to be doing so. I finally had courage. I could finally forget.

"Mariah . . . ?"

I parted his shirt so I could trace his pale skin, and when I did, my hand seemed to warm on him, the rays he'd talked about apparently spreading as he jolted again.

It must've been the shock of it that sent him into action, and he lifted me, setting me on top of him. I gasped, his sex against mine. What was left of my sanity peeked through the fog in my head. *No more,* it said. *Stop now.*

But under his thrall, it didn't seem so dangerous to continue, and I rested my palms against his chest. This time, I could feel a thrust of pressure molding the shape of my hands.

Imprint?

"I can feel it in you," I said. "The blood. Or maybe that's just my own pulse in my hands."

"It is you. Your pulse is mine."

Something—happiness, the ecstasy of finally knowing someone—washed over me. He hesitated, as if hardly grasping that he had the power to cause such a shift of intimate emotion in anyone.

He's feeling even closer to human, I thought. *And I made it happen.*

He latched his fingers to the hem of my top, then undid the tiny buttons. Heat licked over my face when he eased the material off my shoulders, down my arms. And when he palmed my breasts, his thumbs circling my nipples, I lowered my head.

But it wasn't because of any chiding mother voices in me. My pulse was flailing, springing and taking off, and I was trying to get it back.

He slid a finger under my chin, tilted my head up, caught my gaze and opened himself, offering the peace I'd come here for. I breathed easier, although my heartbeat still rammed the blood through me. Through us. I could feel it in him.

I guided him to the ground, leaning forward, my bare breasts against his chest now. What a feeling . . . What I'd missed out on all these years . . .

The fringes of his irises were ringed with a famished red, his fangs edging past his lips, but he didn't seem feral. Maybe he was still feeling the peace, too.

I coasted upward, my nipples combing over him. My short, chopped hair wisped against his throat as I turned my face so that my lips were against the underside of his jaw.

"You're so cold, Gabriel. Hard underneath the skin."

"That's what you get."

"I know what comes with you. At least, I think I know."

"If you're asking if I react like a human guy during all this, then the answer's yes. And no."

What did he mean by that?

"The only way I can have children," he said, "is through a blood exchange. I can't impregnate because vampires are sterile that way."

"But you can . . . do other things."

In answer, he took my hand and rested it over his sex, where the blood rushed, making it harder.

I sucked in a breath, taking my hand away. I'd imagined what it might feel like, but . . .

Then a rush of his vampire sway overcame me again, and I put my hand on his belly.

Relaxed again. I was fine.

"I was raised by my mom to think that you shouldn't share yourself freely," I said. "Not with all the STDs and the movement to purify young women round the country."

Cults had sprung up—"purity enforcers." They were as crazy as the people who'd made a religion of worshipping pop stars.

"But you're not like others," I said.

I skimmed down, over his stiffness, wanting to undo his pants. But he took care of that for me, his expression showing that he was curious about how far I'd go.

When he was bared to me, I hesitated. He looked different from the sketches I'd seen in the mild erotica that had flashed at Dallas intersections via the TV-channel collages that drive-by artists showed in their transport windows.

This was flesh, swollen to hardness. I took him in my hand, my temperature rising even higher.

He groaned, closing his eyes, his fangs needling his gums. But then he seemed to recover, quickly helping me out of my pants, settling me to my back. Then he lay against me, my entire body imprinting him, seething energy buzzing back into me, too.

I was wet, and when he slipped inside me, I wiggled my hips to get him past my tightness. I held to him, one of my legs wrapping round the back of his. It was uncomfortable at first, because he filled me all the way. But his body felt like it was my own.

I could sense his appetite climbing, up, up as he drove into me. Harder, faster, I moved with him, my fingers clawed against his back, my nails biting into him again as I heated up, my blood simmering, my bones going to a melt, tempered only by the peace he gave me as he looked into my eyes, balancing everything.

For what seemed like endless hours, I saw in him the red of blood cells scrambling round. Felt it, too, as crimson blinded me, banged at me, stretched me and fought the peace until it expanded, bubble-like, warped, pushing, near to breaking—

I tensed round him, my muscles convulsing. His body rhythms copied mine as we strained, my nails ripping into his skin, while a low, warped cry shuddered out of me.

There was no bite, no blood, but he took something from me as I came—a blast of fluid heat, running inside us, coating us.

Afterward, we didn't move for a minute, but it seemed

like forever as we panted, coming down into that body of water that held me up in my floating place of peace. But then I glanced at my fingers, and I saw his blood on them.

I was too mellow and content to scream as I would have any other time.

He took my hands in one of his, then folded his fingers over mine, shielding me from the red as he sank down to the blankets, bringing me on my side to face him. Without thinking, I cozied my leg between both of his while he kept soothing me with more of his gaze.

Soon, I was under that imagined water, looking at the wavering surface until everything went as blank as slumber.

Next thing I knew, there was barking, and I bolted up at the same time Gabriel did.

Chaplin?

Had he realized that Gabriel was in here with me?

Then my dog barked again and I heard his true message.

"No," I said.

"What?" Gabriel asked.

I was already putting on my nightclothes. "Chaplin's saying that Stamp's on my main outside visz screen." My voice was unsteady, but it would've been worse without Gabriel's remaining sway. "Stamp's telling us that all's forgiven, and he'd like to explain just why that is if we'll all gather up top, outside, in twenty minutes."

He started to get dressed, too. "I want to be the one to go out there and have a word with him."

I stopped cold.

"Are you all right, Mariah?" he asked.

I still had some peace in me, but now that Stamp was here, I didn't know if I'd be able to get through it. Not unless . . .

Would Gabriel give me more of his vampire tranquility? Or would I be a coward forever without it?

He seemed to turn the decision over in his mind for only

an instant—one in which I supposed he felt torn between the vampire he'd been trying to leave behind and the man he'd just been.

Still, he came to me, cupping my face and looking into my eyes, offering the only peace I knew.

19

Gabriel

After Gabriel finished soothing Mariah, he wrapped her in one of the blankets she'd brought downstairs. She was in her nightclothes, and even if matters were hectic, Chaplin, who was still barking, would surely notice her state, then come after Gabriel. The dog had told him to stay outside, and the vampire hadn't obeyed.

Besides, what had gone on between Gabriel and Mariah was just . . . private. None of anyone else's business. Not even Chaplin's.

As Gabriel finished tucking Mariah up, then grabbing the lantern she'd brought with her, he found her peering up at him. Because of the peace that still filtered through her gaze, there was something in her eyes that he could almost identify. Even when he'd been all the way inside her, she'd never truly let him in.

"Thank you, Gabriel," she said, and the emotion behind her words spoke to him more than the actual syllables did.

She reached up to take the bandages from his head, slowly unwinding them, unveiling what he knew to be all the healed injuries from when Stamp's men had roughed him up outside several nights ago.

When Mariah finished, she dropped the bandages to the ground, then pulled the blanket around her so that it swallowed her from neck to ankle. Then, with a small smile—the last one he thought he might see for a while—she took the stairway.

Gabriel didn't follow at first. He just loitered under what might turn out to be the final moments of a good thing.

She'd been grateful for what he'd brought her tonight, and he realized that he'd come out here to the New Badlands for Abby, but he'd instead found someone—or something—else entirely.

He followed her up the stairs, noting that Chaplin wasn't barking any longer. When he got to the top of the landing, Mariah was waiting, sans lantern, her hand on the door, which she'd already opened to a slit. He didn't know why she was hesitating, but he had his own reasons for doing the same.

The smells, the sounds beyond the door . . .

Gabriel put his hand on Mariah's shoulder and opened the door the rest of the way, revealing the crowd of Badlanders gathered in her home.

Zel, the oldster, Sammy, Chaplin . . . even Hana and Pucci, all in front of Mariah's bank of glowing visz monitors.

And they didn't look happy. In fact, they seemed stunned at the sight of Gabriel with Mariah. . . .

Head down, she bustled out from behind Gabriel in her blanket and went straight to her quarters, where he guessed she was going to change into real clothes.

Everyone's gazes followed her. But when she disappeared, that left Gabriel to take the remainder of their scrutiny. Luckily, he was used to it by now.

Chaplin, who seemed to scent what had transpired between Gabriel and Mariah, had his head cocked, as if he were stunned to realize that his mistress had survived being near Gabriel and his vampire hunger.

Gabriel used his mind to say, *Don't worry, boy.*

And that was the extent of it. The dog, or anyone else, didn't have to know more than that.

As if still attempting to reconcile this with that, Chaplin turned his back on Gabriel to look at the monitors, and Gabriel guessed that the dog was punishing *him* now instead of Mariah.

Well, then. After this matter with Stamp was concluded, Gabriel would take more time to assure the canine that he wouldn't be around much longer as a threat to any person or relationship.

He came the rest of the way into the room, and everyone but Chaplin stirred, crossing their arms in front of their chests, wiping at their noses with odd, fidgety don't-know-what-else-to-do motions.

The oldster, with his eyes squinty as he peered at one of the viszes, pointed to an outside view, the volume turned up so they had a clear show of Stamp standing near Mariah's main entrance. "There he is, counting down the minutes until we either come out or stay in."

Gabriel watched Stamp on the night vision. The kid's tall, slim body was garbed mostly in a material that hugged his long legs, just as leather would. Behind the kid, Gabriel could see flashes of Stamp's crew as they leaped by the lens while wearing their FlyShoes. They all had white kerchiefs in hand, as if bringing positive intentions with them.

To Gabriel, it seemed like one big game, those hankies a mocking salutation. They had come in peace.

Sure.

The oldster added, "We all met here because Mariah's got the best bunch of visz screens, thanks to her father. Also, she's got the finest weapons."

Sammy, his stocky body swaddled in all that orange-and-brown hemp clothing, nervously licked his lips. "Stamp keeps telling us that there's no need to fret about coming outside to meet him. He's here on the up-and-up."

"He says," Zel added, standing by the monitors, holding an old pistol at her side, "that they caught whatever's been attacking his men, and they want to have us take part in a 'memorial service.'"

What was this? "They *caught* it?"

"That's what he says," Zel added. "He didn't say how, but I have to admit—this situation could be a mighty relief."

The others agreed most emphatically, and Gabriel kept his eyes on them, because he wasn't sure why they'd be so suddenly optimistic when the mood had been wary.

Strange, these people. Remote, secretive, and contrary. Again, Gabriel thought of Annie and what they might be hiding about her.

"It could get Stamp off our backs," Zel said, "if we go out there and accept this truce."

"But," the oldster said, coming back to that abandoned wariness, "there's a great chance that he's none-so-subtly luring us out, like they tried to do with Chaplin last night."

"I don't know," Gabriel said. "I can't believe I'm saying this, but why doesn't he just bust on in here and attack if he means harm? Why put on such an elaborate ruse unless they really are offering a resolution?"

From the way the others nodded, Gabriel knew that this had occurred to them, too.

"Either way," Sammy added, "I'll be janxed if this is any kind of real memorial service for a creature they caught. From the way those jerks are partying out there, an execution would be more like it, and I don't have the stomach for that."

"Yup." The oldster finally met Gabriel's gaze. "Make no mistake—Stamp's here to drive home some kind of point. I only wonder if we refuse to come outside as he asks, how sharp that point's gonna be."

Gabriel looked to the visz, where Stamp was standing, watching his men while he casually planted his hands on his hips. Despite his faults, the kid had it in him to be reasonable. But any relationship he did develop with this community would be on Stamp's terms. He'd be the one defining what a good neighbor should be, as he'd proven during the previous house call.

On the visz, Gabriel saw Stamp hailing a vehicle in the near distance, directing it into the monitor's circle of vision. A rumbler, boasting a jetlike body held up by massive, thick, sawlike wheels that spit up dirt as it came to a spewing halt. Three men spilled out, jumping from the heightened body to the ground, all of them in joyful spirits.

Gabriel came closer to the group, and the Badlanders shifted, as if his very presence still unsettled them. But maybe it wasn't him at all. Maybe it was the danger outside, and he was the only one who'd been able to get them to move.

Zel spoke. "We need to decide what action to take. *Now.*"

From a spot in the corner, Hana ducked out from under Pucci's protective arm and wandered closer to the group, her wide brown gaze fixed on the visz. But Pucci latched onto the back of her robes, impeding her.

At the same time, he put forward his idea for how the community should proceed. "Let Stamp tell us a little more about what's happening, and then we can decide."

Hana glanced back at her man but didn't contradict him.

"Well," the oldster said, "I seem to remember you were the one in favor of waving our own white flags in Stamp's face. Shouldn't we just go out there and pussify ourselves first off, Pucci?"

The man seemed to bulk up even more under his brown shirt, lowering his head, using his heft as an imposing response. "Stamp's got backup out there. So far, I've counted seven men as they've crossed the lens's fields, and we don't know if there're even more out of range."

"So much for your career as a diplomat, Mr. Big Talk. . . ."

While the oldster continued dealing out stings, Gabriel wondered what was keeping Mariah. He gravitated toward her quarters, arriving at the dark fringe of her room, where he was halted by the sound of her—the angry vital signs lulled by the peace he'd instilled. And it was the peace that seemed to draw a line from him to her, yet at the same time, it kept him calmer than he'd ever been, less hungry, more satisfied.

"Mariah?" he asked.

A pause. Then, "Still in here."

With a glance behind him to make sure no one was around, Gabriel stepped all the way inside her room, where the walls didn't hold anything decorative, nothing that might hint at what Mariah liked, what kept her occupied during all this time under the ground.

Maybe her weapons wall said the most, Gabriel thought, as he approached, finding her dressed in her regular attire. Lace-up cloth pants, boots, and a roomy white shirt.

Fighting garb.

But she didn't look so ready to kick any ass while sitting on her bed, aiming at him a beaten look that he'd seen too much lately.

"You know," he said, "it'd be great to have someone stay below the ground to watch your visz bank, just to keep a wider eye on what Stamp has going on outside. The different camera angles might come in handy and keep at least one of us aware of the bigger picture so we can be warned about any planned surprises. I'd have my ears tuned for anything you'd have to tell us from your spot down here."

"Are you making an excuse for me to stay inside?"

He'd done the same last night, when Chaplin had been taken, and, now, he saw that she suspected what he'd reluctantly thought she might be—the ultimate victim.

Something broke inside him for her. "It's not an excuse. The viszes would show us if any of Stamp's men are infiltrating the community through the common room via a different outside entrance. That's what they might do if they're using this 'memorial service' as a distraction to take us over."

He didn't really believe that; he still subscribed to the notion that Stamp would've just used surprise and force if he were bent on destruction.

Mariah pushed a hand down her thigh. "I can't stop thinking of how I went out there, far beyond my safe point, not even twenty-four hours ago. I did it just to prove to Chaplin—and myself—that I could. And I made it without bringing about any terrible consequences."

She looked as if she wanted to add something, but seemed to think better of it.

"Yes," he said, thinking only now that maybe Chaplin hadn't been such a bully. "You did, Mariah."

"If you gave me some more peace, maybe I could—"

He was already denying her, shaking his head. He'd known she was going to ask, but it was false courage, and she shouldn't get too used to it.

More unsettling, though, was the fact that he *wanted* her to remain inside, no matter how much he'd previously encouraged her to go out. And she should stay put until Stamp was taken care of. Then she could run around up there until the skies turned blue if she wanted to.

"Indulge me this time," he said. "Stay down here. No matter what your friends choose to do, I've already decided that I'm definitely going up top to see what Stamp has going on."

She stood. "Gabriel, tell me you're not going to . . ."

She gestured at her mouth, and he knew that she was indicating his fangs.

"No," he said.

Her shoulders sank in obvious relief, and that made him tense up.

"Don't worry about my getting you and your friends in deeper trouble," he said, sounding . . . what—wounded? It would make sense, especially after she'd brought out more than the possibility of humanity in him—she'd made him become temporarily alive with her hands on him, her heated imprint, her skin against his.

All she was doing now was pointing out that he was still a vampire to her. She also did it every time she asked for more peace.

He wished she didn't know what he was, just like the other people in the community, who seemed to believe in *him*, not in the abilities that'd driven him into the Badlands.

"I'm not going to need"—he gestured to his mouth, just as she'd done—"that. I plan to weapon up."

He turned around to leave, and after a second, he heard

her follow, her steps deliberate. He didn't know if it was because she was conflicted about her or *him* going outside.

When he got back to the domain's center, Zel, Sammy, and the oldster were gathered by the ladder, and even though it wasn't obvious, Gabriel knew from the shape of their pants and shirts that they were hiding weapons.

Pucci and Hana were gone.

At seeing Gabriel, the oldster brightened as much as the circumstances allowed. "We're down to the slim pickings of us because Pucci and Hana won't have any part of our 'madness.' You could say I'm shocked beyond belief at that, but then you'd have to cut my suddenly grown nose right off." Then, as if realizing what they were about to undergo, he got serious. "We know Stamp's not leaving, no matter what we do, and we need to get this out of the way. You with us?"

"You know I am."

When Zel, Sammy, and the oldster shook Gabriel's hand, it was with a true welcome to their family, as if he had finally earned his way in.

Before he could feel too good about that, he sensed Mariah behind him, her presence a series of snaps over his flesh. Without acknowledging it, he grabbed a revolver from the wall, making sure it was loaded. Then he tucked it into the belt line of his trousers, pulling his shirt over the weapon.

Zel pointed at Mariah. "You're staying here?"

There was no neighborly concern, just a matter of logistics. Gabriel wasn't sure where Zel's tone stemmed from.

Mariah sighed, then retreated toward the viszes. "Yes, Zel, I'll be down here."

Good to know he wasn't the only one looking out for Mariah.

"You know," Gabriel said, indicating the ladder, "using this exit will give its location away."

Sammy said, "I suspect if they don't know of it now, they soon will."

The oldster motioned to Zel. "You should stay below with Mariah and Chaplin."

Though the old guy would've hated to know it, he had a softness in his gaze, and Gabriel even thought that Zel recognized it before she pulled her hat onto her head and adjusted the strap beneath it.

"If I didn't know better," she said gruffly, "I'd think you had some archaic notion of excluding females from holding down the fort. Surely I'm mistaken."

"That's not it, Z—"

"Move on it, oldster," she said, taking the ladder first.

As she climbed up, all business, Sammy followed, his expression grim. The oldster avoided Gabriel as he went up the ladder, too.

Gabriel ascended just as Zel popped the entrance door open to the night and began to climb out. Though he didn't look back, he felt Mariah's gaze on him, and it made him think this meeting with Stamp was going to be okay, just as long as she was down there, secure with Chaplin by her side.

As Gabriel exited, with the dusk-mellowed dragon's-breath air greeting him, Zel shut the door while Stamp and his men stopped all their running around. They'd planted solar-powered lights, the sticks stabbed into the earth. In the distance, the whir of a second rumbler gnawed over the ground, louder and louder, and coupled with Stamp's version of a welcoming smile, it raised Gabriel's hackles.

"Excellent," the kid said, as if there were no hard feelings between any of them and he was happy to have them at his soiree. "I was hoping I'd get to apologize face-to-face for my misconceptions about your killing my men. I'm grateful for this opportunity to smooth the ground between us."

As four of Stamp's crew gathered around, the gasping sound of their FlyShoes stilled. Thanks to the accoutrements, the guys—and even a couple of women—towered over Gabriel and the group as the white hankies went limp in the crew's grips. The three others who'd arrived in the first rumbler ambled on over, too, minus the FlyShoes.

Zel was tense, her fingers spread low on her hips, just under where Gabriel knew she'd stowed her weapons.

"I can speak for us all when I say we, in turn, appreciate

the apology, Mr. Stamp," she said. "Now we can be good neighbors, just as you wanted."

"Yes, we can." As Stamp smiled, his fathomless eyes crinkled at the corners. But that smile did more to freeze than a glare would've. "And, as neighbors do, we wanted to share what we found sniffing around our place shortly after we discovered Cedric Orville dead a few hours before dawn. We figured you would want to know that this menace was taken care of. You'd warned us about the wildlife, and you were right, so we owe you at least this."

The whirring sound of the second rumbler got even louder as it chopped over a hill, mangling everything under its speedy path. Sparks shot from the wide wheels as it consumed rocks and bushes.

While it pulled up a few yards from the group, the driver halted the vehicle, and two men alighted from it, their hands full with what, at first, seemed to be a shapeless form.

Zel, Sammy, and the oldster drifted closer to Gabriel.

The crew's baggage became far more recognizable—a man wearing a black hood. After the crew set his feet on the ground, he stumbled while pulled along, his wrists, covered by the cuffs of his shirt, bound behind his back by some manner of gleaming substance, brassy in the reflection of the solar torches. He was wearing tattered clothing, as if it'd lasted him through a long, hard journey.

A man? Gabriel thought. *He'd* been the scourge of the Badlands?

Gabriel's shoulders hunched as he felt the terrified energy from the others, their adrenaline racing through them and fluttering their heartbeats, the scent of fear and bewilderment in the air.

The crewmen were heading for Stamp with the hooded captive, but the kid held up a hand to stop them about ten yards away. Disdain slashed over his otherwise smooth, young face.

Gabriel couldn't stand the silence anymore. "That's a man, not a . . . thing."

Stamp turned his gaze on Gabriel, but when he talked, it was to his employees.

"Truss him up," he said, his voice without inflection.

And his heartbeat was the same, Gabriel realized. As flat as a projectile's course.

The crew seemed tickled to be taking part in such a job. One man wrapped more brasslike cable around the hooded one's pants-shrouded ankles, and the captive tried to fight as other crew members jumped over to spike three long stakes into the ground, which they crossed at the top. Another guy wearing elevated FlyShoes was up high enough to lash the poles together.

Then they turned the hooded man upside down and handed him up, ankles first, so that the employee with the FlyShoes could tie the captive's cords to the apex of the poles.

An execution. Wasn't that what Sammy had said?

Gabriel leaned a little closer to Stamp. Not near enough to let the kid sense a lack of scent about him or to feel the absence of warmth from his skin. Just enough to whisper in a rough voice.

"Is this necessary?"

At Gabriel's proximity, there was a bump in Stamp's heartbeat. Otherwise, he remained unruffled, only offering another smile.

Cool customer, Gabriel thought.

Then the kid made a small gesture, and one of the crew stripped the hood off the captive, revealing long, stringy black hair that hung to the ground, swarthy skin, and a muzzle clamped over the lower part of his face.

"Jesus," Zel whispered.

Gabriel flinched at the curse—or maybe it was a plea—but he couldn't look away.

As the oldster had said, Stamp did have a point to make, but Gabriel wasn't sure how much it had to do with keeping the Badlands safe. Maybe it had more to do with how Stamp treated those who needed taming . . . like his neighbors.

The kid nodded, and one of the crew, a guy with an old-fashioned miner's hat and a blond braid winding down his back, took out what looked to be a brass dagger.

"This *thing*," Stamp said, "is what's been sneaking around these parts."

With a grin, the braided man pressed the brass blade to the captive's forehead, and as flesh steamed, the victim convulsed, shutting his eyes tight, flopping around as the muzzle cut off his cry.

The crew member yanked the dagger away, but not before the oldster came to step in front of Zel, who'd groaned while lurching forward, as if she intended to stop this torture session. Sammy helped hold her back.

"Now open that monster's eyes," Stamp said to his crewmen.

The employees enthusiastically forced the captive's lids open so that his eyes were big and glaring.

Eyes that were a spangled black—as startling and bright and endless as the old star-ridden sky.

Gabriel's mind raced. What was this man? Better yet . . . what was this monster Stamp had caught?

And why hadn't Gabriel been able to identify it right away?

At Stamp's next gesture, the blade-wielding crew member pressed the dagger to the captive's neck, creating another sickening hiss. The other thugs laughed, as if this were a prelude to some live carnerotica.

Stamp's low voice scraped over Gabriel. "Do you know what this piece of work is, Mr. Gabriel?"

"I'm not . . . sure."

The kid paused, as if deciding whether Gabriel was lying. Then he said, "A demon."

Gabriel tried not to respond. He'd never knowingly met a demon before. Shouldn't he have some kind of violent instinctual reaction to or sympathy for a fellow monster . . . or was it all too true that the other kinds were too hard to identify?

Worse yet, should he be glad it'd been caught because it was Gabriel's rival in the race to survive off the remaining humans in this area of the fractured earth? Should he *want* his competitor's death?

He wasn't sure if vampires were supposed to be allies or enemies with other preters. According to the vague pamphlet his creator had given him, vampires had long ago nursed a preferred avoidance for anything else supernatural. But the rules had changed during the scramble for survival. Every creature did its best to keep to itself out of necessity, never exposing what it was so that it might test any theories of who were friends and who were foes.

As the torture continued, Stamp put his hands on his hips again, as if taking in a sporting event like mash baseball or killfight. "When one of my men caught sight of this loser prowling around Cedric Orville's gutted body last night, he thought he saw it changing shape, from man to red cloud and then back again."

As the demon flailed under the brass knife once more, Gabriel strived to appear untouched by the creature's pain. It'd been out there, somewhere, last night, maybe even yards away from Gabriel and Chaplin, and he'd never even known it.

Wild things, he thought. What else did the New Badlands host? No wonder the community stayed close to home.

He managed to respond to Stamp. "A shapeshifting demon."

"Yes, but it's not shifting now; brass can bind and harm this one. And also?" Stamp's words got graveled in obvious bitterness. "It's clearly a man-eater."

And it'd been feasting on Stamp's crew.

The kid added, "The employee who spied it thought fast enough to take a jetpack closer to the hubs, where she was able to secure Nets reception. She did some quick research about ways to handle situations like this, then persuaded a bunch of fellow employees to catch it, with each of them trying different methods. Fortunately, one of the boys was slinging brass, and it worked to bind and disable this scourge. I didn't even know about the hunt until they were done." Stamp smiled. "Now, that's a crew a boss can hold some pride in."

Zel was breathing hard, a hand clamped over her mouth. The oldster and Sammy just seemed frozen.

Questions rained down on Gabriel. The community had existed out here for years and had to have known a creature of this order was near. Had they been doing something to appease this demon, to keep it from coming to their home?

Gabriel searched his mind for any evidence of that, but he came up with nothing.

As the crew kept at the creature with the brass blade, one of the men pulled down his arm glove and accessed his personal computer screen, reading out loud from it. He must've uploaded the information into his own database.

The words weren't familiar to Gabriel, but his best guess was that they were Hindi, and they made the captive squirm even more.

Expelling the demon from its shell, Gabriel thought.

He shut his mind to the sight, thinking that this torture could've been his own if he hadn't been so determined not to flaunt his vampire powers, even on the night he'd arrived here and Stamp's men had roughed him up.

As the crew member's words got louder, faster, the demon stiffened, then . . .

Much to Gabriel's horror, the captive's body burst open, letting loose with a group of ten screeching black heads, all with long necks and mouths that snapped at the air, then began tearing into each other. While the crewman raised his voice at the peak of his incantation, the heads whirled into one screaming mass of red, then ripped away from the prone host body, hovering in the air, then seeming to melt into a flood of gore as it fell to the ground, seeping into the dirt until there was nothing.

In the aftermath, all went still. No one spoke. Not until the crew started whooping and high-fiving each other, taking kicks and swipes at the decimated mass of flesh and bone dripping upside down from the poles.

Gabriel turned away, expecting the blood from this body that the demon had possessed to tweak his appetite, though it was from a dead man whose blood would be no good for him.

But . . .

He smelled it—the polluted blood of an urban hubite. And the sustenance didn't pull at him as it usually did.

The peace he'd shared with Mariah. Her imprint was still alive in him, wasn't it? And it'd strengthened Gabriel against himself, even temporarily. That had to be it.

He straightened, looking Stamp in the eye, confident that his monster was pushed so far down that the kid wouldn't detect it. And when Stamp just smiled, then looked away to watch his men kick around like giddy idiots, Gabriel knew he was on firm ground.

Then Zel burst out from behind the oldster and Sammy, and Gabriel caught her before she got to Stamp.

"You fiend," she yelled. "That was—"

"Justice," the kid said, sending her a collected, and even somewhat puzzled, look. "And isn't justice beautifully simple in a place like this?"

Maybe, as a cop, she'd seen too many bad guys like Stamp, and she knew when to back away. Whatever the reason, she put distance between her and the kid as she headed for Mariah's entrance.

"There's a place for people like you," Zel said, sounding different, as if some vital portion of her had flipped.

"Believe me," Stamp answered as she opened the domain door, "I've already been there."

Sammy followed her, but the oldster went only half-way in.

"Our squabble has been settled, I take it," he said.

The glimmer in the kid's black-hole eyes sent chills over Gabriel.

"Just being a good neighbor," Stamp said, "keeping us all informed and safe. You can count on cordiality from now on."

And then, as Gabriel settled himself at the entrance, too, the kid walked away, toward a rumbler, signaling to his men, making it unnecessary for the Text-fluent crowd to read his silent intentions of leaving.

They followed their boss, deserting the carcass of the former demon in what Gabriel took to be a dire warning for anything else that might decide to go hunting in the night.

20

Mariah

All I could do was watch the visz to see that the vehicles and men wearing FlyShoes left the area before Gabriel shut the ladder door behind him, then descended. Everyone surrounded him, just as numb as I was, even before he got to the ground.

"That wasn't just about Stamp clearing out a killer," Sammy said. "That was about showing *us* what he's made of. He's declared himself at the top of the chain."

"Not only that," the oldster said. "I get the feeling that above all, Stamp would love to see us run. He plans ahead, that boy, and I'm sure he's got his sights set on what we've claimed here, namely water."

Zel was huddled into herself, arms wrapped round her legs as she sat on the ground. Her hat was still on her head, but the off-kilter angle of it didn't cover a ten-mile stare that told me she was in another time, another place, when the world had started to go crazy. Now it was happening here, again.

"What the hell did we just see?" Her voice was low and

garbled, so I went over to her, knowing that this was the first sign of Zel losing it. I put my hand on her shoulder, just to steady her and, underneath her shirt, I felt the heat of her skin.

Oddly, I seemed to be the calmest person round. Irony at its best.

Zel's "hell" curse had jarred Gabriel, but he hid it well by training his gaze on the visz bank, which featured a screen that showed a clear view of the torture device Stamp's men had set up. Maybe I was calmer than the rest because I'd only seen the tragedy from a distance. That, coupled with the peace that was still in me, probably made a difference.

"All we did was stand by while they went at him," Gabriel said, his words barely audible.

Everyone grew quiet, even though the victim had been a demon. I wasn't sure how we should feel about its termination. Lore had it that demons were awful news, but a possessed man had been involved in this case, and it might not have been a voluntary possession. If it wasn't, killing him was appalling. As Gabriel had told me before, some bad guys are grouped in with the rest, even though they might not have thoroughly earned the title.

His comment still hung in me, like that body outside, swaying in the wind.

Pucci and Hana stayed away from everyone else. He was gaping in that fretful way one had when he could barely believe what he'd just seen. But that was Pucci for you.

"We can't have demons here, anyway," he said. "A demon! The lowest of the low—a monster that'd suck the life out of any of us." He laughed a bit, his nerves clearly addled.

Idiot. "Now's not the time to lose it, Pucci."

"Then when *is* the time?" Pucci chuffed. "Correct me if I'm wrong, Mariah, but didn't Hana and I come back here to your place in time to bear witness to . . . what the tar do they call it . . . ?"

Hana was standing next to Pucci, but there was a space between them. "An exorcism."

As Pucci nerve-laughed again, Hana stayed silent. She was a thoughtful one, as if she might already be a step ahead of us all about how to build that bridge with Stamp she'd suggested last night. I'd wished many a time that she'd leave Pucci in the dust, but she always stuck with him. I couldn't understand why such a smart girl stood for him unless she got something out of all his yelling and bullying. Something a little sick, if you asked me. But it wasn't like we were a template for normalcy out here.

The oldster had bent over, resting his hands on his thighs. He'd seemed fine before, but now it looked as if reality was just hitting him. "A demon. In all my life, I've never seen one of 'em. I heard about 'em, but . . ."

We all just looked at each other, excluding Gabriel from what passed in our gazes. But the oldster didn't need to say it out loud, anyway.

How was it that there'd been a demon running round the New Badlands and we hadn't known it?

Gabriel leaned back against the ladder. "So you all had no idea it was out there."

"No," we said in unison.

"You weren't doing anything ridiculous like making sacrifices to this creature so it'd hunt away from your community?"

God-all.

The oldster looked horrified. "Are you kidding, Gabriel?"

"After what we just saw, I'm afraid not."

Blowing out a breath, the old man stood straight. "Fair enough. But when we spoke of wild things outside at night, we never included a demon in the equation."

Sammy asked, "What do you think brought it here?"

I had an answer. "Some sort of exodus from the hubs?"

Even while I said it, I didn't like what it meant. If monsters started moving out to the New Badlands, this community might end up restarting the cycle of violence we'd tried to flee in the first place. To protect ourselves against this magnitude of threat, we might have to become a new version of Shredders, killing stray monsters who'd bring attention to us out here.

Monsters like Gabriel.

But there was no way I'd reveal his secret. He was worthy of my efforts, because . . .

Was it because of the peace he could give me and that was it?

Zel glanced at one of the viszes, where the remains of the demon swayed in the night.

"This isn't justice," she whispered, sounding far off, eons away from where any of us were right now. "Not all monsters are beyond hope. I've even heard of demons who could bargain for a decent cause if there was a good trade in it for them."

I tightened my grip on Zel's shoulder, wanting to keep her contained. She could have hair-trigger emotions, like me. Like all of us. And it would only come to harm.

Sammy ignored her comment, lowering to his haunches. Now he was belatedly spent, just like the oldster. "So Stamp got his kicks. Maybe that's all he wanted."

"I don't think so," Gabriel said. But then he didn't seem to have any more answers than we did. Tonight he was one of us—unsure and slightly pissed off because he'd just stood there, too, letting Stamp do what he'd done. Gabriel seemed the type to have higher ideals, and here we were, dragging him down to a place where those standards couldn't exist.

"Stamp's gonna turn his attention back here, certainly enough," Gabriel finally said. "You know he will."

Suddenly I wasn't just thinking about Stamp. I pictured the men who'd attacked my old home.

"He's the type who likes live torture," I found myself saying. "Mental, physical—it does something for him. Carnerotica isn't enough because he can't smell it or be next to it. Beings like him, they do it because it's the only way for them to feel alive. Filling his emptiness with someone else's pain is all that keeps him going."

Zel spoke again in that drifting voice. "Stamp'll get away with it, just like they all do."

The oldster gave her a worried glance, then gestured toward the exit, where the night waited outside. "Hate to break in with this, but there'll be carrion feeders arriving to pluck that demon's body clean. And we all know that shades tend to think that there's more to come, and they sometimes hide among the rocks to swoop down on anything else that comes by. We should clean up before that happens."

As if the oldster hadn't said a word, Zel again set her gaze on the outside visz screen, with its focus on the skeleton of the three joined poles where the demon had been executed and the shell of its body twisting in another gust of wind.

"With every passing day," she said quietly, "we good cops saw things get worse, not better. And every time we managed to put a bad guy away, a technicality would surface due to a rotten cop purposely screwing up procedure for a payoff. Or there'd be a command from the government and their corporate interests to release the criminal. After a while, there was no use in keeping on with it."

"Zel . . ." the oldster said.

But she wasn't listening. "The . . . time . . . came when I had to leave the hubs—"

I clamped my hand on her shoulder, and she blinked. Stiffened. Regrouped.

Then she added, "A rogue psychic—a criminal informant who set up a secret fortune-telling business in a free-housing reservation—told me to head west. That's all he said. Out of not knowing where else to go, I did. And I found you guys."

The oldster was looking at the ceiling, as if it were an old movie screen showing the day Zel had arrived. He was smiling slightly until her next words.

"Out here there was good. There was some bad, too, but it wasn't beyond redeeming." She reached up to hold my hand, and I gripped her, my throat getting choked. "I thought I'd outlive the day when I'd encounter pure evil again, and I can't watch it grow and take over now. I won't." She gazed at us. "Tell me we're going to do something about it."

Seconds ticked by. No one volunteered. I was afraid to

because of what it might bring on this time. We were already
in too deep.

It was as if Zel had been drilled through with a bullet,
and she slightly jerked under the impact of it. Then she
wobbled to her feet, pushing her hat off her head as she
wandered out of our circle. We let her be as the talk turned
back to Stamp and our options. And our non-options.

The discussion grew loud and heated between the oldster
and Pucci, in particular. But we didn't get anywhere further
than we'd been before.

About fifteen minutes in, Pucci said, "Maybe we should
just up and go to another place before we're taken over by
people like Stamp. This area we once thought of as a sanctuary has been found, my friends. There could be more of
him to come."

A laugh chopped out of me. I didn't mean to use it to get
everyone's attention, but that was just what it did.

I made use of it. "Hiding. Always hiding."

Pucci shirked back, then frowned. He was the kind of
man who didn't take kindly to any female lip. Too bad.

"Mariah," he said, "I wouldn't be so uppity if I were you."

I stared right back at him, and he knew he'd gone too far.
I could see it in the twitch of his mouth.

On the other side of the room, I could sense Gabriel
tensing. He watched Pucci closely. Was he . . . protecting me?

"Antonio," Hana said.

She didn't even raise her voice, but all the same, it seemed
to slap Pucci.

He walked back to where Hana was standing, then leaned
against the wall next to her, as if all were well. But he was
grinding his teeth as he gradually slid his gaze to Hana.

A split second before Pucci raised his hand with the obvious intention of grabbing her robes and bringing her
face-to-face with him, Gabriel rushed over—not vampire-
fast, but quick enough—and inserted his arm between them
as a barrier.

Hana looked up at Gabriel with her big brown eyes,

utterly calm. She wasn't afraid, and Gabriel seemed surprised at that.

He looked straight at Pucci, and Pucci just stared right back until the oldster spoke.

"Hey," he said. "Where's Zel?"

We seemed to come out of the malaise that the strained moment between Gabriel, Pucci, and Hana had wrought. None of us had been paying mind to Zel. She must've slipped through the door, through the common area and to her domain, during the distraction.

Damn. Damn it all . . .

Chaplin, who'd remained quiet up until now, talked to me.

Check on her, Mariah!

But I'd already sprinted to the common-area tunnel door and opened it, letting Chaplin through. I ran off after him toward the common room, which was empty. Then I yanked open Zel's unlocked door.

Her domain was empty, too.

I barreled back to my place, just as Gabriel was halfway up the ladder, obviously intending to check if Zel was outside, beyond the scope of the viszes.

I stopped him by yelling, "Gone!" while rushing toward the weapons wall.

God-all, we knew what Zel was going to do, and she needed to be stopped. If things were bad now, they'd only be worse if—

The oldster was at my side, echoing my thoughts. "You don't think she did something foolhardy, like going off to Stamp's with her sense of righteousness on fire."

Gabriel jumped down from the ladder. "She wouldn't be that careless, especially all by herself."

I whittled my explanation to its safest, taking a double-barreled shotgun from the wall, plus a bag of ammunition. "Zel's gone into worse situations. She was a cop, and if you saw what was on her face tonight, you know that she wasn't about to tolerate a minute more of what she considers to be injustice. Besides, Zel . . ."

A flustered Sammy cut in, editing me. "Zel can do damage. It's only a matter of *having* to do it. You can only push a woman like her so far, and . . . I think she lost it tonight, you guys. Really lost it."

We were all watching each other in front of Gabriel—what was said, what was done—but he didn't seem to notice.

"This is on *me*," he said. "I was the one with all the talk the other night."

The oldster walked over, clearly sensing that Gabriel wasn't about to stand idly by. Not this time.

"We can catch up to her," the old man said.

Pucci's enraged voice cut in. "And what then? Goddamn it, is every one of you forgetting what the hell's at stake? This is just what we've been trying to avoid!"

Gabriel flinched at the curses, but he moved toward the common-area door, anyway. The oldster was right behind him.

Sammy called, "Oldster, what are you planning—?"

The old man held up a revolver. "Here's my strategy, and it's enough. I've got control of this."

Nobody halted them as Gabriel laid his hand on the door, clearly thinking about how to proceed. Was he wondering if he should run as fast as a vampire was capable, taking the risk of exposing his monster side to whatever was out there?

Whatever he wanted to do, I ached to go with him. I felt good enough to do it, too, with the peace over me. But Gabriel had made it clear he wanted me to stay inside, and I knew that I'd only complicate matters if I made an issue of it. We couldn't afford to lose any more time. I'd hold down the fort here, just in case Zel pissed off Stamp and he decided to pull another stunt like he did with Chaplin—capturing one of our own and then exploiting our imbalance during his attack on our home front. The oldster would keep Gabriel in check. He'd make sure we weren't exposed.

He took Gabriel's arm. "I've got a zoom bike. We'll catch up to Zel that way."

"Is it fast enough to overcome Zel's vehicle?"

None of us answered.

Instead, I went over to Gabriel, giving him the double-barreled shotgun with modified night sights as well as an ammo sack. I wanted my meaning to be clear. *Use the weapon, not your fangs.*

As he accepted the weaponry, his finger slid over mine, and both of our blood flows surged, bringing up what was left of the strength we'd shared, the peace.

Slinging the ammo sack over his head so it rested against his chest, he exited, not looking at me. But I felt like I was still in his mind.

"We'll be back soon," the oldster said. "And if I find that any of you have gone outside after us, I'll kick your asses."

As the door swung shut behind Gabriel and the oldster, Pucci impetuously called out, "Oldster, make sure Zel doesn't—"

Sammy clapped his hand over Pucci's overly emotive speech before anything else got out, and I was right there with him, aiming a revolver at the man's big mouth in case he tried to finish the sentence.

21

Gabriel

The door slammed, and Gabriel didn't hear the rest of what Pucci said. But his mind was in high gear, thinking about what lay ahead as he ran down the tunnel to the common area, then the oldster's door.

They jogged through his tunnel, too, into his domain, where the contents made Gabriel come to a halt.

It was nothing more than a garage, with tools and chains hanging from the walls and various vehicles waiting, some with their innards spilled on the floor, some gleaming and some beautifully intact.

"Shit, oldster," Gabriel said.

The old man had already climbed onto a dark gray, streamlined zoom bike, turning it on to rev its quiet jets. There was enough room on the back for Gabriel, and once he sat behind the driver, the oldster wasted no time in gunning the engine, aiming the bike's twisted hornlike nozzle up, and blasting toward a trapdoor in the ceiling.

Gabriel was just about to yell that the fucking thing was

closed when the oldster pressed a button on the handlebars and the door blasted open.

They barged up into the gray-spun night, curving around toward Stamp's place as the oldster put pedal to the metal. It was all Gabriel could do to hold on to the shotgun as the old man clipped by rocky hills, leaving the *whish* of the engine echoing behind them.

During the short trip, Gabriel ran through scenarios: what they would do if Zel was there. What they'd do if she wasn't.

When they arrived at the base of a large hill, the oldster cut the engine to a near-silent stalk. Gabriel sniffed the air, trying to find a scent that would lead them to Zel or even Stamp's place.

In the near distance, he heard men laughing just over that hill. Then he scented a hint of tangy, luring, coppery aroma, too.

Blood.

Gabriel climbed off the seat and landed on the dirt, then checked his shotgun while easing toward the hill, knowing he couldn't make much noise and alert Stamp to their presence. Though Mariah's effect on him wasn't as potent as it'd been earlier, there was enough of the peace left for him to resist the draw of the blood.

Midway up, he waited for the oldster. The gray moon provided thick illumination as the other man hopped off the zoom bike just before it came to a gentle settling on the ground. Gabriel signaled to let the oldster know they needed to go up and over the hill.

But the guy was already on his way, charging toward Gabriel, then right past him. He was even holding his revolver high.

Gabriel followed him. His blood was thudding, his fingers wrapped around the shotgun.

He and the oldster reached the top, and as they leaned forward against a boulder to see what lay before them, they heard the first of Zel's screams, which sounded much more like an echoing screech.

Gabriel stopped himself from cringing, but the oldster's veins were raised from the skin of his neck, just as if he were gearing up to do something stupid and give them away.

Before Gabriel could grab the oldster's arm to restrain him, a crumble of rocks rolled down from a higher perch.

Then something whacked Gabriel upside the head.

It hit him with enough force that he went down, but he was up again just as he saw their assailant—a massive man—swinging a club at the oldster.

As the weapon connected with the old man's forehead, he fell, but Gabriel was already wielding the butt of his shotgun at their attacker.

With a crack to his skull, he knocked the guy out.

A lookout, Gabriel thought as he first checked on the assailant. He was dead.

He heard the oldster's vital signs, which were weaker but still going. Gabriel wondered if he could heal something in a human that wasn't a laceration or other external wound.

Zel screamed again, the sound drilling through him, and he peered over the boulder to Stamp's spread, which wasn't marked on the surface by much more than a vehicle-strewn cave where the rumblers were stored.

And against the side of that cave was Zel, her arms outspread as if in flight, her front against the rock, her hands clawing at the wall. Blood marked the back of a shirt that was nothing more than strips of white, and the dark streaks traveled down equally destroyed trousers. There was a knife embedded in her shoulder, and that was what was causing her to scream.

Mariah had said Stamp was the type that thrived off the pain of others. Gabriel knew the kind, because he'd soaked up Abby's terror on the night he'd found her running from danger. He'd fed off Mariah's bruised psyche, too.

He knew Stamp, all right, and Gabriel was going to kill him. *All* of them.

His sight threatened to go red, but he knew losing control wasn't the answer, so he called on the solace of what he'd shared with Mariah.

During that flash of an eternal second, Gabriel witnessed what happened next: Stamp standing to the side, his hands planted on his hips casually, as if he were again watching a show his crew was putting on. Then one of his men—a woman, actually, judging by her shape—holding another knife. Then the rest of Stamp's crew, a few more than Gabriel had seen back at the community, circled around, lazy accomplices.

But there were a couple of employees on the ground, too, as if Zel had taken them out. And with Gabriel's heightened sight, he could see that their faces were bloody messes.

He brought up the shotgun. One man against all these foes with weapons wouldn't last, but with any luck, he'd get enough of them from up here to allow Zel to run.

The woman with the knife seemed to be aiming it at Zel, and Gabriel fired, hoping his friend had enough energy to escape and hop on her own vehicle to zoom away.

The shot blew the knife handler forward with such force that she slammed against the cave face-first. As she slipped down the surface of it, the gaping hole in her middle caught on an outcropping of rock, and she hung there, the knife dropping from her hand.

The others turned around, and before Gabriel could shoot again, one of them had his own gun out—a deathlock, small and viperish and smart, with computerized bullets that mapped out and tracked human heat near its path.

For the first time in a while, Gabriel was glad he wasn't human.

Still, the shooter aimed close to where Gabriel had fired, so the bullet sought out the oldster on the ground. Gabriel threw himself over the old man just in time for the bullet to nick his own shoulder, taking out a chunk of his skin and flinging him to the side.

Running footsteps—from only one attacker, another

lookout—came at Gabriel, and though he was losing blood in gushing spurts, he aimed . . .

As the man, his long hair flying behind him, appeared over the boulder, Gabriel fired, and the guy flipped backward, his torso a thing of the past.

Gabriel struggled to get back to the cover of the boulder, break open the shotgun, and reload before the deathlock gunner could do so; it always took a few moments for the computer on the other weapon to reset. His arm would be fine if he could just start self-healing, but who knew how weak he'd be with the blood loss.

He reloaded and managed to cover the oldster's body with his own just before another deathlock bullet whizzed overhead. Then Gabriel peered over the boulder, finding that Stamp's crew had taken cover inside the cavern, behind the rumblers. Their boss was nowhere to be found, but Zel was frozen, panting, looking up at his location, shocked to have a savior among the rocks.

Then another gunshot rang through the air, and Gabriel started. It hadn't sounded like a deathlock, and he sure hadn't fired.

But someone had.

He looked back at Zel to see a bloom of darkness spreading over her heart. She sank to the dirt, her final sound again reminding Gabriel of a screech.

Zel . . . ?

Gabriel ducked back down, his senses fritzing.

A rock tumbled down near him, and he hazily swung the shotgun in its direction, but a blade got to his other arm first.

Fire split down the wound, and Gabriel knew that the blade had been silver—poison for a vampire.

Out of pure agony, his monster instincts took over, his vision going red, his fangs jutting out as he hissed at the attacker, who'd raised the silver knife again, the blade glinting in the baleful moonlight.

But Gabriel was quick, and he brought the shotgun up just in time to fire at him.

The bullet caught the man in the side, and he spun away, but Gabriel thought he still heard vital signs. He also detected a stampede of feet coming up the hill, and he looked at the oldster just lying there, knocked out. Then he thought of Zel, shot through the heart.

He wasn't going to let another one of them die.

So he grabbed the old man, speeding down the hill and back to the zoom bike, tossing him over his lap and revving the vehicle into fast motion before Stamp's men could catch up.

As he flew away, he held tighter to the oldster than he'd ever held to anything before, unwilling to let the man fall, as he'd allowed Zel to.

It was only when Gabriel sped the zoom bike over the hills leading to the community that he remembered the demon's decimated body.

And the carrion feeders that'd been sure to find it.

The flock of shades was indeed pecking at the former demon's skin with their grotesquely large beaks, their eyes as red as the devil's fury in the night as they cocked their heads at Gabriel's approach. Hoping that the oldster's body was balanced enough on his lap, Gabriel gripped the shotgun, which he'd nestled next to the old man, raised it at the carrion feeders, then fired.

The blast scattered their large, gargoylesque bodies, and they rose toward the waning moon until they covered his view of it. As Gabriel veered up to Mariah's entrance, he shut down the zoom bike, tumbled off while it eased down to the ground, and dropped the spent shotgun because there was no time to reload.

Next to him, Mariah's door busted open, and there she was, training her own shotgun around to catch sight of any hiding shades with her weapon's modified night-vision equipment.

"Hurry!" she yelled.

Gabriel didn't need any urging as the flock hovered in the sky, preparing to dive back down.

When they descended, their screech-howl cries pierced

the air, louder, closer. Gabriel grabbed the oldster from the bike, flinging his slight body straight at the entrance, where Sammy was now reaching out his arms.

The oldster's body banged into the other man as he caught the old guy, then fell backward.

The shades' cries got even louder.

Mariah took a shot at them, and she must've hit one because it wailed just before she ducked aside to make room for Gabriel, who was already jumping inside, grabbing the door at the same time and arcing it to a close while he careened toward the ground.

As he hit the floor, his vampire reflexes making his landing graceful, he heard Mariah bolting the door behind him.

But no one seemed to notice the strangeness of his entrance because the rest of the crowd were trying to revive the oldster, whom they'd already laid out on the ground.

"He got a good knock to the skull with a club," Gabriel said so they could start medical work on him. Then he bent to his haunches, weakened.

But before he could remember too much about the silver that'd gotten into his system with that knife blade, he checked the visz screens to see the carrion feeders swooping past the lens, near Mariah's door, then pulling back up. Outside, he could hear their frustrated cries, like the sound of metal against metal.

The shades went back to the demon's body, plucking apart the rest of it, and Mariah came to Gabriel's side. She was breathing quickly.

"The feeders came before any of our group could get out there to clean up the demon," she said. Then in the next breath, "Zel?"

While the others looked to Gabriel, he wasn't sure how to break the news to them. So he merely shook his head.

Pucci, who had his hand on the oldster's shoulder, let out a defeated moan. Sammy hung his head. Hana sat near the oldster's head and paused only a second before she set her jaw and gently placed her hand on the old man's wound, near the trickle of blood from his injury.

Mariah's face had gone a livid red, her eyes light and glassy with what he recognized to be helpless, feverish anger. Her blood screamed through her veins, and Gabriel could tell that the remaining peace was all that was keeping her from losing it.

Chaplin skulked in a corner, one mournful howl his only response as he presented his back.

Mariah closed her eyes, and a tear rolled out. Gabriel could tell she was trying to retain composure, that she was telling herself that now wasn't the time for grief—not with the oldster still able to be saved.

"What happened to her?" she asked, opening her eyes, and he could see it—the determination to not fall apart. He could also feel their connection tugging at him, the renewal of the peace.

He wanted to touch her, but he knew it'd only lead to more—him feeling her despair when they didn't need any more of it to infect them.

Gabriel told them everything: about finding Stamp's place, seeing Zel with the knife in her back, being unable to get to her before she'd been shot.

Pucci got to his feet, his massive form unsteady. "Was she dead, Gabriel? Really *dead*?"

"Certainly looked it." As he grew even weaker, Gabriel met Mariah's stare, and he knew she'd understand an entirely different meaning than the rest of them when he said, "I couldn't . . . test . . . her vital signs to know for sure."

Or, more to the truth, he hadn't been able to *sense* Zel's vital signs.

Mariah understood what he was really saying, but as she went back to watching the oldster, he could see that there was a little part of her that hoped Zel might still be alive with this lack of indisputable proof that she was dead.

Desperate, Gabriel thought. No one wanted to believe

their friend was gone, least of all him. Not when he'd been so close to rescuing her.

He even wondered if flagrantly using his vampire powers would've mattered, if he would've made things better . . . or worse.

Now all the neighbors were huddled over the oldster, shielding him so Gabriel could barely see the man's whiskered face. Hana had used her spit and her robe to clean off the blood from his scalp, and she was still running her hands over his wound, murmuring to him.

Gabriel looked at Mariah, who was holding her shotgun in her arms, almost cradling it.

"What's massaging him gonna do?" Gabriel asked.

A jittery Sammy glanced up from the group, to Mariah. She shook her head.

Was there something they didn't want to tell Gabriel about Hana's methods?

Before he could ask, he noticed that Sammy's gaze was focused on the blood splatters over his shirt, from the wounds inflicted by Stamp's cronies.

The other man turned to the oldster, where the rest of the group were covering their faces, as if barring their sorrow. Sammy did the same.

Mariah was staring at his wounds, too, but she had a furrow to her brow, as if bewildered. "Hana was a new-age science nurse. She knows what she's doing, Gabriel. But you . . ."

She motioned toward his shoulder, where his ripped shirt marked the grazed deathlock bullet wound that had already mended enough to pucker together. Then she glanced at his other arm, where the knife had formed a gaping, unhealed slice from the silver blade. Weakness had already unfolded from the wound and outward, toward his chest. From what he remembered reading in that little vampire introduction pamphlet, it wouldn't be long before the silver poison traveled to more of him, unless he could cleanse it with an infusion of fresh blood.

As the others helped the oldster, Mariah took Gabriel by the shirtsleeve, and he realized that she wanted privacy.

She spoke to the group. "Someone pay attention to the viszes." Then she guided Gabriel to her quarters.

The Badlanders huddled together over the oldster, watching Mariah with something in their eyes that Gabriel couldn't understand.

22

Mariah

When we were ensconced in my private quarters, I set the shotgun down and guided Gabriel to my bed so he could sit. "What do you need me to do?"

I was half in shock from Zel's death. Survival mode. And the blood on Gabriel . . . I was fighting that off, too.

"A drink," he said, as if hating that it'd come to this. "Just a little blood to wash the silver out . . ."

I began unbuttoning my shirt.

"Not like that," he said, latching his fingers round my wrists. Then he explained how he'd gotten these wounds and the consequences of them. "The knife injury is minor, but the weakness is still traveling. I only need enough to keep me."

He brought one of my wrists toward him, then rested his fingers on the inside of it, over my escalating pulse.

Regulating my responses—breathing, trying to find that peace he'd given to me—I sat next to him on the bed.

My offer seemed to move him. Yeah, a vampire affected by emotion. Maybe it was because he felt my sincerity in the rhythm of my heartbeat, the constant dance of it against his fingers. He laid my hand against his cheek, then turned his face against my wrist. The skin there tingled, and the damage traveled up my arm, all over the place, clashing with the peace until my awareness fizzled like sparks all over me.

"Thank you," he said against my wrist, with just a little sway in his voice, enough so that I was under the thrall of it. I knew he was tranquilizing me so I'd feel no discomfort.

With the utmost care, he used a fingernail on my flesh, cutting me. Under the sway, I didn't mind the slight sting. I was a world away, watching, disconnected from the action while still connected to him.

He drank, sucking my blood, the pale of his skin flushing a little with the intake. He shivered, and I imagined that it was because the blood was wrapping itself round the silver weakness in him, stifling and choking it.

When he was done, he covered my wound with his fingers to heal me. Even in that small movement, he seemed much stronger.

"Are you okay?" he asked, and I was sure he wasn't just talking about the effects from my blood donation.

I nodded, and it seemed to jar something in me. Tears sprang to my eyes. I was a liar, all right, and not just to other people. I was particularly good at doing it to myself.

"Talk to me," he whispered.

I didn't want to. I wanted him to just look into me, put me under more sway so I could spend the rest of the night in that mental pool of water, floating, forgetting.

When he spoke, he included some peace. "Tell me what's addling you."

And, before I realized it, I was chatting, even if I wanted to pull my words back. I suppose I actually wanted to talk about this, even though I didn't know it.

"I knew I wouldn't ever get away from it." *Stop . . . talking . . .* "It follows you everywhere."

It. The violence, the never-ending legacy of a society that had looked too far into the abyss and then jumped right in.

Gabriel rubbed my healing wrist, as if hoping it would

make me feel better. It almost seemed like doing that would improve him, too.

"I know what you mean," he said. "I tried to save Zel. She'd taken down a couple of the crew by the time the old-ster and I got there, and it looked as if she'd been in a real fight with them."

Had he seen much more than that?

"She was feisty, and that's the reason Stamp's guys were knifing her," Gabriel added. "There were more of them, too. Stamp might've already called for reinforcements from the hubs—those connections everyone feared he might have." He hunched, as if blaming himself for everything. "It all happened so fast that I wasn't able to think all that much about the details at the time."

"It always does happen fast," I said.

Always.

He was done healing my wrist, but he kept holding my hand. "I'm only relieved that the oldster didn't have to see Zel die. I would've knocked him out myself if I'd have known they were gonna do that to her. She must've ridden a fast vehicle to Stamp's, then thrown down with the crew. Why did she think she could take on all of them by herself?"

I swallowed, treading lightly round his assumptions. "That was Zel. She probably even went for Stamp directly before the crowd stopped her." I concentrated my gaze on our entwined fingers, not at him. "Zel had a real sense of honor, and she would've called Stamp out to suffer for all he's done. I'm sure, for her, Stamp stood for *all* the bad guys who got away with wrong during her watch as a cop. Tonight was just the last straw. She—"

Someone cried out from the other room.

The oldster?

Even through the flow of the peace in me, I struggled to get up from the bed as a ruckus exploded outside my private quarters.

Gabriel helped me up as the oldster stumbled in, his face a naked arrangement of loss and disbelief. Sammy and Pucci were right behind him, each one grasping the oldster's trembling arms, restraining him. Hana slipped round to the front of him to whisper low, soft assurances.

When I saw that the oldster's eyes were light and livid, my heart pistoned.

He pushed past Hana toward Gabriel. "Is it true? They murdered her?"

Gabriel nodded, as if in prelude to saying that they'd tried their best to save Zel, but the oldster was already crying out, his voice mangled in primal grief. His scream was hollow, inhuman.

Panicked, I started forward, but Pucci had already wrapped his thick arm round the old man's neck. The oldster tried to squirm out, his sorrowful fury making him strong. Hana helped Pucci by forcefully pushing the thrashing man back toward the other room.

Sammy put the oldster in an armlock. "Don't do this, old-timer. *Please.*"

But the oldster still fought them off as they pulled him back into the tunnel. His screams of rage continued until a door closed, chopping off the terrible cries, which had almost become garbled sounds, altogether.

The oldster's emotions had gotten to me, too, and my body began echoing those cries by heating up. . . .

Gabriel just sat there, as if trying to find his own way in the swarm of emotion. Meanwhile, Chaplin rushed into the room, his ears plastered back. Thank-all he came to sit in front of me, murmuring just as Hana had done to the oldster.

It's fine, Mariah, he said. *They've got the oldster in check. . . .*

Thanks to Chaplin's soothing voice, plus what I had of Gabriel's peace, I was merely trembling now. "There're so many of them out there, and then there's . . . us."

Stamp would be no match for us if it came right down to it, Chaplin muttered, and I knew that he'd shut Gabriel out of hearing that comment.

I just shook my head. "They're gonna have all weapons drawn."

"Weapons," Gabriel said. He looked crestfallen as he

continued. "That silver knife. My reaction to it . . . They might know what I am. When one of the men came at me with that silver blade, I turned. I couldn't stop myself. I shot him, but I didn't have time to confirm his death because more of them were coming, and the oldster couldn't defend himself. It was either save his hide or give him up, so I took him and ran."

What else could go wrong? I bent down to Chaplin, who was talking again, obviously including Gabriel this time.

The demon's presence here was enough to warrant action, Gabriel. We're already in a spot. If there are any Shredders left in the hubs, Stamp will call on one now. Or he'll bring out every supernatural weapon his crew might have on hand. Maybe Stamp already sent some men to the hubs to gather better tools. . . .

Gabriel slowly rose from the bed, his motions weary. His body told me what he wasn't saying: He'd tried to do such good, but he couldn't get away from the bad.

"Maybe," he said, "vacating the premises wouldn't be such a misguided idea at this point. It would keep everyone safe, at least."

Me and Chaplin whipped our gazes over to him. Was this the guy who'd tried to put some fight in everyone?

My fingers clawed against my thighs. "You know it doesn't matter if you run *or* fight, right? Me and my dad and Chaplin . . . we've tried both before now. Fighting only made everything worse. Then we tried running away from our problems, and it seems as if that hasn't worked, either."

"And what happened back when you fought to make you think there's no solution at all right now?" he asked.

Memory shattered my peace: the men coming into my family's house. The blood. The screams.

Chaplin rested his paw on my boot, and I ran my free hand over one of his pressed-back ears. He was my constant, my comfort. Unlike Gabriel, he wasn't going to leave once business in the Badlands was done.

"We'd moved round so much, because of my father's science career," I said. "He was needed here and there, but

after the government took his tech research over and had
him start designing weapons to be used on the populace, he
elected to retire. So we went to the outskirts of Dallas, which
turned out to be one of the last places to fall in the old States.
And we were there when the final degradation started."

I looked to Chaplin, seeing if I should say any more. He
nodded, telling me it was okay to go on.

My fingers dug into my thigh even deeper, burrowing
into my pants. "You'd always hear about the bad guys—how
they were everywhere—but my father had only met up with
white-collar bads in his work. We never thought we'd see
the lower kinds, with our fancy alarm system and all the
safety we thought we possessed in our nice living unit. But
they came one night. They disabled the alarms and entered
our home before I even knew they were there. They bound
up my mom and brother, Serg, first. I've never stopped hearing their screams." I sucked in air, my voice quivering.
"Such screaming."

Gabriel lowered his head, as if he were hearing Zel's
screams, too.

"For a few seconds—they seemed like hours—I couldn't
move from my bed," I said. "But when I finally started to
get out of it, I went for the pistol under the mattress frame.
Then one of . . . them . . . barged through the locks on my
door and—"

Chaplin let out a soft, woeful yowl. Gabriel stared at the
ground. Was he picturing me under the greedy hands and
bodies of human monsters?

Maybe, because when he glanced back up, his eyes had
gone red.

I let him assume what they'd done to me. It hadn't been
full rape, but there were other nightmares bad guys brought on.

"I wish," he said, "I could've been there to bleed for you,
to take all the pain. *I* could've quickly healed from it."

"Maybe on the outside." We all healed faster on the outside.

He didn't answer.

I went on. "Before my dad had quit his job, he'd grabbed

Chaplin from the lab, so my dog was young, fresh out of training. But by the time those men got to my room, he'd already been shot. They thought he was dead, yet they had no idea he was an Intel Dog. Still, Chaplin was in no shape to help me. It was my dad who barged into my room with his gun, and he wasted some of the men. The others escaped."

I ran my hand to the side of Chaplin's head. He leaned against me. "Then Dad took me to the panic room, where we had to watch on screens as my mom and brother were set upon with a . . ."

Careful, Chaplin said, shutting Gabriel out again.

I righted myself, thinking of clear water and of being held up by its cleansing cradle. I thought and thought of it until I was ready to talk again.

"I wanted to get Mom and Serg into the panic room, too, but my dad started grabbing weapons and told me not to move an inch. Then he left. He . . ." I paused, minding my words, then whispered, "He accidentally killed Mom and Serg in the gunfire. Accidentally." I swallowed. "I'd turned off the screens by then. I couldn't watch."

"What about your dad? What eventually happened to him?"

Dad.

I'd said enough by now.

Chaplin came to my rescue, telling Gabriel only what he needed to hear. *Dmitri brought Mariah out here and spent years making sure she'd have somewhat of an existence. Then, when he thought he'd done his job, he ended his life.*

We all sat there. No condolence or platitude would fill the emptiness.

Chaplin—logical, stalwart Chaplin—put a merciful cap on the conversation. *This is Mariah's bottom line—running somewhere else ends up being as useless as staying. So what's the choice? Is there ever one?*

"But if you stayed," Gabriel said, "Stamp would ultimately come into your home, just as those intruders did."

I thought of Chompers on my visz screen, then the other

bad men who'd crept into our territory—scum who deserved what they'd gotten.

"Not necessarily," I said.

Gabriel was taken aback at the force and roughness with which I'd said it.

I leveled off my voice. "If anyone comes round these parts with the overt intent to harm me or mine, they'll pay. And now that Stamp's done with all his good-neighbor talk, he's going to pay. Believe me. Zel was right—there comes a time when enough is enough."

I could feel the heat in my eyes, the fever, and Gabriel seemed to notice, too. Chaplin rubbed his face against my leg, bringing me back.

Gabriel looked at us, as if the sight of me and my dog touched even a vampire. He looked so isolated sitting across from us, but I wondered if finding out what'd happened to Abby would erase it.

As if he'd taken up some sort of personal stake in protecting me and Chaplin, he started to walk out of the room. "I should check on the oldster, then round the group up again. There'll be better safety in numbers now that the shit's really hit. We can't sit here waiting to get plugged one by one. And we need to decide whether we're going to run or . . ."

I followed him out, Chaplin trailing as Gabriel halted near the exit to my room, resting his hand on the doorframe.

"I'm sorry to hear about your trials," he said, as if believing he needed to say something to me. Anything. "I truly am."

Cold, even for his sort.

Chaplin said, *And what now, Gabriel?*

"You tell me." Gabriel peered down at the dog, and there was a hint of a sad smile on his lips. "You had plans all along, didn't you? Did you plan on using me, the vampire, to kick Stamp's ass in the end? Is that why you shielded my identity? Well, the time for that is gone. I'd get one bite in and, if Stamp is as smart as I think he is, he'd have a machete handy to lop off my head. Then he'd rain down fire on all of you because you were harboring a monster." Gabriel cocked his head. "I'm sure that's not the outcome you'd been hoping for."

Gabriel had to be right, and the plan shamed me. Chaplin had promised my dad to protect me to the end. That was just what he'd been doing.

The dog sighed as Gabriel continued to the lounging area. I followed, wanting to apologize for the deviousness. But when we saw the living area, we all stopped at the overturned crates and scuffed-up dirt. The oldster had gone overboard.

Good thing the others had gotten him to his domain.

Before any of us could comment, a spasm of movement lit over a visz screen—a woman I'd never seen before, her mouth moving as she sat in front of the lens outside. In back of her were the three lashed poles. A bare, hanging rope was the only reminder that the demon had ever been there. The carrion feeders had taken their fill, and they'd obviously decided to go somewhere else instead of waiting in ambush round here tonight. Lucky her.

Gabriel turned up the volume as I stood next to him with Chaplin.

The woman was in the middle of a message to us, using Old American speak. Her dark hair was slicked back, her eyes Asian-exotic, her skin dark in the night vision.

"—hope you won't ignore this invitation, Mr. Gabriel. A good night to you."

Then the woman nodded, as if tipping a nonexistent hat to the visz. The image disappeared, only to be replaced by the beginning of the same transmission.

What the . . . ?

"Did she hack into the lens box to send a looped message?" I asked.

No one answered as the woman continued.

"I've been sent by Mr. Stamp to cordially invite the man who shot up the compound to a . . . diplomatic meeting," she said. "Mr. Gabriel, I believe, is the one who paid us a visit." The woman's eyes seemed to darken. "He killed a couple of my friends tonight."

And it was warranted after what they did to Zel, I thought.

"Mr. Stamp," she added, "requests neutral ground—the gully a mile off, over that old mine where the loom trees are thick. The time is midnight, stroke of twelve. And he comes alone, because Mr. Stamp is going to show up solo, just as a display of his faith in our continued attempt to work matters out with your lot." The woman came closer to the lens. "And here's a personal message from Mr. Stamp. He knows what the community's been hiding, and if Gabriel shows up, Stamp will think twice about telling. We hope you won't ignore this invitation, Mr. Gabriel. A good night to you."

I didn't move, even when the message started again, because I was still hearing the one part of that message: *What the community's been hiding . . .*

Gabriel spoke over the repeated request. "So Stamp does know I'm a vampire and that you've been sheltering me. The crewman who saw my fangs didn't die and he lived to tell."

"You can't go to that kind of meeting," I said, ignoring his take on what was happening.

"I *can* go," Gabriel said. "You heard her. I'm a menace to Stamp but your community will surely learn how to obey now, because of Zel's death. You're not in his sights. Stamp aims to clear the monster out, just as he did with that demon. And I'm not about to put the people who've sheltered me in any more danger than you've already experienced." He paused. "But maybe there's even a way around this."

"What?"

"What if I could show Stamp that he's wrong? That I'm *not* a vampire."

Was he bent? "But you are."

"Maybe I can convince him otherwise, in spite of what his employee might've told him. For all Stamp knows, what his man saw was a trick of the night or the result of an excited imagination. Besides, if I end up needing weapons—which I probably will—I'll bring enough to show him I don't depend on fangs." Gabriel turned off the visz, blanking the messenger. "If I can show Stamp that I'm not bringing my vampire to any fight, then it takes the heat off the community, and there'll be nothing for the kid to tell anyone about your sheltering a monster."

He was taking too much on himself, like some kind of willing savior. Like he was taking that longing for humanity that I'd sensed in him when he'd peered into me too far.

"But—" I said.

"Mariah, be logical. Stamp showed up here earlier, willing to make amends in his own way. He strikes me as having his own code, just as Zel did. I can take him on." He grinned with the bitter weight of truth on him. "I have a code, too, I suppose, and it's not something a man turns his back on."

My blood began a slow simmer, and I knew the fever was reflected in my eyes.

"What was it that Zel told us before she went out there?" he added. *"I thought I'd outlive the day when I'd encounter pure evil again, and I can't watch it grow and take over now. I won't."*

I felt myself twisting up, getting more upset as Gabriel continued.

"Zel was right about all that, Mariah. There're bigger things in this world to fight for. I even watched Zel die standing up for those things. And if you're going to stay here, refusing to run, I don't intend to sit by and watch ever again."

"You can't win in this," I said, my voice gnarling. The peace had faded. "That's logic enough. You go there without using your powers and you definitely die."

"I'm already dead," he said.

"Are you?"

My impulsive question put a memory between us: when he'd been inside me, pure and almost human again. When he'd been a man, not a vampire. It hovered, almost melting the air.

As the palpability of it singed into me, I felt a weight, because Gabriel was willing to sacrifice himself for us, and for ideals that seemed to keep his world—mad as it was— together. But I couldn't let him. It just wasn't right.

No matter how useless it might be to fight, I didn't see any other choice.

I blocked him from going anywhere. "You're not doing this."

He only smiled, as if thinking that I had to put up such a front. He'd end up going because there was no other way to get Stamp to leave us alone.

He began walking toward the weapons wall, obviously intending to extend this human thing all the way by using ammunition other than fangs, speed, and strength. He wanted to keep from relying on the powers that would betray us all if he used them.

Knowing there was no other way to make him see some sense, I extracted my knife from its sheath, then moved quietly behind him. Then I put the blade to his throat.

"I told you," I said, my voice almost unrecognizably rough as my emotions escalated. "I'm *not* letting you go out there."

23

The predator hunched on the boulder where, earlier in the night, Gabriel had hidden himself, killing and maiming the employees with the aid of a shotgun. Obviously, the bloodsucker had needed such a weapon to pick off Stamp's men at a long distance; the firearm had taken the place of close-range fangs.

Using the tips of his fingers to test the dried blood that the vamp had sprayed on the rock when he'd been shot, the predator marveled that the texture could be the same as a human's. One of his men—dead now after Stamp had ordered a crew member to put the severely wounded guy out of his misery—had seen Gabriel flash fangs, and that was enough to go on. Luckily, the dead man had been in the group who'd hunted the demon and, like others in the party, he'd been carrying a silver-bladed knife as a possible weapon to control the monster. They hadn't known what sort of demon it was before they'd discovered that brass was its bane.

At any rate, the silver had brought the fang out in

Gabriel—a vamp who'd covered his true nature with a respectable decency that spoke of constant vigilance.

It'd been a long time, but the predator had always ended up cornering his vampires and were-creatures, although he couldn't say the same about demons, really, since he'd never hunted one before.

He stood up from the rock, then wound his way down through the gauntlet of boulders until he reached the clearing, where the crew was cleaning up the dead bodies, including Zel Hopkins's. The carrion feeders were stalking the blood and gore from above, circling, but the crew had their own guns out, warding the grotesques off.

One of the employees, who was preparing to drag Zel Hopkins's corpse to a grave, glanced up, his lower face covered with a kerchief. The moonlight revealed a stunned glaze to his eyes. None of the men had expected this when they'd signed on to come out to the New Badlands to work the land for water. None of them had expected to go after a demon, much less fight off a vampire with a hero complex.

"Mr. Stamp," the crew member said, addressing the predator.

Stamp, a.k.a. the man who was going to wipe away the last of their worries when he met Gabriel at midnight, nodded back. While he was busy with Gabriel, some of his men were going to take advantage of the distraction and go to the scrub community to clean them out once and for all. After tonight's rites of passage, his crew certainly had enough confidence to go about it.

It was a shame, though, because Johnson Stamp really had wanted to find good neighbors out here. But he'd taken enough of the scrubs' crap. At first, he'd been loath to kill the settlers because he had no proof beyond suspicion that they were outlaws. Now he knew, and there was justice in going after them. After facing down Zel Hopkins, he'd seen that they were *all* beyond redemption. He wanted to separate Gabriel from the community because vamps could be stronger and prone to inflict more mental as well as physical damage than many other monsters. More important, the vampire just might have it in him to play the hero again and screw up an attack on the scrub sanctuary.

Odd, how the vamp was so protective of the scrubs. Stamp had never seen the likes of it. He only wished his men had realized Gabriel was a monster when they'd found him in that cave several dusks ago, roughing him up for trespassing on Stamp's territory. The guy must've tried hard to hide his vampiness during the scuffle. Kudos to him for that.

Gunshots blasted as the crew worked at holding off the carrion feeders, and the employee who'd greeted Johnson Stamp got back to dragging Zel Hopkins's corpse away, kicking aside a blood-soaked feather at the same time.

As Stamp walked off, he was glad he'd brought most of his past life with him into this new one, because some things should never be let go of, including weapons. After one of his crew had identified that demon tonight—and thank-all the employee had been savvy enough to interpret the signs of a monster in time—Stamp had realized that no matter how hard you labored, the past would always be there.

He'd tried everything to get rid of it early on, though, after his parents had gone from smiling shoppers in a marketplace to bits of blood and bone after a suicide bomber for a monsters' sympathy group had come at the wrong time to the wrong place. After their deaths, Stamp had been scooped up by the government and deposited into an orphan camp, where he'd been educated, his talents and bottled aggression then put to good use early on as a civil servant who kept society clean. But just as he was getting good at his job, they'd told him that his efforts were no longer needed. The dirt of society was under control.

The layoff had left Stamp aimless, even at the age of twenty. But then, after the government had given him a pretty severance check to keep quiet about his service to them, he'd heard about a place out west, still pure enough after the bombings and brutal weather, and he'd redirected his verve for sweeping up the garbage from the street to something else.

He'd collected humans instead, liking how it made him feel, because where things like the dregs of society could never change, people like him could. Someone like Stamp could teach his new employees right from wrong, so he had set about doing it.

He'd even tried to prove this tonight, when he'd offered apologies to the scrubs for being wrong about them killing his men. He'd only meant to show them with the demon that they could all work together. But they hadn't seemed to see it that way.

Yet with what they'd been hiding, it was no wonder they had a tolerance for monsters.

Stamp rolled down the protective glove on his left arm and checked his personal computer screen for the time. 23:04. Almost one hour until midnight, when he'd meet the vampire.

There were more gunshots while his crew fired at the carrion feeders. But as Stamp looked to his right side, where some men were burying the employees whom Zel Hopkins had killed tonight—both of them with their damned eyes scratched out—he knew the feeders would be gone soon with the lack of dead bodies to compete for. And if the shades decided to stick round to hide and ambush him and his guys, they'd be sorry.

But soon the last of the grotesques was indeed shooed off, and Stamp was just about to go inside when he heard a noise from the boulders. In quicksilver time, he turned toward the sound, his weapon drawn from the holster at his side.

Just as fast, he raised his arm in the air, the revolver aimed toward the night sky, when he saw that it was only Montemagni, the woman he'd sent to the community to deliver the meeting invitation to Mr. Gabriel.

Mags had her hands raised as she descended. "Whoa, there. It's only me."

"You got the message to Gabriel?" Stamp asked, holstering his weapon. "No hassles from carrion feeders or scrubs?"

His employee nodded, lowering her hands as she came

to stand in front of Stamp. She was one of a few tough females on the crew—a former white-collar thief—and she'd taken to Stamp's second-chance program with gusto. "The shades had all gathered over here, attracted by the newer bodies. As far as the message to Gabriel goes, I looped it into all the viszes I could find above the ground."

"I guess," Stamp said, "we'll see if the vamp shows then."

"He will. If they have a brain among them, they'll give up one to save the many."

Stamp glanced at the bulging portion of moon in the sky. Then he caught Mags's frown.

"What is it?" he asked.

"Well, not that I doubt our capabilities here, but instead of meeting Gabriel tonight, do you need me to go to the hubs to find help in taming a vampire? I hear they're rough to face one-on-one."

"You want to find a retired Shredder who specialized in vamps?" Stamp asked.

"It's worth a try, I think."

Stamp smiled, but the gesture was stiff. "There's no need, Mags. We've already got a Shredder handy."

It took Montemagni a second to catch on to what her boss might be saying, but Stamp was already walking toward the cave-hidden entrance to his domain, ready to unearth the past he'd hidden in that baggage he hadn't been able to get rid of.

The silver bullets. The ash wood stakes.

Tools he'd used back in the day when he'd been recruited as a young Shredder on the government's payroll, special-izing in the termination of vampires and were-creatures.

24

Gabriel

The edge of the knife blade scratched against Gabriel's throat as Mariah held it against him.

She'd told him that she couldn't let him go to the meeting with Stamp, and he hadn't taken her seriously. Until now.

He didn't move. "If you know me at all, Mariah, then you know that a regular blade is only going to do temporary damage."

She brought the knife closer to his jugular, and he noticed her hand was shaking.

"I realize I need more to restrain you," she said in that anger-torn voice. "But don't make me—" It sounded as if a whimper chopped off her words, and she leaned her forehead against his back. "Don't make me force you to stay," she finished on a rasp that reminded him of the anguished strain in the oldster's voice as he'd been dragged away earlier.

He could hear her vital rhythms thrashing, stretching through the disorder of her emotions. As her other hand gripped his shirt, twisting it, he heard the material protest, seams popping.

Gabriel still didn't move, but this time it was because he didn't know what to make of her reaction. He'd witnessed . . . *felt* . . . her anger before, but this seemed beyond even that.

What was going on with her?

"Come on," he finally said. "Ease off now."

"I'm the one with the knife."

"And I'm the one who can disarm you within a blink."

Out of the corner of Gabriel's gaze, he saw Chaplin slinking out of his corner, shadowing the wall.

He appealed to the dog. *I might need your help here, boy. Mariah's not thinking straight.*

Chaplin sat on his haunches. *No, she's not.*

The dog's words had a tinge of fatefulness to them, and an accepting smile dawned over Gabriel's mouth. So here was the truth—Gabriel was, in a way, their hired gun. Chaplin had paid him by taking him in, saving his hide, and now the dog was expecting Gabriel to return the favor. He'd seen right through Gabriel, and he'd known early on what this particular vampire was looking for out here.

Redemption.

And he'd known Gabriel wouldn't have any other choice but this if he wanted to find it.

Smart dog. Dumb preter.

You got me, Gabriel thought to Chaplin. *But I suppose there was bound to come a time when I'd have to answer to someone for what I am, anyway.*

The dog seemed to smile, too—a sad acknowledgment. *Just don't let Stamp know what you are, Gabriel. Do it for you . . . and maybe even for us?*

It was a brassy request, but Chaplin knew Gabriel wouldn't give himself—or the sheltering Badlanders—away. He'd rather face Stamp as he was now than live as what he'd put behind him. An eternity of that was his idea of true death.

Mariah, who hadn't heard the silent exchange, spoke to her dog. "Chaplin, jump up to the weapons wall and bring me that steel cable."

The canine circled back and leaped up, catching a loop of low-hanging cable with his teeth. Then he veered over to Gabriel and Mariah, dropping the coil near her feet before backing up, his gaze on Gabriel, who knew exactly what the dog wanted him to do, even without any mind communication.

"There comes a time," Mariah said in that grief-warped voice as she used the tip of her boot to hook into the coil's center, then kick it up to where her free hand could grab it, "when we have to step out of the places that shelter us. Me and the rest, we always thought we could avoid that. And we did for a while."

"You still can," Gabriel said. "I'm not sure you're entirely clear on what could happen to you if you don't let me go."

"Oh, I know. We might have to pay with our very lives."

"Zel sure did. Do you want to end up like her?"

Mariah's breathing was quick and tight. "That's the other thing, Gabriel. There's no steel-clad proof that Zel's dead."

"I saw her die."

"You thought you did. But were you able to detect any life left in her body? You were too far away to be sure."

This was ridiculous. "Mariah . . ."

"Zel wouldn't have gone down that easy," she said. "There's a small chance that Stamp's still got her, and while everyone stays in a safe location for the time being, I could go to this meeting in your place, kill him, make my way to his domain, then find out whether Zel's dead for certain, and . . ."

That was where her crazy plan seemed to end, and Gabriel wondered where it'd all come from. Then again, if he were human, and his friend had been killed, wouldn't he be running on adrenaline, too? She spoke to Chaplin, her heartbeat churning in Gabriel's ears. "Cover him?"

Obeying, the canine sat in place, guarding Gabriel, who wasn't about to remind Mariah that wrapping him in mere cable would do even less good than using a blade on his throat. But she was apparently binding him and hoping that the time it would take for him to break out of those cables would give Chaplin an extra, valuable second to launch an attack.

She took the knife away from him and undid the length of cable. "After everything that's happened with Stamp, I can't imagine what price I wouldn't pay to see a reckoning for Zel's sake. She set out to do what none of us have had the guts to."

"Didn't you tell me not fifteen minutes ago that nothing—not fighting or running—would do any good?"

She grabbed one of his wrists, winding the cable around it, creating a cuff by using a catch on the end of the length. Then she slid the rest of it across his back and to his other wrist, where she made another useless bracelet.

"Now that Stamp has called you out," she said, "I know I was wrong about the fighting. With the bad guys who ruined my family, I never got a chance to do any while I was in that panic room. Maybe this is where *I* make up for it—not you, Gabriel."

He let that sink in. He realized that she'd gotten feisty after Stamp's invitation to meet up in the gully. It'd taken a threat to *him* to break her out of the fear that'd controlled her for so long.

But it was too late for that. "Mariah, I've got to go now."

She was roughly pulling on the cable, bringing his wrists together at his back.

"Mariah . . ."

She began to wind the cable down and around his legs, vising him.

Regretfully, Gabriel tensed, intending to yank apart the cable and get on out of here.

But Mariah was ready for that.

"No," she yelled, kicking his legs out from under him.

Off balance, he crashed to the floor, disbelief handicapping him for an instant—one in which Mariah flew into action.

Levering a leg onto his throat to keep him down, she

somehow found the angry strength to pull up his legs and continue wrapping the cable around them.

Survival mode kicked in, and Gabriel's sight reddened. He vamp-hissed in a warning.

When she looked at him, her chopped hair covered most of her face.

"Don't," she said in that garbled voice he barely recognized.

But he'd had enough, and he burst out of his bonds, then sprang to his feet.

Mariah was prepared for that, too.

She whipped out the knife she'd used at his throat, plus a longer blade that she crossed together to form the sign of the cross, which she knew would freeze him.

It was as if a bolt of silver split him in two, and he fell to all fours, agonized, not only because of the hopelessness embodied in the cross—the mental flash that he'd never win forgiveness, ever—but because Mariah was the one doing this to him.

"Chaplin," he heard her say in a pained tone, "fetch the crucifix billboard poster. The sight of it'll bind him. Hurry."

But the dog didn't move.

"Chaplin!"

He barked viciously at her, and through the haze of Gabriel's anguish, he thought he heard a snarled response from Mariah that was just as ferocious.

Then the canine sprang at her, knocking her over, breaking apart the blade crucifix and shattering the hold Mariah had on him.

Gabriel leaped to his feet as Chaplin pinned her face-down on the ground, her fingers digging at the dirt, guttural cries of rage making her thrash beneath the dog like a wild animal.

This wasn't like Mariah. She was so different—

Go! the canine mind-said to Gabriel. *Get your weapons and get on that zoom bike.*

With a cry, Mariah reached back at Chaplin, clawing,

and the dog snapped at her hand. Then he almost blew Gabriel's brain apart with the force of his next words.

Get out of here before I chase you out myself!

Gabriel didn't try to override the Intel Dog's brain, because there was no reason to. Besides, his familiar's rejection was too thick inside him for much else to rise above it.

So while the dog restrained Mariah, Gabriel grabbed everything he could—a revolver, a machete, knives, a grenade—from the wall, jammed them into his clothing, and then ascended the ladder, unlocking the door to the night.

He glanced back once more to find Chaplin giving him a look of such apology that Gabriel couldn't help but respect the dog's determination to save his mistress by whatever means possible. And with Mariah beneath Chaplin, moaning and fighting, her voice going low, hollow, Gabriel wished he didn't have to remember her this strange way if Stamp ended up getting the best of him.

He started out the door, and just as he was about to close it, Mariah cried out.

"Gabriel . . ."

His name ended on another moan, so twisted and tortured that he could only shut the door on it. If he didn't have to leave, he might've stayed to revel in the warped fact that he'd earned such a reaction from her—that he'd finally done something in his pitiful existence to deserve such an entreaty to come back to someone.

But he needed to leave it—*her*—behind, and he went to the waiting zoom bike.

He was going to show Stamp that no further warring was needed—that he wasn't hiding anything.

Testing the bullet wound on his arm, Gabriel found that it had almost healed to normal, unlike the injury from the silver on the other, which was still mending. Then he tried to wipe the last feral sight and sounds of Mariah out of his head, yet couldn't.

He revved the bike's engine and took off toward the loom

tree gully, the night drained of color around him while, in the sky, a lone carrion feeder that'd broken away from its group tracked Gabriel, just like a long, never-ending shadow.

25

Mariah

Chaplin still had me pinned to the floor, my face against the ground as my body roiled, heating, exploding in my frustration and grief.

Don't fight me, the dog kept saying. *I'm doing what's best for all of us.*

"It's over," I said, struggling to form words now. "Zel, the demon, Gabriel . . . I can't live with myself if I stay here while he does what we should be doing—"

Calm—down! Chaplin put his mouth to my neck, as if he were going to tear into it if I didn't obey.

I sank all the way into the floor, rage pushing through me as I half-cried, half-whimpered, my body pulling at itself, hurting so bad that I clawed at the ground. Through my unrestrained sobs, I asked, "Do you . . . *really* think Gabriel . . . is gonna satisfy . . . Stamp?"

If he doesn't, we'll be ready, Chaplin said. *But there's no reason for us to put ourselves out there when Gabriel's willing to do it for us.*

I panted, and with every passing second, my body

regained some calm, my fever cooling, my body pressing
back into itself so it felt near normal again. Only the vivid
memory of peace from Gabriel was what did it in the end.
The gift he'd given me.

And this was how I was going to repay him?

The dog backed off of me slowly, still keeping watch. *No
funny moves, Mariah.*

I let myself sob some more, still facedown on the ground.
Minutes went by while I scrabbled at the floor, my fingers
bleeding, my very bones hurting with all they'd been through.

It was only when I heard Chaplin sit on his haunches that
I stopped lying to him.

No more lies . . .

I sprang at him, grabbing him by the neck and pinching
a pressure point—a sure way to overcome an Intel Dog.
Soon enough, Chaplin passed out.

My breath heavy and hollow in my chest, I arose. I picked
up my knife from where it was lying and, in the blade, I
caught a demented glimpse of my eyes.

My livid green eyes.

Sprinting, I clamored out of my domain to the oldster's
quarters, where I knew my neighbors were tending to him.
I burst through the unlocked door, and they all looked up at
me: Hana tending the prone oldster, who was chained to his
bed. Pucci. Sammy.

"*Goddamn* it, Mariah," Pucci said, looking me up and
down, as disgusted as usual. But he had more reason to be
right now, while I was in this terrible state. Every time I got
like this brought trouble.

My breath came raggedly, hollow in my chest. Body,
gnarling inside. Hot . . . stretching . . .

Sammy was already coming toward me, motioning to
the others. "Mariah, it's a good thing you came here. We'll
take care of you. Don't worry."

He sounded as scared as I felt at the thought of getting
outside our domains.

But for the first time, I *needed* to go out there, no matter
the consequences. I couldn't be afraid of what I would do.

Sammy reached for me, but my voice was a near growl as I lashed out at him. "Wait—listen to me. Please . . ."

And I told them about Gabriel and what he was doing on our behalf. I even told them what he was.

Before I was even done, the oldster had asked Hana to unchain him, and he got out of bed, stripping off his clothing.

"What the hell are you doing?" Pucci said.

"What we should've done before it came to this." The oldster wouldn't meet my gaze, and I didn't blame him. "It doesn't matter how you or I or anyone feels about Mariah. Stamp's people killed Zel. And if you just sit here like we've been doin' . . . then *fuck* you, Pucci."

One by one, they all came to their senses, too.

One by one, blood screamed, bones melted, bodies stretched, as we fully gave in to what we'd tried so hard to control.

And to hide.

. . .

26

Gabriel

Gabriel arrived at the gully all too soon, the throttled glow
of grayed moonlight spilling over the gulch's craggy
walls and flooding over the spindled loom trees, whose dark
branches were like webs, ready to catch prey.

As he veered the zoom bike into a copse of them, he tried
to scent out another presence. Or many presences, to be
more accurate, because he suspected it wasn't above Stamp
to put together an ambush with all his men in attendance.

But Gabriel only sensed one person nearby, somewhere
among all the trees, and he recognized the deliberate, cool
vital signs as Stamp's.

The kid had been waiting here for him, right on time,
stroke of twelve.

Images of Zel washed over Gabriel: her body helplessly
pasted against that cave wall with the knife in her shoulder.
Her screams.

Gabriel cut the quiet motor and got off the bike, and when
his boots hit the ground, he felt and heard a hollow thud

beneath his feet. The old mining shaft, he thought. Dead space beneath him.

Stamp's voice floated down the gully, filtering through the spun branches. "Mr. Gabriel. I had a feeling you'd be wise enough to come out here. Alone, too."

The kid probably had surveillance equipment on him, so Gabriel took casual shelter behind the bole of a tree, under the hunch of branches. "That's what you asked of me, Stamp."

Unless the kid was an expert with any vampire-killing weapons he'd managed to rustle up within the last few hours, this could be a manageable confrontation. Gabriel would just make the case that he and the other neighbors would pose no further danger—he'd prove they were all human and willing to call off any brewing wars between them. He could fix this situation, but he was definitely prepared should it go awry.

Stamp got to the meat of the matter. "As my messenger said, I know what's been going on in that community of yours. You, Mr. Gabriel . . ." His disembodied voice seemed to wander among the branches, getting lost until he started up again. "To think—when I initially met you, I saw a man I could've come to respect. Someone who seemed to have low tolerance for rudeness and wrong, although he'd inadvertently fallen in with a crowd of scrubs. But I was mistaken. And I'll give it to you—you hid your baser qualities."

"And what would those be?" Gabriel rested his hand on the butt of the revolver he'd tucked into the waistband of his trousers.

"Let's not treat each other like asshats," Stamp said, sounding as if he'd come a little nearer. "You know what you are, and you were smart to keep it hushed for as long as you could."

There was a bladed nick to the kid's voice, and right off, Gabriel could tell that Stamp had some kind of history with monsters. Maybe one had gotten to his family. Or maybe he'd only been set down to sleep each night, nursed by tales of the bogeymen who ran the streets, waiting to feast.

Gabriel kept looking around him, sweeping his gaze over the unfriendly landscape—the seething sky, the rocks, the grasp of branches over his head—but didn't see any sign of the kid moving around.

"Stamp," he called out. "Just say what you brought me here for, because I'm not in the mood for beating around any bushes. I want to know what you intend to do with my friends."

A stretch of near-silent night.

Then the kid spoke, and he sounded even closer. "I'm focused on only you right now. A dirty abomination. A *vampire*."

"No. I'm as human as anyone."

Gabriel said it with all the conviction he owned, because he'd started half-believing the lie, and hearing Stamp define him as a monster when he'd made such strides away from it caused him to clutch the butt of his revolver even tighter.

"Come out in the open and prove me false," Stamp said.

"So you can take a potshot at me with a gun?" Something like anger screwed into Gabriel. "Listen—if you're keen on exacting an eye for an eye because of me taking out some of your crew as they were killing Zel, that's one thing. I'd understand your ire. We might as well make this a fair fight without an ounce of cowardice involved."

Unbidden, Gabriel realized that he wasn't even halfway through making up for what Stamp and his crew had done to Zel. But that wasn't why he was here.

Reason, he thought. He had to see if he could reason with Stamp.

He could hear the kid's vital signs getting closer, the measured thump of his heart the most ominous sound in the night. Gabriel's fangs itched to come out, but he pushed the defensive urge back.

"What I did to Zel Hopkins was necessary," Stamp said. He'd halted his progress where the acoustics were deceiving, where his words bounced off the gully walls, making Gabriel think he was here when he could've been there.

Gabriel didn't stir. He only waited, just as Stamp had been so patiently waiting.

The kid said, "She attacked us first, and, insultingly, it was just after we'd come to you with white hankies waving. The only way we could initially stop her was with a weapon that a member of the crew had at hand. My employee had one of the knives we'd tried on the demon earlier."

The blade sticking out of Zel's back . . .

But . . . that knife had been used on the demon hunt? And what did Stamp mean when he said that using it was the only way they could initially stop her?

Before Gabriel had time to figure anything out, he heard a scrape over the dirt—footsteps that caused reverberations under Gabriel's own boots—and a shift of what sounded like hard leather against soft. Suddenly, Stamp was in the open, twenty feet in front of Gabriel, framed by the loom branches.

He looked . . . different.

Part of it was the clothing he wore. Leather armor that caught the glower of the moon, long gauntlets, heavy boots. The other part was the weapons he was carrying—the guns holstered at his hips, the bandolier of bullets worn over a shoulder and across his chest . . .

. . . and the complicated mass of steel peeking up from the sling on his back.

Gabriel recognized the last piece of equipment, just from the design. He'd heard about chest punchers before.

A Shredder, Gabriel thought, the hair on his skin rising. It was said that only a Shredder who hunted vampires used punchers to anchor to a monster's chest, rip it open, then mangle and burn a heart in one fell swoop.

It hadn't been only the monsters who were undertaking an exodus from the hubs, Gabriel thought. It was the out-of-work hunters, too, and Stamp . . . yeah, Stamp . . . must've been one of the young ones the government had recruited without shame.

Gabriel's spine arched, just like an animal that'd been cornered. But it'd be the end of him if Stamp saw him now.

Again, he realized that Stamp had no scent, but now he knew why. The kid had neutralized himself with Shredder expertise. Still, Gabriel acted as a human would, refusing to run or beg for his existence. If he could fool Stamp, it might work, because Shredders were supposed to have strict codes about killing only monsters. . . .

The kid's arms arced by his sides, as if he were ready to draw at the slightest hint of Gabriel's vampire. In turn, Gabriel strained under the urge to spring at Stamp and tear him apart before the Shredder could do the same.

"The knife," the kid said, clearly taking up the conversation about Zel again, "was silver. You should know all about silver and how it affects you as well as how it tamed Zel Hopkins."

"Zel was no demon," Gabriel said, even though the words sounded weak. He was recalling how those two men Zel killed had died with their faces mangled. . . .

"You're right," Stamp said. "Zel Hopkins wasn't a demon. Thanks to my security cameras, after I heard my men screaming outside and I saw their faces being ripped off with Zel Hopkins's freakish claws, I had a pretty good idea of what she was."

Claws?

Stamp turned his head so he was assessing the spot where Gabriel still took cover with a sidelong look. Then he laughed.

"If I didn't know any better," he said, "I'd think you had zero idea."

Everything was falling in on Gabriel now—Zel disappearing so quickly, Zel's strange death screech . . .

Stamp added, "And the longer I stand here, the more I do believe it, Gabriel. Then again, your ignorance makes sense. You were masterful at keeping your monster from me, but Zel Hopkins was, too—were-creatures can contain themselves much better than your sort. They're absolutely human when the moon or emotion doesn't pull at them, but when they change . . ." The kid laughed freely now. "How was it that the community didn't tell you what she was?"

Gabriel was speechless, and Stamp was enjoying taunting him too much to stop.

"I never caught a vampire living alongside a were-creature. Both species would run with their own kind out of preference, and vampires used to be a bunch of loners, to boot. Of course, there's ancient lore about alliances between the two groups, but this is rich. You and Zel Hopkins, in the same community. Did she know about *you*?"

"There was nothing to know," Gabriel finally said.

Laughter again. The more Stamp found this amusing, the more Gabriel burned, his gaze flashing deep red until he had to close his eyes so Stamp wouldn't see the glow through the branches.

The kid obviously knew he was getting to Gabriel, even without a weapon, and he put more verbal firepower into his attack.

"Know what my crew told me? They said that Zel Hopkins appeared from behind the hill, stalking over it, her clothes in shreds because of the change from this to that form and back again after she flew to us from your place. But we only figured that out afterward. At first, she was aiming her pistols and calling me out, just as if she wanted to do this the human way, without giving up her true identity. A couple of my men told her to back off, and when she didn't, they got out the guns."

Stamp's words sounded as if he were saying them with a tight smile. "She was so outraged that I suppose she couldn't help what came next. She turned, Gabriel. Turned into a were-owl—a cross between a bird and human, something whose systems underwent mutations until she became a creature of blood appetite. I hear it happens to all those weres, even what used to be plant eaters. That's how they get their water out here when they're in animal form, I suppose. Accidents of nature, just like a lot of things out here in the Badlands.

"She winged into the air in that awful half-human, feathered body, flew around, then gained momentum, attacking with her claws extended, her wing-arms spanned. She mauled my men but good with her claws and beak until that employee who'd been on the demon hunt earlier got her with the silver knife. The silver gave Zel Hopkins a decent shock, weakened her enough to take away her preter powers, and she turned all the way human again, yelling for me to come out and face her the entire while until I did emerge. I just had enough time to fit a silver bullet or two into my revolver before you rode to the rescue and I terminated her." He shook his head. "A monster. A thing way out here where I least expected to find any more. I thought you all were extinct."

Gabriel had been sieving Stamp's comments, taking what he needed and letting the rest fall away. It was the only course he had left if he wanted to restrain himself.

"Is that what you did with your life?" Gabriel asked. "Killed?"

Stamp's amusement seemed to disappear, his tone going flat. "I did my duty to humanity. And I'll keep doing it until your kind presents no more problems to the good of the world."

Thinking he'd calmed enough to open his eyes, Gabriel did, relieved that his sight was normal. He'd done it—gotten through Stamp's verbal assault.

He'd taken it like a man, too.

Now he stepped away from the tree, confident in the good he knew he had in him.

They faced off, Stamp ready to draw, Gabriel willing to do it, as well, his hand just above his revolver. The longer he didn't change into his vampire, the better his chances for survival, and he could see that in Stamp's expression as it went from utter cool to containing a shade of doubt about Gabriel's monstrosity.

He was thinking that Gabriel should've turned into a vampire by now, not be squaring off in a fight with just a bullet as an ally.

"I'm going to be departing this place soon enough," Gabriel said, "but I won't do it until I know that you're going to leave my friends alone."

The oldster. Sammy. Hana.

Mariah.

Some kind of emotion must've come over Gabriel's face, because Stamp was still hesitating. Then a sympathetic yet pitying expression consumed the Shredder.

Gabriel knew what it meant. Stamp was thinking how naïve his opponent was. He hadn't changed his mind about Gabriel's vampirism at all. . . .

Instead of fearing Stamp's perseverance, Gabriel's anger at Zel's death rose up, inflaming him just enough to provide courage for what needed to be done now.

He went for his revolver, and Stamp drew, too.

But the kid wasn't raising his firearm—no, he flicked up a hand and a cross snicked out of the wrist of his gauntlet.

The silhouette of the holy symbol was black against the gloom of night, and before Gabriel's body jerked into itself, he reached for his revolver, skinned it, and fired.

He fell to his knees right before he heard Stamp dive to the side, dodging the bullet. With the cross out of sight, Gabriel rolled behind a tree.

Then he heard the eerie whirring sound coming at him.

Automatically, he sprung up to the branches of an adjacent tree, grasping the weave of them and flipping himself up into cover in the mass of darkness just before Stamp's bullet zipped by.

A Shredder bullet. The professional killers had gotten their nicknames from the projectile that would open into ripping blades upon impact, shredding a vampire's heart at longer range than a chest puncher required. If it didn't disable the heart thoroughly, it'd at least give a Shredder enough advantage to descend on the incapacitated vampire and behead it to ensure termination.

Gabriel stayed still in the hive of branches, waiting to see what Stamp would bring at him now. Next to his hand—the one that wasn't still gripping the revolver—he felt a tiny pinch. When he glanced over, he saw a little jaw bird opening its sharp-toothed beak to take a bigger bite of him.

Gabriel flicked it aside and bent down to get a view of where he thought Stamp had gone, behind another loom tree.

When he saw the nose of a weapon peeking around the bole, he knew Stamp was there, using a corner shot gun, which boasted a screen that extended away from the weapon, showing the target, even from around a barrier.

"Come on out, Gabriel," Stamp yelled, his voice echoing. "I'm going to get you in short order, anyway. You might as well not prolong the exercise."

"I'm not what you think I am." The statement surprised even Gabriel. But here he was, still trying.

Still believing.

Stamp didn't answer right away. Gabriel could see him scanning around with that corner shot gun.

Then the kid said, "Fair enough. I'll admit, the vamps I met back in the hubs would've turned full monster by now, just out of a desperation for survival. But you . . . You've got some discipline for a preter."

Gabriel knew why that was. Mariah. What she'd given him when he'd shared his sway with her. It was with him, even vaguely.

"Yes, sir," Stamp added, "you did react to the cross."

"You drew on me, and I thought it'd be a bullet, not a tired religious symbol."

He could see the corner shot gun's nose lower, then pull behind the tree.

Gabriel leaned forward. Stamp *did* have doubts.

But then the corner shot gun appeared once again, and this time it was focused on Gabriel's branches, as if the weapon had some kind of close-up mechanism that would unmask him.

Stifling a curse, he quickly slid down the bole, hitting the ground and slipping to another nearby tree. Then another. Then more . . .

Stamp's voice came from way back now. "Just make this easy."

Gabriel listened for the Shredder, but the kid was stealthy, and it wasn't until he saw Stamp's corner shot gun poking around the tree two down from his that Gabriel targeted his own weapon and fired.

Stamp's surveillance screen exploded with the impact of the bullet, and the kid dropped the gun altogether. But then Gabriel heard the rustle of dry twigs to his left, and he aimed there, seeing, too late, that it'd only been a tossed rock.

Then he felt a chill on his right side.

Gabriel darted his gaze over to find Stamp just ten feet away, his gun pointed up into the tree, the nozzle sparking and the Shredder bullet gnawing through the air toward him.

Diving to the ground headfirst, Gabriel let go of his revolver, feeling Stamp's bullet grind into his calf. He grunted as it dug through him, exiting the other side of his leg.

Silver. It'd had silver in it, and the weakness spread like a bloom of shriveled skin.

He gripped his leg, crawling for his zoom bike, which was only about six feet away. If he could just get to it, he could speed off much faster than his silver-addled powers would allow. Then, back at the community, he'd ask someone, anyone, for help in cleansing him with a drink of their blood.

Shit, why hadn't he thought to bring his flask?

The regret weighed him down as he crawled, inch by inch. Always it came back to this . . . being a vampire . . .

He slowed down, so weak, so tired.

Was it even worth going back to the way he'd been before?

"Gabriel!" Stamp was stalking him, approaching. "Damn it, you freak, why don't you just turn and then face me like a real vamp?"

Even as Gabriel flinched at the curse, he heard the frustration in the kid's tone.

The silver—much more than what he'd gotten from the cut of the knife earlier—spread up Gabriel's leg, breeding weakness, and he knew that aside from the knives and the machete and the grenade he'd grabbed back at Mariah's, playing on Stamp's frustration was all he had left.

Funny, but now, when he truly could use his powers, they weren't so available.

He saw the kid come into the open. Finding Gabriel near his zoom bike, Stamp holstered his revolver and reached over his shoulder, whipping out the chest puncher.

It resembled a long crossbow with clamps and cables. Unable to control his body, Gabriel felt his fangs needling his gums, and he groaned.

"You're not going to win!" Stamp said. "The way of the world won't let you win!"

Then he was right in front of him, the chest puncher aimed. But Gabriel had already slid a knife out of his back pocket, bringing it up to target Stamp's neck, where there would be no leather armor.

Neither man moved.

At least, not until Stamp started laughing again. This time it sounded real unsure.

"Mutually assured destruction?" the kid asked. "Is that how this is going to end?"

"Seems like we've been hurtling toward that conclusion all along."

The nose of the chest puncher dipped. "I could use that cross on you right now, you know. I could cuss up an unholy storm that would make you writhe until you screamed for me to stop. I only wish I'd had the chance to hunt down any remaining holy men in the hubs for holy water, too. That'd get a confession out of you."

"Do your job, then." The silver had rolled up to Gabriel's chest, lulling him, and he smiled.

It flustered Stamp. "Why do I have to resort to crosses and words with you?"

Gabriel could only whisper. "Because you were wrong about me."

"No. I can't be."

He wasn't looking Gabriel in the eye, probably because he'd been trained to avoid it with vampires. But Gabriel would use his knife rather than hypnosis or his voice, anyway, especially since the silver had doused his power.

The blade started to fall from his grip. He couldn't hold it up any longer.

"Silver," Stamp said. "It got to you, Gabriel. Open your mouth. Show me that fang. Show me some red in the eye."

"You're pathetic." The knife dropped to the ground.

A muffled sound of rage pushed out of Stamp, and he swung around with the chest puncher, using it as a club. A bang of agony splintered Gabriel's sight when the weapon slammed him in the skull.

Stars. Gabriel hadn't seen such clear stars in a long time, thanks to the red haze enveloping the atmosphere. . . .

"Turn, damn you to hell! You should've already turned!"

Nothing less would be good enough for Stamp, and that made Gabriel even more determined to stay a man, even though his chest was tearing itself apart at the curses.

Stay a man. No fangs . . . no red . . .

Stamp delivered another blow to Gabriel's head, then prepared for another—

Still ringing from the curses, Gabriel gathered what remained of his strength, lifting his hand and catching the puncher, and it trembled in his grip as he kept it between him and the Shredder.

He opened his eyes, still seeing through those stars, seeing Stamp hovering above him, breathing hard, smiling a little at Gabriel's determination not to turn.

Carrion feeders began to gather overhead.

When a burning sensation sizzled against Gabriel's skin, he was barely aware that the kid had struck without him knowing it, pressing a cross into his forehead.

Gabriel couldn't hold on to the chest puncher anymore, and he slumped all the way to the ground as he lost the weapon to Stamp.

"There!" the kid said. "See? We are what we are. There's always something that'll betray it in us."

Forehead crisped, Gabriel struggled to push himself back up, to show Stamp that he . . . was . . . a man.

No matter the common definition, nothing could take this moment from him.

Stamp pressed the cross against Gabriel's cheek this time, and Gabriel went down, again, eating dirt.

"I really am sorry it turned out this way," the kid whispered, taking the cross away. "I'm sorry for you, for Zel Hopkins . . . for everyone else in the scrub compound who's been hiding."

Gabriel was so discombobulated that the last part hardly registered.

Everyone else . . . ?

Everyone else?

A voice cried out from somewhere in the gully, and Stamp faced it. Gabriel remained on the ground, the grit of dirt in his mouth, the chars of the cross branding him from his skin down to the empty area where he would've stored a soul.

Standing, Stamp hailed the voice and, within a minute, one of his employees had sprinted over on FlyShoes. Gabriel couldn't really hear what the woman was saying, because he was too close to the black, near a place where he wouldn't have to be one thing or another anymore.

Even so, he inched his fingers toward the knife he'd dropped.

"The scrubs aren't there," the woman said in the thick of Gabriel's mental murk. Old American. The messenger who'd called Gabriel to the showdown?

Stamp started asking her questions, but Gabriel had already tuned out, the woman's words swirling around his head as if trying to find a catch to cling to.

He was remembering how Stamp had called Gabriel out via that message delivered by this very woman . . . Remembered how the community had been left unguarded . . .

Stamp wasn't talking anymore. Neither was the woman. There was just a slice of silence.

Gabriel tried to look past the swelling around his eyes to see that all of Stamp's crew had gathered around them by now, and they were glancing toward the top of the gully, frozen.

He sensed what Stamp's crew had just now discovered—vital signs rimming the gulch. Signs that Gabriel had deemed more appealing than any human's when he'd first

sensed them. Signs that *couldn't* have been so different from
any human's just because the air and water out here were
purer. . . .

"Fck," said one of the Text men.

Then, before any of the crew could draw weapons, mass
confusion rained down on the gully.

Explosions from what seemed to be grenades, cries from
a few groups of employees who were torn apart from the
multitude of blasts. Then came enraged cries, howls, hisses.
Human yelps of pain lit the air as whatever was attacking
them overcame the crew.

Gabriel attempted to push himself up, yet couldn't. The
silver was too much, but he did grab the knife. As he opened
his eyes the widest they'd go, he heaved the weapon toward
Stamp.

It hit him, though Gabriel didn't know where, and the
kid dropped the chest puncher, falling backward.

The woman standing over Stamp in her FlyShoes bent
down to catch him, yelling something inarticulate at Gabriel
just before taking a submachine gun and shooting a circle
into the ground around her and her boss.

Then, with a stomp of a FlyShoe, both she and Stamp
dropped down into the old mine, the descent covered by a
gush of dust.

Gabriel tried to yell, to relay where Stamp had gone to
anyone who'd listen, but then a spray of blood dashed over
his face, wetting his lips. Unable to stop himself, he licked
at it.

The taste wasn't sufficient to push out the silver weakness, but he had enough strength left to turn toward the
source of the blood.

The bleeder—one of Stamp's men—was screaming as a
creature gored him with its antlers.

Gabriel's vision wavered. A fever dream from the silver,
he thought. This couldn't be real. . . .

The attacker was only half-man, standing on his two legs
as he bent to thrust his antlers into Stamp's employee again.

The other half of him looked like a massive elk, with hooves, long legs, a short tail, and a tannish brown hide. . . .

It gazed at Gabriel, grinding its teeth, its eyes a glowing yellow in what almost resembled the grimace of a man's face. Then it used its antlers to push its victim's body to Gabriel before it ran away. With surreal fascination, Gabriel heard that the prey's heart had stopped beating, and though he wanted blood, he knew a dead man would poison him even more.

The elk-thing had galloped to where another creature—part woman, part mule deer—was pummeling another member of Stamp's crew with her front legs, rapidly stomping on his stomach. The elk man nudged her aside and gored this thug, too, tossing him away with his antlers.

Gabriel heard the first gunshot from the crew, and he had the presence of mind to pull the grenade out of a pocket, enable it, then toss it at what seemed to be the last bunch of employees who'd huddled behind a nearby boulder to take cover.

Rock and flesh burst into the air with the explosion.

Collapsing, Gabriel watched as he tried to gather more strength. Meanwhile, in his fever dream, he saw a man-scorpion, multiple limbs waving as it used pincers to crush two crew members at once while lashing its tail out to sting a woman who dropped the rifle she had been aiming at him. Next to the scorpion, a Gila monster–man was chewing down on an employee who'd already had his guts clawed out.

Gabriel's sight wavered again just as he heard a howl, an angry roar, and he rolled to his back, finding a wolf creature flashing its teeth, then tearing into two more employees at one time with frightening speed. When it had finished, the woman-animal tossed down its prey, then panted as it hunched and surveyed the scene for more targets.

Like the rest, this monster was bare of clothing. Its reddish fur bristled away from a slim body, its teeth sharp in a snout, its ears canine, its eyes a glowing green.

It paused, as if startled to find Gabriel looking at it. Then,

just before the silver crept over his sight altogether, he heard
the creature's vital signs—how they sounded like a livid
crash of notes that infiltrated him with a song he'd always
been on the brink of understanding. He felt a vague connection, a link he'd forged when he'd looked into those eyes
earlier tonight, before she'd fought him about going
outside—before her voice had become almost unrecognizable, before she'd fought so ferociously with Chaplin.

Gabriel remembered what Stamp had told him.

Everyone else who's been hiding.

He sank into the silver, which felt more like grief, as the
last thing he saw was Mariah's feverishly green eyes glowing in the face of a monster.

27

Mariah

A couple of hours later, my body aching, I huddled into myself while waiting for Gabriel to awaken from his resting spot on the floor of the common room, where all of us had laid him out.

In a way, I didn't want him to open his eyes, which had looked at me with such compassion and . . . Hell, I didn't know what it was, but I knew Gabriel would hold no tenderness for me now.

He'd found out why we'd been so secretive and, from this point on, there'd be no more lies.

No more for anyone.

The hatred I expected from Gabriel didn't mean I'd stopped feeling for him. Back at the loom tree gully, after the melee had gotten under control, I'd turned back to my good, human form. With my senses returned, I'd seen how weak he was, seen the cross wounds that marred his forehead and cheek. He'd passed out, and I'd assumed it was because of silver poisoning, so I'd opened my wrist to allow blood to drop into his mouth. Soon, I'd seen the shriveling effects of the silver on his skin fading, and I'd felt like at least one portion of the world was righted.

But only one.

While my blood had done its work, I'd searched for that bastard Stamp. Didn't find him anywhere—not in the old mine, or even at his deserted spread, where I took Gabriel's zoom bike to also see if Zel was being kept captive.

No.

At not being able to find her, I'd given in to my grief, running, crying out until my pain echoed under the sky. Every time I changed into a full were-creature, it was like I experienced everything from a distance. My rage was a vague thing, like someone else was screaming, howling, aching. It was probably the only thing that allowed me to think distantly afterward, too.

But not this time. Not when I finally had to face what I'd done.

By the time I'd gotten back home, I'd returned to my calmer human shape again. The others had the still-sleeping Gabriel safely ensconced, and I'd fed him more blood, then dressed and gone to a corner until he roused. A corner where, once again, I could beat myself up for all that I'd brought about.

Round me, my neighbors sat in stoic vigil, not a one looking at me, but that was nothing new. I'd forged a lifetime of earning their disappointment.

Even as I sat alone, there was one thing keeping me company. A tiny thrill—a flutter of joy I should've shunned. I'd been free tonight, let loose outside to do as much damage as I could. There were no boundaries I kept myself from crossing, no fear about blood.

No fear at all.

Still, freedom was the real problem, wasn't it? The lack of fear, the wildness, the unrestrained craving for raw, hot blood that I'd promised I would push aside, even to the point of denying it to myself. But I was just as much a bad guy as anyone, and I couldn't block it out or lie to anyone about it any longer.

How could I lie when I'd seen the look on Gabriel's face when he'd spied the animal in me, just before he'd passed out? He was the most honest and open amongst us, even as a vampire, and he hadn't been able to hide his surprise. Repulsion. In his eyes, I'd witnessed that mirror reflection I'd feared—the image of a monster directed right back at me.

I glanced at everyone in the room, knowing I'd have even more penance ahead.

The group had pretty much healed from the injuries sustained during the face-off. Thanks to the explosives and the element of surprise, we'd won—if you could even call it winning. Although Stamp's crew had been decimated, we guessed that he was still out there, thanks to the lack of a dead body for proof. If he'd retreated to the hubs along with the female crew member who'd helped him escape, it would take him a while to round up enough of a mob to come after us. And that was exactly why we'd never dared show ourselves in the first place—because we knew this was the price for being what we were. We just hadn't been willing to pay it before Gabriel had tried to do it for us.

By now, we had all cleaned the blood off our skin, nourished ourselves to revitalize our bodies, and dressed back into our clothes, mostly out of respect for Gabriel when he awakened. Before Stamp had come to the New Badlands, we hadn't minded clothing so much, but afterward . . . ?

Afterward, we had tried so hard to seem as human as we still believed we could be most days.

Across the room, Pucci was pretending I didn't exist. He'd been aggressive during the showdown, using the best weapons he had—antlers, speed, strength. But he hated me more than ever. The only reason he wasn't attacking me was that were-blood was toxic for us—it was Mother Nature's way of allowing different strengths of were-creatures to live together, I guess. It was as if she'd known that, one day, my neighbors would want to chew me apart.

"I can't believe we were brought to this point," he said, rubbing his arm, where he was obviously still sore. When our kind willed a change, it was harder on the body than a change during the call of the moon. "I can't believe we *had* to. If we'd just stayed in human form, Stamp would've never detected us."

"He turned out to be a Shredder," the oldster said. "Who knows what he would've discovered, no matter how well we hid? But now we need to think about the future—where we'll run, how much time we'll have to relocate."

He was kneeling by Gabriel's prone side, dressed in his usual earth-toned denim. The oldster was normally the last one to give in to his were-scorpion change whenever the moon was full; that was when a were-creature couldn't help giving in to the turning, although most weres changed every so often to let off steam. Heightened emotions could also bring on a turning, but the oldster didn't often give in to that sort of change. He had excellent control.

However, after Zel's death, the change had been all too easy for him. He'd been about as able to control himself as I had lately.

Hana was covered by her gray-brown robes again, but I could still see remnants of her mule deer form in her big, dark eyes, which were filled with discomfort from a willed change, too. Like the oldster and Pucci, she'd been true-born—a were-creature because of birth, not a bite, so she lived with all the changes pretty well.

"Zel had to have changed form in front of Stamp," she said to Pucci. "He knew what she was, and that is why he sent his men here while Gabriel was at the gully. We are only fortunate to have already left before they arrived for what no doubt was meant to be a surprise attack."

We'd seen evidence of the crew's presence all over the place in the overturned furniture and careless boot prints. Thank-all Chaplin had hidden from them just after waking up from my neck pinch.

Like Hana, I'd suspected that Zel had changed form in front of Stamp. Knowing what we knew about him now, it would have been only a matter of time before a Shredder identified all of us. If it hadn't been for Zel losing control, we might've even fooled him for a while, seeing as were-creatures didn't have their preter powers in human form and were hard to ID because of that. And we'd had the demon to pin the murders on.

Now I deflated at that, too. God-all, the murders of Stamp's men. That was another thing I'd have to confront tonight.

But at the moment, Pucci was bristling at Hana's comment, which he would take as "backtalk." In my corner, I kept my gaze on him for her sake. I was barely aware of Chaplin, who'd remained far and away from me.

He woofed, cutting the tension in the room, and since Zel wasn't round anymore to translate, I braved a few words to my neighbors about what my estranged dog had said.

"Chaplin says we should begin packing while we wait for Gabriel." I looked at the ground, wanting to do everything I could to win their forgiveness. "I can stay here with him if you all want to get started."

"No," Sammy said, grunting as he shifted position. He'd also be extra sore after changing back, too. "I want to be round when he wakes up, if anything just so he knows how much we appreciate what he did." He had his brown-and-orange hemp clothing back on. Like his mutated Gila monster form, he dressed himself to blend with the earth, but there was no covering his resentment at me right now.

"I cannot imagine a home better than this," Hana said.

"Anywhere that won't get us silver-bulleted to death will be better." Pucci crossed his arms over his big chest, furrowing his brow. "Frankly, it looks as if this territory's time is up, anyway. Bit by bit, we all found it. Then Annie came. And then that demon, who obviously scented out Chompers's mangled, messed-up body before the carrion feeders even got there. Bad timing for that particular monster."

Hana kneeled by Gabriel, checking on the progress of his healing wounds—the bruises and swells on his face, the cross burns. "Gabriel came to us, too."

When no one said anything, I could guess why. They

were miffed that me and Chaplin had never told them our
guest was a vampire or what my dog had planned for him.
But there'd been plenty of reasons for that. First, Gabriel
wasn't intending to stay very long. More important, Chaplin
hadn't wanted them to toss Gabriel out before he could be
of use against Stamp. He had fit right in. He'd even inspired
a few, like the oldster and . . .

Well, Zel.

I hung my head, dwelling on how Gabriel's presence had
brought matters to where they never should've been. As I'd
told him once, he summoned the good in me . . . but also
the wicked—the bad side I controlled in a body that occa-
sionally exploded with the force of my restraint. And Gabriel
had been the only one besides a full moon phase that'd ever
brought out the passion, the anger.

The bad.

I'd never felt half of what I did for him before, and the
learning process had affected us all.

Under Hana's palm, Gabriel moved his head, and everyone shifted, getting to their feet. When he groaned, Hana
murmured to him, just as she'd done earlier while the oldster
had privately self-healed his own head wound under her
calming guidance, which had only speeded his recovery.

When Gabriel opened his eyes, it seemed as if he didn't
know where he was. But then he saw Hana kneeling over
him, and the oldster, Pucci, Sammy, even Chaplin, who was
a few inches back from the rest of them.

Gabriel turned his head, as if hearing my quickened
pulse, seeking it out in my far corner.

The peace he'd instilled earlier was about gone. In fact,
I think it'd mostly left me when I was doing damage to
Stamp's men, obliterating every one of my targets except
for the woman who'd escaped with Stamp.

There was a glint in Gabriel's eyes, and for an instant, I
grabbed on to the possibility that my deceit, and even my
monstrous truths, didn't matter. But then he seemed to
remember how I'd no doubt looked in the raging moonlight

while standing on two feet, not quite a wolf, not quite a woman, teeth sharp and gleaming, eyes glowing, skin covered with fur, fingers clawed and nailed and tipped with human blood.

He kept watching me, and I also recognized sorrow.

A vampire's sorrow.

I heard myself talking. "I never wanted you to know. I did everything I could to keep you from the reality until the time came for you to leave us behind and not think another thought about us."

The oldster joined in. "Mariah's not the only one who was keeping you in the dark, Gabriel. We *all* believed you'd find your fill with Annie and be on your way."

Everyone except Chaplin, I thought.

"But then you stayed," I whispered.

"When . . ." Gabriel started to ask. Yet speaking seemed to be painful for him, even with the healing. Still, he forged on. "When were you thinking of telling me?"

Chaplin mumbled, and I spoke for him.

"Chaplin says that *he* told Zel to relay to everyone that they should stay mum about what we are until you went on your way."

My dog continued talking, and then I added, "He says that by being in your mind, even superficially, he could tell that you didn't suspect the truth. This gave him the leeway to introduce you to everyone, then organize his plan to keep us safe from Stamp."

Gabriel stared at the ceiling. "The plan to get me to fight for you. Isn't that right, boy?"

Chaplin nodded, then sank to the floor, burying his head in his paws and flashing those brown eyes in apology.

"I know," Gabriel told the canine, and I realized that Chaplin must've offered even more sorries mind-to-mind with the vampire. There was no need to hide a thought-link from us now.

Then he talked to the entire room. "It's gonna take a while for me to understand. To get over how you deceived me. But at the very least you came to help me when I needed it."

The oldster shrugged. "Took us long enough, but when Mariah told us you were confronting Stamp for our sake"— he shot a chiding glance to Chaplin, who'd sent Gabriel out there—"that was all that was required. Plus, there was Zel . . ."

His breath caught, and he pressed his lips together, controlling his response before it went too far, as it'd done earlier when he'd learned of Zel's death.

"There was no other choice but to go out there," Sammy said. "Having you fighting for *our* problems just didn't sit right."

"Besides," Hana added, "we were already revealed to the Shredder because of Zel."

Gabriel seemed as if he were still coming out of his silver-addled daze. "I remember when the oldster and I were going after her, and Pucci said to 'make sure Zel doesn't . . .' Then he was cut off by the door."

Pucci gave me a dirty look. He'd also been cut off by the sight of my revolver in his face because he'd been about to say too much in front of Gabriel.

I didn't regret *that* one bit.

Gabriel stared at the ceiling again. "Pucci was about to tell the oldster to make sure she didn't change in front of Stamp, wasn't he?"

The oldster coughed, and I knew he was hiding something like a sob.

"If you're still wondering if Zel somehow survived her attack," Gabriel said, "she didn't. I found out that Stamp used a silver bullet on her."

The confirmation stabbed at me. Earlier, when Gabriel had let us know that Zel had been shot through the heart, we hadn't known it'd been with silver. A regular bullet wouldn't have killed Zel. That was why there'd still been hope.

"I only wish," the oldster said, "I'd had more to offer during the fight than what my abilities allow."

And I wished I'd gone after her. I'd regret it for the rest of my life.

"All of your abilities," Gabriel said, "seemed to work just fine on Stamp's men. You were fast, strong. Every one of you held your own, especially with the aid of the explosives. But . . ." He shook his head, as if he still couldn't believe he'd seen us so altered.

Sammy said, "It's just that we believed we could finally live as humans out here. There was no point in telling a stranger like you about us. We'd be endangering our safety, and believe me, we had enough to worry about besides that."

Although none of them acknowledged it, I knew Sammy was talking about me. There was still so much Gabriel didn't know. So much I'd have to tell him.

No more lies, though.

Pucci had taken a seat on a crate chair. "We were all drawn out here because the land gave us what we needed and, person by person, we found each other. Until about a year ago, the oldster would watch for preter activity, then invite us in. Eventually we formed a clan." He laughed a bit. "Poor Sammy wasn't a birth-were, so when he came to us, he took some coaching."

Sammy said, "I'd left the hubs as a human, thinking I could make a go of it out here. A survivalist, they called me. But on the wall border one night, I came across a Gila—half-man, half-creature. It bit me and that's the last I ever saw of him. I continued on here, thank-all. I'm not sure I would've known what to do without the clan."

What he said was true for me, too. The community had helped. But help in and of itself hadn't been enough.

Hana said, "We were not open to accepting new members when you came."

"Probably a good thing, seeing as I don't quite fit the mold," Gabriel said lifelessly.

"Maybe not, but the Badlands actually treats us in particular better than most places," the oldster added. "In were-form, our bodies acquire, conserve, then recycle water, just

like all good desert animals. Actually, every were adapts
out here."

"And what about you, Mariah?" Gabriel asked.

I startled. He was talking to me in a civil manner.

"Are you a born were-creature or are you bitten?" he
asked, but there was a coolness in his eyes.

"Bitten." I locked gazes with Chaplin, letting him know
that I wasn't hiding behind half-truths this time. "When
those men attacked my family in Dallas . . ."

I hadn't told Gabriel everything before because it
would've exposed me.

The oldster took pity on me, just as he usually did.
"Those bad guys had a chained werewolf with them. They
thought it'd be funny to threaten people with it. That was
their big weapon of the night."

"The werewolf is what got to Mom and Serg," I said, the
lining of my stomach starting to quiver. "After my dad got
me to the panic room, he grabbed a silver letter opener from
his desk. It was the only silver we had, but it took care of
that wolf when he stabbed it and it went back to human form.
Still, he . . ." I grabbed a fistful of my shirt. "My dad didn't
see what happened to me before he took me out of Dallas,
out here."

"The story you told was a lie, then," Gabriel said. "You
didn't mention a wolf."

"Again, Gabriel, you were going to leave. We didn't want
you to carry the knowledge of what we are with you."

Hana spoke. "Mariah . . ."

No more lies. "Things are different now, so I'll say it
truthfully. Before the bad men brought the creature to Mom
and Serg, half of them cornered my mother and brother with
more conventional weapons while they let the werewolf
loose to stalk me. The other half laughed and laughed as
that . . . thing . . . bared its teeth, nudged my legs with its
snout, nipped at my nightgown, tore at it. They taunted me
while I tried not to scream. I . . . I couldn't move, not even
when it brought my gown up. They laughed and laughed

more, goading it, and it nicked me on the thigh with what I thought was its claw. I had my eyes closed. I didn't know. Then my dad came in with his guns, but he didn't see what came before."

I hunched into myself even more. "Dad killed some bad guys in my room, and the rest were wounded as they escaped, but not the werewolf, because he didn't have any silver in him yet. So the thing ran to where my mom and Serg were. My dad got me to the panic room, and while he was fighting everyone off, I cleaned my wound, thinking that would be enough. Just a scratch, I kept thinking. That's all it was. Chaplin was passed out, so he couldn't do anything. My dad thought the wound wasn't a real bite, either—nothing like what my mom and Serg had, and that's why I think they probably begged him to end their lives, because they knew. They were torn up from the bites and their self-healing abilities hadn't kicked in yet, but they still knew. Then, a couple weeks after we'd left Dallas, the first night of the full moon came."

The room was quiet.

The oldster said, "By then it was too late. Dmitri wouldn't kill her. He told me once it was because guilt was eating him about being unable to save his wife and son, and he was going to make it up to them by seeing that Mariah got better. He wasn't going to give up on her. He tried to invent a bunch of were-creature cures, but none of them worked."

I could testify to that, because I'd tried all of them—wolfsbane potion, feyweed smokes. "The thing is," I said softly, "I didn't want to die. Dad kept telling me we could overcome what I'd been infected with, and I thought our prospects were looking up when we found the New Badlands, with the others here. He even did his best to chain me and then fortify himself in his room during a full moon phase or trouble."

"But," the oldster said, "it was all too much for Dmitri." Everyone seemed to be waiting for me to tell Gabriel just why that was, but I wasn't going to do it in a room full of onlookers.

"All your vital signs," Gabriel said, oblivious to my dilemma. "I should've realized right off that you were different from humans. Especially . . ."

He glanced at me.

"Especially *my* signs?" I asked. "Do I sound different to you?"

He looked so bruised that I could barely stand it.

"Yeah, you do," he said. "It's almost . . . a calling." His light gray eyes cut through the swollen tissue round his eyes, which had been healing even since he'd gotten back here. But there were still the fading marks of the cross on his skin. "I have to wonder if I hear you that way because I'm connected to canines as a vampire. That's why I was able to have Chaplin as a close familiar, not just an animal to summon. Not that it did me much good."

The dog twitched, but there'd been no bitterness in Gabriel's tone.

The oldster reached out to take Gabriel's hand. "You did good, and we thank you for that. A million times, thank you."

The others joined in, and even though it sounded as if that was that, I knew the night was far from over.

"I'd like to speak to him alone," I said.

Hana offered me a sympathetic glance. But then again, when Pucci wasn't round, she'd been one of the most relatively tolerant of my issues, besides Zel and the oldster. Hana had been like that with Annie, too, always going behind closed doors to talk with her, never telling anyone else a word of what was said.

As everyone but Hana and Pucci moved toward my door, I didn't tell them to stay out of my domain. The viszes were the most varied there, and I suspected that Sammy and the oldster would want to listen in on the common-area link besides scanning the outdoors for any signs of Stamp's premature return.

Pucci and Hana went to their own domain, where there would also be a common-area visz, but Chaplin went into my place, too. I watched him go, wishing things were better between us. Wishing I hadn't hurt him in so many ways.

After they were all gone, I sat on a crate near Gabriel, sucking in a breath at my soreness. If only I could get nearer to him. But even though he seemed to accept what we were as a community, there was still an invisible wall between us.

A lack of trust. And I'd built it.

"They've put up with me for a long time," I finally said. "I suppose it's because of my dad and how much he did for the community before he poisoned himself with some calantria from outside. But before that, he made them all promise to protect me—just as Chaplin did—and teach me to forget all the anger and how to survive in calm like they have. And as much as I'll always be grateful to them for doing that, sometimes I wonder if I shouldn't have left months ago."

Gabriel didn't say a word, and it wasn't because he was too tired. He looked better now that the silver had been chased away. It was just that he had nothing more to say to me.

I tried not to let that stop me from the inevitable. "Once, you told us that the passage of time wasn't going to erase our problems, and it disturbed me more than you'll ever understand, because, without you knowing it, *I* was the cause of those troubles."

I allowed that to sink in for him. But his only reaction was the tensing of his jaw under those bruises.

"Maybe," I added, "I even made matters worse by not telling you exactly how I work—how I'm like a spring that's always being pressed down until it shoots up when the controlling force can't hold anymore."

"What're you trying to tell me?"

I blew out the breath I'd been holding for . . . how long now? It felt like years.

"Just as I said," I whispered. "I'm the cause of everything. It wasn't a demon that was killing Stamp's men, Gabriel."

He sat up, and the horror on his features made me feel like I was a monster through and through, even in human form.

God-all, I couldn't look at him, see that reflection glaring back at me—the self-hatred he'd carried along with him through all his travels. It was mine now, and I wished I could go back to a time when no one outside the community knew just what I was.

Then he lowered his head, pressed his hands over it. Was he thinking that he'd touched and been inside this brutal, bloodthirsty *it*? That he'd taken some of such a creature— my blood—inside *him*?

But wasn't he a monster, too? Hadn't *he* wanted to bite *me*?

"At first," he said, "I thought I was the one killing those men."

It was another stone on my chest, making it harder to breathe. "I'm sorry. You don't know how sorry I am for everything."

He struggled to his feet, and I stood, too, afraid he was going to leave. Explanations wouldn't condone my actions, but maybe it would . . .

What? Pave the way for my rehabilitation?

Even though I doubted that, I said, "We don't have heightened powers in our human forms—only when we're changing. That naturally happens every twenty-eight days, when there's a full moon phase, sometimes for three nights in a row as it waxes, gets to its peak, then wanes. When the night's at its darkest, that's when the full moon is at its worst for us, and we're compelled to go out and hunt for whatever we need to soothe the wild were-creature side of us."

Gabriel stalked away from me, but didn't leave.

"We can't stop ourselves from changing during a full moon," I said, "although the more mature we get, the more control we have on other nights. We can also force a change to happen, just like some of the others did tonight when we needed to fight. But there's a price for that, because it's not organic." If I'd forced a change during a less emotional time, my very bones would be groaning, my skin burning— although both elements had become more elastic since I'd been bitten. "It's not a natural change, like when the moon calls or when we're so angry or passionate that we have to battle for control. I'm a newer were, and I don't have the restraint of the others in the community."

"Anger," Gabriel said, as if fitting everything together. "Passion?"

I could see that he was remembering all the times I'd been close to changing in front of him. "Like the night when Chaplin was captured . . ." I said, urging him along. "Or when we were . . . together."

When he'd bitten me and entered me in a way that had made me think that I'd been missing so much by staying inside, secure, untouched.

"I had no idea how passion affected me until you got here," I said. "Your peace was the only saving grace for me."

He seemed beyond that right now, and it broke me.

"Your voice," he said. "It would get rough. And your eyes . . ."

The fever. Unless I could summon every ounce of restraint, my disturbed state went livid in my eyes. "When you gave me the peace," I said again, "it helped. Helped so much. That's why I asked for more of it. To calm me, to keep me inside."

He laughed without humor. "So your fear of venturing too far from your home—"

"Truly is about what's out there—the bad guys like Stamp and the ones who attacked my family." I held out my hands in an appeal. "I was honest about that. But staying inside is also about keeping myself together. Every time I've strayed too far from the domain, I've been a monster who's brought pain to the community. Forcing myself to stay in kept me away from trouble. I hate what I do when I wander too far, and I've never been able to accept that about myself, mostly because it makes me a bad guy, too."

I was getting worked up now, upset, and it made my blood simmer, my bones begin the first melt of a slide into my bad, were-creature form. My mother would have screamed, had she seen what I'd become. My dad would have killed himself all over again, just as he'd done when he'd realized there was no hope of conquering my bloodlust.

Chaplin had told me that fear destroyed control, so I shouldn't fear. But I feared what my body did, feared the anger and passion that sometimes made me that way. And when I feared, I gave into all of it.

Fear had been our downfall out here in the New Badlands.

"Some scars never heal," I said, "even though were-creatures mend just as fast as any vampire when we're in preter form."

"All this time," Gabriel said, "I thought you were such a coward for not going outside."

"I am."

He looked at the ground, as if there were answers there. "Once Zel told me that I had no idea about the damage that was going on. I guess I brought on that anger . . . passion . . . in you."

Although I didn't want him to suffer any blame, I was going to be genuine. "You had an effect. But, as I said, you also found a way to balance me."

"Balance." He didn't seem to believe in it. "So when Chaplin forced you outside, to face that fear of yours . . ."

I nodded, knowing where he was going.

"He said that having me with you would do a world of good. That was because it was a test—having me near you when you were at your most vulnerable, outside where you wanted to run free."

"He wanted to prove two points. That I needed to toughen up, and that I could be strong in your presence, too." I glanced at the visz, where the others were most likely listening in. "They all have tried to teach me. Only I'm a hopeless student."

"Don't say that." Gabriel seemed as if something inside him still wanted to protect me, even from myself. "Nobody's beyond learning."

Our shared gaze was so intense that the heat rose in me to an even higher degree. But as I'd done so many times before, I pressed it down, priming that spring inside me to let loose. I didn't know another way of handling myself other than blocking the emotions. Shielding from the truths that could break me for good.

He continued. "There was also a time when Chaplin told me that, normally, he would've been the first to order me to get myself out of here, away from the community. He wasn't talking about how he couldn't overcome my sway to do what he wanted me to. He was saying that if he hadn't had that grand plan to match me up with Stamp so my sacrifice would protect your true identities, he would've kicked me out because of how I affected you. Because of what damage I was doing."

"I suppose it took the dog a little time to control the sway you had over him. So he was slow in recognizing your effect on me until I killed the man in the whale-hide hat. . . ."

Gabriel wandered toward the wall. "Maybe you'd better tell me all of it, Mariah. Every kill. I'm still trying to get it all straight in my mind. You'd think as a fellow preter, it'd be easier for me to accept everything."

Yeah, one would think that. But I didn't say that maybe I was a worse kind of monster than he was.

"What happened with the first death?" he asked. I could only see his wounded profile. "I know it occurred just before I got here. Stamp's men thrashed me, and then I came to your place."

"Do you remember how the moon looked the night before?"

He hesitated, then nodded, shaking his head. "Full."

"The last night of the full moon phase." I felt as if I were sliding down a slippery slope, no way back up. "All of us were outside that night, running free. Before that, for almost a year, I'd been doing much better at controlling myself, so no one was worried very much about me. Not yet."

Of course, the others had avoided me that night, as usual,

because of what I'd done to earn their worry. The terrible, terrible truth I'd also been lying to Gabriel about.

But I'd get to that soon enough.

"Stamp's men had just started coming round," I added, "harassing us via the visz lenses, so the thug who'd appeared on my screen was fresh on my mind. But all of us promised each other we'd leave them alone. I really did mean to do just that, and I even had the others bind me with cable and chain that night so I could prove my good intentions." I exhaled. "I don't clearly remember how it all happened, though—things are always a blur except for bits and pieces—yet I recall the fear that Stamp's man would find my home. Then I remember breaking out of the bindings while the others gave in to their full moon changes. Then I was trying to catch that thug's scent round my visz lens, tracking him, waiting near Stamp's place to see if any of his crew would be out. And there he was. He'd wandered off with some drinking buddies, then branched off by himself. . . ."

Now that I was allowing myself to, I remembered the aftermath of blood, the taste of him in my mouth, the buzz of fulfillment. Regret.

"Afterward," I said, a catch in my throat, "I came home, cleaned myself off, healed. There was so much blood—more than my usual meals produced. Then, even though I rarely even visited the common area, I found Zel and Sammy there, chatting after their own hunts. I told them what I'd done. They didn't want me outside from that point on, so that only encouraged me to stay inside my home—I guess it even enabled me. But then you came, and what I felt for you only built on the fear I hadn't quite let go of yet with Stamp moving in nearby."

I lowered my voice so the others wouldn't hear on the visz. Even now, he was stirring the appetite in me.

"You made me hunger in a way I'd never done before, and it got worse and worse until I couldn't stand it."

"I'm sorry," he said.

"No. Don't apologize *for* me. You can't correct this."

"Can't I?"

He'd altered his tone, hinting at the sway he'd used on me before, and my body went soft, my mind open, my chest and limbs light. Peace. It'd even quelled the bloodlust when our connection had been in its waning period, earlier tonight, after he'd come back from trying to rescue Zel and he'd appeared with his wounds, blood decorating his shirt. The others had turned away from the red, not wanting it to affect them, but I'd found that I hadn't reacted to it in the normal way.

I kept linking to his gaze, yearning for him, for what kept me good, not bad. Still whispering, I said, "Then there was the second killing. You'd told me that the guy in the whale-hide hat had hurt the oldster with the taserwhip. I suppose that planted the seed for his death, made me focus on him rather than any of the other thugs. But, even more, *you'd* gotten to me, Gabriel, and I thought I might be able to relieve myself of the building hunger for you. I couldn't. When I touched myself, I made the anger, the confusion worse, much, much worse, until my blood heated and my bones began to melt. You'd gone outside on your own by that point, and I gave in to the change."

"And you went after Whale Hide."

"Any one of them would've appeased me, but yes." Red, splash, heat in my throat and stomach. That was all I recalled besides the rage and the satisfaction of killing him. "After that, I came home, then changed back. I couldn't sleep, even though my body needed it. Then you returned, and I stayed downstairs, mostly because I was hoping you hadn't seen what I'd done—not with pleasuring myself or with the change."

His gaze had gone hazy, a hint of red at the edges of his irises. I knew he was thinking of that night. It'd awakened the monster in both of us.

"After that killing," he said, "Chaplin told me to stay away from you. Now I know why. It wasn't because I'm a vampire and he was worried about what I might do to you. It's because of what I raised in you."

The memories—the way he'd watched me, the way I'd gone on fire for him—were overlapping now, rolling over and into me. But I breathed. I had to block it just for the time being, because it was proving to be too much.

"I never realized," I said, feeling halfway sane again, "that you might think you'd committed any of the kills. I never thought you'd suffer because of that."

"I have a tendency to overindulge, if not properly checked."

Just like me. I hated that part of myself as much as I hated the men who'd made me this way. Most of all, I hated that it brought me a thin memory of pleasure.

"The night Chompers was killed," he said. "That was because of anger. Because they'd taken Chaplin."

I'd been close to turning, right in front of Gabriel, but he'd gone after the dog before the change had consumed me. "I held off turning as long as I could, and I made it outside just after you did. I tracked Chaplin down, freed him, and took care of Chompers." The sight of my dog had pained me—Chaplin, so afraid of me as he'd tried to persuade me not to kill again, so out of his drugged mind with the resurrection of my uncontrollable urges. The worst part was the memory of Chaplin crawling away from me, as if he thought I was going to come after him next.

And if I'd still been hungry enough after doing away with Chompers, my fever might've led me to it. . . .

Shaking out the thought, I knew that if it weren't for Gabriel and his sway, I might be even worse off now. Chaplin always tried to counsel me, and as a fellow quasi-canine, I connected to him and his compassion. But he only had so much of it, as he'd shown when he'd forced me to go outside shortly thereafter.

I said, "I made it back to the community long before you and Chaplin did."

"You're fast. I saw that tonight."

"You were also slowed down by all of Stamp's men still

hanging round, but I used Zel's entrance to avoid them. I washed off the blood and went to the common area."

"You had that cap on," Gabriel said. "The blanket, too, so I never knew you'd even changed clothes or gotten your hair wet. I didn't smell any evidence of a kill on you because you'd gotten rid of it." His smile was stone-hard. "All of you were so proficient. You took such pains to fool me."

"Yes." But we'd already explained why. I could see by his growing impatience that I didn't need to do it again. "When I arrived at the common area, everyone got on me about the man in the whale-hide hat. They hadn't seen me since they'd gotten the news, and I'm sure they would've been even angrier at that juncture if they'd known about Chompers, too. I just hadn't told them yet."

Gabriel looked up, as if mentally focusing on what he'd seen just after he'd arrived back at the common area with Chaplin. "They were all standing over you, but I thought it was out of comfort because Chaplin had been captured."

I'd actually taken solace from how they'd yelled at me. I'd even hoped that I could use their anger to restrain myself in the future.

But then, I'd always hoped in that way, and it never seemed to work. The hunger was too strong, and not a one of them was as dominant as their crazy lone wolf. There was nobody who could overcome me in were-form, so they'd allowed me to stay, depending on my desire to get better. Meanwhile, I holed myself up, away from them, so they wouldn't have to deal with me.

Then Gabriel had come along, and he'd been the only one who could match me.

He said, "And here I thought that the tension I felt when I walked into the room was due to me. Then again, they weren't too happy with me, either."

"By that time, they'd realized you had a strong influence on me. But Chaplin wanted you round, and none of them would challenge me, knowing I would best them. They thought I wanted to keep you, just as Chaplin did."

"But you wanted to kick me out, too."

"No," I said. "I didn't. I couldn't."

His gaze locked onto mine, as if he were trying to decide the extent of this truth, too. But my whole soul had been in the confession.

Too bad that what I had to say next would push him away for good.

"Those aren't the only killings." My eyes heated with oncoming tears. "Annie didn't disappear, Gabriel."

The words sounded sharp, an excision that we both needed. I only wished I didn't have to be the one who'd made the cut, because I would've gladly taken the bleeding side of it, especially while I sat there watching Gabriel's expression fall.

I reached for his hand. "I told you before—I'm sure Abby wasn't Annie."

He was having none of it. "What happened to Annie?" His eyes were getting redder, his hands clenched. "Was she a were-creature, too, like the rest of you?"

All I wanted to do was get through this, to arrive at the consequences—his raging at me, his well-caused yelling.

"She was," I said, "just like all of us here. She was a wolf, like me."

His eyes were all red now, but I wasn't afraid. I only felt numb as the tears came and my throat made it impossible to say more.

"Her domain," Gabriel said, his voice near a hiss. "When I searched Annie's domain, there were scratched-out tally marks on the dirt wall. Twenty-eight marks. The lunar cycle. Why didn't I realize that?"

"I was in her domain before you were. I tried to erase those marks, but I was working so quickly that I guess I didn't do a good enough job."

"You messed with her possessions to keep me dumb and happy?"

"To keep you from knowing our secret."

He reared back his head in clear anguish, and my chest seemed to crack because so much was weighed against it.

"Everything about Annie's disappearance . . . it was all a lie, too."

Tears attacked me. "She was so happy to find us. But, as I said, she was another werewolf, and I wasn't used to the proximity of a second one. Just by being round, she made my hackles rise, and I did the same to her. During the first two full moon phases, my dad was able to restrain me with chains and cables before I turned. But the full moon after that, I escaped them."

Gabriel looked as if he couldn't take any more, but I kept talking. "I didn't wish her any ill while I was in my human form, but when the wolf took over, the fear did, too. She felt like a threat to me, and Annie felt the same way about me, because we faced off that night. It was in our nature to fight, to see who would dominate."

"And you won," he said.

"No," I said. "There wasn't any winning. She was trying to rip my throat out, so I had to do something worse to save myself. I killed her."

I'd clawed her stomach out, getting to her first while she'd choked on my poison blood, because that was what were-creatures' blood did to each other . . . poisoned.

He went into a hunch, but I was going to finish this, no matter what he did to me.

"That's when my dad gave up," I said, brushing back tears. "And after he died, I stayed away from the others because I knew they were afraid of me. But I wanted to show everyone that I would stop. I kept myself underground and didn't go outside during the full moon until I felt as if I could hunt without the bloodlust absolutely taking over. I gave my neighbors more water that I pumped from my system than ever, and some of them started to talk to me over the viszes when they saw I meant well. Zel believed in me, because I was trying so hard. Same with the oldster. Even Hana and Sammy, to a certain extent. But not Pucci. He's a black-and-white kind of guy and doesn't forgive easily. He thought I was still beyond redemption, and he ended up being right."

"And who was going to throw you out when you were the deadliest among them?" Gabriel asked, his tone thoroughly mangled now.

"No one."

When he flashed his fangs, I was thankful.

I sank to my knees, my blood beginning its lethal boil as I got out the silver-bladed knife I'd tucked into a pocket, ready to do what was needed to stop all this from ever happening again.

28

Gabriel

Gabriel's reddened vision took in Mariah on her knees as she pulled out the knife, and he opened his mouth, baring his fangs even more, shuddering with such rage he could hardly keep still.

He didn't have sure proof that Annie was Abby, but he'd smelled a trace of the woman he'd loved in the domain. He knew enough.

But why hadn't he known before now? It'd all been in the vital signs. Mariah's and Abby's, so similar. He'd been thrown off by the variance, two different songs—one using angrier, more desperate notes than the other—played on the same instrument.

Canines. He was drawn to them: Chaplin. Mariah. Abby.

But the more he thought about her, the more he realized she was gone—that she'd been away from him for a very long time—and it left him feeling disembodied, more apart from himself than he'd ever been.

Mariah was trembling now, her eyes light green. Gabriel

hoped she'd turn. Hoped for a fight, a showdown that he would win this time.

"I should've left you all a long time ago," Mariah said through her tears.

She brought up the silver blade, and it glinted in the solar lamps.

Death. She was going to kill herself.

Shock blazed through Gabriel, and like the live wire it was, the connecting line between him and her buzzed to life. He realized in a lightning instant that it might've even been her were-blood that created such a link between two preters. . . .

Without thinking anymore, he sprang toward her, wrenching the weapon from her grip.

She gasped at the pain, and the weapon stuck point-first into the ground. Mariah slowly raised her head to fix her gaze on Gabriel.

That light green shade of uncontrollable emotion . . .

"Let this end the way it needs to," she said, her voice low and rough, just as it always got when her beast overcame her.

He hissed at her, flashed his fangs, not sure if it was because she was putting every ounce of his instincts on high alert or because he couldn't watch her self-destruct.

Then she began her change, too.

It happened quicker than he'd expected, with Mariah shaking just as if her blood were so hot that it bubbled under her skin, with her bones seeming to change shape in a rapid melt that reconstituted her skeleton into a bigger, badder form: her limbs stretching, ripping her clothing as she yell-howled until she loomed over him, her back going into a morbid arch, her face pushing into a snout that held rows of long, pointed teeth. Hair burgeoned over her skin, her ears pointing, her fingers clawing.

She growled, the deep, hollow sound warning Gabriel to back off, and though he could still see the tears in her green eyes, his vampire was in charge, and he gripped her throat with one hand, raising her off the floor and far above him.

Justice, he thought. Zel had died for it, and Stamp had come close to getting it tonight.

Abby deserved justice, too.

Gabriel heaved the wolf to the other side of the room, where she hit the opposite wall, causing crumbles of rock to slither down to the floor around her. But she was up in a blink, leaping at him with a quickness that left him no time to react before she barreled into him, sending him into the opposite wall with such force that he embossed his shape into the rock.

As Mariah's claws wrapped around his neck, he hissed. "You gonna kill me like you killed her?"

Her eyes emptied of anger, just for a split second, and Gabriel hissed again, striking out with his arm, spinning her across the room near the oldster's art wall with its roots sticking out. She barely avoided slamming into a curved one, instead grabbing onto it to swing back and forth.

When she looked at him again, it wasn't with rage, and that bewildered Gabriel.

But the confusion only stoked his fury, because he didn't know how else to rectify what she'd done.

Zel, he kept thinking. *Stamp.*

Abby.

He flew at the wolf, but she pulled herself up the roots, climbing with ease and coming to a claw-wielding hunch while balancing on the wood bar Zel had once used for exercise. But she wasn't so far up that he couldn't reach her, and he sprang upward, yanking her back down to the ground.

They came to a grunting crash, sending up a huff of dirt, and Gabriel pinned her. Maybe he could've swayed her into obedience with his voice or gaze, but that would've given her what she wanted—peace. And Mariah didn't deserve any. She'd earned an eternity in fire, the kind of anguish that was driving him right now.

When he met her gaze, expecting to see a refueled anger, he froze, because there was no ire at all.

Just water. *Tears.*

They'd become the eyes he'd looked into when the two

of them had been together in the most transforming act of his existence.

Though he couldn't define what it was, some form of emotion traveled from his brain and down to the place in his core where his soul used to be. But he spurned it, bunching his fists in her fur, pulling her up, hearing her whimper.

Then he bared his fangs, readying himself for a righteous bite. He'd tear out her throat, then shove her silver knife into her heart.

Another look into her eyes told him that she would accept this, but something else was in there, too. She didn't want this bloodlust that had been ruling her. She'd tried to outrun it.

He hesitated, seeing himself reflected right back at him. Then she closed her eyes, waiting.

He held her by the hair like that, knowing he had nothing to look forward to but endless battles. He was tired of them already. So tired.

His fangs receding, he pushed her to the ground, backing off from her.

He didn't look behind him as he went to Abby's door, pulling it off its hinges and slamming the thick wood to the ground. Nowhere left to go. No direction. No Abby to find anymore, no sense of purpose now that his codes and beliefs had lost the fight.

He bolted through Abby's room, using her exit to go outside, where the sun was on the cusp of its rise.

Thankful for the coming mental darkness that would swallow him up, he madly dug himself a shallow grave in the Badlands dirt, then covered himself for what turned out to be several blank nights where he wouldn't have to recall the tears in Mariah's feral eyes.

Where he wouldn't have to ask himself how *any* monster could have it in them to cry.

29

Mariah

It wasn't until a few nights later that I saw Gabriel again.

I'd gone to Abby's room in what had become a ritual since he'd disappeared. There, I would sit, using her domain as a cathedral of sorts—a place where I wanted to find forgiveness, if it would have me. My neighbors left me alone to do it, too, and for that, I was grateful, if not even lonelier.

Before tonight, I'd known just where Gabriel had buried himself. It wasn't far from Abby's entrance, and the dirt was so disturbed that it was obviously a quickly dug grave. A section of Gabriel's shirt was even sticking out, so when I'd ventured outside in a heat suit with Chaplin accompanying me, I'd covered him all the way up, wondering when Gabriel would come back.

Or if he ever would.

But here he was tonight, in Annie's place, clearly having straightened up, all the handmade rugs piled neatly near the common-area tunnel door, all of Annie's scant possessions tucked away so that it seemed as if a new occupant were ready to continue on from where Annie had expired.

As I entered through the common-area tunnel door, he didn't say anything.

"I'm sorry," I said. "I thought I'd find myself alone here."

He kept packing up his carryall bag, which he'd, at some point, fetched from my domain. It was the final sign of his moving out and on.

Didn't he still want to kill me?

"If I didn't know better," I said, "I'd think you planned to stay in this place."

"Abby's?" he asked, as if he wanted to hear me say the name.

There was no cruelty in his tone, and his loss of passion saddened me. But he was talking to me, and he wasn't doing it while trying to maim me, either.

"You still think Annie was Abby." My heart sank a bit.

"After talking to Hana, I know for certain now. She found me at the beginning of the night when I came out of the grave and sat me down for a chat."

I blinked at him. Hana had been Annie's only real friend here, but the woman had never revealed any secrets between them. That was probably what friends did for each other.

"Hana said after the other night, when she found out I was a vampire, she put two and two together. She thought it'd only be right to tell me her thoughts first, before any of you were privy to them."

"Okay." It seemed as if his time in the grave had robbed him of much response, his voice dull, his movements slow. Or maybe he just wanted to make me feel even worse before he left.

"Hana started off by telling me about a dress Abby gave to her once," he said. "Abby told her that there's more to life than wearing robes. Hana thought how beautiful this dress was, and she couldn't resist trying it on. But when Pucci saw her in it, he didn't like it. He said he preferred the robes, but she thought he merely didn't want her accepting anything from a wolf. He always told her 'Annie' was a troublemaker, and he wanted nothing to do with her."

I could hear the doubt in Gabriel's tone. He still didn't believe Abby had been a werewolf who'd challenged me.

But how well had he really known Abby?

"Abby," Gabriel added, "told Hana to keep the dress, because she might wish to wear it again someday." He stopped packing. "Earlier tonight, Hana took that dress out of its box for me. It hadn't been disturbed. Still had Abby's scent all over it."

And there it was. Utter, total devastation. Mostly in me, although from the sound of his voice, the destruction could've been all round.

"Hana never mentioned the dress to anyone—especially after Abby's death," he added. "She said that you all agreed as a community never to speak the truth about her again. It kept you together, even in delusion, especially from a stranger who would only come and go. That's another reason none of you would talk about Annie to me."

"I'm—"

"Don't say you're sorry. There's no use for that anymore."

I nodded past the lump in my throat. "The two of them confided in each other. They would disappear and then return, all quiet and secretive. We knew they were close."

"True, but Hana said she wouldn't have called them the best of friends."

I watched him carefully. He still sounded as if he were taking and choosing what he believed, and since we'd deceived him, I couldn't see why we deserved the benefit of any doubt.

"Hana also told me," he said, "that Pucci was right about Abby. She did have a wild streak that kept Hana cautious, no matter what the two of them might have talked about with each other. She said sometimes, there're people who are easier to unburden yourself to than others. People who listen better than anyone else on a certain subject, though that's as far as your relationship might go." Gabriel began packing again. "We never show all of our true selves to anyone, she said. We share different pieces with different people, and all that's left in the end is to fit what we know of that person together."

I didn't ask him if Abby had showed him only a part of herself. I didn't need to, because I could hear the suspicion of that in his voice.

"Abby never revealed her real name to any of you. She must have changed her identity out here to start her life again. But she did offer Hana a reason for coming to the Badlands." His voice broke. "She told Hana of a sanctuary where she'd been hiding back in the hubs. There, she expended a lot of effort to cover her condition—she had been a werewolf for years, and she was weary of it. Then there was a night she was out for food, and a group of robbers saw her and chased her through the streets. She screamed, thinking they were going to find out what she was. But just before she was about to change form to defend herself as a last resort, someone interceded. She found out later, after he joined her in the sanctuary, that he was a vampire." Gabriel came to an abrupt stop, then started up again. "Hana didn't realize until the night of the showdown that I must've been that vampire."

I was never that great at consoling, but I wished I had the chance to try it with Gabriel. Could be I'd fail at it, but just standing here was so much worse.

"I can see that night all over again," he said, "but in Abby's view. Her screaming and running from the bad guys, me being so attracted to the sounds of her—the terror, the beat of her body. She was a monster, just like me, and that colors everything in such a different way. She was capable of rescuing herself from those bad guys, but I saved her first, and that allowed her to masquerade in front of a vampire whom she thought to be a man."

"Why didn't she tell you?"

"She came close. But she saw the writing on the wall. A vampire and a were-creature should never be together. That's what common sense said, and she was practical enough to believe it. So, though she was tempted to stay with a vampire, she didn't. She left before I could find out what she was. She said I looked at her in a way that she could never live up to in reality, and for me to find out that she wasn't the woman I seemed to think she was . . ."

He trailed off, the blunt fade of it hurting, because even now, he obviously hadn't fully accepted that Abby had been a were-creature.

Not "his Abby."

"So she came out here," he said. "It was no less dangerous than the hubs. Far less, in fact. Back at the sanctuary, she'd been living on the canned goods smugglers brought in, because fresh meat was so chancy to come by. She'd grown weaker. I almost resurrected her with my bite, and she was thankful for that. But she couldn't accept what I had to give. She couldn't accept *me*."

He shoved his flask into the bag. "But I won't be around too much longer for anyone to do any more accepting. I know you and the others have also been looking at other locations to move to, because Stamp, if he survived, or his female sidekick, could bring back a mob of humans at any time."

He'd left talk of Abby behind, but it bothered me, because it meant he'd done what he thought he needed to do before leaving—clear the boards.

"The community's ready to flee at first notice," I said. "We posted lookouts round the area. Sammy's out there now."

"Hana said that you yourself have taken up most of the dusk-hour shifts, on top of the nearest hill."

It was true. Night by night, I was venturing even farther than the lookout hill. I had no other choice.

No more lying, even to myself.

Gabriel picked up the revolver he'd been using, but he didn't pack it. "Anyhow, it sounds as if your friends haven't given up on you. Chaplin already told me that you volunteered to stay behind while the others look for a new place to live. After they move into it, you're planning to go to them, but only subsequent to any return by Stamp."

"If I can report what kind of assets he's brought back

with him, the community will be that much better prepared if he finds the new place." I fisted my hand. "But they don't know that I *won't* be joining them there."

He jerked his attention over to me, and I didn't meet his gaze.

"I'm going to do anything it takes for them," I said. "For the first time, I'm not going to disappoint them."

I'd do just as much for Gabriel, too. Yet he'd always meant to leave, and nothing I could say would change that.

"You'll be a sitting duck here," he said.

"Maybe."

He considered me, and for a moment, I thought that he meant to talk me out of it. But then he stuffed the revolver into the bag with more force than necessary. "Never in my life did I think I'd ever be so angry at another that I would bury myself for nights on end."

"If I were you, I would've wanted to kill me, too."

Like father, like daughter. Suicide apparently ran in the family.

But Gabriel, of all people, had stopped me. I wasn't sure why. I only wished that he would lend me even more forgiveness now—that he would stay with us and give me another chance. My neighbors had done so, in spite of Pucci's protests, but I thought that they might only still be doing it out of respect for what I could do to them by were-force.

Yes, the community would be better off without me.

When Gabriel got to that pink bit of material I'd seen that first night he'd come to us, he held it, as if unwilling to stuff it away. It had to have been Abby's.

"She was the best human I knew," he said.

I wanted to sink into the earth, because he wasn't mourning the fact that *Abby* was a were-creature. She'd been enough to make him come out here across the miles to find her again. I was nothing compared to that.

"Before you knew that Zel and the oldster and Sammy were were-creatures," I said, not daring to use myself as an example, "didn't you think they were good humans, too?"

"I thought you all were."

Finally, he met my gaze. "I'm trying to reconcile myself to everything, but I can't. I can't wrap my mind around how the thing I so hate about myself was also deep down inside her. But most of all, when I found out that you killed Abby, I can't imagine her as the kind of beast that would merit such an action."

A flash of "Annie," with her flaring eyes, her pointed claws and teeth, flying at me in the night, consumed me.

"Why imagine that when you have much better memories of her?" I asked.

Then I filled myself with one last look at him before I began to leave.

"Mariah." It was the first time he'd said my name since almost killing me.

I halted, helpless to do anything else.

He took another glance at the pink patch, then put it back on the table, obviously intending to leave it here, along with everything else that'd be abandoned. "I don't know what to think about anything. When Stamp killed that demon, half of me thought it was okay, because I believed it was a murderer. When I found out about you, I wanted you to suffer, too." He put his hand on his bag. "But monsters don't function like the rest, and I don't know how I can look at the bunch of you and think you're not like I am. I wonder if I still think too much like a human sometimes. And I wonder if I've even got the same prejudices as one."

Was there some hope for me in his confession? No, it couldn't be that simple. "Your philosophical crisis doesn't wipe away what I did to Abby."

"You're right. And it doesn't wipe away everything *I've* ever done to survive, either, before I decided I didn't want a part of it anymore."

The hint of forgiveness put a spark in me, but it died as he merely closed his bag, then slung it over his shoulder. He was wearing his long coat, appearing almost the same as when he'd come to us, except without the injuries now. At least not the physical ones.

"Where will you go, Gabriel?"

He seemed to wonder, too. "I don't think there's much direction for me. All I know is that leaving might bring me to a place where I'll find more answers about all the things I'm not able to figure out here. Or maybe there's even a cure out there for vampires—besides having to terminate my own maker. Or a cure for were-creatures, and it isn't the one for lycanthropy we talked about. If I find one, I'll . . ."

What, be in touch?

That wasn't true, yet he tried to act as if it were, anyway. I pushed back more tears. Hateful, damned tears that wouldn't do me much good.

"Mariah, don't."

He sauntered over to me and, in his gaze, deep in his irises, past the gray, I saw that a part of him did still feel for me, in spite of everything.

And it was that part that made me throw my better instincts away and take hold of his coat. I stifled sobs—a woman who'd rarely given in to them before he'd shown up to heighten my troubles with his very presence. A woman who'd never shown much of anything to anyone.

Then Gabriel gently took my hands and made me let go.

He couldn't stay here, because that would force him to think about Abby every night. Abby only brought out the truth about me and about himself. They were matters he'd rather leave behind.

But wasn't that what he'd been doing? Leaving it all behind in the hopes that there'd be something better in front of him?

He released my hands, yet as soon as he backed away, he seemed to realize he couldn't leave me guilt-ridden, leave me here to clean up a mess he'd taken a role in, as well.

For a second, I thought that he might be thinking that I was the one who was here now, not Abby.

But he was going to go—I knew it—and as a good-bye, he looked into my eyes and shared the only gift he seemed able to give anymore. The peace. A lengthy dose that wouldn't last as long as I'd need it to.

In his eyes, I saw thoughts of the world as it had been:

children, laughing in a field while throwing round a football. Candlelight glowing on the faces of neighbors in the streets in memory of that long-ago day on 9/11. The warmth he'd felt when I'd laid hands on him, imprinting him, just the two of us bared to each other.

Then he disconnected, obviously because he hadn't meant to include the last image. He donned his bag and walked toward the ladder, as if he needed to go before he changed his mind and the terrible cycle he'd started here began all over again.

Never looking back, he climbed up and opened Abby's entrance door, then got out and shut it behind him. Meanwhile, the peace whirled in me, and things became clearer than they'd ever been before.

I exited the door, also, and low dusk rushed over me, baked and forlorn in the moonlight. Joshua trees bent in silhouette, creaking in the wind. Nearby, the upset dirt from Gabriel's temporary grave mocked me.

He was already off in the near distance, but he walked slowly, as if deciding which direction to take.

Was there anywhere left in the world that would welcome him?

Yards away, where the rest of the community had come out to see Gabriel leave, Chaplin barked. But Gabriel didn't look behind him.

Chaplin barked again, and I bit my lip, realizing that my dog was forlornly calling Gabriel back.

But he just kept going, his gaze on the hill in front of him. I'm sure he thought that, once he got over it, it'd be easier.

Then the oldster cried, "Gabriel!"

His steps faltered, but he kept on.

The others called for him, and I finally joined in, even though the rest of my community was separated from me by what felt like an ocean of desert.

"Gabriel?"

My cry seemed to linger a split second longer than theirs.

I could've been wrong about this, but it was like he only heard my voice.

It was as if his gaze were pulled back as he glanced over his shoulder to the other group. Individuals, each with their own power, who hadn't amounted to much until they'd taken themselves back.

And then he looked at me.

I closed my eyes, thinking hard, hoping he'd somehow pick up on it with his vampire mind. *Don't you know that we have something you wanted to find so badly? Don't you realize a community can keep you sane during the darkest times?*

When I opened my eyes, he was cocking his head, as if he *had* heard.

He turned all the way round.

My legs moved without my telling them to, and I walked toward him, closer, closer, so unsure.

I stopped about ten feet away. "Don't go. I promise, I'll do good from now on. I can be that way, especially with you here, Gabriel."

He looked at my boots, as if noting that I'd come past the border of the community's caves. Encouraged, I stepped over that invisible line I'd always drawn, going the rest of the way.

"Just come back?" A question. A hope.

Then I saw something I'd thought never to see: Gabriel's eyes going wet, affected by something that wasn't red, and I knew it for what it was.

He'd recognized acceptance. Here, in the last spot where it should've been, there was purpose and togetherness. A place where he belonged.

I backed away, having said all I could. If he turned round and walked off, I wouldn't be able to stop him.

Don't leave, I thought again.

Gabriel closed his eyes, just like he could hear my pulse inside him. Then, opening them, he began walking to me.

A sob welled in my chest and throat, my gaze going teary, although I was sure it remained the darker green of my humanity. I continued on back to the community, and he followed, the rest of the group coming forward to meet him now—others he'd have to accept, too, if he wanted the redemption he so needed for himself.

As the moon looked down in graying calm, our stride grew surer and surer, bringing us both back to a sanctuary we'd always been meant to find.

Turn the page for a special preview of
Christine Cody's next novel of the Bloodlands

BLOOD RULES

Available September 2011 from Ace Books!

Mariah

Even though the moon had been in its waning phase for a few nights now, I was seething, my bones shifting in what felt like a brutal melt, my skin hot as it stretched during the fever of were-change.

The murky midnight sky flashed by, blue swishes in my emerging monster sight, while I sprinted over the New Badlands, trying to get away—

But he was right behind me.

"Mariah!" he yelled, his vampire voice gnarled.

A fractured second later, Gabriel crashed into me, driving me to the dirt near a cave in a hill, my chin and palms skidding on the ground and abrading my skin to rawness.

Backhanded, I swiped at him, but he caught my half-human claw. Everything was starting to happen as if I were watching from a near distance, remote.

I panted like the animal I was becoming as we struggled, him flipping me to my back as I arched, growled, snapped at him. His eyes blazed against his pale skin, his fangs sprung.

"Stop it, Mariah!" he said.

"Can't . . ."

My voice was just as warped as his own. Hollow beast voices.

Before I could bite at him again, he grasped my head, looking into my eyes, slipping into my mind. My thoughts went watery, as if I were suddenly a pool and he'd dipped into it.

Peace. He was trying to give me the peace, and I opened myself fully, still panting. My temperature was already cooling in the hope of receiving his calm.

Easing. Serene.

As he infiltrated me, my vision wavered; he was on the top of water and I was under it. I felt the flow of his sway over my skin, smooth and numbing.

Thank-all, I thought as my bones started flexing back to their human shape.

I floated in sensation for a few more moments, almost afraid of it ending. I sucked in the dragon's-breath air, which was still hot during late spring here in the nowheres.

Gabriel kept looking deep into me, and I breathed some more, letting him take the place of my turmoil. Then . . .

Then I saw it in his eyes—the resentment. The stifled hatred for what I'd done to the woman he'd come out here to find nearly two months ago.

Abby.

As soon as her name entered my head, it seemed as if the water that'd been calming me boiled. And I could feel it in him, too—he was thinking about how I'd killed her.

The boiling intensified, the water parting, splashing out in a roar that I felt in my own lungs—

Our peaceful connection shattered, my body straining against itself again with the start of another change, my breath rasping. I could also feel the scrapes on my chin and palms healing with preter speed.

"Get . . . off . . ." I growled.

But Gabriel kept pinning me, putting more effort into

giving me the peace. With his stronger sway, my body whipped back toward humanity—the watery hush of it, bones and muscle slipping and sliding. For a second . . . then two . . . then more, I stayed in my good, human shape, whimpering because I ached. Ached so bad.

As he pushed me toward that better place, I hurt some more. Were-change had been natural when me and the rest of my community had been taken by the full moon. My neighbors had chained me up in our new homestead, and afterward I'd thanked them for keeping me restrained. They hadn't dared let me run free after what'd happened with Abby and the rest.

Natural moon change was so much better than the turning that consumed a were-creature because of emotional upheaval. Anger, passion . . . it all hurt a lot less during those three or so nights a month when the darkness combined with the moon's peak to compel a were-creature to madness and terrible hunger.

Gabriel whispered, "There you go, Mariah . . ."

I grunted. A tiny fever still had hold of me.

"Just a little more," he said. "Come on."

My teeth were still long, and I bared them at the vampire, not because of any innate hatred or a need to war against a different breed of preter, but because my wildness just couldn't stop itself.

Yells and barking arose in the background. More than one person was running, no doubt also keeping to the shadowy, hiding cover of the Joshua trees and standing rocks. I didn't want them to see me like this.

My dog came to a dirt-spraying halt next to me in the sheltering cove.

Mariah? he asked. *Running over open ground . . . why . . . ?*

Even in the hazy near-completion of my change cycle, I thought that Chaplin sounded inarticulate for an Intel Dog. I growled, flashed my teeth at him, too.

Chaplin barked at Gabriel.

What set her off this time?

Gabriel could translate Chaplin's sounds because they were communicating mind-to-mind, vampire to familiar.

Although Gabriel was still pinning me, he wasn't breathing heavily, like a human, because vampires didn't breathe. "I don't know what it was, but the peace isn't working so well anymore. I can't soothe her like I used to."

At the mention of something so personal, I turned my face away. It helped not to look at Gabriel, even though my breaths still came hollow and deep, my sight still a little blue-tinged. I just wished he'd get off me, because it reminded me of the first time he'd given me the peace, with his body flush against mine. We'd done sex, and with him being a vampire and me being a were-creature, something strange had happened.

We'd imprinted on each other in some way. I could calm him and he could calm me. It seemed we weren't so much monsters anymore when we were intimate.

But that had been before I told him the truth about the woman he'd loved—how Abby had been a fellow werewolf who'd attacked me, challenging my place in our secretive were-community. Now Gabriel's hatred of me polluted the peace, and I was flailing without it.

Then again, I'd never been the most stable of werewolves. I'd been bitten, not true-born, and my violent initiation had screwed me up but good. I hadn't had much control over my changes—not until Gabriel's peace.

And without it, now? I was back to being a disaster.

By this time, more of the community had arrived. I closed my eyes and willed myself to go all the way human. My bones and muscles obeyed grudgingly, making me buck beneath Gabriel and moan while my skin undulated with the chaos beneath it.

God-all, Chaplin had been right about my running over open ground nowadays. The group was usually so much more careful while in were-form, but I'd taken off, so upset, that I'd just run as fast as I could without thinking about keeping to cover. . . .

When I opened my eyes, breathing shaky, my sight had adjusted to filter in the regular ominous gray cast of a New Badlands night. I saw Pucci first, his bulky chest and grinding teeth belying his true-born were-elk form.

"What the tar is it now?" he asked.

The only reason I never attacked his ass was that, in human form, he could easily take me. But in monster form, another were-creature's blood was like poison, so I had an aversion to his blood—I sought out much more appealing prey instead of turning on the weaker were-creatures. So we were all one big, happy family, except without the happy part.

Another true-born, Hana, had the decency to pretend I was lucid enough to answer. "Mariah, what upset you?"

I couldn't find my voice as I glanced up at her—the mule deer brown eyes and skin, the African-inspired robes and scarf she wore over her head. Hana's and Pucci's animals used to be herbivores in the years before the world had changed, but with the lack of plant life, regular elk and deer had died off, and only the were-creature versions had lived on because their digestive systems had long ago adapted. Same with every other were-form I knew of—like me, they craved blood, which also gave water out here in the nowheres. When we were in regular form, we didn't have were-powers, so we didn't go after blood then.

Gabriel saved me from everyone's interrogation. "I'm not sure chatting about this is going to improve the situation."

But now that I could think more clearly, I *wanted* to talk. I'd spent so much time keeping my rage bottled in that airing it out seemed safer than exploding. My neighbors deserved at least that much from me. They'd let me stick round. Actually, no one had the power to kick me out, except maybe Gabriel, and he was giving me the chance to redeem myself.

I finally found my voice, tangled as it was. "I was unpacking, and I found my dad's journal. I couldn't help it— everything came rushing back. . . ."

My dad's grief after the attack in Dallas, the deaths of my

mom and brother, the fallout from what those bad guys had sicced on me. They'd used a werewolf, and that was when I'd been bitten. Because of that, my dad had smuggled me to our first home in the New Badlands—the one we'd had to leave a little over two months ago. When he'd been alive, he'd taken care of me as well as he could until Abby had come along and we'd had our showdown. After that, Dad had given up on trying to cure me, taking his life and leaving me alone to deal with it.

Oh, Mariah, Chaplin said, as if he were exhausted because of me, too. Then he turned to Gabriel. *I thought we buried sensitive items for the time being.*

"Did you think I wouldn't stumble on them?" I asked. "I spent a lot of time camouflaging the entrance to the cavern, so I'm familiar with every speck of dirt and sand near it." I held my tongue as my last bone locked in place. Then I breathed a bit easier. "I found those journals, Dad's old pipe, his collectible geek dolls without hardly even trying."

Hana had bent to me, running a hand over my forehead, murmuring a foreign chant that she'd learned as a new-age science nurse before having to go underground. Her voice helped me as I tried to stay in control.

Gabriel still held me down while Chaplin and Pucci hovered, ready to take me on. Smart, because I didn't trust myself, either.

"I shouldn't have come with you all here," I said as Hana pushed back my hair. "After I found this new homestead, I should've kept to my original plan and struck out on my own—"

"Do not say such things," Hana said. "If we do not help each other, what is left of the world will surely fall apart."

Chaplin put a comforting paw on my shoulder. *And God-all knows the world's crumbled enough.* I *wasn't about to leave you behind.*

It was true that he'd eventually persuaded me to come with the community when we'd moved, but that was back when Gabriel's peace had been working. Before his resentment had grown and polluted our connection.

Although Hana couldn't translate what Chaplin had uttered, she must've sensed that he was consoling me. She added, "Johnson Stamp is still out there, and we need to see that he *never* catches up to any of us."

"Yeah," Pucci said. "If Mariah had broken off with us and Stamp caught up to her, he'd probably have tortured our new location right out of our pet psycho. Might as well have her here where we can keep an eye on what she says and does. Unless, of course, she turns into a werewolf and runs all over the place like she's inviting someone to catch her."

His concern would've been heartwarming if I knew Pucci had any love for me.

Chaplin barked, then muttered and whined. *Let's get inside. We can't afford to get caught by anyone, especially if Stamp made it back to the hubs to announce we're out here.*

He didn't have to add that you never knew when Stamp might be round, either, if he'd survived his confrontation with us.

Stamp—who'd been a Shredder, or government-sanctioned hunter, before the powers that be had deemed preternaturals under control years ago—had almost died while accosting the community. Out of defense, we'd killed all his employees except for him and his female lieutenant, but he'd been so torn up that his wounds might've proven fatal.

As I said, you just never knew with Shredders.

Gabriel translated Chaplin's words. Then Pucci turned to me.

"How many times is it going to take until you really do us in, Mariah?"

Gabriel shoved him away, warily backed away from me, then turned and walked off, keeping to those shadows.

I watched him go, my throat tight.

Hana helped me to a sit, and I made a low sound of unease because of the tweak of my bones and joints. She checked me over, seeming to ignore the rips in my clothing, then peered into my eyes. But since they weren't glowing with the fever, I passed her inspection.

Pucci yanked on her robes, almost dragging her up so that she followed him as he walked away, both of them taking care to seek cover, too.

I watched Pucci's treatment of Hana, who never fought back. I could never figure out how such a strong-minded woman loved such a jerk. She always seemed to hold her own against him, but she never left when he seemed to give her good reason to.

As I stood, my legs wobbled, and I sucked in a breath at the piercing reminders of the shift. Chaplin nudged me into a shaky walk, keeping up with my unsteady pace as we sought the boulders, then other camouflage.

Chaplin, my remaining friend. I knew that he also resented me sometimes, but we'd been through a lot together, including the Dallas attack and my dad's death. Hell, my father had trained Chaplin as an Intel Dog in the lab, way back when Dad had still been a scientist, so we'd both lost a father.

"Then there it is," I said quietly so the rest wouldn't hear, although maybe Gabriel would pick up my words because of his heightened vampire hearing. "I didn't mean to put us in danger."

You had a moment, and it's over, Chaplin said. *We'll need to watch those visz screens to see if anyone comes round, but we're very well hidden, Mariah. You've just got to be more careful.*

"Right. I just had a moment." But there'd be more and more moments as the years wore on, and we both knew it.

The metal-gray of the sky made Chaplin's brown coat look drab as we darted out of the shadows and into the safe cover behind rocks or more Joshua trees.

It'll be a long time before everyone forgets what happened back at the first homestead, Chaplin said, chewing on his words.

"My lack of control made us vulnerable to Stamp, so I earned the wariness."

Before the big showdown, I'd killed a few of Stamp's men when they'd encroached upon our territory, threatening us. We'd suspected they wanted our aquifer-enhanced dwellings, and, in my anonymous were-form, I'd made sure they didn't get them. Then Gabriel had appeared one night, wounded, and Chaplin had invited him into our home. My dog had been under his sway, but Chaplin had overcome it, manipulating Gabriel into confronting Stamp for our sakes. But I, and the rest of the community, hadn't been able to stomach his sacrifice, and we'd gone to the showdown to defend him.

So if you went right back to the beginning, the death and destruction had all been because of me.

Mariah, there's always . . . Chaplin began, then cut himself off.

I wasn't dumb enough to believe that my dog had an unfinished thought. He was luring me into something. Intel Dogs had been genetically bred and trained to be practical and lethal when the time called for it. He was my best weapon and, sometimes, my worst.

"Spit it out," I said. A sand-rabbit leaped out of some brush in front of us, causing a rustle.

Everyone ahead of us startled toward the sound, even if they were under the cover of the shadows, but when they saw it was only a little flit of an animal, they moved at a faster clip. Anything could be a Shredder or even another preter who'd deserted the hubs. We didn't need to be discovered by either one.

My heart was blipping in my veins because of the interruption. "You gonna say it, Chaplin?"

I could've sworn my dog smiled at my vinegar. It meant that I was fully back to being human. For now, anyway.

There's always hope for a cure, he said.

And that was all, but that final word had the power to give me pause.

A were-cure—that was what he meant, and he'd been mentioning it in private ever since we'd moved into our new digs. He hadn't ever expanded on his thoughts, but it was as if he'd been watering a seed every time he muttered it. Although it was a ridiculous idea, his comments had made me think. They also made me ache that much more, and not in my joints and muscles, either.

"There's no cure for monsters." I'd discussed this with Gabriel before he even knew what I was, and Chaplin had been in the same damned room. Obviously, this rebuttal bore repeating. "Stories about cures are just legends, and every bad guy who doesn't believe that monsters were eradicated probably uses the rumors to lure what's left of our kind into the open. That way, they can beat the location of any hidden preter communities out of the idiots who take the bait."

What if you're wrong about there being a real cure? Chaplin asked.

And there it was—he was about to grow that seed into something I'd have to confront right here and now, fresh after losing control to the point where I hadn't even thought to hide while I was running outside.

"Dad tried every panacea he could think of on me," I said, "and nothing worked. And if he couldn't figure it out, who could?"

He wasn't the only scientist round, Mariah. Maybe Gabriel was right when he said that there was such a sharp drop in preters in the hubs because a cure was found.

Up ahead, hills rose out of the ground like the curves of a serpent's spine. Pucci and Hana had already run ahead to access a trapdoor to a tunnel that led to our homes, but it looked to me as if Gabriel had slowed down before going inside. The moonlight skimmed over his beaten white shirt and pants. His close-cropped hair looked darker than I knew it actually was, and his face, with that slightly crooked nose, had gone back to its normal stillness—like the façade of an abandoned house, the windows gray and cloudy.

His head was cocked.

Was he listening?

His possible interest lit something in me. Hope.

Actual hope.

If I improved my disposition, would that make him look

at me differently? Would he feel whatever he'd started to feel for me back before the truth about Abby had come out?

Sorrow and anger began to simmer deep in my belly, but I tamped it down before it resulted in another change . . . and in more trouble.

More than anyone, I needed some kind of cure, and the only one I could think of right now was for me to end my life. I'd already tried that after Gabriel had found out the truth about me, but he'd stopped me for some reason. Now, I still figured he would've been better off.

I realized that, maybe, Chaplin was really going at this subject right now because Gabriel was near, and my response might be affected by that. It was also becoming more obvious that my dog might've asked me to come to this new homestead not only because he loved me, but because he'd wanted to lead me to accept the idea of a cure, all while making it seem as if I'd agreeably arrived there with minimal assistance.

Too smart for his own good, this dog.

If there is *a cure,* Chaplin said, *what would you do to find it?*

"If it were true, I'd do anything." The comment was out before I could even think, but I knew with all my heart that it was what I'd been feeling for a long time now.

And if the cure required more than just swallowing the contents of some vial?

"What do you mean?"

I mean, what if it involved conditioning, Mariah? Ultra-shock therapy. Mental tooling—

I recalled how Gabriel had tried to slay me after hearing about Abby's death. How, beneath his words and actions, he hated me even now because I was a killer who couldn't help herself.

I suppose, in life, there's always a moment where you run into the wall of yourself. That was what I was feeling now, the crash of knowing there's nowhere else you can go because you can't turn back.

"As I mentioned," I said, "I'd do whatever it takes."

Up ahead, Gabriel glanced partway over his shoulder until he met my gaze.

His eyes . . . red glows in the night.

I held my breath, then used my energies to think to him, willing his vampire mind to pick up my inner voice.

Believe me, Gabriel. I want to be better.

His only answer was to turn round and slip into the cavern entrance, leaving me behind with an Intel Dog who gave me a sympathetic look, then stranded me, too.

**Explore the outer reaches
of imagination—don't miss these authors
of dark fantasy and urban noir who take you
to the edge and beyond . . .**

Patricia Briggs	**Anne Bishop**
Simon R. Green	**Marjorie M. Liu**
Jim Butcher	**Jeanne C. Stein**
Kat Richardson	**Christopher Golden**
Karen Chance	**Ilona Andrews**
Rachel Caine	**Anton Strout**

penguin.com/scififantasy